Deepening Homefront Shadows

Michael Staton

A Wings ePress, Inc.
Historical Romance Novel

Wings ePress, Inc.

Edited by: Jeanne Smith
Copy Edited by: Joan C. Powell
Executive Editor: Jeanne Smith
Cover Artist: Trisha FitzGerald-Jung

Wings ePress Books
www.wingsepress.com

Copyright © 2020 by: Michael Staton
ISBN-13: 978-1-61309-589-8
ISBN-10: 1-61309-585-9

Published In the United States Of America

Wings ePress Inc.
3000 N. Rock Road
Newton, KS 67114

Dedication

To the men who fought in the Civil War,
both Union and Confederate.
Some survived the war, although many suffered from war-related ailments for the rest of their lives. Others never made it home, dying on battlefields or in winter camps.

* * *

One

Tar Heel Private Bill Stamford fisted his hands as he awaited his new future just a few minutes away.

Feet restless, Bill waited expectantly in the foyer of the Grove Presbyterian Church in Kenansville, North Carolina. His best friend Charlie, also a private in the Army of Northern Virginia, stood beside him, chuckling at Bill's unease.

"My, my, you look more pathetic than when you took the shell sliver in the back." Charlie brushed his stump against Bill's shoulder.

Bill offered a skewed smile. Charlie didn't often fling a wisecrack, not since returning from Gettysburg minus his right arm.

The son of the town's newspaper editor understood Charlie's frustration and melancholy—to a degree. Bill too had suffered a life-threatening battlefield wound, but at least he'd healed without the loss of a limb. Always a Casanova, Charlie no longer chased after bits of frock, pretty girls who loved to flirt and spoon. What girl would want him now? Charlie had repeated those very words to Bill at least half a dozen times since returning home in early August.

The organ music stopped. As the organist, Julia Dickson, one of Kenansville's sacred protectors of virtue, began "At Cana's Wedding Long Ago," the Reverend James Sprunt emerged from a side room and gestured for Bill and Charlie to follow him into the sanctuary.

Grinding his teeth, Bill fished inside his pants pocket, grateful when his fingers touched Grandma Newton's wedding ring. Soon it would grace the left ring finger of Franny Neale.

"Last chance to run away." Charlie turned and eyed the foyer's double doors.

"Think I'll keep her." Bill caressed the white gardenia pinned to his shell jacket.

Stumbling, he recovered quickly and shadowed the preacher down the aisle. Charlie walked nimbly beside him.

Kind eyes were fixed on Bill as he strode to the altar. So many friends and loved ones were seated in the pews—older folks who had welcomed Bill's mother to Kenansville when she arrived as a young bride; girls Bill's age, many who had hoped to snag him; Franny's mother who made the trip from Fredericksburg, Virginia, and his momma and papa, dressed in their frayed Sunday best. Clarence Stamford sported an ear-to-ear grin; perhaps he remembered his own wedding up in Arkona, Ohio.

His father's smile was the only feature on his middle-aged face that didn't look frazzled—sunken cheeks, sleep-deprived eyes and pale skin. Icie Belle appeared young and vibrant, as if watching the wedding of her oldest son had removed more than twenty years of life. Even the strands of gray speckled in her flower-bedecked hair were hardly noticeable. Seated next to his parents, his younger siblings, Mark, a newly minted teenager, and nine-year-old Laura, beheld him with hero worship glinting in their eyes.

"Maybe Franny's the one who has skedaddled?" Charlie whispered. "Poor Bill...left at the altar."

"Hush! You're the one who'll get left at the altar, chuckaboo." Bill jabbed his friend in the ribs.

Mrs. Dickson's organ music faded. The sanctuary grew silent as the pastor settled in behind the pulpit and rested his hands on the congregation's eighty-year-old Bible. Behind him, the choir loft gleamed with an array of colors—lilies, chrysanthemums, roses, lavenders and marigolds.

We can't get married in war-damaged Fredericksburg, Bill thought. *Hopefully, Franny finds Kenansville a wonderful substitute.* As if on cue, Mrs. Dickson launched Mendelssohn's "Wedding March." Everyone in the sanctuary, Bill included, turned to ogle the bride, standing alongside her father just inside the foyer.

Lordy, Franny's beautiful. Bill wiped away tears welling in his eyes.

He'd almost lost her in the spring. They had met in the aftermath of battle. Together, they nursed the wounded. A few days later, they tipped the velvet in the overseer cottage of Fredericksburg's Yerby Plantation. A fairytale love, he believed, until she flew to Tennessee to nurse her sick fiancé.

Heartbroken, Bill had soon gone into battle and fell wounded, shell shrapnel embedded in his back. Sent home to recuperate, he found solace in the arms of another, Becky Powell. But she too fled—not to another lover, but to Europe to escape the sadness of war.

Bill feared he'd die an old, decrepit bachelor—until Franny barged back into his life during a Union cavalry raid that saw a Kenansville sword factory burned to its foundation. She sought forgiveness, promised to always love him—and here they were about to marry.

Franny whispered into her father's ear; as if getting an order, he escorted her into the sanctuary. With the blockade preventing the purchase of a new wedding dress, Franny wore the carefully preserved linen and muslin wedding gown of Bill's mother. A tiara of glass flowers held her mother's wedding veil. Ringlets of wheat-blonde hair fell to her shoulders.

Bill heard the swish-swish of hand fans as Franny's father, Howard Neale, ushered his daughter up to the altar where she nuzzled against Bill. When he reached to hold her hand, the petals of her bouquet tickled Bill's wrist. "Charlie thought you'd change your mind and head for the train station."

"I may if you don't stop joking at my wedding." She winked.

Franny smelled delightful, a subtle scent of violet. He wanted to press his nose against her skin and let the fragrance saturate his senses. His thoughts drifted, turning carnal, imagining her naked on a hotel bed in Wilmington. A couple of passionate nights at the Purcell House would have to suffice for a honeymoon; Paris or Niagara Falls perhaps after the war.

"I don't know who's been happier about this wedding?" Franny whispered. "You and me or my mother. I think deep down she wishes she could marry you."

Bill rolled his eyes. "Your father's going to hear us."

"I did," Howard said.

Julia Neale adored Bill and thought him a fabulous catch, not due to his family lineage but because he wanted to share in Franny's literary dreams. Even after he'd been wounded and lay in a hospital tent, Julia had worked relentlessly to keep Bill's love for Franny as fiery as the Northern Lights glowing over Fredericksburg after the battle. She knew Franny's stuffy ex-fiancé offered only misery for her daughter. Franny would come to her senses. And she had, making a long, dangerous train ride to Bill's home county to profess her love. Her charms proved irresistible. They made love.

Franny intruded on his thoughts, "Wake up! I want to get—"

The Reverend Sprunt cleared his throat, a sound much louder than Franny's whispers. "Miss Franny, your mother's motionin' to me." He acknowledged Julia with a nod. "As the Bible says, 'He who finds a wife finds what is good and receives favor from the Lord.' Let's get these two deeply-in-love young'uns married."

A boy screeched the rebel yell. Shocked protests echoed within the sanctuary, mainly from middle-aged matrons who weren't dressed in black.

Bill whirled around and recognized the guilty party, eleven-year-old Donnie Matthews. His mother sprang to her feet, grabbed Donnie by the ear, and lugged him into the foyer and through the double doors.

"Now that harmony has returned, let's get Franny and Bill hitched." The pastor explained the holy purpose of the marriage covenant and asked, "Who gives this woman in marriage?"

Franny's father answered, "Her father and her mother."

Told to face each other, Bill and Franny joined their right hands. The Reverend Sprunt led them through the sacred ring vows, instructing the couple to "publicly commit everything they are and everything they possess in a covenant relationship." As had been said for centuries, Franny and Bill promised to leave their families, forsake all others and become one with their spouse.

Grandma Newton's ring slipped easily onto Franny finger. When it became her turn, he expected the preacher to revise the ceremony, since she couldn't put a ring on Bill's hand. Doing the improbable, Franny drew out a man's ring and slithered it onto his digit. He gazed at the dazzling ring. Bill had no idea how it had come into her possession.

"I declare Franny Neale and Bill Stamford are now husband and wife and one in the eyes of God," the Reverend Sprunt intoned. "To our wedding guests, I introduce Franny and Bill Stamford, Kenansville's newest married couple."

Mindful of the guests in the pews, Bill gave Franny a pristine kiss. Franny turned the innocent peck into something much more primal and took his hand. Together, they made their way toward the foyer and twin doors to the yard. The guests stood and clapped. A few of the holier-than-thou ladies whispered about Franny's kiss.

Ahead, beside the Seminary Street curb and under a near-cloudless sky, a buggy awaited them. Cans had been rigged to the rear and colorful paper fastened to the doors. They'd ride it to the train depot in Warsaw and head for Wilmington to consummate the marriage in a Purcell House bed.

"You really had me believing we'd have a one-ring service," Bill kiddingly admonished his new wife once they were in the foyer.

"I like surprises."

"I should have suspected. So how did you come by it?" Bill arched an eyebrow.

"From a friend of your father's." They passed through the entryway into the sun-drenched yard of flower beds. "The jeweler Wayne Laird. We'll have to return the ring after the honeymoon."

"What?" Bill wondered if his voice sounded like a small girl's. He glanced at the ring shining in the light as sunbeams warmed his face.

"I'm kidding."

He groaned. "You've done it to me again."

"Nothing's for free, though. We're going to have to pay for it after the war."

"I can't complain. Sounds fair to—"

Screams from inside the church stopped Bill cold. Releasing Franny's fingers, he fixed his eyes on the double doors. Julia Neale waved frantically.

The buggy's darkey driver tossed an alarmed look in Bill's direction. "Better git in the church, sir. Screamin' gittin' louder."

"What in the world?" Franny said, bewildered.

Bill took off running as if chased by a troll. Encumbered by her floor-length veil, Franny struggled to keep up.

On the church steeple, a robin sang its whistling song, so lyrical compared to the unsettling screams inside the sanctuary.

"Bill, it's your papa," Julia cried out.

Sidling past Julia, Bill's sister Laura darted out the double doors, shrieking "Bill! Bill, something's happened to papa!"

Laura slipped on the uneven footpath and fell to her knees, scraping them and the palms of her hands. Kneeling, Bill helped Laura to her feet as Franny rushed past them into the foyer.

"Calm down, Laura," he said, his own voice not so calm. "Papa? What happened?"

"I don't know. He's on the floor. I'm scared, Bill."

He took her hand. "Come with me."

Bill and Laura stopped briefly in the doorway as guests stared stupidly at the altar where a dozen men and women were congregated, some standing, others kneeling. Julia seized his right shoulder with both hands. "Your father needs you."

Still gripping his sister's hand, Bill wove past gawkers to where his momma, Howard Neale, and the Reverend Sprunt knelt beside his father, pallid and barely conscious. Icie Belle cradled her husband's head and dabbed his brow with a hankie. She swung her despairing gaze to Bill. "Your papa, he collapsed. No warning, Bill. He never said anything. Just went down."

"I didn't expect this so soon." Bill drew a curious look from his momma.

Eyes glazed and seemingly staring at something beyond the church ceiling, Clarence tried to speak, but gurgling smothered his words. Slowly, agonizingly, he fixed his eyes on his oldest son. Bill lowered his head. *Papa knows I'm with him.*

"Don't die, Papa." Laura's voice quivered.

Bill searched for Mark and found him sitting on the first step of the dais, weeping copiously. "Laura, go to your brother. Help him."

She looked at Mark, returned her gaze to Bill and nodded. "Papa, I love you," she told Clarence before going to her brother. Wrapping an arm around Mark's shoulders, she kissed him on the cheek.

Bill yelled out to others in the sanctuary, "Where's Doctor Graham?"

"Chauncey couldn't make it to the wedding," Icie Belle said. "Had to deliver Florence Sampson's baby."

Clarence tried to speak again. Closing his eyes, grimacing, he choked out, "Ruined your wedding."

"You didn't, Papa." Bill's voice cracked.

Franny's words glided past Bill's ear. "You stop that kind of talk, Mister Stamford."

Clarence strained, "You married a humdinger, Bill."

"Indeed, I did, Papa." Bill caressed Clarence's cheek.

"My Clarence adored you from the moment Bill ushered you through our front door," Icie Belle told Franny as she wiped perspiration beading on her husband's forehead.

"And I adore you." Franny kissed Clarence's chin.

Bill turned and spotted his best friend. "Charlie, let Doctor Graham know we need his help, then send a telegram to Doctor

Iuppenlatz in Wilmington. Tell Iuppenlatz his fears have come to pass and to rush to our house."

"Gladly, Billy Boy."

Bill nodded toward his father-in-law. "Sir, help me get Father to the honeymoon buggy. Let's get him to the house."

Howard Neale's gaze held respect. That had not always been the case. Franny's father would have preferred his daughter marry the Tennessee officer. Better family connections, better bloodlines, more wealth. Nonetheless, the man had helped Bill get the job at the War Department. Franny... always persuasive when she wanted something from her father.

Bill helped carry his father to the buggy's back seat. He patted Clarence's feet. "It won't be long and we'll have you in your bed."

He helped his momma and Franny into the front seat. "Laura, Mark and I will ride with Howard and Julia," he told Icie Belle.

Bill caught a glimpse of his father as the buggy's darkey driver reined the horse into motion. In his short life, Bill had seen a half-dozen halos flame around people. The nimbuses meant death, sometimes in days, sometimes in weeks. The last one had surrounded Rose Greenhow, the Confederacy's famous spy. She still lived—for now. No halo had surrounded Bill's father. Perhaps it meant Clarence would survive this attack. Yet people died all the time without the appearance of halos. As Bill climbed into his father-in-law's carriage, he looked skyward. *Lord, please make it clear. Why me? Why the halos?*

Bill did thank the Lord for one mercy. He was grateful God hadn't put a halo around his papa. No way would he have wanted to know ahead of time.

The carriage lurched into motion. Bill's thoughts melted away like morning dew before the glory of the rising sun.

Two

A Loved One Lost

Above Kenansville, lightning streaked across a menacing sky. A few seconds later, thunder rumbled, jarring the Stamford home. Beyond the dining-room window, the vegetable plants in the summer garden whipped about in a frenzy, portending a coming drencher. Bill took notice of the outside fury. *Never can be a sunshiny day when a soul streaks heavenward.*

As another flash lit up the window, Bill gazed at a bowl of fruit salad on the table in front of him. He poked his fork into the compote of strawberries, blueberries and blackberries, but made no effort to lift a mouthful to his lips. Mark, Laura and Franny's parents had also left their bowls untouched.

Franny flitted around the table, the serving bowl of fruit compote cradled in her hands. "No one?"

Mark looked at his brother's wife like she was mad.

Bill sighed. "Please sit, Franny. No one's got an appetite."

Perhaps in an effort to lighten the gloomy mood, Franny's father Howard quipped, "Too many parties and balls, daughter. Not enough cooking lessons."

Franny feigned outrage. "Oh, Father, stop it!"

"With so many slaves bolting to Fort Monroe and Yankee protection, you're going to have to learn to like your daughter's cooking—and mine." Julia tendered her husband a crooked half smile.

"You too, Mother! Stop it!" Franny settled the serving bowl on the end of the table and went to sit beside her new husband. Before plopping down, she lingered behind Bill and massaged his neck. "Your muscles are knots."

"What do you expect?" Bill squeezed his fork tighter, and when it hurt his fingers he let it fall to the table and judder until the vibrations dampened.

"I want to see papa," Laura said plaintively.

"Me too." Mark wiped his sleeve across his eyes, drying tears.

One day after his heart attack Clarence lay in his upstairs bed, Icie Belle at his bedside along with Doctor Iuppenlatz, who arrived just before four o'clock. Doctor bag gripped in his right hand, he'd promptly climbed the stairs to see his patient and hadn't been downstairs since. At Iuppenlatz's order, no one else had been allowed in the bedroom.

"The doctor says silence is best for now." Bill steepled his hands. "Just Momma. Anymore would be too taxing."

"He's dying, isn't he?" Tears spilled faster than Mark's sleeve could soak them up.

"Don't say that!" Laura pounded the table.

Franny bolted from her seat, rushed to the girl's side and seized her hands, keeping them in a vise-like grip until Laura calmed down.

At that moment, all heard the old-house creaks of someone descending the stairs. Bill sprang to his feet and scampered for the steps. His siblings and Franny trailed him.

"Please, God in Heaven, let it be good news." Laura's gaze drilled through the ceiling upward to Jehovah's throne.

All waited at the foot of the stairs, except for Franny's mother and father who remained seated, concern stamped on their faces.

His steps leaden, the doctor descended the staircase. He stopped one step short of Bill and squeezed his shoulder.

"Please come upstairs. It's time to say your goodbyes."

The doctor's words prophesized death—maybe in mere minutes. Bill didn't want to surrender hope, yet Iuppenlatz's expression offered none. Bill knew something his momma didn't. His father had told Bill he'd been diagnosed with a failing heart. Clarence had made him promise to keep it a secret.

Franny squeezed his hands, and then Bill, his legs wobbly, climbed the stairs. His new wife stayed behind with her parents. This goodbye wouldn't include the Neales.

Led down the hallway by the doctor, Bill, Mark and Laura approached the bedroom with trepidation. Bill had seen men die on the battlefields of Fredericksburg and Chancellorsville, but those ghastly scenes hadn't prepared him for his own father's death. Iuppenlatz opened the bedroom door. Bill paused in the entryway, his lips locked shut, hands clenched.

Barely any summertime light penetrated past the drawn curtains. The wick on a nightstand oil lamp emitted a faint amber glow that made the room's shadows stand out. His father's pride and joy, a Frederic Edwin Church painting, remained shrouded inside the shadows. Bill's mother sat in one of the spoonback chairs, a water-filled porcelain bowl on her lap. She smiled at her children then dribbled water from a damp handkerchief onto her husband's lips.

"Clarence, the kids are here."

Wheezing, he opened his eyes. "Bring Laura and Mark closer."

At the end of the bed, the family cat, Indy, turned an ear toward the sound of Clarence's voice. The white-furred cat eyed the door, leaped from the bed, and flew through the doorway. Soon, he'd be in the dining room pestering Franny and her parents for scraps.

Bill took his siblings' hands and led them to the bed. Icie Belle patted Clarence's veiny right hand. "They're beside you, my love."

His body quivering, Clarence lifted his left arm maybe six inches, and grunting, gave up. It flopped onto the bedspread. "Wanted to...touch...can't."

"It's their turn to do the touching, sweetheart." Icie Belle nodded to her two youngest children. "Laura and Mark, stroke your papa's arm and kiss his cheek."

Laura caressed Clarence's wrist, tickling the hairs. "Hello, Papa. I love you. Tell Grandma and Grandpa Stamford howdy for me. Tell Grandma I miss her strawberry pies." Sniffling, Laura kissed her father's forehead, drew back and looked helplessly at Bill.

Ruffling her hair, Bill squeezed his baby sister against his side. "You'll see him again. That's Jesus's promise."

"Mark?" Clarence's voice sounded like a baby's rattle.

"Yes, Papa. Feel my hand?" Mark rubbed Clarence's cheek. "Is an angel here?"

Dim eyes suddenly brightened. "Just appeared. Says it's time."

"Really?"

Bill rested his hand on Mark's shoulder and motioned him to back away from the bed.

"Clarence, Bill's here too." Perhaps Icie Belle saw the irony in Bill's presence beside the bed. Without the shrapnel wound, he would have marched to Gettysburg. No telling what could have happened. A wound suffered at Little Round Top or Cemetery Ridge? Maybe the loss of an arm—like Charlie—or a leg? Even death and an unmarked grave in Pennsylvania?

"See a halo?" Clarence barely managed a fleeting half-smile.

"No, Papa. Thank God." Bill meant that with every fiber of his body. He would have been devastated had he seen one flashing around his father.

Clarence shifted his eyes to a part of the room without people. He laughed or groaned, Bill wasn't sure which. "All this talking has wearied me. Not many heartbeats left."

"We've had twenty wonderful years together," Icie Belle found a new use for the damp handkerchief—wiping away her own tears. "Don't worry about us. Mark, Laura and I will be fine. I promise to keep publishing the *Gazette* so I won't need to marry a man I don't love to keep us out of the poorhouse." She kissed her sweetheart on his parched lips. "And don't fret about Bill. Remember, he's going to Richmond to work in the War Department. He'll be safe." Again, she kissed him. "Go with the angel. I'm sure he's telling you to listen to me—after all, I'm your wellspring of wisdom." Smiling, Icie Belle took Clarence's right hand in both of hers and pressed her forehead against it.

Bill's father closed his eyes and said nothing more. His breathing slowed, sometimes as long as a minute between breaths. Just when Bill thought he'd passed, there would be another breath.

With the goodbyes said, Doctor Iuppenlatz stepped up to the bed. "He's been given laudanum to ease his passage. There'll be no pain, no suffering."

One thought pricked at Bill's conscience. His momma intended to run the newspaper. She didn't know the *Gazette* was about to be sold to the publisher of the Wilmington *Daily Journal*. He wondered if he should try to convince her to let the sale happen. Yet his father hadn't protested when she told him about her plans. Then again maybe he hadn't been conscious enough to understand her meaning. Bill came to a decision; he couldn't go against her now. He would help her break off negotiations for the *Gazette's* sale.

Dropping to his knees, Bill leaned forward and whispered into Clarence's ear, "Go to God."

Doctor Iuppenlatz helped Bill to his feet. The doctor must have heard Bill's whispers, for he said, "He's gone. And may I add...a life well lived."

Three

Another Southern Funeral

As the organ trilled "My Faith Looks Up To Thee," Bill grimaced. In spite of torturous efforts to think of something else, he kept coming back to the image he wanted cleansed from his mind—his father inside the coffin. When he looked at the bier and the coffin on top, Bill saw only the glass lid. That's why he kept staring at the floor.

He tentatively lifted his head and saw his father in the coffin dressed in his Sunday-best suit, worn and frayed thanks to the out-of-control inflation. Bill's momma had been devastated she couldn't buy him a new one. His hair had been perfectly combed by Wilbur Scott, the undertaker. It usually looked windblown, a casualty of breezy walks to and from the *Gazette* office. His hands were crossed and rested on top of Laura's favorite doll, bought early in the war as a Christmas gift. Mark's Jacob's ladder toy lay on a satin pillow beside his head. Bill had personally placed a composing stick between the side of the coffin and Clarence's body. The lead type and the slugs spelled out Icie Belle. It made him think of his momma's intention to run the newspaper.

Bill still needed to find the proper moment to tell Icie Belle about the pending sale of the *Gazette* to Tanya Gleeman's father John, owner of Wilmington's *Daily Journal*. When the right moment came, it would entail revealing his father had told Bill about his failing heart, but had made him swear to say nothing to his momma. She'd be upset, but hopefully she'd understand. The sale was meant to give Icie Belle, Mark and Laura a financial cushion if Clarence died before the Lord's three score and ten years. Bill's papa wanted Icie Belle to be able to open a flower shop. Clarence never considered she might want to run the newspaper.

Franny squeezed Bill's right arm. "Are you all right?"

He must look as bad as he felt. A glance at his lap brought a folded newspaper into focus—the *Gazette's* latest issue, his father's last. On his left, his momma patted her eyes with a handkerchief. He couldn't say the truth, not with Icie Belle seated with them. "I'm okay. Memories keep spinning in my head."

Julia Dickson tapped the last notes of "Rock of Ages" as the Reverend Sprunt took his place behind the pulpit. He led them in prayer, reciting the words of the Twenty-Third Psalm. Then he eulogized Clarence. "Today we gather to honor the life of one of our own, a fair-minded man who never held political office. Mayors, city councilmen and county commissioners came to him hopin' for a favorable word in his editorials. Clarence Stamford was a newspaper editor, not an easy job in these troublin' times when overzealous patriots burn down newspaper offices."

The reverend told of a business trip to Ohio to purchase a printing press. "When in the Buckeye State, Clarence met a comely young woman on a walk in a park and resolved to court her. This stranger from North Carolina overcame the woman's reservations and gained permission from her father to call on her. Against great odds, Clarence won the heart of the Ohio woman, Icie Belle, and made her his wife. We all now consider her a Tar Heel."

The mayor and the chairman of the city council spoke glowingly of Bill's father. Their eulogies irritated Bill. They were mad at him more often than not. Many times they marched to the office to complain about an editorial. They were stingy with city money even in the prewar days, and Clarence Samford loved pointing out their failings, especially since April 1861.

Newspaper in hand, Bill sported a grin as he walked up to the podium to talk about his father's work as an editor. Clarence's eldest son intended to turn the politicians' words against them. "Good afternoon. All of you know me. Back in the day I was the kid on the boardwalk playing jacks, the one you had to step over before you could enter the *Gazette* office. When I got older, you often saw me inside the building, sometimes at the composing board, sometimes helping out with the press. I'm Bill, Clarence's oldest son, the boy who joined up a year ago with his chuckaboo, Charlie, and took the train to war." He pointed out into the mourners. "Charlie's out there somewhere. Oh, there you are. He lost an arm at Gettysburg. I've a scar on my back, a sliver from a Yankee shell. It's mostly healed so I'll be returning to the war." Bill regarded the coffin to his front. "Look around town and you'll see lots of fellas like Charlie and me. We're the flotsam of this war. We're the ones my papa looked out for every time he wrote a harsh editorial taking the politicians to task."

Bill held up the newspaper. "This is my father's last edition of the *Gazette*. I'd like to read a portion of his final editorial." He positioned the newspaper on the podium and rested his hands along the newsprint's edge. "The *Gazette* has championed the lame soldiers, the war widows and their children since First Manassas. We thought we could finally announce a small victory in that humanitarian fight. We were wrong. Our efforts to see nominal funding in the city and county budgets to help the innocent victims of this war came to naught. The money has been zeroed out. There will be no farm markets for soldiers' wives nor government aid for soldiers horribly wounded." Bill folded the newspaper and set it back down on the pulpit, then let his gaze travel from one end of the sanctuary to the other. He found it hard to believe that a few days earlier he'd been married in this very room. "My father has gone to Heaven, but I can assure you his fight for the plight of lame soldiers and widows isn't finished. My momma will pick up Papa's sword and continue his fight. Icie Belle Stamford will be the new editor and publisher of the *Gazette*." He nodded to his momma and she blew him a kiss. "Just like Clarence Stamford, Icie Belle will put into action the words Jesus preached throughout his three-year ministry. Know this, politicians! Icie Belle will defend the war's lame soldiers, the widows and the orphans."

When Bill resumed his seat in the front pew, his momma leaned against him. "I didn't expect that from you. Now you leave me no choice but to take the *Gazette's* helm, not that I had second thoughts." She patted his arm.

As soon as Icie Belle stopped whispering, Franny offered her opinion. "Way to give 'em hell. You're definitely your father's son."

The funeral service concluded with Mrs. Dickson playing "Holy, Holy, Holy, Lord God Almighty," and the Reverend Sprunt leading the mourners in prayer. And what Bill had been dreading… pallbearers carrying his father to the hearse.

The brass handle felt jarringly cold as Bill helped cart the coffin out the front doorway. A chill crawled along his skin when the pallbearers slid the coffin into the hearse. A few days before, Bill's honeymoon buggy had been parked in the exact spot.

As Bill stepped onto the floorboard of the undertaker's carriage, he swiveled toward the line of conveyances that stretched for several blocks. The pastor told him it was the largest procession ever seen. Nature cooperated with a partly cloudy sky where the occasional cloud offered momentary shade. Bill had heard many stories that rain invariably impeded funerals. Not his papa's, though.

Bill settled into the carriage seat, joining his momma, Franny, Mark and Laura. His poor momma had no one from her own Ohio family to help dry her tears. Another cost of the war.

Drawn by two horses, the hearse led the procession to Grove Presbyterian's burial ground on Routledge Road east of town, a half-mile journey. On the way, Icie Belle kept fiddling with her ragged purse, bought a week before First Manassas at Brown Mercantile on the town square.

"Bill, I had the oddest dream last night." She put the purse aside. "Clarence came to me, stood at the edge of the bed. It felt real. My dreams are usually a mishmash of chumpy images. He spoke. 'Have Bill find out about Wilson and Malinda.' Then he walked into the hallway. I threw back the sheet and got up to follow. By the time I reached the doorway, he was gone." She sighed. "I'm still not sure if I really got up or it was part of the dream."

Wilson and Malinda were the family's slaves. She ruled the house, he the yard. With his father's blessing, they'd fled with the Yankee cavalry after July's sword-factory raid. Bill too sometimes wondered how Wilson and Malinda were faring. He hoped the North Star had led them to a happier life.

"I don't discount anything anymore, Momma." Bill swiped at a fly buzzing around his nose. "I'm the boy who sees halos."

"Halos?" Laura asked, her voice hesitant.

"Not now, Laura," Icie Belle said.

"If it is a message from Papa, I don't see how I can learn anything," Bill pointed out. "Malinda and Wilson will be in Yankee-occupied land and I'll be in Richmond."

The darkey driver—Bill wondered why the fellow hadn't shadowed the Yankee Cavalry to New Bern—followed the hearse into the burial ground, guiding the carriage through the gate with its inscription: Here I Wait For You. In the distance among newer gravestones and an ancient oak tree, Bill could see an ugly hole in the ground and next to it an oilcloth covering a mound of dirt, their stark destination.

Again, Bill helped carry the coffin, this time to a grassy spot near the hole. As he held tightly to the brass handle, he watched more than a hundred of his father's friends gather at the gravesite, some from as far away as Wilmington more than a hundred miles to the south. Not all had been in the church for the memorial service—not enough room. Yet they valued their friendship with Clarence so much they took time off from work and farming to make the melancholy trek to the cemetery. Tears washed down Bill's face. With his hands clutching the handle, he couldn't get to his handkerchief.

The Reverend Sprunt joined Bill, his mother and Franny. "Splendid location for a final restin' place. The stately oak tree will provide shade for Sunday visits. One couldn't ask for a better place to rest until the resurrection."

"My husband picked this spot several years ago." Icie Belle swept her hankie across her forehead and neck, not for tears but sweat. "Of course, he'd thought today wouldn't happen until far in the future. The Lord has a habit of undoing all our calculations."

The pastor nodded. "Naked came I out of my mother's womb, and naked shall I return thither: the Lord gave, and the Lord hath taken away; blessed be the name of the Lord."

After all the words heard earlier in the day in church, Bill found his mind wandering as the Reverend Sprunt led the mourners in prayer. Later, he watched graveyard workers—darkies—lower the coffin into the hole. He dumped a shovelful of dirt into the grave, a task he found morbid. Yet it remained time honored for the sons of a dearly departed father. Bill handed the shovel to Mark. Gritting his teeth, Mark gripped the handle so tightly his knuckles turned white. One, two shovelfuls went into the hole.

"Our duty is done, Papa," Bill whispered.

The eldest son put his arm around Mark's shoulders and led him back to the carriage.

Strong faith ensured Clarence celebrated with the saints in Heaven. There'd be no celebrating in the Stamford house twenty-nine months into the war.

Four

A Time to Unwind

Deepening shadows crept into the Stamford parlor, chasing away the light except for two lit oil lamps, one next to a game board table and the other beside a tufted linen couch. Bill coached Laura on tactics as she competed against Mark in a cutthroat game of checkers. Across the room, Franny had burrowed into the couch to read a novel by lamplight. Icie Belle lay back in a velvet chair, her eyes closed, exhausted after nearly a week of constant strain—a wedding, her husband's heart attack and death, and just a few hours earlier, his funeral and burial.

"Not fair," Mark crossed his arms against his chest. "It's two against one."

Although Bill didn't feel particularly humorous this night, he tried to crack a joke. "The blue-bellies always outnumbered us two-to-one. It didn't matter; we always whipped them."

Mark yawned. He too fought to stay awake. "I'm really playing against you, Bill."

"I understand." Bill rose from a game-table chair. "It's Laura versus you. May the best player win.

Right leg cramped, Bill took a wobbly step and nearly went down. He righted himself and settled beside Franny.

Laura giggled at her brother's clumsiness, then clammed up. Her papa had just been put in the ground. "Forgive me, Papa," she whispered.

"It's okay to laugh, Laura," Bill told her. "Papa would want you to…I did look silly."

Grinning guiltily, Laura quipped to her thirteen-year-old brother, "I'm going to slaughter you. Move your confounded piece."

Bill leaned forward to see the cover of Franny's novel, but couldn't make it out. "What are you reading, sweetheart?"

"Herman Melville's *Moby Dick*. Mother left it with me before she and father headed to Virginia." Franny bookmarked the last page she'd read and shut the novel. "Ahab's one obsessive man."

Icie Belle glanced at her Bible on the small tea table next to the chair. "Ahab reminds me of King David and his obsession with Bathsheba."

"Like many of the politicians in Richmond," Bill inserted. "An independent Confederate States of America has become their whale."

Franny cocked an eyebrow. "You'll soon be one of them, darling."

Bill offered his wife a sour smile. "Not me. I'm a soldier, not a politician."

She pursed her lips. "You'll be working for a politician, James Seddon, malleable as they come."

"I can't make up my mind about your father." Leaning closer, Bill squeezed Franny's hand. "One minute he seems to like me; the next, he gives me the cold shoulder."

"Father's a reserved man. Along with Chaplain Anderson, Father helped get you the job at the War Department. I'd say that's a vote of confidence."

Bill shrugged. "Since we'll both be working there, he's going to get to know me a heap more. Hopefully, he won't come to regret the decision."

"Father rarely changes his mind." Irony sparkled in Franny's eyes. "More than once he has said God will not allow the Yankees to win the war. He's a man who refuses to acknowledge the concept of doubt."

Near the fireplace, Mark jumped to his feet and glared at the game table. "Look at what Laura has done, Momma! She's ruined the game!" The pieces lay scattered all over the table and the rug.

"I nodded off for a second, Momma," Laura responded, her expression one of confusion.

"That's all it took," Mark grated. "Her head hit the table and the pieces flew."

Laura rubbed a red spot on her head. "Not that hard. The table didn't tip over."

"Hard enough," Mark hissed.

"I'm sorry." Laura slapped a hand over a yawn. "I'm so tired. I can't keep my eyes open anymore."

"It couldn't have been that hard of a head knock." Icie Belle yawned herself. "I didn't hear it. Anyway, pick up the pieces and go upstairs to bed."

When the game pieces had been placed inside a table drawer, Laura and Mark gave their mother a goodnight kiss and plodded upstairs.

Franny set *Moby Dick* on the tea table next to the lamp. "I'm tuckered. Think I'll turn in." She took Bill's hand and kissed it. "See you in a bit."

"I'll be up shortly," Bill said as Franny rose to her feet.

Franny approached her mother-in-law. Stooping in her hoopless mourning dress, she kissed Icie Belle's cheek. "I know Clarence was a special man. He chose you to be his wife and the two of you shaped the man I love."

"My Clarence knew Bill made the best choice." Icie Belle leaned forward, took Franny's hands and kissed each palm. "He joked once he couldn't believe Bill actually made a wise choice in the courting game." She gazed heavenward as if she could see her husband. "Your son won a sweet, precious heart, didn't he?"

"Indeed, I did," Bill affirmed. "I didn't even have to chase her. She chased me all the way to Magnolia."

What a shocking July morning that had been for Bill. After a nighttime trek from Kenansville to the Confederate headquarters in Magnolia, Bill had warned the commander of the raid on the sword factory and then gone to bed. A knock on the door awakened him. Not one of the commander's greenhorns as Bill expected, but Franny come to claim his heart. They'd had a melting moment, and she'd never been far from his side since.

When Franny's footfalls up the steps faded, Icie Belle pressed her palms into the armrests. "My thoughts agree with Franny's sentiments. I can't keep my eyes open any longer. Hear it, Bill? My bed's calling out to me." She scooted to the edge of the chair.

"Wait, Momma. I need to tell you something." He'd put off his father's prospective sale of the *Gazette* long enough.

"You sound so serious. I didn't think this day could get any more serious." Icie Belle settled against the backrest and hitched herself up straight.

Bill lugged a footstool to the chair and sat, facing his momma. "Back in May, Papa went to see Doctor Iuppenlatz. The heart attack wasn't a surprise, Momma. Papa knew he'd die soon."

Brows knitting over her nose, Icie Belle frowned. "He knew and kept it from me? That doesn't make sense. I used to be a nurse."

"He didn't want you worrying." Bill knew he was making a mess of things. Nonetheless, he forged on. "Papa made plans to ensure you, Mark and Laura were financially secure just in case. He didn't want you forced to marry someone you didn't love to stay out of the poorhouse."

She shook her head in dismay. "How far did he get?"

Icie Belle realized she might not get the *Gazette*. "Bill, the sale… can it be reversed?"

"John Gleeman, the *Daily Journal's* publisher, has the contract. On our office calendar, he marked Thursday, September twenty-fourth as an appointment in Wilmington with Gleeman." Slithering off the footstool, Bill knelt on one knee. "I figure September twenty-fourth is the day they're to sign the contract and make it official."

"Your papa's a very good man. I need time to think about the contract. Maybe it's for the best we sell the newspaper. I could spend the money to open a flower shop."

Her thinking surprised Bill. She'd seemed so committed to running the *Gazette.* Just the thought of coming into a windfall of cash had her pondering a flower shop. Maybe it would turn out to be irresistible, and Gleeman would soon own the Stamford newspaper. Bill's belly churned. "Whatever you decide, Momma, you know I'll back you."

His momma turned her head toward the stairs, perhaps thinking of the bed she shared with his father for twenty years. "It's his legacy. So many people came to his memorial service, some from as far away as Wilmington and Raleigh. They loved and respected him. I hate to sell his legacy. Yet the money could let me have my flower shop, a dream I've always had."

"I know, Momma." His eyes welled with water, forcing Bill to wipe them with his handkerchief. "You'll make the right decision. As to the *Gazette* as Papa's legacy, the same people who now praise and honor him were ready to burn it down earlier in the summer— simply on rumors he might print something seditious. He softened his editorials about the conduct of the war. Papa didn't want to put your life and the lives of Mark and Laura at risk."

Concurring, Icie Belle said grimly, "Sometimes I think the South has gone—"

"Momma, I can't sleep." Laura rubbed her eyes as she lurched into the room.

"Come on over here, daughter. Let me hold you. This week has been terrible for you."

Laura let Icie Belle's arms enshroud her. "Did Papa think people wanted to hurt me, Mark and you?"

Icie Belle stared intently into her daughter's huge eyes. "Remember what he would tell you when you heard us talk about adult matters in the house? No loose lips when you're with your friends." The older woman ran a finger along the girl's chin. "Lips always sealed. We don't take chances."

"Yes, just like Papa told me, keep my lips sealed. I thought he was jesting. He wasn't, was he? He didn't want me, Mark or you getting hurt." Her lower lip quivered.

Bill spoke up, "Lots and lots of people have been hurt by the war. They deal with their pain by hurting people they think aren't strong patriots like themselves."

"I promise, Bill," Laura said in a subdued voice. "What I hear won't leave the house."

"We've been talking about the *Gazette*, Laura. What do you think? Do we sell the newspaper?" Bill smiled when his sister pursed her lips thoughtfully.

"No!" Laura's near-shout sent the cat Indy scurrying out of the room. "It wasn't just Papa's newspaper. It was all of ours. Even me. I'll help out after school. You mustn't sell it."

"I'll think long and hard on it, Laura," Icie Belle promised. "Come, take my hand. We'll head up to bed."

~ * ~

Even with the lamplight, the room felt cold and empty with everyone but Bill upstairs in their beds. Bill spanked his forearms to dispel the chill. He considered starting a fire in the fireplace, but laughed. It was summertime. While the nights were getting cooler, it was still not time for smoke to rise from the chimney. The cold in the room was all in Bill's mind.

Scrambling to his feet, Bill noticed two errant game pieces under the table. As he dropped them into the game-table drawer with the others, Bill wondered if his momma would invite Laura into her bed. The night would turn out less lonely, less forlorn, if they shared it together.

Had Laura's words swung Icie Belle's decision toward keeping the *Gazette*? With the date to finalize the sale coming up fast, Bill would get the answer soon enough. He extinguished the lamps, and as the darkness enveloped him, headed for the stairway. Nearby, Indy meowed, then tore up the steps to the second floor. Bill could hear the cat's paws slapping each step. "Who's bed are you contemplating, Indy?"

As Bill followed Indy up the stairs, he yearned to slip into bed next to Franny. Maybe her warm body would dispel the cold that had settled uncomfortably in his mind. He suddenly realized that his birthday approached—September 28. No one remembered, not even his momma. Then again who felt like eating cake just days after a loved one's passing?

Five

A Night of Seeking Warmth

He rested his palm on the banister handrail and let it slide along the mahogany. Whatever the *Gazette* decision, Bill knew his momma would have no regrets. She'd love to grow flowers in her own greenhouse and sell the roses, azaleas, peonies and lilies in the attached shop. But if she chose to keep the newspaper, she'd put all her heart and soul into keeping it the politicians' worst nightmare.

Bill knew the way to his bedroom so well he could reach it in darkness, blinds closed and curtains drawn so even moonlight couldn't leak through. Once on the top landing, he reached out with his arm and touched the wall. As a kid, he'd count the number of steps to his room. He took longer strides now, so instead of eighteen it took just fifteen. Sometimes he wished it still took eighteen so he could wipe away everything bad that had happened in the years between ten and nineteen, except for Franny.

Nearing his momma's room, he heard two voices, hers and Laura's. He smiled. Laura had indeed sought the familiar warmth and love of their momma. The night would be less cold for them both. With Franny in his room, Bill knew he would bask in her warmth once he slipped between the bed sheets. *Sleep well, Momma and Laura.*

Ahead, light seeped out from the narrow space between the plank floor and the bottom of his bedroom door. Franny hadn't extinguished the bedside lamp. She must be reading. *Moby Dick* had been left on the tea table, so she must have grabbed one of his books stored away on the bookcase his Granddaddy Newton built for him. He wondered which one she'd chosen. Maybe *Westward Ho* or *Tom Brown's Schooldays.*

Bill turned the knob and tiptoed into the bedroom. Franny lay asleep on the bed, snoring softly, her head cushioned by a pillow, a book resting on her belly. The window was open, allowing a breeze to cool the room. Soft room light fluttered as puffs of air skimmed against the bedside lamp's glass shade.

Sighing, Bill settled onto the edge of the bed and tugged off his boots. Feminine lips brushed against the back of his neck. Long manicured nails stroked his chest. Franny had awakened. Bill glanced down at his groin and groaned. His penis had refused to engorge. It hadn't since his father's death. His melancholy proved more powerful than his desire to make love to his new wife. Each night since his father's death, he'd spent his bedtime crying into the pillow as Franny nestled against him, massaging the tension in his shoulders and neck.

Wearily standing, Bill discarded his uniform, and wearing no more than his cotton drawers, slipped between the bedcovers and savored the touch of Franny's nightgown against his chest. Her satin nightdress meant she acknowledged they'd not consummate their marriage this night. She knew he needed more time to grieve.

"In the past week, I've barely thought about the halos," he told her.

She kissed his bare shoulder. "Not surprising. You've a lot on your mind, darling. You're worried about your momma, Mark and Laura—and no doubt your father's newspaper."

He drew her into a tight embrace. "I've been scanning the Raleigh and Richmond newspapers looking for Rose Greenhow's name. In August, she sailed for Europe with her daughter and Becky."

Franny rubbed her face against his cheek and chin. "Looking for Rose's death notice, eh? And maybe Becky's too? Don't forget, Charlie's still alive—and you saw a halo around him. I expect Rose, her daughter and Becky are having a fizzing good time."

"It's been three months since Rose's halo." Bill caressed his wife's exposed arm. "You could be right. For whatever reason, the Lord's showing me mercy. I've prayed for no more halos, and perhaps He answered my prayers."

Franny draped a leg atop his thigh. "I've also prayed that God sends no more halos. So far good news, right?"

"I still worry. At least I didn't see a halo around Papa. That would have shattered me." He let his mind wander: *How's Heaven, Papa? Please ask the Lord to let Rose, her daughter and Becky live. Please, for me. The Lord took General Jackson instead of Charlie. Let that be enough. The halos are wearing me down. I'm not sure how much more I can—*

"Charlie's putting on a good front for you, Bill." Franny danced her fingers along his chest, fiddling with the hairs circling one of his nipples. "I worry about him. I know you've said he hasn't been his old self."

Taking her hand, Bill kissed her fingers. "Maybe a woman much like you will show him he doesn't need that arm to be a man."

"Plenty of women are glad to have their husbands and beaus alive even without an arm or leg." Franny pushed Bill onto his back and clambered atop him.

"Sorry, Franny," he said, his tone regretful. "The soldier won't salute. I realize I have a bride who hasn't been made love to since our wedding. We can try."

Tapping Bill's chest, Franny glided off him and lay on her side, her breath stroking his week-old whiskers. "Our morning of lovemaking in the Magnolia mansion will keep me satisfied until you're ready. When we do tip the velvet, I know you'll leave me exhausted but begging for more."

"I'm so lucky to have you."

"Indeed, you are, Bill Stamford." Franny toyed with Bill's whiskers. "You know I don't like a beard. You're going to have to shave it."

'I know. I just didn't feel like shaving since the wedding." He kissed her. "Then you're not angry that we haven't joined giblets?"

"Giblets? Lordy, you men have such awful ways to describe the act of love." She moved closer and let their noses rub together. "A wife who isn't a best friend isn't much of a wife. Our lovemaking can wait. Now's the time to hold you close and let you cry without judgment or reproach."

"Thank you, my love." Bill wiggled closer to Franny and caressed a buttock. "And thank you for giving me time to mourn."

Chewing his lower lip, he let his head sink into the feathered pillow. Franny rose up on her elbow and extinguished the lamp, turning the flame knob until the wick disappeared then blowing across the top of the chimney. The light flickered and went out.

"Good night, my love," she said.

"I love you."

His chest still tingled from the touch of her fingers. That was a good sign. Maybe his deep glum would soon lessen and his plug tail would start doing what God intended.

So much to worry about, though, uneasiness he couldn't control. Fretting about Laura and Mark; Papa had left them at the most important time of their young lives. Momma forced to make the most crucial decision of her life since accepting their father's marriage proposal. Should she keep the *Gazette* or sell it and use the cash to go into the flower business? Make the wrong decision and she could leave herself, Mark and Laura penniless. *No, that won't happen as long as I'm breathing. If need be, I'll take care of them.* Except the war could ruin his fallback plans if orders came to return to the Army of Northern Virginia.

Next to him, Franny snored, much to his relief. Bill didn't want her fretting all night, worrying about him. In the morning, he intended to gather up the toys and games from his dressertop and store them in the armoire. He wanted no reminders of a lost childhood. Too many children in the South had lost their childhoods due to a mini ball, artillery shell and disease. He'd been lucky enough to have a father until the age of eighteen...almost nineteen. Thousands of young ones no older than seven or eight would grow up with a stepfather and dimming memories of another man who marched off to fight a war and never came home.

"You're tossing and turning. Try to get some sleep," Franny said drowsily.

Once again his new wife made sense. Bill tried to empty his mind of all the nerve-wracking thoughts. Not something easily accomplished, he admitted, and then chastised himself for cluttering his mind when he needed slumber. *Listen to her. Maybe if you get some sleep, you'll be able to perform your bedroom duty to your wife.*

Bill turned onto his back and let the breeze wafting from the window cool his face. Soon he felt himself drifting....

Six

A Newspaper's Future is Decided

Bill and Icie Belle strolled from the Wilmington and Weldon Railroad depot onto the Front Street boardwalk. Almost immediately the noise inside the depot's waiting room faded. As the mother and son made their way toward Wilmington's Market Street and the *Daily Journal*, sprinkles dampened Icie Belle's mourning dress and Bill's Confederate uniform. Fiddling with the umbrella he clutched like a Springfield rifle, Bill glanced upward into a sky filled with churning clouds. Raindrops splattered his face, forcing him to look away.

"Bill, the umbrella?" Icie Belle repositioned the satchel strapped to her shoulder.

"Sorry, Momma." Bill unfurled the umbrella he had brought along from Kenansville when the morning looked ominous. "I can almost see the beginnings of a tornado sinking from one cloud."

Icie Belle drew closer to Bill so she'd get the umbrella's full protection. "A tornado? Hope not. Wilmington doesn't need another disaster, not after last year's yellow jack epidemic."

"Don't see it now." Bill ducked his head back beneath the wide-brimmed umbrella.

Lightning lit up the sky above Wilmington followed by thunder that rumbled along the waterfront. On the Cape Fear River a block away, ship masts and blockader smokestacks swayed wildly, buffeted by the blustery wind.

"Better think of something, Bill." His momma squeezed his arm as if she feared the wind might send her tumbling down Front Street. "The umbrella's going to turn inside out."

They scampered into the Mermaid Tavern, passing beneath a noisily swinging sign of a long-haired mermaid perched on a rocky foreshore. Bill closed the umbrella and looked for a vacant table. All were occupied by folks seeking shelter from the rain. Normally, the tavern's tables would have only four or five customers on a Thursday afternoon. With nowhere to sit, Bill and Icie Belle stood at one of the windows with other customers watching raindrops splash in the puddles on the street.

They'd been riding the rails for more than four hours, traveling from Magnolia to Wilmington aboard a dilapidated train depleted by nearly thirty months of conflict. The locomotives, passenger coaches, freight cars and tracks themselves needed major maintenance, but that wouldn't happen until after the war. It took all of the Wilmington and Weldon Railroad manpower to just keep the rail system operating at a maddening crawl.

Bill stared at the waterfront and the sundry tall masts and smokestacks dominating the harbor skyline. The rain fell in a torrent, veiling the dockside scene, cloaking everything behind a misty curtain of water.

"I love the waterfront," he blurted out.

Several men around him agreed. "Never get tired of the bustle at the Dock Street warehouses," one mustached fellow said.

"This rain's cleansing everything," a businessman with a British accent observed. "It's going to wash away the factory soot."

"My mind's on yellow fever," Icie Belle said. "This is my first trip since the epidemic. I'm nervous. I want to get my business done and get back on the train."

"Where do you hail from, ma'am?" The mustached man tipped his bowler, revealing a thick mane of coppery hair.

"Duplin County," she told him. "Kenansville, best small town in North Carolina."

The sound of the rain proved mesmerizing as it pounded the cloth awning. Bill swore he could smell a perfume-like scent leaking through the closed front door. Across the street, under another awning, a young woman in a mourning dress and bonnet clutched a broom, but not for sweeping. Instead, she poked the broom's handle into a gutter downspout hole, clearing a plug of leaves. Rainwater gushed from the downspout and washed across the boardwalk. Not far from the broom woman, a girl clad in a flowery dress skipped through a milliner shop doorway, leaped across the boardwalk and landed in a substantial puddle. Rainwater sprayed upward, drenching her. She danced from puddle to puddle as a horse and buggy splashed along the brick street, adding to the girl's soaking.

"You're going to get run over, Shirley Long," someone in the buggy shouted. "Get out of the street!"

Even inside the tavern with rain smacking the awning and glass separating Bill from Front Street, he easily heard the shrill voice of the woman inside the buggy. Another voice just as strident came from inside the milliner shop. A woman in a dress with the same flower pattern stamped out the doorway and shouted, "Shirley, get inside now! I'll never get that dress clean! Naughty little sprite!"

The spat-spat-spat of raindrops spraying the awning diminished even as the little sprite's mother hustled her back inside the milliner shop. Bill ushered his momma out the tavern door ahead of others who also considered the downpour nearly over. Just before he opened the umbrella, he spotted a sliver of green on the horizon beyond the Cape Fear River.

"We could have stayed home and done this by telegraph. Missed the thunderstorm." Bill leaped across a puddle on the boardwalk. His momma came up short.

"Well, aren't you the gigglemug!" Icie Belle snorted, glancing at the soaked hem of her dress.

"Sorry, Momma. Still, the telegraph sure looks good after all this miserable weather."

"I want to be fair to Gleeman. I think it's the right thing to do—face to face. The fever, though, makes me nervous." Icie Belle scowled. "The telegraph doesn't sound so bad when I think of yellow jack."

"No reports of any outbreaks. And we'll be back on the train headed north soon enough." Bill wiped a raindrop off his nose. The breeze still swirled, occasionally sneaking sprinkles past the umbrella and against his face.

At the intersection of Front and Market streets, Bill and Icie Belle headed for the *Journal's* office.

Three front pages of recent editions covered the *Journal's* storefront window. Icie Belle pointed to one headline, an announcement of a recruiting drive by a convalescing soldier with the Fifty-First Regiment attached to the Army of the Tennessee. "Just three months ago you were doing the same for the Eighteenth Regiment," Icie Belle remarked. "I remember you mentioning an ad the *Journal* did for you."

"Yes, and those few days included my major transgression—Becky." Bill shared a remorseful half-smile.

"You survived it and gained the forgiveness of the only person who should matter in this whole silly mess. Not Becky, not her father, not me or your father—Franny." Icie Belle stuck her hand out beyond the umbrella. "No rain."

At the *Journal's* entrance, Bill stepped aside to allow his momma to enter the newspaper's reception foyer. Closing the umbrella, he shadowed Icie Belle into the room as the overhead doorbell jingled. Behind the counter, Tanya Gleeman, the owner's daughter, beamed when she recognized Bill. "Private Bill Stamford, you're the soldier who put on that nanty-narking good time at the recruiting drive. Bob Wright? Remember him? He owns Wright's General Store and plays the saxophone. He lined up the community band for you. Bob still talks about it."

"Nice fellow. I couldn't have had as good a drive as I did without his help." Bill swung his gaze to Icie Belle. "This is my momma. She's here to speak to your father."

Tanya wore an odd expression of bewilderment and apprehension followed by shock. She'd obviously just realized Icie Belle's widowhood was barely a week and a half old. "I'm so thoughtless. Please forgive me, ma'am—and Bill. I'm so sorry for your loss."

Most women in Wilmington were dressed in black in the late summer of 1863. Easy to be dull-witted when yet another black-clad woman walked into the newspaper office.

"Thank you, dear," Icie Belle said, her voice muted. "It was sudden and I'm still trying to make sense of it. The Lord's will, I guess."

"He didn't suffer long." Bill stored the umbrella on the parasol stand and bellied up to the counter. "Better than the deaths of some amputees. Done in by gangrene. Or consumption, the cough of death."

Grimacing, Tanya nodded. She reached for a datebook and eyed it. "Oh, you've an appointment. Follow me."

Tanya shepherded them into a conference room. In an adjacent area, the steam-powered press growled like a Wilmington and Weldon locomotive trundling toward the downtown depot. The floor, the walls, the ceiling, even Bill's chair vibrated.

John Gleeman strode into the room; soon the noise lessened and stopped. Clad in work clothes and an ink-stained apron, a straw hat atop his bald head, he bowed to Icie Belle and shook Bill's hand. "I'm so sorry to hear about your husband, Mrs. Stamford. I wanted to attend the funeral, but pressing business prevented me."

"In these times, life's so fleeting. Every household's dinner table has an empty chair." Icie Belle raked back damp graying hair from her forehead. "I feared Bill would fall on some distant battlefield and the Good Lord would claim him. Instead, this terrible war wore down my husband and God called him home."

"My wife and I have no sons, just four daughters." John looked toward the open door. "I've sent the oldest, Tanya, to summon my lawyer who has my sale papers. He has an office down the street. He should be here shortly."

"You're a lucky man, sir," Icie Belle responded. "Lucky to have four delightful daughters, and lucky that you haven't had to bury a son like so many families in North Carolina."

"I fear for Tanya, though." John took off his hat and set it on the table in front of him. "Her beau is with the Fifty-First North Carolina out west. There's been fierce fighting at a place called Chickamauga. We wait for the casualty lists and pray her Dempsey isn't among the dead and wounded."

"We will pray for a great Confederate victory, and that the Lord protects Dempsey from Yankee mini balls." Bill's shrapnel scar suddenly itched.

"Yes, a prayer that Dempsey emerges from the battle unscathed," Icie Belle concurred.

"I think I hear my daughter and the lawyer." The doorbell jingled.

"I hate to see you go to all this trouble." Icie Belle reached into the satchel and produced her copy of the contract. "Without my knowledge, Clarence put out feelers to sell the *Gazette*. Doctor Iuppenlatz told him he had a failing heart and could die at any time. My husband wanted to provide for me and the children in case..." Sniffling, Icie Belle wiped her eyes with a handkerchief. "He married an Ohio girl and feared she could face troubles without him there as a buffer."

"Very understandable," the Wilmington newspaperman said. "Too many Tar Heels are looking for scapegoats as the war drags on."

"He didn't get my okay," Icie Belle stressed.

Tanya escorted the lawyer into the room and returned to the front counter to wait on customers. Once seated, the lawyer unstrapped his satchel.

"Dennis, we've had a change of plans." John grinned sourly. "I think Mrs. Stamford is having second thoughts. Icie Belle?"

"Yes, I'm uncomfortable selling." Icie Belle stripped off her wet gloves and pocketed them. "I want to run my late husband's newspaper." She leaned closer and rested her elbows on the table. "I don't intend to marry a man I don't love to keep me and my youngest kids from destitution. Or sell the *Gazette* for onetime money to start up a flower shop that may or may not be successful. The *Gazette* is already highly successful. I know the business. I've been working alongside my husband for twenty years."

Bill wanted to cheer. His momma had chosen to keep the *Gazette*. After the war, if he chose, Bill could partner with her. And Mark, perhaps even Laura, would grow up during their school years helping out in the print shop.

"My momma's a force of nature," Bill wisecracked. "If she says she'll run the *Gazette*, it'll soon be the best newspaper in North Carolina."

"You're right, soldier." John eyed the ink stains on his fingers then switched his gaze to Icie Belle. "Ma'am, your husband and I initially agreed to the sale with a handshake. We had my attorney, Dennis here, draw up a contract, one copy for your husband to peruse and mine that Dennis brought along today. Now it appears there's no need to sign them, Dennis."

The lawyer plucked the contract from his satchel and handed it to John. "Hope you're not making a mistake, ma'am." Dennis's brows knitted over his nose.

"Icie Belle made the right decision. She has fire in her eyes. The *Gazette's* in good hands." John tore the contract in half.

"Fire in her eyes? Wonderful description, Mr. Gleeman." Bill reached across the table and shook the man's hand.

John stood and again bowed to Icie Belle. "Good luck, ma'am."

Icie Belle retrieved her version of the contact and handed it to Bill. "I do believe this should be the eldest son's duty." Bill ripped the contract into six pieces.

"Still enough time for you two to make it back to Duplin County." John led them into the reception foyer and toward the front door. "But, ma'am, if you change your mind at any time, I'll be more than happy to make you a lucrative offer. In these inflationary times, the offer could prove a godsend."

"On the contrary, I intend to someday buy the *Journal*, sir." Icie Belle grinned.

With the *Gazette* safe, Bill and Icie Belle were soon headed back to the depot.

Seven

Some Shooting and Dying

The Reverend Sprunt passed through the entryway into the Warsaw Depot just as a locomotive steam whistle blew, heralding a train's arrival from Magnolia. The Wilmington and Weldon train would transport Bill and Franny up into Virginia where they'd board a Richmond and Petersburg train for the final leg to the Confederate capital.

"Your momma's going to miss you, Bill." The pastor settled on a bench behind Bill and his family. He'd just stabled his horse and buggy so the animal could be fed and groomed for the return trip to Kenansville.

"I got to keep him for a few weeks more than I anticipated." Icie Belle let her words out in a sigh nearly as long as the blast of the locomotive's whistle.

If not for my father's sudden death, Franny and I would have taken the train north to Weldon weeks earlier. We would have accompanied my recruits, with the new soldiers joining the Army of Northern Virginia while Franny and I caught a train to Richmond.

Leaning forward, Reverend Sprunt palmed Franny's shoulder. "I hope in time you'll remember the joyful parts of your wedding, not that terrible ending. I know in Heaven there's no sadness, but I expect Clarence is still chastising the Lord for the heart attack at the end of the ceremony." The clergyman laughed softly.

"Bill's father offered me only love and kindness from the moment we met." Franny patted the Reverend Sprunt's hand still resting on her shoulder. "Indeed, I can see him upbraiding the Lord for the ill timing." She summoned a rueful smile.

"I won't try to guess the Lord's purpose for taking Clarence when he did." The preacher withdrew his hand from Franny's shoulder. "I'll only say it'll become clear in time."

Clear? Like the halos? Bill kept that thought to himself. "I gained a wife and lost a father. The happiest day of my life—and the saddest. One of those times that test one's faith."

The train drew nearer, its arrival announced by quarrelsome sounds—pounding pistons, hissing steam, clattering wheels on the tracks, and the whistle wailing like women weeping at a funeral.

"This must be how demons sound in Hell." Reverend Sprunt rose to his feet.

"I don't intend to find out." Standing, Bill grabbed the handles of two carpetbags.

When the train stopped and the only sound came from steam escaping the chimney, everyone made their way to the loading platform. Bill transferred the carpetbags to a luggage handler then returned to hug and kiss his momma, Laura and Mark and shake the Reverend Sprunt's hand.

Laura clung to Bill. "I don't want you to go. I'm afraid something bad's going to happen."

Bill ruffled his sister's hair. "I'll be fine. I'm going to help run the war, not fight in it. As soon as Charlie gets over the rot in his stump, he'll join me. Do lots of praying for Charlie, okay?"

Laura nodded. "Every night before I fall asleep. The rot's not good, right?"

"Yes, not good, sweetie." Bill kissed his sister's forehead. "Doctor Iuppenlatz's looking after Charlie and he'll have the stump healed up in a few weeks."

Franny tugged on Laura's earlobe. "I heard a little birdy tell me you're going to marry Charlie someday."

"Ugh! No way. I'm not crushed over him. Charlie's a gal sneaker." Laura pulled a face.

"Lordy, girl, where did you learn those words?" Franny tapped her foot. "Your momma's going to wash out your mouth with soap."

Laura winked. "I listen well. I'm like an old man's ear trumpet. Convalescing soldiers like to talk about filly-and-foal stuff, especially Charlie."

"Daughter, be a lady!"

"Yes, Momma. Always a lady." Laura danced up to the passenger coach Bill and Franny would soon board. "I wish I was going along. Sounds like I'd have a bang-up time in Richmond."

The dreary sky on this Wednesday meshed well with the new month of October—a cool autumn day. With the windows open in the coach, the ride north into Virginia would be pleasant and hopefully uneventful.

Climbing up onto the steps leading to the vestibule, Bill helped Franny onto the first step. Normally, mourning dresses were austere, a style from the 1820s dyed black. Always a revolutionary, Franny had done some modifications to the dress, donated by one of Icie Bell's friends. Not just discarding a hoop, but sewing a brooch in her decolletage above her heart. A tiny tintype of Bill's father lay pinned inside the brooch. A circle of lilies had been stitched around it.

When Franny stood on the vestibule alongside Bill, she regarded him with eagerness and an almost undetectable flash of guilt, which she quickly quashed. "Sweetheart, you look quite dashing in the new uniform. You must write a letter to the Kenansville Ladies' Aid Society and thank them for sewing the uniform."

The ladies had done a remarkable job of keeping their project a secret from not only Bill, but from his father and mother as well. The gossipers could indeed keep a secret if their cause was noble.

"When the ladies came to the house with the uniform, I told them Charlie deserved it more. He left his arm at Gettysburg."

"I was there, remember? I heard your speech." Franny ambled into their coach as the locomotive's whistle blared then ceased. "Your wound was far more serious than you're letting on, husband. Mother says that had the fragment sliced into your back half an inch higher, you'd have died."

"But it didn't." As Bill and Franny made their way along the aisle, he peeked through the side windows looking for his family on the loading platform. "That damned rot that showed up after papa died has been a nuisance for Charlie. A new uniform presented to him by pretty girls will do him a world of good. I hope the ladies got my hint. Be nice to see him in a new one when he arrives in Richmond,"

Franny slipped into a window seat, one without a torn cushion. Bill plopped down beside her.

"They'll take care of him." Franny grinned. "I expect one or two of the younger ones sneaked off for a nighttime engagement with our Charlie."

"Probably more than two," Bill joked.

"A bit stuffy in here." Grunting, Franny opened the window to get fresh air.

Bill leaned across her to take in the loading platform. Assembled with others saying goodbye to love ones, Bill's family and the preacher waved. Laura jumped up and down. "I love you, big brother!" She blew kisses.

Bill craned his head through the window. "I love you, Laura! Mark and Momma too! Hey little sister, maybe you can come up to Richmond and visit us?"

Pushing through the crowd, Laura ran up to the window. "Yes! The spring! If Momma let's me."

Bill had second thoughts as he relaxed in his seat. He hoped his momma would veto the offer. Trains weren't reliable or safe. Yankees still occupied New Bern from where they sometimes forayed into the countryside and tore up track. Just three months before, Yankee cavalry had struck hard in Kenansville and burned down a sword factory, and when the troopers withdrew they ripped up Wilmington and Weldon track.

The cars the locomotive pulled reflected the South's wartime troubles—fewer passenger coaches, replaced by a boxcar filled with track and bridge repair materials and darkies to patch up any raid damage. Sprinkled throughout Bill's coach were Home Guard militiamen who looked old enough to have fought with Andrew Jackson at New Orleans nearly half a century before.

As the locomotive shuddered into motion, Franny elbowed Bill. "Look at Laura."

Near the window, his sister scampered like a rabbit, trying to keep up as the train pulled away from the depot. "Bye, Bill! I'll make sure the ladies make a suit for Charlie."

"A uniform," Bill shouted, correcting her then laughing.

Bill took Franny's hand and intertwined his fingers with hers. The coach swayed as the locomotive gained speed. "Delayed a bit, but we're at last on the way to Richmond."

"No regrets? No second thoughts about not rejoining the Eighteenth?" Franny's index finger tickled his palm.

"None. I survived my wound. Figure I won't be so lucky next time. I'm fine with a War Department desk job."

"Good. And once Charlie arrives, you'll have your possum with you. Richmond will never be the same."

Bill knew he had the War Department job because of Franny's family connections. Her father was an assistant to the War Department's chief of conscription. The first time Bill made love to Franny after the New Year's ball had led to so many twists and turns in his madcap life. He stared at his ghostlike reflection in the window and thanked his stars he was on the way to a desk job in Richmond, not the Army of Northern Virginia like so many other healed-up soldiers in the coach.

With nearly all the windows open, the train-stirred breeze ruffled the hair of veterans returning to the Northern Virginia front and recruits who'd soon get their first taste of battle, the sulfurous taste of black powder, the stink of copious blood, the foulness of decaying bodies. At Fredericksburg and Chancellorsville, Bill had seen the worst the war could serve up. At Weldon, he'd be glad to transfer to a train bound for Richmond.

He found himself thinking back to his train ride home a few weeks after the Battle of Chancellorsville. He chuckled.

Franny settled her head against his shoulder. "Why the laughter?"

"Remembering another train ride. From Fredericksburg to Warsaw."

"That was just after you were wounded, right? Momma told me in one of her letters. Worried me sick. I can't imagine why you're laughing. I was so mad at myself for running off to Tennessee to be with that jackass."

Bill cocked an eyebrow. "The stitches were still in me. Even with Dover's powder, I could barely tolerate the pain. Spent the whole journey to Warsaw sitting on the edge of the seat. Whenever I'd accidentally lean against the backrest, I'd nearly faint. Why do I laugh now? It's better than crying. I've done enough of that since Papa's death."

"All that's in the past. We're about to start a new life in Richmond. Next year at this time, who knows? Maybe I'll be bouncing a little boy or girl on my lap." A smile flitted across Franny's face.

"A baby? Are you..." Bill pursed his lips, blinked eyes he knew were ballooning.

"No, silly. Not yet. We're making a new life for ourselves. I think a baby needs to be part of it. Don't you?"

"Everything's so new, and Papa just passed away, and I haven't really given it much... oh hell, yes, I want a baby boy or girl I can dote over."

"Sounds like we won't be using a rubber."

"Maybe. This needs further discussion."

Less than an hour out of Warsaw the steam locomotive suddenly braked. Franny and Bill banged against the seats in front of them. The train screeched to a juddering stop. A conductor strolling along the aisle toward the vestibule staggered and dropped to his knees.

His black hat with its leather visor tumbled along the aisle and came to rest near the vestibule.

"Lordy," he wheezed. "I think I broke my arm."

Bolting from his seat, Bill reached to help the conductor to his feet.

"Be careful with him," a businessman in a seat across the aisle warned. "He's squealin' about that arm you're about to grab. The left one, he's babyin' it."

"Won't touch it," Bill assured the businessman.

The conductor hugged a backrest in front of the businessman, ready to try to rise to his feet. Bill swung his right arm around the trainman's back. Careful not to brush against the man's left arm, Bill lifted him to his feet, plunked his hat atop his head, and led him into the vestibule.

"Thank you, Private. I can handle it from here," the conductor said through gritted teeth.

Letting go, Bill watched the trainman lurch into the next coach.

Profanity greeted Bill when he re-entered his coach. "Damn, no-account railroad!" a Tar Heel corporal growled. "Good track's scarce as hen's teeth."

Shots rang out. Everyone in the coach traded nervous glances, except for a Palmetto State private with a mangled right ear and mutilated forehead. "Probably a militiaman shooting at a farmer's runaway bull that's blocking the track."

Seconds later, a Home Guard grandpa stumbled out of the front vestibule into the coach. "Yank cavalry," he bawled, teeth chattering. "Any volunteers? Sure could use some help."

The corporal snorted, "Damn!" Standing and sidling into the aisle, the soldier patted his holstered sidearm. "So not bad track or a bull. Well, gramps, you got one volunteer."

Most of the soldiers furloughed home to recover from their wounds didn't have a weapon on the train, certainly no rifles, and only a few possessed a revolver. Like the cussing corporal, Bill carried a Colt Navy revolver. He'd been given the weapon by a Confederate officer assigned to the Magnolia District to guard Wilmington and

Weldon tracks. With the Kenansville raid fresh in his mind, Bill had the weapon with him when he climbed aboard the Reverend Sprunt's buggy for the road trip to the Warsaw depot.

Bill leaned forward. "I'll help out!"

"Me too!" the South Carolina private echoed.

Franny's eyes flared with fear. Her fingers gripped Bill's hand, nails dug into his skin. She started to speak, but instead prayed silently. He gently untangled her hand from his and joined the Palmetto State private and the Tar Heel corporal.

"Well, let's go see what all the fuss is about," the corporal told the militiaman.

"Be careful, Bill," Franny blurted.

Bill blew her a kiss.

Near the train the Home Guard troops stood in a ragged battle line. The militiamen numbered no more than thirty, all with quivering legs. They faced four Union cavalrymen one hundred yards away, dismounted with three down on one knee, Henry repeaters aimed at the old-timers. The fourth one held the horses. Bill suspected a whole lot more cavalrymen were beyond the next hill tearing up track. That's all he needed...to spend rest of the war in a Yankee prison on a Lake Erie island.

Not squeezing into line, Bill and the two other veterans clambered over a fence and took cover inside an apple orchard near the Home Guards. Bill would have preferred a breastwork in front of him, but made due with a tree trunk. Standing in line out in the open like Revolutionary War soldiers displayed the naïveté of the old men.

"Those first shots were probably aimed at the boiler and chimney," the corporal opined, cuddling with a trunk. "Thought they were going to capture a train and ride back to the main force with a whole bunch of Home Guard prisoners."

"Still could," Bill remarked. "We got to make sure it doesn't happen. I've no intention of becoming a jailbird."

The kneeling Yanks resumed firing, rat-a-tat-tat, four shots per cavalryman, twelve in all.

A bullet whizzed by Bill's head, proving the Yanks had noticed him and the other two concealed in the orchard. Well, not really concealed. That bullet had nearly put a hole in Bill's skull.

Groans and a scream at the train drew Bill's attention. Five militiamen were down including their commander, an ancient captain with a belly button-length white beard and a splendid uniform newly stained with a spreading blood splotch. The commander held both hands over the wound, trying and failing to stop the bleeding. He moaned as if he'd realized he would never get a chance to prove his courage in a clash. Then his whimpering stopped.

The legs of two wounded militiamen in the battle line twitched as blood pooled around their heads. A third wounded Home Guard soldier wobbled on his knees, musket on the ground before him, his hands pressed against his heart as if he expected it to stop beating momentarily. He keened, "Momma! Help me, Momma!" Heartbreaking—his momma hadn't been on Earth for decades.

Holding their ancient muskets, the remaining militiamen began backing up. Three whirled around and ran like rabbits chased by a bobcat. Bill sprang from the orchard, scrambled over the fence, and raced to where the commander lay dead or dying. "Damn it! We haven't fired a shot." Bill aimed his revolver at the cavalrymen and fired. "Stand your ground, soldiers! Dress your line! Load your weapons!"

"They are loaded, sir." A militiaman without one hair on his head but so many freckles they hid most of the white on his face saluted Bill as if he were a captain, not a private.

"Well, damn it, fire!" Bill pointed at the Union cavalrymen and their Henry repeaters.

The militiamen discharged a ragged volley. A bullet ripped into Bill's shell jack along his side. Fearing blood, he probed the tear. No wetness. He'd been stupidly standing in front of them.

A sheepish grin on his face, the freckled militiaman mumbled, "Sorry, sir."

In the distance near the track, the blue-belly cavalry looked untouched. The graybeards had missed. The cavalrymen fired off more rounds, and three more codgers toppled. "Load!" Bill bellowed over the wounded men's wailings. These one-leg-in-the-grave Home Guard graybeards had become Bill's first command. "Fire!"

Flames erupted from the barrels of the graybeards' muskets. One of the kneeling cavalrymen dropped his Henry rifle and clutched his right shoulder. Even from a hundred yards away, Bill could see how pain clouded the cavalryman's face.

Bill spared the old men behind him a quick glance. Pale as an autumn moon, they looked like they'd break at the next rifle fire from the Union cavalrymen and skedaddle back toward Warsaw. He needed them thinking about something else. "Load! Fire at my command!"

The oldsters bit off the cartridges, inserted the balls and black powder into the gun barrels, then wrenched the ramrods from their holders. Before the ramrods could be shoved down the barrels, the Yanks mounted their horses and rode off. The Home Guards howled a rebel yell. Now shaking himself, Bill breathed a sigh of relief.

The two veterans left the orchard and joined Bill. "Good, fast thinking," the disfigured private told Bill.

Inside the train, Franny shouted out to Bill, "You wounded?"

As he made his way to coach, he shook his head. Once at the open window, he leaned forward on his tiptoes and kissed Franny. He liked the feel of her smooth skin against his palm nestled at the back of her neck.

"Sweet Lord...I don't think I've ever been so scared." Color gradually returned to her face.

"Just four Yank cavalrymen." He gestured toward the locomotive. "I want to see what's on the other side of the hill. And I need to know what the engineer and fireman saw." He kissed her again then tramped up to the locomotive.

Grabbing the handrail, Bill climbed up into the cab. The engineer seemed confused by Bill's uniform. No gold braiding or chicken guts. "The Home Guard captain's dead," Bill told the engineer. "They were about to bolt, so I stepped in."

"Thank God you did, sir." The engineer removed his blue-and-white pinstripe cap and wiped sweat from his forehead. The steam engine idled as he returned the cap to his head. "Anyone who sends the damned Yankee raiders runnin' got my respect. Bastards put a couple of mini balls in the chimney. Goin' to have to do some patchin'. Can't have embers escapin' and settin' fire to a passenger coach."

Bill considered the engineer's words. "So you think they planned to capture the train?"

"No. They would've shot us up more if that had been their intent. They were toyin' with us."

"Probably givin' their rail busters a chance to git away," the fireman spoke up. "Sometimes we've Warsaw garrison troops aboard, not the Home Guard. We'd have captured a bushel of them—and they knew it."

Bill leaned out the engineer's window and eyed the distant hill. "Those volleys I ordered convinced the Henry rifle boys to run off."

"Yep," the engineer agreed. "They didn't want a fight. Not worth losin' men over wreckin' track."

"Especially when one took a wound in the arm," the fireman added.

Bill started down the locomotive steps. "I'm going to take a walk up that hill and see if it's safe to proceed."

"We'll start the patchin' while you're explorin'. Hopefully, we'll have *Deerhound*"—the engineer slapped a steam gauge—"movin' soon after you return."

As he approached a blood spot near the tracks—the place where the cavalryman had been wounded—Bill heard men running to catch up with him. He turned and grinned, eyeballing his pursuers, the Tar Heel corporal and the Palmetto State private.

"Figured you might want company," the corporal said.

"Glad to have you."

They proceeded past the splotch of blood, and huffed and puffed to the hill's summit. At last, Bill had his look at what lay beyond.

"It could be worse," the corporal muttered.

"Far worse, Corporal." Bill traced the track down the hill through farmland bordered by split-rail fences that separated the crops and orchards from the railbed. "We ruined their plans."

The Yanks were gone, but telltale signs of their handiwork remained, maybe fifty feet of demolished railroad track and fencing. The tracks lay at the bottom of the railbed. The crossties and the fence posts were gathered in a pile for burning, but the train had shown up before they could be torched.

The corporal laughed. "The Yanks think our locomotives can't go any faster than five miles per hour. Fools! We can get 'em up to eight miles per hour."

"I don't even know your name, Corporal. Or yours, Private Palmetto."

"We've been too busy to deal with niceties," Private Palmetto said. "My name's Joe Bowden."

"And I'm Dempsey Glidwell." The corporal held out his hand.

"Glad to meet both of you." Bill shook Dempsey's offered hand, then gripped Bowden's. "My name's Bill Stamford." He glanced back at the train. "Let's go give the engineer the latest news."

At the *Deerhound*, passengers were escaping the coaches, unbearably hot with the locomotive stopped and no wind reaching the people inside. Home Guard men were carrying the wounded and the dead back to their car. Slaves milled about at the back of the train near the maintenance car. Not one had tried to escape with the Yank cavalry. Probably too risky, Bill figured.

One of the passengers, a woman in a black dress, hastened toward Bill, Dempsey and Joe. Franny's hips swayed as she scurried around the smudge of blood left by the wounded blue-belly cavalryman.

"Lordy, now there's a nice bit of jam tart," Joe declared.

Dempsey belly-laughed. "The Good Lord forgot to give you smarts, Joe. You just called Stamford's wife a jam tart."

Joe swallowed hard and his face turned crimson. "I'm sorry, Bill. Sometimes my mouth runs faster than an out-of-control buggy."

"Apology accepted. You didn't know Franny's my wife."

Joe grinned. "She's pretty. You're a lucky man, Bill."

Franny met Bill near the bottom of the hill. "No Yanks?"

"Nope. Not one." Bill gave her a quick hug and a peck on the cheek.

"Some wrecked track, though," Joe said.

"Yep, we're going to be delayed a bit more." Bill scrutinized the two newly bolted metal patches on the locomotive's chimney. "Track's got to be repaired."

Dempsey and Joe supervised the Home Guard fellows while Bill led Franny to the locomotive, helping her up into the cab.

"Howdy, ma'am," the engineer greeted Franny then turned his attention to Bill. "Your jaunt show any Yanks still around?"

"Didn't see any. They'd started a necktie party, but we arrived before they were expecting a train. They skedaddled. Those cavalrymen with the Henrys were giving the necktie boys time to get away."

The engineer chuckled. "They don't have much respect for Wilmington and Weldon timetables. I'm crawlin' real slow, but the Yanks act like old *Deerhound* here can't even manage two miles per hour. Arrogant fellas, ain't they?"

"I'm just glad the necktie party figured a few burned-up rails and a tumbledown train weren't worth dying over." Weariness crept into Bill's voice.

"Necktie?" Franny blinked in confusion.

Bill rolled his eyes. "You never heard the phrase?"

She shook her head. "Not until now. And don't roll your eyes at me, mister."

"Sorry, sweetheart. It's a term we and the Yanks use to describe tearing up track. Heat the rails over burning ties and bend them around trees or whatever's at hand."

"Folks, if you could," the engineer began, "please help the conductor get everyone seated. I'll get *Deerhound* runnin'. We'll mosey up to the wrecked tracks and get them fixed." He snickered. "Got a schedule to keep."

"I'll be glad to be away from here, Bill. I don't like seeing you get shot at."

"Me neither." Bill drew another exasperated look from Franny.

When the passengers were back in their coaches, the fireman fed wood chips from the tender car into the firebox. The fire began heating up the boiler. At Kenansville's Grove Academy, Bill had been told to think of a boiler as a giant kettle inside the locomotive. When the water in the boiler had produced enough steam under pressure, a valve released steam into the engine, pushing pistons back and forth. As the pistons turned the locomotive's wheels, *Deerhound* moved at a snail's pace, chugging up the hill.

"Maybe we'll make Rocky Mount by midnight," Bill wisecracked to Franny, then began to explain the operation of the locomotive's raucous steam engine.

Franny yawned, bringing Bill's explanation to a premature end.

Deerhound stopped a few feet short of the gap in the tracks. The slaves piled out of the maintenance car and began to lay new rails and crossties.

"They're not going to set a speed record." Franny fanned herself with a folded periodical having the flowery title *The Englishwoman's Domestic Magazine.*

"Except maybe for the slowest repair job ever done." Bill enviously eyed the magazine. It was growing stuffy in the coach.

Franny leaned against Bill and whispered, "The darkies are probably regretting they didn't run to those Yank cavalrymen."

"Lincoln thinks the war's God's punishment on the South and North for what's been done to them." Bill slipped his arm around Franny's shoulders.

"He's right." She kissed Bill's earlobe.

Once underway, the train continued to travel at a snail's pace with the engineer and fireman keeping a sharp lookout for severed track. Normally, trains didn't travel at night. This one had no choice. A nearly full moon in a star-studded sky made enough light to provide a small measure of warning. The conductor, his face racked with pain from his broken shoulder, came back to the coach. "We'll be traveling at night, but don't worry. The engineer and fireman have keen eyes. We won't derail."

Franny shouted out to him, "Willing to make a bet on if we're derail before we reach Rocky Mount?"

"Nope."

The conductor would have won the bet. They didn't derail or even have to stop to fix severed track. The train reached Rocky Mount just before midnight.

Eight

A Marriage Gets Consummated

Bill stripped off his shell jacket, vest and shirt, but the room still felt stuffy. Franny lay in bed, the top sheet and quilt thrown back, revealing her nakedness. No cotton nightgown on this warm mid-October night. Striding to a window, Bill drew back the curtains and threw open the sash, allowing in cool night air. The breeze stirred the hairs on his chest, tingling his skin.

The owner of the Clermont hotel next to the Rocky Mount Depot kept the downstairs Kettle restaurant open, allowing the *Deerhound's* passengers to get a bite to eat before turning in for the night.

"The breeze is wonderful," Franny said from the bed. "Come lie beside me, dear."

Bill turned to the sound of her voice. Her right hand, fingers wagging, beckoned him. Her unused nightrobe lay folded on the end of the bed. She looked intoxicating as the breeze tousled loose hair, but Bill figured she didn't expect any romance this night, not after the afternoon's deadly skirmish.

It's time, Papa, isn't it? Bill knew his father wouldn't want him to ruin his newly minted marriage. He looked up at the ceiling, his imagination reaching beyond the clouds, and pictured his father saying: "Time you two have your first melting moment of your married life. Show her how much you love her."

"I'm ready for some tupping," he told Franny. "Today's fight has me eager to play a game of loll tongue." Bill knew Franny deserved an attentive husband keen to dote on her. And he needed to drown in her passion.

Unable to mask a frown, Franny turned on her side and eyed him suspiciously. "Are you sure?"

He gaped at the contours of her body, her thighs, hips, ribs, her breasts. "At this moment, I want to make love to you more than anything else in the world."

Her eyes lowered to his loins, to the bulge in his trousers. "So I see."

Those azure eyes were mesmerizing; they made him hurriedly peel off his gray wool pants and waist-high longjohns. So eager to feel the touch of her breasts against his chest, he kicked the pants and longjohns across the room. Franny laughed when they landed on the floor inside the open armoire.

"Like my aim?" He launched himself onto the bed and sought her mouth.

Their eager hands explored each other's bodies as they kissed, their tongues probing. Franny caressed the back of his neck and spine, then stroked his Chancellorsville scar.

"Thank God the shell sliver didn't damage anything vital," she said, her voice languorous.

"The only organ vital right now is my tallywag." Bill rubbed his loins against hers.

"Not so fast, mister." She turned away from him and reached toward a bedside table. "While you were opening the window, I was taking precautions—just in case you decided you were ready."

"Ah, one of Franny Stamford's rubbers. You get the honors, my dear."

"Gladly." Franny sucked in air and let it out with a soft moan.

She kissed his rigid arbor vitae, then slid the rubber onto its tip and stretched it out.

"You ready?" Bill kissed her left breast then licked the nipple.

"Your terms, please? I'm ready to surrender."

"Let your love shower over me like a warm summer rain."

"Done." She dragged her fingernails from his tallywag up his belly to his chest where she finger-walked each rib.

Franny purred softly, warm and inviting, as Bill mounted her. Soon, they were drenched in sweat as they gyrated wildly—and then it was over as Bill collapsed against Franny. She closed her arms around him and drew him firmly against her breasts.

"Thank God you weren't wounded again today." She started to cry.

Their bodies glistening in lamplight, they lay in each other's arms. He draped a hand across her exquisitely long legs and let his fingers wander to her taut rump. Snuggling closer, Bill kissed her tears, tasting the salt.

"Why the tears?" he asked gently. "We just made love. No sadness allowed, just moans of passion—our married melting moment." He kissed the end of her nose.

"I know. I am happy." Franny tickled his shoulder then his upper chest. "I can't get it out of my mind...those Home Guards getting shot. You could have died in front of my eyes. I hate this war."

"But I didn't." His fingers brushed her silken hair and brushed strands away from her forehead. "Some men would have felt mollycoddled allowing a lover to wrangle a job for them away from the fighting. Not me. One bad wound's enough. I don't want there to be a next time. The odds are against me. You can mollycoddle me all you want."

Franny laughed, her saucy eyes dancing. "The halo-seeing man isn't a fool. He knows when Death lurks just inside his shadow, waiting to claim him."

"There's only so many battles in a man. I'm lucky to be alive." Bill brushed his hand along Franny's leg, stroking pale skin from her ankle to her thigh. "I'm glad you went to the chaplain and your father. I'm more than ready to fight my war in Richmond. Seen too many mini balls at Fredericksburg and Chancellorsville...I've fought enough battles."

Franny played with his belly button, drawing circles around it. "The chaplain and my mother were working on your behalf soon after your wounding when I was still in Tennessee. They make a fine team and can be persuasive. My father never stood a chance. I'm evil. I took credit for your transfer to Richmond."

Bill ran a finger along Franny's lower lip. "Really? You had nothing to do with my transfer?"

She shrugged; blonde curls rippled. "Okay, darling, that's not entirely true. I did write mother asking her to talk to father and the chaplain. Your wound terrified me. I just wasn't sure you'd agree—until we made love in the upstairs bedroom of the railroad magnate's mansion. Only then did I know you liked the notion of working for the War Department." Sighing, she interlocked her legs with his. "I don't think you ever realized how scared I was that you'd return to the Army of Northern Virginia."

Bill leaned across Franny's body and kissed her rump. "I didn't think you had a scared bone in that pretty body of yours. Now I have to convince the War Department to let Charlie be my aide."

"You will," she said, her voice sassy. "Secretary Seddon likes me. If he was thirty years younger, he'd try to court me. He did whirl my mother around the ballroom a few times when she was a teenager. He'll okay Charlie's transfer."

"We should try to get some sleep, Franny. It's well after midnight and the train will be heading out in the early daylight hours."

"Sleep?" She giggled. "I thought you'd want to wear out the bedsprings."

"We will—on our first night in our Richmond apartment."

"I've a confession, Bill." Franny's eyebrows scrambled up her forehead. "I almost asked you if you wanted to forego a rubber."

Bill shook his head, as if he needed to shake loose the cobwebs in his brain. "These are not the times to raise a baby. Just a few months ago some of Richmond's mothers rioted over food prices and scarcity."

"Yes, the bread riots of April. You're right. Not the best of times to make us a family of three. Still, it'd mean we see the hope promised in Psalms Thirty: 'Weeping may endure for a night, but joy cometh in the morning.' Bill, someday there will be a morning free of war."

"And a day with no more halos?" Bill rolled over and turned down the bedside lamp's wick. The room's amber light winked out. "I hate to sound selfish, but I want that nearly as much as I desire peace."

"You haven't had any more halos, have you?"

"No. Not since Rose Greenhow."

"Maybe God has answered your prayers, Bill."

"I hope so. I am so weary of the halo burden."

She kissed him goodnight. "We will revisit the baby question once we settle into our new apartment." Not satisfied with one goodnight kiss, she smothered him with more. "A baby brings balance. Your father left the world. A baby will fill that void he left behind."

He chuckled. "I agree to another discussion or two, Franny, my love. Nothing more."

"Yes, we'll talk."

With the room plunged into darkness, Bill lay on his back while Franny rested on her side, nuzzled against him. She snored softly, the air leaking from her mouth and tickling his ear. He couldn't sleep. Voices from the boardwalk and street drifted through the open window into the hotel room. Not as loud as the voices, sprightly piano music wafted into Bill's ears. Straining to recall the song, he remembered. "With My Banjo on my Knee" came from a tavern on the other side of the livery stable. He found its name amusing, Fiddler's Green, a place in Heaven where people did nothing but dance and sneak kisses.

"You awake, Bill?"

"Yes, Franny."

"Those voices belong to amorous men and women who will soon be doing what we just finished doing." She chuckled.

"Railroad men. Gal-sneakers and their bangtails. You're right. They're aiming to do some prigging."

Done talking, Franny turned over and lay on her other side, her rump pressed against his buttocks. The autumn night continued to be summer-like with no need for a cover sheet or quilt. The outside voices and music subsided, and soon all Bill heard was the sounds of crickets, stabled horses, the breeze rustling trees, and Franny's breathing. The sounds were mesmerizing.

Almost asleep, he felt his wife shift and her fingers play with his chest hairs. "There I go awaking you again, Bill. I'm dastardly."

"Yes, you are, Franny." He brought her fingers up to his mouth and kissed each one.

"After the day's fight and seeing those wounded and dead Home Guards, I thought I'd have nightmares tonight, but you made this a perfect night for us, Bill. I hope the rest of the trip to Richmond goes without a hitch." Drawing her hand away from his lips, Franny rolled onto her back and skated her right foot across the bottom sheet so her toes perched on his left foot. "If our loved ones can look down on us from Heaven, then your father must be proud of you right now. I love you, Bill."

He heard her words, but before he could reply, he'd fallen asleep.

Nine

Bustling, Sinful Richmond

The Richmond and Petersburg train turtle-crawled through wheat and tobacco fields. Bill figured he could jump off the train, run to Richmond and get there faster. They'd been traveling since seven in the morning, switching trains at Weldon and then Petersburg. At six o'clock they were still maybe ten miles from Richmond.

"I expected the worse. Thank the Lord no Yankee cavalry, no shooting." Franny grinned. "Good day all around. Except for having to stop near Weldon to fix track."

Bill turned away from the window. "Back in May, I changed trains in Richmond. All I remember seeing is Chimborazo Hospital up on that hill east of the downtown. Too much pain to enjoy the short visit."

"The times I've been there since the war...I barely recognized the place," Franny repressed a sigh. "Four times as many people living there since it became the Confederate capital. It's a modern day Sodom. There's more gambling dens and whorehouses than theaters and restaurants. Can't walk downtown without getting rolled by gang scurf. Too much for the coppers to handle. General Winder now has day-to-day control."

Bill rolled his eyes. "Brothels? Charlie will love it here once he gets over his melancholy."

"As long as you don't go with him." All humor died in her voice.

"No chance of that, not with you waiting for me to come home."

"The wagtails all have the clap anyway."

The train wheeled by an army camp on Richmond's outskirts, a miniature town of tents and soldiers drilling in the late afternoon under a sky of dark clouds. The steam whistle wailed as the locomotive pulled the passenger carriages and boxcars into the Richmond and Petersburg Railroad's Byrd Street depot on the north bank of the James River. Once on the loading platform, Bill scanned the horizon. The Thomas Jefferson-designed Capitol building could be seen in the distance. Brick residences of the city's elite perched above a string of tobacco warehouses, flour mills and ironworks that lined the banks of the river.

A darkey porter toted their carpetbags and traveling trunk through the depot and out to a line of Hansom cabs parked along Byrd Street. He flagged down a bowler-hatted cabman, and the two of them loaded the luggage into the baggage platform. After tipping the porter, Bill helped Franny into the cab and then seated himself beside her. He closed the folding wooden doors designed to protect passengers from splashing rain and mud. Craning his neck, Bill opened the trapdoor above his head and addressed the cabman, "Take us to two-o-six East Franklin Street. I've been told it's a four-story brownstone apartment house called The Willows."

Seated in his sprung seat behind the cab, the cabman chortled, "They're all brownstones, but only one's The Willows." The horse pulled the Hansom along Byrd Street then a quick right onto Fourteenth and a left onto Canal.

Unlike a coach, the cab gave Bill and Franny a splendid view of all the waterfront. Jabbing Bill in the side, Franny pointed toward an isle in the James River. "That's Brown's Island."

"Damn! What in tarnation happened?" Ruins dotted the island. There had been a newspaper story he'd read back in winter camp. He struggled to recall the details.

"Back in March—a Friday the Thirteenth—there was an explosion on the island at the government's ordnance laboratory. More than sixty women and children perished. Halted production briefly."

"Sabotage?" Bill twisted around for a last look at the island.

Franny shrugged. "Don't think so. It's a dangerous business— war."

Bill nodded as the cab bounced along the brick road. "I recall a fire along the industrial waterfront. Read about it in the *Richmond Daily Dispatch* while recovering from my surgery."

"The Crenshaw mills. Terrible fire. Spread to some of the Anderson and Company's machine shops. Wrecked them." Franny swept some wild strands of hair back under her stylish pork-pie hat. "And then there's the bread riot back in April. Women got fed up with the speculators and commandeered food for their kiddies."

Unseen behind the cab lay the Chimborazo Hospital. Bill was glad he'd decided to go to Kenansville to convalesce. Too many soldiers left Chimborazo in pine boxes.

"My job may require me to go there, but it'll be a sad trip," he told Franny, his voice quiet for the first time since sitting in the Hansom.

Franny arched an eyebrow. "A sad trip?"

"Chimborazo Hospital."

"Oh. Maybe I'll do some volunteer nursing work there."

"The men will perk up seeing your beautiful face, Franny."

The Hansom made two more right turns—onto Second Street and then onto Franklin—and soon came to a bumpy stop. The trapdoor opened and the cabman's voice drifted through the hole: "Two-o-six East Franklin Street, soldier. Sixty-five cents."

Bill dug inside his vest pocket and produced his coin purse. He transferred the fare through the hole into the cabman's hand. The front folding doors opened, and Bill and Franny stepped down to the street and onto the boardwalk.

Franny waited near the brownstone front steps as Bill and the cabman unloaded the luggage. The building's double doors squeaked open, revealing a one-armed sergeant. "Private Stamford?" He descended the steps, stopped on the boardwalk and bowed to Franny. "And Mrs. Stamford?"

"Yes," Franny said, offering her hand.

"I'm Sergeant Frank Davis." He brushed his lips against her fingers. "I'm here to help you and your husband get settled in. Fourth floor, apartment thirty, I believe."

Franny glanced at the trunk on the boardwalk. "Four floors, eh? Getting the trunk to our apartment's not going to be fun."

"I can help," the sergeant offered. "I've learned since Sharpsburg that havin' one arm ain't no bother."

Bill turned to the waiting cabman. "Looks like I won't need your assistance this evening, sir. But I'll need a ride to the War Department in the morning. Be here at seven sharp and I'll make it worth your while." Bill jangled his coin purse.

"Rest assured I'll be here on time, soldier." The cabman doffed his bowler, climbed back into his seat and prodded the Hansom horse into a trot for the trip back to the depot.

"Let me take the lead." The sergeant grabbed a handle.

"Franny, please get the door." Bill gripped the other handle.

Bill feared Davis might have exaggerated his ability to lug the trunk up three flights of stairs, but the sergeant handled his end with no problems. In fact, Bill was the one who had to stop on the second landing for a breather. He hadn't realized how out of shape he'd become since the surgery five months before.

At the door to apartment thirty, Bill let his end of the trunk drop to the plank floor with a thump.

Davis chuckled then gently lowered his end. "Drained?"

"Yep, all played out," Bill acknowledged, panting. "I've a friend who lost an arm at Gettysburg. Charlie's scared, thinks his life's all but over. No woman will want him. Not any good for work."

Davis nodded knowingly. "I was the same way. Had to work through it. Hopefully, he'll come out of his funk."

"Bill plans to seek War-Department approval to bring Charlie to Richmond to be his aide," Franny spoke up. "We don't want him cooped up in North Carolina feeling sorry for himself. He's smart and can do a lot of good here."

"If you get the transfer, I'll talk to him." The sergeant drew a skeleton key from a pants pocket and handed it to Franny. "I'll knock some sense into your Charlie." Davis rapped his stump. "Sometimes a one-armed sourpuss needs to see another soldier with a missin' arm doin' everything he did before the surgeon cut it off."

Franny unlocked and opened the door and the sergeant and Bill carried the trunk into the parlor. She reflected, "Well, here we are. Our home until the war ends."

The sergeant sat on the trunk. "You're a lucky couple. Not many in Richmond have such fine accommodations. It's not unusual to see several families livin' in cramped, unheated apartments. We've faced threats of smallpox last year and durin' the summer this year. Before the war, Richmond's population was thirty-eight thousand. More than one hundred and thirty thousand here now."

Bill surveyed the parlor and tiny kitchen with its Hathaway coal-fired, two-burner stove and oven then peered down the hallway toward the bedroom and water closet. The apartment was humble, but he couldn't say so, not after hearing the sergeant's words.

"I love the apartment," Franny enthused. "Perfect for newlyweds."

Bill caressed Franny's back. She'd grown up living in a Fredericksburg mansion, but the last year had seen her town bombarded and many of the grand homes including hers blasted into rubble. Maybe this humble apartment did look wonderful to her. As for Bill, at least he wasn't sleeping in a lean-to on the eve of battle.

Bracing himself with his arm, the sergeant stood. He retrieved another key from his pocket and presented it to Bill. "Stamford, I'll see you in the mornin'. Secretary Seddon's a big believer in punctuality. Most of the day will be spent introducin' you to the various department personnel." He winked. "And we do have a special surprise for you, Private."

Franny clapped in delight. "I'll probably be out at the hospital offering my volunteer services. I do wish I could be present for the surprise. Oh well."

"Thank you for your help, Sergeant Davis," Bill said, "and for your offer to set my friend Charlie straight."

Once Davis left, Franny moseyed over to a frayed sofa settee and sat. "Prepare to be seduced on this divan, sir. Perhaps a dozen times before we leave our first home."

Chuckling, Bill plopped down in the worn parlor chair. "I can't wait."

Franny glanced into the kitchen. "The oven looks like a little girl's plaything. Let's get a closer look." She stood and stepped through a miniature archway into the teeny kitchen.

Bill smiled as he watched his wife fiddle with the levers and knobs on the Hathaway stove and oven. The kitchen coal bin was empty. Bill would have to pick up a load of coal and groceries so there'd be food for a late-night snack and breakfast. Franny sidled to the icebox and opened it. "Empty," she said absentmindedly. "Well, that's not entirely true." She unfolded a piece of paper with inked words. Franny began reading, "We heard you're newlyweds. We thought you deserved a belated wedding gift. Enjoy the canned green beans and strawberry jam." She rifled through the cupboards and showed Bill the results of her expedition—two cans. "Don't look spoiled."

"The house is cold as a snowball," Bill observed. "I'm going to have to make an evening run for firewood, ice, coal and some groceries."

Franny corrected him. "We'll need to make a run. You won't be able to cart all that stuff back to the apartment."

"I can see where a kid's wagon could turn out to be a wise purchase." Bill sat in one of the two kitchen chairs. "Of course, that will depend on how close the ice house and general store are to us."

Franny returned the cans to the cupboard then sat in the other chair. "You know what this apartment needs?"

He wondered if she intended to mention a baby again. He'd know soon enough when they again tipped the velvet. "Some pictures on the wall?" He pointed to a forlorn parlor wall.

"No, not paintings, but a cat like your momma's Indy."

"Lots of feral cats running around outside. Catch one and you'll have your Indy." Bill grinned evilly.

"If I see one, I'll offer some scraps. If he eats out of my hand and lets me pet him, he'll have himself a nice home with a couch to sleep on and plenty of food to give him a fat belly."

"He won't sleep with us?"

"We'll see." Now it was Franny's turn to grin.

~ * ~

Bill and Franny left the apartment building just as a gray-furred cat paused at the bottom step and eyed them curiously. When Franny knelt to pet the green-eyed cat, the critter scarpered away, darting down an alleyway.

"Well, that cat won't be joining our family." Bill stepped down onto the boardwalk.

"Don't be so sure. I can win him over. He's so beautiful with the jade eyes and white paws. I want him."

"He'll never let you get close, sweetheart. He's a rake and the reason for the burgeoning neighborhood feline population."

Bill looked both directions along Franklin Street and decided to head away from the Capitol Square. On the Hansom ride, he hadn't seen a general merchandise store near the apartment house. He was hopeful they'd find one in the next few blocks.

They walked two blocks under a sunset sky, their hands entwined. Old ladies rocking on their porches no doubt considered them to be uncomfortably spoony, a couple who needed to pull down the blinds so to speak.

A boardwalk sale announced the presence of a general store three blocks from their apartment building—tricycles, commonly called dandyhorses or boneshakers, lawn chairs, toy soldiers, model trains, dolls and red toy wagons.

"Looks like we've got ourselves a wagon," Franny joked as Bill ushered her into the store.

With daylight nearly gone, they bought cornmeal, molasses, canned vegetables and firewood.

"War Department, eh?" the skinny, fortyish store clerk said as Bill paid with Confederate scrip.

"Starting the job tomorrow," Bill answered.

"Good luck. We do what we can for the cause and for soldiers like you." Nodding, the clerk helped Bill load the purchases into the kiddie wagon. "But I don't aim to go out of business either. These are tough times. I'm proud to say I wasn't targeted by the bread-riot women."

"You have my business," Bill assured the clerk. "Where's the nearest butcher?"

"Turn left at the next intersection, then one block down on Randolph. Butcher's my big brother. He'll be fair to a soldier assigned to the War Department. Means you've been wounded." The clerk opened the door for them, and Bill and Franny were soon on the way.

At the butcher's shop, they chose bacon, a side of ham and a block of ice stored in an attached icehouse. Franny gave the butcher a smile normally reserved for men like General Lee. "We're newlyweds soon to spend our first night in Richmond. My soldier husband starts his job at the War Department in the morning. Your brother sent us to you."

The butcher bobbed his head to Franny. "We send each other business. You live at the Two-o-six East Franklin Street brownstone?"

"Yes, moved in a few hours ago," Bill answered.

The butcher shook Bill's hand. "I'm your landlord. Got a contract with the War Department to house some of its families."

They dashed back to their apartment, their goal to save as much of the ice as possible.

~ * ~

Near their brownstone, the white-sock cat scampered alongside them, sniffing the wagon. He still tailed them when they climbed the steps to the two-door entrance. They lowered the wagon onto the portico, and Franny knelt down and offered her hand to the cat. The tom sniffed her fingers.

"You want food and a home, don't you?" He let her stroke his fur below an ear then the back of his neck. "This is the one, Bill."

Franny opened the door; the cat dashed between Bill's legs and into the lobby with its postal boxes. Bill rolled his eyes as he picked up his end of the wagon. "Our first child, eh?"

"Yep, a four-legged one." She batted her eyes at him as she picked up her end of wagon.

Once up the steps and on the fourth floor, the cat jumped up on the cornmeal bag and rode the wagon to the couple's apartment.

"He'll leave us for the streets as soon as you give him some scraps." Bill sighed theatrically. "That's my prediction."

"We'll see soon enough." Franny opened the door to apartment thirty.

The cat darted under the settee then meowed loudly. Bill kept the door open for a minute or so, thinking the cat might choose to escape. The critter stayed under the settee, though, still meowing. Shrugging his shoulders, Bill closed the door and unloaded the wagon's food, leaving the ham, bacon, cornmeal and canned goods on the kitchen table. His teeth chattered as he transferred the ice to the icebox insulated by tin. Rubbing his chilled hands against his pants, Bill returned to the parlor and stacked logs in the fireplace. Soon flames danced up from the grate. Bill glanced back into the kitchen where the cat brushed back and forth against the hem of Franny's hoop-free dress.

"He's definitely your cat."

"Don't be so sure, Bill. Men have probably been mean to him. Once he trusts you, he'll not give you a moment's peace." Franny unwrapped the ham, cut off a sliver and left it on the floor for the cat, who gobbled it up and meowed for more. "Ah, you're still hungry, little guy." She sliced off a bigger piece for him. "Can I call you Tessir?" The cat meowed, then chomped down on the ham. "I will assume that's an okay, Tessir."

Bill sat at the kitchen table and swiveled his gaze between Tessir and Franny, who stocked the canned goods in the pantry and slipped the ham and bacon into the icebox.

"So can you cook?" he joshed. He dumped the coal into the bin and went about lighting the oven.

"Yes. It's a shock, isn't it? I loved the smells in our kitchen. Our darkey cook, Florina, noticed my fascination and taught me. Scandalized Mother and her friends."

Bill and Tessir watched Franny cook a meal of cornbread, greens and ham. She rummaged through the upper cabinets and soon had plates, cups and utensils arrayed on the table. He said grace, and soon they were gobbling down the late-night meal and finishing it off with Carnation milk.

Franny prepared a bowl of scraps for the cat and handed it to Bill. "Best way to gain Tessir's trust is to feed him, dear. Give it a try."

"Hey, I'm buddies with Indy, so I expect Tessir will come to see my good side." Bill put the plate of scraps on the floor between the oven and the coal bin. Tessir immediately attacked it.

"We're lucky to be eating this well." Franny carried her plate up to the sink. "We didn't break the bank to buy the food. I kind of feel guilty. Desperate women were rioting in the streets back in the spring. I feel like I should do something to help them."

Bill joined Franny at the sink. Fumbling with cabinet handles, he found a pot large enough to become a washtub for the dirty dishes. He tugged on the water pump and soon had the kettle filled with soapy water. "I feel guilty too, Franny. Maybe at Christmas we can do something to help out the women and their children. I'll do some thinking on it." He wrapped an arm around her waist and drew her against him. "That was a fine meal, sweetheart."

"Florina would be proud of me."

Franny put the last of the plates and mugs in the cabinet then took Bill's hand and led him into the parlor and onto the settee. Scooting forward, she unlaced her boots and wriggled them off her feet. "Have you ever done any tupping on a sofa?" She giggled.

Bill studied the settee, much smaller than a regular sofa. "The bed would be better.”

“Who says? The settee is much more romantic. Some people call it a love couch.” Franny cupped his chin and kissed his mouth. “We’d make it official.”

Standing, he again skeptically eyed the settee. “It’s awfully small, but I’m game. Don’t always have to use a bed, eh?”

Franny stood. “Undress me.”

“Not before I stoke the fire.” He opened the damper. “Now what were we doing?”

“Acting like lovers.” She tugged off his boots then unbuttoned his shell jacket, vest and shirt, and left them puddled by her feet. “I still have my clothes on.” She dragged her fingernails across his bare chest.

“Not for long.” He unclasped each fastening of her dress and underthings, and soon a mountain of lacy clothing lay atop his uniform.

Returning to the settee, Franny reclined on it, her legs drawn up and apart. Bill knew he’d never grow tired of ogling her breasts, belly and thighs. He’d yet to kiss her boobies, but the nipples had already hardened.

“The rubbers are in my carpetbag,” she reminded him.

So tonight they wouldn’t try to make a baby, he thought as he extracted a rubber. *Hey, we got a cat. Who needs a baby? So where’s the little guy?* Bill looked under the settee. No cat. Then his eyes returned to the perfect angel waiting for him on the love sofa.

Engorged, he let Franny draw him down onto her bubbies. He sought her mouth for a feast of kisses. As Bill took Franny’s hand and guided it to his crotch, he felt a thump on his back and then claws digging into flesh.

“Damn cat!” he cried, partly in pain, partly frustration. He squinted at the settee’s backrest. Tessir sat atop it, staring at him.

Franny snorted. “Bad boy, Tessir. I’m supposed to scratch his back, not you.”

Ten

An Alleyway Mugging

Bill sat on the edge of the hospital-style bed and tugged on his boots. He'd just finished fishing through the armoire and donning his uniform. Behind him, Tessir stalked Franny's feet.

"Stop it, cat!" Franny wiggled her toes, prompting Tessir to renew his attacks. "Confound it! Okay, Tessir, I surrender." She squirmed from beneath the top cover and swung her legs to the cold bedroom floor.

In the wee morning light, shadows shifted on Franny's naked body as she rose, padded to the armoire and wrapped herself in a lacy day-robe. She stepped back to the bed, petted Tessir's head and kissed Bill.

Bill's nose twitched as an unwelcome smell soured his nostrils. He turned toward the source—cat poop in the corner near the dresser. "The cat's going to smell up the place."

Franny pivoted and gazed down the hallway. "Get a large pot from the kitchen and fill it with dirt. He'll use it from now on."

Pot in hand, Bill went down the stairs and out the front entrance where he filled it with clumps of dirt from flower beds along the brick front. Soon the pot lay in the water closet. The smell of the dirt immediately attracted Tessir, prompting him to squat and pee.

"That's a good boy," Bill told the cat.

Tessir meowed. Bill scratched where the cat had clawed his back during the couple's lovemaking. He gave Tessir an accusing look.

"I don't want to hear any more complaints from you," Franny jawed at Bill. "You're acting like Tessir's claws were worse than the shell sliver."

"He's jealous." Bill almost grinned, but kept a straight face.

"Stop it! Cats like to sleep on backrests. You should know that, Bill."

"My back isn't a resting place," he growled, continuing his charade.

She studied his face and he lost his battle. A wide grin spread across his mouth. "I knew you were jousting. You're no good at lying, Bill Stamford."

Bill fired up the Hathaway stove and Franny cooked cornmeal pancakes smothered in molasses syrup. Fortified for his first day at the War Department, he headed for the door.

"I'll be catching an omnibus out to Chimborazo. I'm volunteering to keep the soldiers company. Hopefully, I'll be back by the time you get to home." Franny pecked him on the cheek. "Wish me luck. With track going to make cannon and horses lost to the military, I hope I don't have to go far to find one."

"I'll walk to the War Department building, Franny. You take the Hansom out to Chimborazo." Bill ambled to the window. The cab waited at curbside.

"Tell the cabman to wait, Bill. I need to put on my coat and hat. It shouldn't take long. No more than five minutes."

Once down the steps and out the double doors, Bill fastened his shell jacket's top collar button and stepped to the Hansom. "There's been a change of plans." He withdrew his coin purse from a pocket.

"Instead of me to the War Department, you're to take my wife to Chimborazo." Bill extracted four bits from the purse, and stretching on his toes, put the coin in the cabman's hand. "That's the tip. Franny will pay the fare."

The cabman bit down on the half-dollar coin and grinned. "Thank you, sir. It's smart lettin' your woman ride in my cab, not hike to an omnibus stop. The gangs are gettin' bad. Not safe fer a lady. Don't worry about a ride back from the hospital. There's always cabmen parked and waitin' to provide a ride."

Just as Franny promised, she pushed open the double doors and bounced down the steps no more than five minutes after Bill started yakking with the cabman. Bill helped her up into the cab and waved goodbye as the cabman pressed the horse into a canter. The Hansom disappeared into a flamboyant coppice of trees clothed in autumn colors. Shoving his slouch hat partway down onto his ears, Bill headed to the Capitol Square eight blocks away, its Palladian-style hilltop Capitol building blocked by four-story brownstones and graystones on Franklin Street.

A sooty pall hung above the apartment buildings, the smoke from the chimneys of ironworks lining the James River. Bill hoped the morning would be free of showers. The raindrops would leave dirt splotches on his uniform. *Ah, city life.*

Barely past seven, Franklin Street already teemed with wagons, buggies, cabs and carriages. The apartment buildings thinned out closer to the Capitol Square, giving way to milliners, dressmakers, grocers, toymakers and butchers. Even closer, every building seemed to belong to a lawyer or doctor.

A scream pierced the hum of foot-traveler voices and wheels rolling along the street's bricks. Half a block ahead, near Fifth Street between the Yorktown Tavern and a milliner shop, shabbily dressed boys—no more than fourteen years old—were dragging a well-dressed elderly man into an alley. Brandishing a Bowie knife, a one-armed corporal sprinted toward the alley. Unarmed but game, Bill hustled to catch up. His boots pounded the boardwalk as he accelerated. Bill passed the milliner who nonchalantly swept her shop's front steps as if a mugging meant nothing.

Inside the alley, two teenage thugs lunged at the corporal, jabbing at his belly with carving knives. Nearby, a third youthful goon straddled the old man, rifled through his billfold then ripped a pocket watch from its chain.

Bill eyed barrels and crates lined up along the tavern wall next to the side door. He tried to pick up one. Too heavy. The one next to it turned out to be half the weight. Whatever it contained rolled and rattled when he lifted it.

Getting a running start, Bill heaved the barrel at the two scurfs. It thumped into the one closest to Bill just as the youth tripped on broken bricks and stumbled. The lid went flying as the thug fell backward and struck the alleyway pavement. Bottles, some intact, others broken and jagged, rained down on him. The cask hit the ground beside the ruffian and rolled away from him. The knife slipped from the scurf's sweaty hand and skidded across the alley, stopping near Bill's feet.

Groaning, tears raining down his cheeks, the youth scrambled to his feet. He glanced at the glass slivers in his palms. "We was just scarin' the old man and the cripple. Do some stealin' and be on our way. Ya'll didn't have to hurt me."

Bill picked up the butcher knife and waved the serrated blade. "Scaring soldiers with this pig-gutter? You and your buddies are going to end up dead if you don't change your ways."

Screaming swearwords a thirteen year old shouldn't know, the bloodied boy tore between Bill and the corporal, and disappeared among the throng of wagons and buggies on Franklin Street.

Bill snatched up the barrel's lid with his free hand, and using it as a shield, advanced on the other scurf waylaying the one-armed soldier. The thug lunged; his knife grazed the lid. The boy pounced again. This time the knife plunged into the wood. He yanked on the weapon, but it wouldn't budge. His eyes ballooned in alarm. The hooligan released the stuck blade, and screaming a litany of curses, fled past Bill, following his panicky friend's trail.

"Thanks, friend," the one-armed corporal grunted, panting. "One left. Too stupid to run."

The scurf straddling the old-timer twisted around and settled his scared gaze on the two of them. Leaping to his feet, the boy pressed the elderly man's watch against his chest and tried to scurry past Bill and the other soldier. The veteran stuck out his foot and tumbled the bully. The boy did a somersault and smacked the pavement, bloodying his forehead and tip of his nose. Watch still clutched in his right hand, he rolled over and glared at the corporal.

"That doesn't belong to you." The corporal seized the watch.

Bill leaned over the kid, grabbed him by the hair, and jerked him to his feet. The boy barely reached Bill's shoulders. He reckoned there was a gal somewhere in Richmond who loved this lad because of his beautiful tresses and ocean-blue eyes. *Poor, wretched girl.* Bill kicked the scurf in his back avenue, sending him stumbling away toward Franklin Street.

Kneeling beside the old man, Bill rested his hand on the fellow's shoulder. "Anything broken?"

"I don't think so." The timeworn gentleman, dressed in his Sunday-best suit, tested his arms and legs. "Not sure I can get up, though. These skinny legs don't support me very well nowadays." He laughed sourly.

Clutching the elderly man by the armpits, Bill helped him to his wobbly feet. "Need some help walking to the boardwalk?"

"No, don't think so. I'm just glad the thug didn't rough me up more."

"Here's your watch, grandfather." The corporal handed the railroad-style timepiece to the old man.

He took the pocket watch and fixed his gaze on its glass face. "It's broken. Retirement gift. I was an engineer for the Weldon Railroad. Best job in the world." He rubbed his sleeve across his face, wiping away tears.

"It can be fixed." Bill patted the elderly man's shoulder.

"If I was a rich man," the old-timer snapped, scowling as he shuffled toward Franklin Street.

The two soldiers exchanged weary looks. "Name's Craig Arnold," the corporal said.

"Bill Stamford."

"Delighted to meet you, Bill." Craig leaned down on one knee and picked up the old-timer's billfold. "If it had bills, they're gone now." He stuck it in a pocket. "If I see him again, I'll return it." Turning slightly, he gestured toward Franklin Street. "I'm headed to the War Department."

"That's fortuitous." Bill grinned. "I start my first day at the War Department. Care if I join you?"

"Glad to have your company, Stamford."

Drawing closer to the square, Bill at last could make out the very top of the Confederate Capitol rooftop. Its resemblance to ancient Greek and Roman buildings became more obvious as the square's parkland became visible. The architect, Thomas Jefferson, had designed a government building that had become the template for statehouse buildings all over the South and the North.

"The building housing the War Department fronts the west end of the square," Craig said. "It's fairly nondescript. No one passing by it would suspect it's the brain of the Confederate war effort."

To Bill, the ugly four-story building looked like it could have been designed by a bored Mechanics Institute freshman. "You're right. It's nondescript. I might have walked right by it and not noticed."

"I'm working here because I lost my left arm at Mechanicsville and chose to continue contributing to the war effort. What's your story, Stamford?"

Bill's back twitched. The wound might be healed, but it did like to occasionally remind Bill of the folly of politicians who chose to fight wars. "I've been healing up since taking a shell sliver in the back at Chancellorsville. I thought I'd be returning to my regiment, but the chicken-gut buggers had other ideas."

A laugh rumbled up from the corporal's belly. "This sounds like a tale I've got to hear."

"Seemed like Secretary Seddon needed a writer with reporting experience to be his new press contact. Normally, I'd never be considered for the job—except my bride's father is a civilian bugger in the conscription branch." Bill rolled his eyes. "And Seddon can't say no to my wife." He found his thoughts drifting back to Chancellorsville. "I've been in two battles. I'm more than willing to let some new volunteers and conscripts do their part."

"That's my sentiment as well."

"I start this job with sadness weighing heavy on my heart," Bill told his new friend Craig. "I buried my father a few days ago."

"I'm so sorry, Bill." Diffidently, Craig hugged him.

"Yep, a new job, a new bride and a new grave."

Eleven

First Day at the War Department

Bill and Craig entered the War Department building along with a crush of workers trying to beat the clock.

"Need directions to Secretary Seddon's office?" Craig inquired.

"I'm assuming it's on the first floor." Bill shrugged. "Not sure which direction, though."

"It's down there." Craig pointed to the right where there was little foot traffic. To the left took folks to a wide stairs, the choice of almost all the workers flooding into the building.

Bill reached out to shake Craig's hand. The corporal brushed the hand aside and hugged him. "Again, I want to say how sorry I am about your father."

The corporal headed up the stairs and disappeared from view. Bill wondered if Franny's father would be waiting for him in Seddon's office. *Well, I'll get my answer soon.* He proceeded down the hallway toward an approaching colonel.

"Lost, Private?" the colonel queried, an elitist tone in his voice.

The young officer was all spit-and-polish down to his neatly trimmed Suvorov mustache and slender sideburns. His perfectly pressed uniform said the colonel had never been close to a battlefield.

Bill saluted the chicken-gut greenhorn. "No, sir. I'm to start work here today."

"You're on the wrong floor." The colonel motioned toward the stairs.

"No, sir. I'm supposed to meet—"

"Follow me. I'll show you where the clerks work."

Bill shrugged away his frustration. He decided to let the peacock take him up to the clerks' chamber. Later, he'd shed the bugger and go find Seddon's office.

As they climbed the stairs, the colonel said neutrally, "Most of the soldiers in the clerks' pool are missing limbs."

Bill ignored the slight. The fancy-dressed officer obviously had family connections that kept him away from the battlefield smell of black powder. But a lowly private didn't dare point that out. Instead, Bill buried his irritation then said, "I'm lucky in that regard. Took a shell fragment in the back at Chancellorsville. An iffy wound. An inch upward and I'd be playing the harp in the Lord's heavenly symphony. Healed up now except for an occasional pinch of pain."

At least one hundred clerks—some soldiers, others civilians—worked diligently at their desks inside the vast third-floor chamber. When a toddler, Bill had loved to observe worker ants scurrying to and from their anthill. Now he was surrounded by them.

The colonel took Bill to a clean-shaven civilian wearing a leather apron and a green eyeshade. "Here's your new worker, Pete." He nodded toward Bill. "It may look overwhelming, soldier, but it'll get easier. You look smart. You'll catch on quick." Whirling around, the colonel left lickity-split.

"I don't have a new worker." Pete brushed a hand through his disheveled, ink-black hair.

Bill held out his hands, palms up. "That's because I'm Secretary

Seddon's new press guy. I tried to tell the colonel, but he didn't seem interested in listening."

"Colonel Sam Stone loves to hear himself give orders. You may make an enemy when he realizes the trick you played on him."

"No trick. He wanted to take me upstairs. I saw no reason to correct him. Hopefully, he has a sense of humor."

"Sorry. He doesn't."

"Then the next time he sees me should be interesting." Bill drew orders out of a vest pocket. "These say I'm to see Captain Beardsley."

"He's the gatekeeper for Secretary Seddon. Let me escort you to Beardsley lest another bugger officer tries to send you back up to me. I'm Paul Kelly, by the way."

Kelly ushered Bill out the door and toward the stairwell. Sneaking a last look, Bill eyed the clerks, many missing an arm, a few even a leg, before Kelly shut the door. No wonder suspicious looks fell on him.

Bill and Kelly bumped into a friend on the way down the steps—Sergeant Frank Davis, the one-armed soldier who helped Bill lug the traveling trunk up to the No. 7 apartment.

"I knew I'd seen you in the crush of workers and then you disappeared," Frank told Bill. "I promised Captain Beardsley I'd find you. Figured you took a wrong turn."

Kelly laughed. "A wrong turn engineered by Colonel Stone. Private Stamford made the mistake of listening to him."

"Ah, that explains his tardiness." Comprehension gleamed in the sergeant's eyes. "A rank conscious man. A private can only work in the clerk pool."

With the colonel's mistake allayed, Sergeant Davis escorted Bill to Captain Beardsley's office. Bill snapped a salute. Rising to his feet, Beardsley returned the salute. More than six feet tall, the captain towered over his oak Partners desk and leather-upholstered chair. He looked the part of a battlefield-tested veteran. He wore an unpretentious uniform, not bedecked with chicken guts. His eyes cast the faraway stare that said *I've seen men die.*

"Stamford?" the captain inquired.

Bill sensed he'd discovered a kindred soul. "Yessir. Glad to meet you, Captain."

"Secretary Seddon will see you, Private." The captain turned and eyed a closed door that apparently led to Seddon's office.

Bill thanked Sergeant Davis. "Hopefully, you'll soon get a chance to help out my possum, Charlie Kurtz. Together, we'll pierce his melancholy and resurrect my happy-go-lucky buddy."

"That's my aim," the sergeant reaffirmed. "He'll definitely get my two cents."

Davis closed the door behind him, leaving the captain and Bill alone. "The sergeant likes you, Stamford, and he's a good judge of men. Men like Colonel Stone love the trappings of being an officer, but find ways to avoid battle. I can tell you're different. I've read up on your service record. To be honest, I don't understand why you're a private. Had you returned to the Army of Northern Virginia, I imagine you'd have gotten a promotion."

"I'm satisfied being a private, sir." Bill pursed his lips thoughtfully.

"Ah, a man not sure he wants to take on life-and-death decisions. Makes me respect you even more, Stamford." The captain stepped up to Seddon's office door.

Seddon sipped a cup of steaming coffee when Beardsley and Bill strolled in. With a George Washington glass paperweight holding a document in place, Seddon picked up an ink pen and scribbled his signature to the bottom of the paper. He placed the pen back in its stand and sipped more coffee.

"Mourning, Captain Beardsley. I see you have our new press attaché." Seddon glanced at his pocket watch. "A bit late, but I'm sure there's a good explanation?"

Beardsley chuckled. "Colonel Stone."

"Ah, now I understand his tardiness. I really should send Stone to Lee, but the general would probably never forgive me."

"General Lee would ship him back to us." Beardsley's lips shivered with amusement.

"Hopefully not before the colonel got his pretty uniform dirtied." Seddon turned his gaze on Bill. "So you're Franny's new husband. I admit I wondered what you'd look like. Far different than I expected. She made a good choice. I never liked that Tennessean."

"I'm lucky she chose me." Bill settled in one of the cushy chairs in front of the work desk when Seddon gestured for him and the captain to sit.

"I think she's lucky to have you in her life." Seddon leaned back in his chair.

When younger, Seddon must have been attractive to the ladies. Even in his late forties, he still had an impressive air about him. His deeply set eyes were shadowed by heavy brows and a broad forehead. The mop of hair that had once graced the top of his head had thinned long ago, but ample amounts still grew along his sides, covering his ears. Still a bit vain, Seddon sported a hint of a beard and a full mustache. Gaunt with a sallow complexion, the gentleman wore a black skullcap.

Franny had prepared Bill for their first-time meeting. Seddon was somewhat neurotic and a semi-invalid. If not for the war, the man who'd served in the U.S. Congress in the 1840s and early 1850s would have stayed cooped up in his house. Only President Davis's entreaties convinced Seddon to serve the Confederacy. Knowing he could return to private life at a whim made him impervious to outrageous demands.

Bill leaned across the desk and shook the secretary's hand. "Thank you for this opportunity, sir."

"Franny and her father convinced me of your worth as a reporter and writer. By the way, your father-in-law will be joining us shortly."

"I've been told I possess a flair for writing." Bill crossed his legs. "I was in Richmond once before. A few weeks after Chancellorsville. I was on my way home to recuperate and transferred from one train to another. I don't remember much. Those were days filled with pain."

"Most of us here have taken that train ride," Captain Beardsley reflected. "We know what you've been through. You've earned our respect, Private."

"Private Stamford, I'm pleased to have you join my staff. I have a plethora of ideas for using your newspaper skills. When Howard gets here, we'll share some of them with you." Seddon glanced at his empty coffee mug and groaned.

The captain jumped to his feet. "Let me get you a fresh cup, Secretary."

"And for you and Bill as well, Captain." Seddon handed his mug to Beardsley. "You do drink the stuff, don't you, Bill?"

"Indeed, I do—ersatz and real." Bill rested his hands on his right kneecap. "Almost embarrassed to say the last real coffee came off a dead blue belly."

"Not doing him any good," Seddon said. "And coffee's not the Lord's tipple."

Beardsley returned with the mugs, all steaming. Once all three had their initial sips, Beardsley made no bones about his view of Richmond's newspaper editors. "They don't understand words can prolong the war. Their editorials can surely kill as permanently as a mini ball. I don't like seeing newspaper offices burn down, but I understand how mobs of convalescing soldiers can be incited to torch them."

"I'm hoping that one of their own can get through to them," Seddon explained. "It's better having them work with us. I don't want to turn them into enemies."

Bill mulled the two men's words. Editors were headstrong. They'd fought hard for press freedoms and would be reluctant to surrender them. "They're patriots, Mr. Secretary. Most have sons serving in the armies. I think I can get their cooperation. I'll start this week setting up appointments to get to know them."

"I will need to see results, Stamford," Seddon stressed. "The President expects—"

A sharp knock on the door interrupted Seddon. A moment later, Howard Neale and a surprise guest strolled into the room.

Bill almost spilled his coffee down his shell jacket at the sight of her.

"Franny!" he stammered. "You're supposed to be at Chimborazo." Hand jittery, he put the coffee mug on Seddon's desk. "I'm in shock. Well, not entirely. I'm also delighted."

Grinning, Franny settled into an empty chair. "I wouldn't miss seeing my man made a second lieutenant."

"A lieutenant's bar?" Bill turned his skeptical gaze on his wife. "You're fooling…you're not!" He scrutinized Beardsley. "Captain, you were in on it too, weren't you?"

"I sure was. Now, you don't need to worry about Colonel Stone. He'll have to find another private to bedevil."

Franny scooted her chair closer to Bill and kissed his cheek. "I loved keeping *this* secret, Bill. You really thought you'd stay a private?"

"I really didn't think about it."

Seddon chortled. "Newspaper editors expect to hobnob with an officer and gentleman."

Franny clapped. "Just think, darling, I'll be dancing with a handsome Confederate officer at the Spotswood's Christmas Ball." She stood and pointed to the sheet of paper held in place by the George Washington paperweight. "Sign it, James. Please." Her pronunciation of Seddon's first name was flirtatious, drawing a smile from the secretary. "When I go to sleep, I want to kiss a lieutenant goodnight."

Seddon took the pen from its holder, poised it over the paper and stopped. "Oh, look. There's a signature there already. Your husband's a second lieutenant. I kept the news from him so you could give your officer husband a kiss stronger than that peck on the cheek."

Franny rolled her eyes. Reaching out to Bill, she motioned him to his feet then kissed him full on the mouth per Seddon's instructions. "That meet your expectations, James?"

"Never deny a Southern lady," the Secretary of War said, slapping his desk. "William Stamford, you're a second lieutenant. Congratulations."

Unable to keep a serious mien, Bill shook hands with his father-in-law and Seddon, then turned to get another kiss from Franny. She was gone. The closed door to Beardsley office was now open, so he knew his wife had sneaked out during the handshaking ritual. Eyeing his father-in-law, Bill raised an eyebrow. Howard said nothing.

Beardsley coughed. "She'll be back, Lieutenant Stamford."

Franny breezed through the doorway, an officer's coat draped over her arm. "Get out of that shell jacket, darling."

Once he removed the jacket, Franny helped him don the new one with the second lieutenant's bar on each collar. Again, he got a kiss on the cheek.

"The South's newest second lieutenant," Bill's father-in-law said, whimsy in his voice.

The old shell jacket draped across her arm, Franny headed for the doorway then suddenly turned. "I'll see you after work, Lieutenant Stamford." She shut the door behind her. Bill could hear muffled giggling.

Seddon and Franny's father gave Bill the grand tour. They showed him the basement's printing press, the first-floor telegraph office, the Adjutant and Inspector General's Department on the second, and all the myriad bureaus spread out among the four stories. All but the clerks' pool.

At the tour's end, Bill's father-in-law returned to his department, leaving the new second lieutenant alone with Seddon.

Once Bill and Seddon were seated in the secretary's office, Seddon gave him his marching orders. "I like that you're going to meet with the editors of the Richmond newspapers. Remember, there are newspapers all through the South. The distant ones will require the telegraph. I'll be passing battle reports to you so you can prepare some of them for publication. You're to make each battle's tactics and overall strategy understandable to the editors, especially the Richmond editors. In the event of bad news, caress it so it doesn't sound so bad. As we discussed earlier, I want to improve our relationship with the South's newspaper editors. Too many are turning pessimistic about the war and our cause."

"I look forward to the challenge, sir."

Seddon stood. "Anything else before I put you to work?"

"Just one request, Secretary." Bill scooted forward to the end of the chair and rested his elbows on Seddon's desk. "I want to name my own aide. I have someone in mind, a friend who served with me in my regiment. His name's Charlie Kurtz. We joined together."

"Consider it done, Lieutenant."

Twelve

A Longtime Friend Arrives

"Morning, Ernie," Bill shouted to the cabman as he stepped down his brownstone's portico steps, Franny on his arm.

"Mornin', Lieutenant." The cabman grinned as he pronounced Bill's new rank. "Ya'll look fine with the new second lieutenant bar. I probably said it before, Mr. Bill, but let me say it again. Congratulations." The cabman adjusted the fit of the worn bowler atop his head then swung open the front cab doors.

"Thank you, Ernie." Bill helped Franny up onto the cushioned seat. "And thanks for agreeing to pick us up."

The day before he'd taken a walk down to the Weldon Railroad depot to see if he could find the cabman. Bill had been lucky. The cabman had been parked in front of the depot waiting for a customer. The fellow, too old for army service, had readily agreed to pick up Bill and Franny for a trip to the depot to meet Charlie, arriving from Kenansville. "Looks like I'm goin' to be your favorite cabman," the gent had said just before Bill returned to the War Department. "My name's Ernie McGaul. I'll take care of ya just like ya're my own grandkid."

The cab juddered into motion. The black-colored horse strutted down the brick street as if showing off for them. Franny chuckled. "Our horsey likes to run and Ernie's Hansom can take curbs faster than any carriage. She's begging Ernie to let her give us a ride to remember."

"I hope not. I don't want to end up sprawled on the roadway." Bill leaned against Franny and nibbled on her ear, earning a "Stop that!" from her.

"So your adventurous spirit doesn't go beyond our bedroom?"

"Not at seven in the morning, darling."

Franny shouted out to the cabman, "Ernie, let her rip!"

"Want to see some speed, eh? Hold onto your hubby, dearie."

Off they went at a speed that made Bill almost as nervous as the sound of mini balls whizzing by his head. Borne by just two wheels and the braggart horse, the cab turned on a penny as Ernie went around a corner. Ernie steered through a traffic jam one block from the depot and came to a stop at the curb behind five cabs already lined up to receive train passengers scheduled to arrive at eight, weather and track conditions permitting.

Ernie opened the trapdoor. "Enjoy the ride?"

"Loved it," Franny remarked.

"And you, Lieutenant Stamford?" The cabman sounded amused.

"I felt about the way I did at Chancellorsville just before a shell exploded above my head."

Ernie burst into laughter. "Your wife wanted some excitement. Just like comin' down the ice slides in Russia. Whoopee!"

Bill exhaled a raucous sigh. "What's the fare, Ernie?"

"Sixty-five cents—for the ride of your life. You folks are fun."

Bill handed him two fifty-cent pieces. "All for you if you promise never to do that again." Bill's tiny laugh turned into a hoot.

"I can't promise that, not with your daredevil wife aboard." The cabman opened the front half-doors. "I expected you to be the daredevil and her the scaredy cat."

Bill helped Franny step from the cab onto the boardwalk. In the distance, he could hear a train whistle. Charlie would soon arrive. Bill hoped his friend had conquered the melancholy, but doubts remained.

Franny read the look on Bill's face. "Don't worry. He's coming here. That means he's fighting what ails him. He'll see how others like him are persevering."

Bill nodded. "I hope you're right, sweetheart." He put his arm around Franny's shoulders. "Charlie needs a woman to whisper sweet nothings to him."

"I might be able to help there. I know some women in the Ladies' Aid Society who have unmarried daughters. I can arrange an introduction or two." She gave Bill a seductive glance. "Southern ladies love heroes."

Bill raised an eyebrow. "Then why did you choose me?"

Franny rolled her eyes. "A hero never knows when he's a hero."

Sighing, Bill waved to the cabman. "You're going to wait for us to return with Charlie, right? Not skedaddling with other customers?"

Ernie saluted Bill. "Don't worry. I ain't goin' anywhere. A promise is a promise."

The locomotive's steam whistle blew again, much louder, a sheer noise that announced: hey, folks, come on out and greet me. Above the chug-chug-chug sound of the locomotive's drive driveshaft turning the wheels at a slower and slower rate, the brakes squealed, signaling Charlie's arrival.

Bill caressed the back of Franny's neck. "Let's head for the platform. I want Charlie to see us waiting for him. He needs friends right now."

Franny took Bill's hand. "He's going to get sick of me introducing him to my single friends."

"Charlie? I don't think so."

First, stretcher bearers brought wounded soldiers down onto the platform for transportation by ambulance to Chimborazo. Next, the walking wounded joined loved ones on the platform. Bill and Franny watched for Charlie, but the Kenansville soldier was scarcer than a barefoot Yankee on a battlefield. A few nattily dressed businessmen left the train. Still no Charlie. Bill's belly growled, not from hunger but from nervousness. Had his possum got the willies and not boarded the Wilmington and Weldon train in Warsaw?

A curse on the tip of his tongue, Bill turned to go back into the depot.

"Not so fast," Franny chided.

Charlie stood on the top step, eyeing the crowd on the platform. His gaze fell on Franny then shifted to Bill. "Hey, possum! Did you think I chickened out?"

"Crossed my mind."

A carpetbag in his hand, a haversack strapped to his shoulders, Charlie descended the steps and vaulted onto the platform. Franny hugged him. Bill crossed his arms and gave his best friend the once-over.

"You're skinnier than the last time I saw you," Bill remarked dryly.

"We'll have him over for supper," Franny added. "I'll fatten him up."

"You've a trunk?" Bill nodded toward the luggage car.

"Just what I have in the carpetbag and strapped to my back," Charlie answered, shrugging his shoulders.

Franny shook her head, an incredulous look on her face. "Really? That's all?"

"A couple of uniforms, underwear, cloak, winter overcoat and summer jacket...what else do I need?" Charlie bowed to Franny. "Work during the day and settle in at my apartment at night...that's going to be my life from now—"

"No, it isn't," Bill cut in. "I've plans for—"

A halo flared around a young girl no more than five as she danced alongside her mother and her businessman father. *No, Lord, not this little thing.* He'd already dabbled in fate, saving Charlie's life in exchange for General Jackson, or so Bill had come to believe. This little girl deserved to grow up, have children of her own, and in her old age watch grandkids play around her feet. Bill would at least make sure she made it safely into a Hansom, buggy or carriage. He slipped away from Franny and Charlie and trailed the girl and her parents. Longer than usual, the halo still blazed around the youngster.

Behind him in the depot, Bill heard Charlie growl, "What in tarnation is he doing?"

"Don't know. We need to catch up with him," Franny said, her voice adamant. "Bill? Slow down!"

Bill yelled out to Franny: "Halo!"

"Oh, Lord, no!" Franny followed Bill's gaze to the girl, wearing her Sunday-best pink day dress.

"Halo?" Charlie furrowed his brow.

Outside the depot, the mother reached for her daughter's hand as they prepared to step off the boardwalk between Bill's cab and the one behind it. Ernie from his perch atop the Hansom puffed on a pipe, oblivious to what transpired just a few feet from him.

At that moment, a rich woman's lapdog, a brown-furred Sleeve Pekingese, leapt from its owner's arms as she stepped down from the family carriage. "Oh, Sadie, come to Momma," the middle-aged woman pleaded.

"No! No, little doggy," the girl shrieked just before the halo flickered and disappeared.

Ernie the cabman twisted around, saw the dog dart into the brick-paved street. His pipe slipped from his mouth, bounced off the side of the Hansom and smacked the bricks in front of the girl.

"Sadie, stay out of the street," the dog's owner, clad in a flowery dress ten years out of date and a snood hat, ordered—to no avail.

Midpoint in the street, the girl snatched up the Sleeve Pekingese. Twenty yards away, a careening Hansom bore down on her. Holding the doggy against her chest, the girl blinked huge eyes and gaped at the onrushing cab. Drunk out of his mind, the cabman made no effort to avoid the girl.

"Sweet Lord, no!" the Pekingese's owner wailed.

"Oh, my God," the girl's mother shrieked. "Please, a miracle." She buckled, dropped to her knees and Franny smothered her in a fierce hug. "Bill, don't let the halo win." Franny's eyes drilled into his soul.

The girl's father lurched toward the boardwalk curb, tripped, and reeling, fell between parked cabs. He sobbed.

Bill sprinted into the street, scooped up the girl and leapt for safety. Hoofs pounded the brick pavement near him. He could hear the horse's frantic breaths. The dog yelped and squirmed free of the girl. The Pekinese froze in the path of one of the Hansom's wheels. From the corner of his eye, as Bill lay on the ground cradling the girl, someone grabbed the dog just in the nick of time and danced away from the cab.

Cuddling the Pekinese against his chest, Charlie screamed profanities at the inebriated coachman. The Hansom didn't stop. Since the morning the three teenage toughs waylaid the old man in the alley, Bill had carried a concealed derringer. He nearly drew it for a shot at the stewed man, but calmed his anger. They were all safe, though, but not without scrapes and bruises.

A wagon, buggy and a coach were all stopped, people jumping from them to aid Bill, the girl and Charlie, still clutching Sadie. First to Bill was the girl's mother who snatched her from him. "Thank you, Lieutenant," the woman gushed as Bill hobbled to his feet. His pants were torn, his knees skinned and bleeding, as were his elbows and palms. His toes inside his left boot complained and he quickly saw why. The Hansom's iron-clad wheel had scuffed the boot.

The woman's husband shook Bill's hand. "I'm forever in your debt," the businessman said, his voice trembling. "You saved my daughter Tonya. Anything you need just let me know."

Bill nodded then took a few tentative steps. He'd not be racing anyone for a while. Any substantial walking would require a cane for a few weeks.

Tonya's mother spattered kisses on Bill's face—his eyes, cheeks, chin, forehead, everywhere but his lips. She held Tonya close against her side. "The lieutenant saved your life, Tonya," she told her daughter. "What do you say to him?"

"Thank you, sir. Tonight I'll ask God to keep you safe." Tonya took Bill's hand and kissed his palm.

"Oh, Sadie, you naughty dog," said the middle-aged woman, scurrying to Charlie's side and grabbing her Pekinese from him. "You scared me to death. Bad girl!"

"There, there, ma'am," Charlie said, soothing the older woman. "The doggy's fine. She's a face licker, ain't she?"

Sadie lapped her tongue along her mistress's cheek, even washing the woman's eyebrow. The woman swung her focus from Sadie to Charlie. Her eyes lit up with admiration. "Thank you, soldier. God's blessings rain down on you." She grabbed Charlie fiercely, covering his cheeks and forehead with kisses. The Pekinese yelped, getting squeezed too tight.

Charlie laughed. "Ma'am, I saved your Sadie. I don't want to see her crushed."

"Oh? I'm so foolish," the woman blubbered. "I'm so sorry, Sadie. I'm just so glad you'll be sitting on my lap tonight."

A younger woman dressed in an alluring French-style dress emerged from the older lady's carriage and hurried to her side. "Oh, Momma, I've warned you to take better care with Sadie. You're always almost dropping her."

"Daughter, not here!"

The younger woman turned saucy eyes Charlie's way. "Thank you, sir. Thank God my momma didn't have to see Sadie squished"— she swung her gaze to the little girl—"or the child run down and murdered. Thank God you and your friend were here to stop two tragedies. I don't exaggerate; you both are heroes." She slipped by her momma and kissed him on both cheeks.

Charlie blushed, something that would have never happened before he lost his arm. "Couldn't let the doggy get squished." He fingered his wet cheeks. "I expected doggy kisses, not a bunch of sweet ones from a beautiful girl."

Charlie's new admirer regarded Franny. "Franny Stamford, who is this wonderful man?"

"I wondered when you would ask, Avis Thompkins." Walking over to Charlie, Franny looped her arm around his shoulders. "This is my husband's best friend, Charlie Kurtz. Next to my husband, the sweetest man in the South."

Charlie grinned. "Bill's my possum, Franny, but let's be honest. I'm by far the sweetest."

"I must agree." Avis chuckled. The dog barked. "Sadie would love to see you again. So would I. Please call on me."

Charlie insisted on loading his carpetbag and haversack aboard the Hansom, and once the two men and Franny were comfortably inside the passenger compartment, cabman Ernie put the vehicle into motion. Before they boarded, Ernie had assured Bill, "The bastard will get cabman's justice. Read the newspapers. Soon you'll see justice done."

Franny sat between Bill and Charlie. "So are you going to call on Avis?" she queried innocently.

"Probably. Maybe. I'm leanin' that way." Charlie's face showed no emotion.

"She's pretty." Franny caressed Charlie's stump. "I know Avis. She wants to get to know you better. There's sham coffee and sham girls. She's not sham. If Avis wants you to call on her, it means she likes you."

"I'll probably call on her. Like you said, Franny, she's pretty and she did kiss me." Charlie finally grinned. "Her momma likes me. And their dog."

"Probably?" Bill sighed. "That's not the possum I remember. You'd be plotting an after-sunset walk with her in Jefferson Park."

"I'm cleanin' up my act." Charlie smiled.

"Avis would be a perfect partner for the Christmas Ball," Franny pointed out.

"Franny's right." Bill patted his wife's kneecap. "The ball's just six weeks away. You'd better ask her before some desk-bound bugger calls on her."

Charlie's shoulders slumped as raindrops sprinkled the top of the Hansom. "A one-armed gent ain't no good at dancin'—or tippin' the velvet."

"That's cow manure, Charlie," Franny shot back. "You with one arm can outdance all the buggers working at the War Department. Like I said, I know Avis quite well and I'm going to tell her you will soon be calling on her."

"I'd say you're bluffin', except I know you don't bluff." Charlie jabbed Bill. "You picked a humdinger, possum."

"That was one of her selling points. So you don't have a choice, Charlie, you got to call on that pretty girl."

A steady rain pelted the Hansom's top as the cab pulled up to the brownstone. The trapdoor opened. "Sorry about the rain, Lieutenant," Ernie said. "The sky was blue when I hitched up at the crack of dawn."

Bill paid the cabman, and helped Franny reach the boardwalk. He let Charlie get down without assistance. He grabbed the haversack and left the carpetbag for Charlie. The three raced up the steps and into the protection of the roofed portico.

"You're two doors down from us," Bill informed Charlie.

"Good," Charlie said, merriment in his voice. "I'd hate to be kept up all night by your bedroom shenanigans."

"You've a filthy mind, Charlie Kurtz." Franny opened the door into the lobby. "Avis's going to love your humor. Away from her momma, she's quite the firecracker."

"Charlie, once we get you settled in, we're going to have you over for a late-night supper." Bill headed for the stairs. "It's time for you to see what a good cook Franny has become."

Thirteen

Wintertime Arrives

The cool days and nights of autumn turned colder. By early December, the first snowfall covered the streets and boardwalks of Richmond. Snow coated the trees in Capitol Square and the new Washington statue. The walks of Bill and Charlie to the War Department became slogs through ankle-deep slush, the square's squirrels as scarce as steak.

Franny had her volunteer work at Chimborazo and inside the mansions of Richmond's elite families toiling alongside the War Department wives on Richmond Ladies' Aid Society projects. On most days she'd take a cab to the Seddon residence and help James's wife Sarah and other women of the society—including Avis—quilt blankets for Lee's freezing army.

Bill and Franny had spoken only twice about the little girl and her halo. For Franny, Bill's rescue proved the Lord didn't always require a sacrifice. Bill wasn't sure. He found himself scanning the Richmond newspapers hoping not to see the girl's obituary. A man with the halo gift needed to be vigilant.

Charlie had called on Avis as he promised. They'd clicked at first and then she'd gotten frustrated with Charlie's moodiness. Sergeant Davis had chinwagged with him—hard words from a fellow one-armed soldier. Davis's words helped, but Charlie still had to fight the black moments of near-mental paralysis. Weary of Charlie's unpredictable gloom moods, Avis cooled the romance, had even begun to see other men. That left Charlie even more downcast.

One block from the War Department building, Bill found himself rudely wrenched from his inner thoughts. No longer using a cane, he slipped on boardwalk ice and took a tumble onto his buttocks. "Someone's losin' his marchin' skills," Charlie sniggered.

Not angry at his possum, Bill grinned as he took Charlie's hand, glad to see him laughing. In the evening, Charlie would eat with them. Franny planned to double-down and convince Charlie to patch things up. Avis had told Franny something Charlie didn't know—she loved him.

As the snow coating his frockcoat turned to water and dripped, Bill limped into his office. Spying some papers spiked to the message spindle on his desk, Bill slid the top one off the hook and read the first two paragraphs. The words didn't surprise him. A Mine Run battle report from General Lee. Further investigation revealed another report, this one from General Edward Johnson, division commander under General Richard Ewell. Bill grimaced. Lee had stopped an Army of the Potomac's offensive near Chancellorsville. Just reading the name Chancellorsville made him queasy, summoning memories of the day Yankee shrapnel tore into his back. *We just fight for the same real estate over and over again.*

Bill read on...it wasn't a smashing victory. The telegrapher had underscored the word smashing, probably perturbed to see yet another hollow victory. Lee hadn't turned Meade's flanks and wrecked the Army of the Potomac. The opportunity had been there, but the execution had been lacking. Jackson was dead, and General Longstreet and his corps were out west fighting with the Army of the Tennessee. It was the winter of 1862 all over again with both armies in their winter camps, Southern boys eating too little food, and what there was of it awful. Bill tightened his lips. Worst thing was, he couldn't say any of this publically. Times like this he hated his job.

Bill pricked his ears. Even with his inner-sanctum door shut, he heard a fledgling commotion in Charlie's outer office and recognized the strident voice, *Daily Dispatch* editor Michael Russell. In the more than two months since Bill started his War Department job, he'd met all of Richmond's newspaper editors and tried to nurture professional relationships. Russell didn't like to make appointments; he preferred showing up for morning chitchat. Charlie tended to his appointment book the way Santa kept a naughty-and-nice list. The two would good naturedly bicker. Usually Bill would open the door and tell them to pipe down. This time, though, Charlie nudged the door and squirmed his head through.

"The man who doesn't believe in rules wants to see you, Billy Boy. Why bother with a calendar book?"

Unseen, Russell exclaimed, "Stop it, Kurtz. The first appointment isn't until nine. I've got your possum all to myself for forty-five minutes."

Russell strolled into Bill's inner sanctum with cups of steaming coffee in his hands and a sheet of paper held by his teeth. With the cups safely deposited, Russell plopped down in one of the chairs arrayed in front of the desk. He put the sheet beside his coffee cup.

"My reporter with Lee sent this telegraph dispatch overnight." Russell tapped the sheet. "It's his impressions of the Mine Run fighting." He sipped the coffee. "I figured your first job this morning would be to prepare a censored battle report for the newspapers." Russell greedily stared at the handwritten sheets in front of Bill. "You couldn't give me a peek?"

"And get tarred and feathered by the other editors?" Bill raised his coffee cup and instead of taking a swallow, he waved it in front of the editor. "You know I have to be fair to everyone."

"Nothing I can entice you with to get an early look?" Russell picked up his correspondent's dispatch, and with its jagged edge scratched a day-old growth of beard.

"A peek at your correspondent's observations could get you the first look at my version of Lee's battle report." Bill took the first sip of the coffee, took in the rich aroma and let it wash lazily down his throat. Real coffee from one of the War Department's warehouses, Bill's one vice. "I could be convinced to hand-deliver it to you later today—before I visit the other Richmond newspapers or have my telegrapher send it to other editors in the South. You can brag that you were the first."

Russell acted as if he intended to hand his correspondent's missive to Bill then jerked it back. "I need to think about this," he teased.

Standing, Bill took a couple of steps toward the doorway. "Don't think too long. I'm sure the editor of the *Richmond Daily Examiner* will be knocking on my door before noontime. I do believe the *Examiner* also has a correspondent with the Army of Northern Virginia."

"Sit down, Stamford." Russell scowled. "I get General Lee's battle report before the *Examiner* or anyone else, right?"

"Yes—and you can brag about your possum relationship with me." Bill put down the coffee cup and leaned back in his chair. "Of course, I'll say I treat all the editors the same. And that every one of you need to remember your papers are read by the politicians in Washington. Pessimism in the news columns gives Lincoln and his Republicans hope they can outlast us." He gestured for Russell to share the correspondent's words.

The *Daily Dispatch* editor sailed the sheet to Bill who scanned the sentences. "As you can see, the correspondent interviewed a dozen Virginia and North Carolina soldiers," Russell explained. "The boys love General Lee, but believe the generals below him bungled the Mine Run fighting. To a man, they're sick of seeing the Yanks escape and fight another day."

"Your correspondent calls the result a stalemate," Bill said through gritted teeth. "A lot of soldiers died or were wounded. Nothing gained. Yanks and Butternuts are now hunkered down in their winter camps. Damn depressing, Russell."

"That's how the men feel, Lieutenant." The editor shrugged away his annoyance. "We sugarcoated our war stories in the first years of the war to keep the morale high on the homefront. Wives are reading the same dispiriting news in their husbands' letters. When they pick up the *Daily Dispatch* and start reading, the women immediately sniff out the candy-coated manure. Remember, a fair number rioted over food back in the spring."

Bill steepled his fingers. "Of course, you're right, Russell. But when you're putting together your latest Mine Run story, remember it'll soon be Christmastime. Mommas are already telling their little ones Santa won't be able to get through the Yankee blockade. Way too many women are wearing black dresses. They're walking the boardwalks and seeing soldiers without arms and legs." He lifted his half-full cup and drank lukewarm coffee. "I would never tell you to write fairytales. Just be careful with the truth, Russell.

"What are the facts? General Lee stopped Meade's offensive. What's opinion? Soldiers' gripes about their officers. Women and their kiddies don't need their hearts ripped out during the Christmas season. Think twice before you accuse General Lee's generals of incompetence. Talk to any wife out for a stroll on the square and she'll tell you that Lee is one of the Lord's angels come to Earth." Bill handed the sheet back to Russell. "Not far from here on the city's outskirts are the army camps. Those men read the *Daily Dispatch*. Use your head, Russell. You don't want to get them riled."

Charlie intruded with the pot of coffee, topping off the cups. "Newspaper offices have been burned in the Tar Heel state," he said, proving he'd overheard the conversation.

The editor pushed his cup away from himself. "The headline will say 'Lee Wins Mine Run Victory, Our Soldiers Disappointed Yankee Army Not Destroyed.'" Russell swung his gaze from Charlie to Bill. "Every time I write an editorial I think of those troops in the camps. The Yanks didn't retreat, so our readers know it ain't much of a victory. That's something that can't be sweetened over—unless I make stuff up. Like Federals Routed, Yanks Running Back To

Washington. Lincoln Flees To England." Russell hooked a finger around the cup's handle. "The truth's best even if it hurts."

"I have to keep Seddon and President Davis happy," Bill underscored as he picked up his refreshed cup and drank. "Soldiers rampaging through the street, torches raised on high, that's not healthy for me or you, Russell. Be careful about what you write. These are peculiar times."

"Understood. I get the first look at General Lee's after-battle reports?"

"You'll be the first one. It'll be hand-delivered later today." Bill ushered the editor to the outside hallway then returned to the inner sanctum where Charlie had planted his buttocks in Russell's vacated chair.

"It may not be the *Daily Dispatch* office, but one of them's goin' to get burned. Someone's goin' to write an incendiary editorial." Charlie lowered his voice to a whisper. "I don't like the war, but I keep my mouth shut." He grabbed Russell's coffee cup and finished off its still-hot contents.

"When one burns, the rest will be more careful." Bill glanced at his coffee cup, didn't drink. He'd soon need to make a water closet run; no point adding to the volume.

Charlie crossed his legs. "I'm goin' to try to do better with Avis. I know I'm scarin' her off. I'm goin' to call on her, tell her I'm sorry. The girl has such sweet kisses. And she enjoys my company. I've made so many bad mistakes since losin' my arm. No more, Bill. I'm goin' to show her the old Charlie, the South's sweetest lover boy."

"Just be careful, possum. You don't want her father coming after you with a shotgun."

"I'm goin' to be like General Lee plannin' a battle. Goin' to plot a lover's campaign and marry that girl."

"No more black moods that scare her?"

"No more. So many one-armed soldiers walkin' around the War Department doing more than when they had two arms."

"Sounds like you've been having conversations with Sergeant Davis."

"Yep. Several. He got so mad at me when I told him Avis didn't want to see me no more. He scared me to death, said he'd seduce her just to prove me a fool." Charlie laughed sheepishly. "He'd do it too."

"Well, Avis told Franny something about you, Charlie. She loves you. She'll take you back, and I wager she'll accept your marriage proposal." Bill smiled roguishly. "Now if you'd had your nebuchadnezzar shot off, that would be a whole different can of worms. Women like to twiddle with a man's nebuchadnezzar, and it comes in handy when it's time to put a bun in the oven."

Charlie gave out a groaning laugh. "Oh, I know. When I came out of surgery, that's the first thing I looked at when I lifted the bloody sheet."

Fourteen

A Christmastime Protest

On this early December evening, the setting sun had already painted the western horizon a glorious red. Just as Bill and Charlie reached the brownstone's front entrance, a Hansom cab's horse pranced through the snow left from the previous day's storm and stopped at the curb in front of them. Bearing a basket of groceries, Franny exited the cab and greeted Bill. "Darling, sorry I'm late. Stopped to get tonight's meal. We're having Hoppin' John Stew."

Bill pulled a face. "Better than I ate at the Fredericksburg camp." He took the basket from his wife.

Franny tapped her lower lip. "I should say so. Get a fire going in the stove and we'll be able to eat by eight o'clock."

The clock above the Hathaway oven read just after nine o'clock when Bill, Franny and Charlie sat down at the kitchen table and spooned Hoppin' John Stew into their mouths. Bill's belly growled as the mess of bacon, beans and red peppers slid down his throat. Franny's grin grew larger.

"How was your day, dear?" she said.

"You don't want to know, Franny."

"I'm a polite girl."

Bill stopped his spoon an inch from his mouth. "No, you're not. Tell me about your day."

"Since you insist." Franny returned her spoon to the bowl. "At the Seddon house, I happened to mention that I helped decorate the Forest Hills ballroom for the Fredericksburg ball. You do remember the ball, don't you?" She winked at Charlie. "I know it's vulgar to say, but we tipped the velvet for the first time in the overseer's cottage."

Bill chuckled. "My favorite memory, except for my seventh birthday when I got a wind-up locomotive."

"Well, Sarah picked me to head the society's decorating committee. I think sometimes I talk too much."

"You don't want to do the decorating?" Bill sipped his glass of molasses punch.

"On the contrary. I've lots of ideas for raising money to help our soldiers and Richmond's widows and orphans. Overseeing the committee gives me Sarah's ear."

"I can't think of anyone better for the job," Charlie nodded his congratulations.

Franny crinkled a smile. "And Avis has agreed to be my assistant. By the way, I thought you'd be bringing her to dinner tonight."

"Her grandma's not feelin' well, so she decided to go see her." Charlie shrugged. "I couldn't very well complain, could I?"

Leaning forward, Franny shook her head in dismay. "Avis's grandma? It's not too serious I hope?"

Washing down the last of his Hoppin' John Stew with his mug of molasses punch, Charlie cleaned his mouth with a cloth napkin and stood. "I don't know. Avis should be gettin' home about now. She suggested I call on her after I finished eatin' with you. I reckon she needs peppin' up. Her grandma's fifty-five and gettin' up in age. In wintertime, even sniffles and sneezin' can do in an old woman."

Rising, Bill ushered Charlie to the front door. "Keep us posted. And tell Avis we hope her grandma starts feeling better soon."

"I will, possum. See you in the mornin'."

Bill helped Franny wash the dishes. Later, they sat on the settee and kissed. She danced her tongue across his lips then reached to the end table and drew a book to her lap.

"I just started reading these poems, darling." She opened the pages to a bookmark. "I want you to guess the artist. I'm not going to tell you the poem's title. Ready?"

"I'm always ready to hear a poem from your lips."

Tittering, as if eager to disclose something Bill didn't expect, Franny read the first stanza.

"Thou ill-formed offspring of my feeble brain,
Who after birth didst by my side remain,
Till snatched from thence by friends, less wise than true,
Who thee abroad, exposed to public view,
Made thee in rags, halting to th' press to trudge,
Where errors were not lessened (all my judge)."

Bill held up his hand, stopping Franny from beginning the second stanza. "Enough! That's too painful."

"And here I thought you were an expert on American literature."

"Far from it. I'll put up with Elizabethan natter in the Bible. Not this, though."

"That's silly. How about Shakespeare? And the Bible doesn't have great poetry? How about Psalms?"

"I accede you make a point, Franny. Who's the poet?"

"An American lady. Born in Northampton in England, she sailed to New England in 1630 with her husband and her parents."

"A Puritan?"

"Yes, they went to the Massachusetts Bay Colony with the Winthrop fleet." She held up the book. "You really don't know who she is, do you?"

"No idea."

"Anne Bradstreet. And her poem's name...*Author To Her Books*. Lordy, I love this. I finally stumped Bill."

He rolled his eyes. "I prefer love sonnets."

"Well, I'm up for a love sonnet." She closed the book and returned it to the end table. "It's one you'll have to write yourself, but only after you carry me to bed."

"Let's write the love sonnet together." Bill took Franny's hands, pulled her to her feet, and swept her into his arms. "Our shortest but most romantic journey."

Standing next to the bed, they hurriedly undressed and let their clothes pool at their bare feet. The cold air left goosebumps on Bill's skin. Franny crossed her arms and slapped her shoulders, trying to muster heat for her naked body.

"Get a fire going in the fireplace," she entreated as Bill smothered her breasts with kisses. "The fire's more important." Her teeth chattered near his ear.

Regretfully, he turned away and fed logs and kindling into the firebox. He allowed himself a moment to glance back at the bed. Franny lay on her back atop the quilt, her legs spread slightly, her hands covering her breasts. Her golden hair was loose and tousled, the strands arrayed on the pillow around her head.

His hands quivered as he tossed kindling atop the logs. Kneeling, he struggled to extract a matchstick from its matchbox. The stick slipped and fell on the hearth. "Damn! Fingers are numb."

A delightful laugh escaped Franny's mouth. "Get the fire going so you can come to bed and warm me up."

Match in his hand, he struck it along the matchbox edge and it flamed to life. Soon a fire roared in the firebox.

"Let's see if I can stoke your passion, sweetheart." Bill dropped onto the bed, his chest pressed against Franny's breasts.

Squirming, Bill maneuvered until he lay on his side next to Franny. Her fingernails danced along his shoulder blade, stroking skin warmed by the fireplace heat. Slowly, her index finger drew circles on his chest as she tickled her way down to his bellybutton. And further down…

"I see you're ready to show me your sonnet," she said.

"When in eternal lines to time thou growest," Bill said huskily as he mounted Franny, "so long as men can breathe or eyes can see, so long lives this, and this gives life to thee."

"I didn't think you liked Elizabethan." Franny's voice mirrored the urgency in her hands as clasped the back of his neck and drew him against her.

"Shakespeare doesn't count. Besides, I know you like his poetry."

Franny slipped a rubber onto his gaying instrument and desire rolled through him. Lovemaking frenzied, they made love as firelight pirouetted on the wall above them—and then it was over. He heard her suck in air and let it out with a soft moan. Reluctantly, he rolled off her and again lay beside her.

"One of these times I'm going to forget the rubber," she teased.

"And I'll be too prig-happy to care."

"We'll both be nervous nellies worrying if I'll soon be big in the belly." She kissed him gently. "Let's get some sleep. Truthfully, I won't forget the rubber. War's not the time to be raising a child."

~ * ~

A bright beam of daylight streaming into the dark bedroom awoke Bill just after seven in the morning. Yawning, he leaned over his wife and kissed her on the cheek and the tip of her right breast. Moaning, she complained, "Stop it. I want to sleep a bit longer."

Naked, he slipped out from the bedcovers into the frigid air. The fire had nearly gone out. He stoked the flames and fed more logs. The longjohns, pants, shirt, vest and shell jacket were still on the floor beside the bed along with Franny's frilly clothes. Once washed and dressed, he wandered into the kitchen and ate a cold meal of canned fruit and Franny's water-and-molasses brew. Just one more thing to do. Tuck the derringer into his pants pocket. By seven-thirty Bill was out the door, and with Charlie in tow headed to the War Department through slushy snow.

Bill and his buddy didn't get far, and not because of a December snowstorm. The sky was as blue as the dress of a thirtyish working-class woman who rushed past them, a sign and an empty basket clenched in her tiny hands. A gust of wind blew the woman's hat from her head, revealing strands of coal-black hair. Her grip on the sign loosened, providing a clearer view: WE ARE STARVING!

His newspaperman instinct took over. *Follow her!*

The woman, her sign and basket clutched securely against her ample bosom, quick-marched for Capitol Square. Bill increased his pace to keep up, hurrying by the War Department.

Charlie too stepped it up. "Hey, possum, who cares if the woman gets to the square two minutes ahead of us? We'll know soon enough why she's totin' that sign."

"The sign can mean only one thing, Charlie."

Ahead, the lack of leaves on the square's trees provided an unobstructed view of the Washington monument where a multitude of women, all with signs and empty baskets, were gathered. More were flooding into the square, a patchwork of brown grass and snow.

"Ah, another bread protest." The biting wind had scoured Charlie's face, turning it red. "You knew, didn't you?"

"Suspected. It's the Christmas season. Mommas can see what's happening. Speculators live the good life while kids go to bed hungry."

Charlie grimaced. "No sufferin' like this in Yankee country."

Back in April, women protesters had marched to the Executive Mansion begging for help. President Davis had turned them away. Frustrated, the women and their sons had broken into stores and looted the shelves. The city battalion marched against them, breaking up the protest. The generals in control of Richmond wanted to use regulars to suppress the women, but Seddon refused. With the first snowfall and the Christmas season turning out to be dreadful, the women had again taken to the streets.

"We've caught the protest at its genesis," Bill told Charlie. "No reporters on the scene yet. We can get some good interviews, even do some writing. The Richmond editors will eat it up."

"Goin' to start with the woman we followed?" Charlie pointed to where she stood on the throng's fringe, waving her sign as bureaucrats and soldiers walked across the square.

The woman could have been pretty had she not fretted so much over the war's calamities. They'd aged her, leaving crease lines in her face. Three or four kids, he guessed, the oldest no more than ten, and probably at their grandma's house. The frayed green dress and patched coat no doubt hid a still-desirable body, one her soldier husband would gape at when he again saw her naked in their bed—if he survived the war.

"Yep, she's the first." Bill strode toward her.

"You can also give our version to Secretary Seddon, Billy Boy. In case the generals describe the women as rabble-rousers. God forbid soldiers fire on them. If that happens, we just as well surrender to the Yanks."

"I agree." Bill reached the woman's side and bowed. "My name's Bill Stamford. This fellow's Charlie Kurtz. We both work for Secretary Seddon at the War Department." He raised his hands, palms displayed, when distress spread across her face. "Secretary Seddon's your ally, ma'am. I'm going to forward your story to the secretary. He needs to hear the truth."

Charlie spoke up, "Bill's the secretary's spokesman. The stories on the war in the Richmond newspapers...Bill helps get battlefield news to them, the generals' reports and casualty lists."

"How did you lose your arm?" the woman asked point-blank.

Charlie raised an eyebrow. "You don't beat around the bush. At Gettysburg, ma'am. A mini ball shattered too much bone, so the doctor started sawin'. Told me to bite the bullet."

"I don't see where you got wounded," she told Bill in an accusing tone.

"He did, ma'am," Charlie said. "I was with him. A shell ripped out a chunk of his back."

Bill patted his back. "At Chancellorsville. Now we're both working for Secretary Seddon. I promise we'll do whatever we can to make sure you and the other women of Richmond can give your children a wonderful Christmas."

"Thank you." The woman offered up her first smile. "I'm not even sure I can afford a tree for the kids, let alone a meal and gifts. My father died earlier this year. Last Christmas I got help from him."

Bill lowered his voice. "In the meantime, while we work to open Secretary Seddon's heart during this Christmas season, you ladies need to be careful. Up north in New York City, Union troops fired on draft-act rioters."

"You fear the same thing could happen here?" she said in a near whisper.

Bill bobbed his head. "You got away with the rioting in April. This time could bring trouble even though it's the Christmas season. In some quarters you're riffraff."

She scowled. "That's why I left my children with my oldest, twelve-year-old Tina."

Ah, granny's not babysitting, Bill thought, and then said aloud, "Prudence is the best course."

Squinting at Bill's jacket collar, she changed the subject. "You're an officer, a lieutenant. My husband's with the Twenty-Third Virginia Infantry. When I write him, I don't dare tell him how bad it is in Richmond. Truly, I fear my young ones will starve to death. He'd sneak away and come back to me and the kids."

Nearby, a bonneted thirtyish woman clad in a patched mourning dress scurried toward them. "Who're you talkin' to?" she shouted out. "Be careful. Can't trust no one in these times."

"Don't worry," the woman standing next to Bill and Charlie reassured her friend. She swung her gaze back to Bill. "She's my best friend. Her man's six feet under, shot dead at Gettysburg."

When the onrushing woman clad in black reached them, she poked a finger into Bill's chest. "You married, Lieutenant?"

"Yes. Franny's on your—"

"Bet she's a hoity-toity wife," the widow snapped. "Not like us. Rich women look down on us. They got the means to get food for their little ones. Not her or me"—she nodded at her friend—"or all the other poor women in this God-forsaken city." She dropped her sign and basket and perched her hands on her hips. "You with the War Department?"

"We are, ma'am." Charlie's tone projected patience.

The widow grabbed Charlie's shell jacket. "Tell whoever will listen we need help. We don't want to bury our children."

The black-haired woman Bill and Charlie had followed to the square told her friend, "They're goin' to, dear. The lieutenant promised just before you got here." She hugged Bill. "The good Lord bless you, sir."

Bill bowed to both women. "I'll do my best for you. What good's winning this war if we bury our children?" He took a step toward the War Department, but stopped and spun around. "In case you forgot, my name's Bill Stamford."

The two women exchanged knowing looks. The woman with the coal-black hair said, "We fear reprisals or we'd tell you our names."

"I understand your concern and I agree. Better to stay anonymous." Bill tapped the widow's empty basket. "I'm going to do all in my power to ensure these food baskets get filled this morning. Don't leave. Secretary Seddon's a good man. I'm going straight to his office to urge him to come out here and talk to you ladies."

Newspaper reporters were arriving to report on the protest as Bill and Charlie walked through the melting snow to the War Department and Secretary Seddon's office. Bill swore he'd make Seddon see reason even if he had to drag him out to the square to meet with these desperate women.

Fifteen

Help Comes to the Protesters

Even out in the hallway, Bill could hear the commotion. Secretary Seddon was arguing with someone inside his office. Seddon was a sickly man not given to raising his voice, so what Bill heard surprised him. Someone behind Seddon's closed door had upset the war secretary.

For an unnerving moment, Bill wondered if he should reconsider venturing into Captain Beardsley's office, the anteroom to Seddon's domain. Bill knocked on Beardsley's door and walked in warily. He'd promised the two women he'd seek help for them. No way he'd put off meeting with the secretary.

Once inside, he eyeballed Beardsley then swung his gaze to the door leading to Seddon's office. Two angry voices seeped through.

"Who's in there with Secretary Seddon?" Bill raised his voice above the hubbub.

"Northrop." Beardsley grimaced.

Ah, the man responsible for the logistics and supplies, and the man most hated by the protesters. Colonel Lucius Northrop, commissary general of Subsistence. The miles of waterfront supply warehouses? They were Northrop's. In the Confederate Congress, the politicians were questioning why the food inside those warehouses was not ending up inside soldiers' bellies. And the fuming Richmond women wanted some of the food for their children.

"Now I understand the reason for the hullabaloo." Right hand fisted, Bill thrust it upward. "Secretary Seddon must know about the protesting women out at Washington's statue."

"He does. Northrop has some explaining to do. He promised conditions would get better for the armies and the civilians. I heard the secretary say the only ones seeing better times are the speculators."

"A warning, Captain. I'm going to barge in on them." Bill headed for the door. "I've been with the women listening to their pleas. Don't try to stop me."

"Wouldn't think of it." Chuckling, Beardsley beckoned Bill into Seddon's office.

Bill took a deep breath just before slinging open the door. "Colonel, Christmas is coming...we should be able to—"

"Lieutenant Stamford! You interrupted a meeting!" Seddon rocked back in his chair, startlement etched on his face.

"I've just come from a women's march on the Capitol Square." Bill strode into the room. "Those poor women, Secretary, they're desperate, just like in April. Come with me, sir. I told them you'd see them. They need hope."

"You want me to open the warehouses for them?" Seddon's expression turned from surprise to skepticism.

"More rations for their hungry children, sir." Bill went to a window and looked toward the square before turning back to Seddon and Northrop. "Like you said, Secretary, Christmas is a few weeks away. Richmond's kids—the ones not living in mansions—need to wake up on Christmas day and see presents and a holiday meal. Promise the women canned goods, salt pork, cornmeal, desiccated vegetables and dried beans, and not just for Christmas Day. Increase their rations so their kiddies don't go to bed with empty stomachs."

Already agitated in his chair, Northrop bolted to his feet and stumbled, his bum knees buckling. Grimacing, he straightened up. "Yes, I can increase rations for the women and their children, but then the soldiers get less. It's your decision, Secretary. Not as many farmers are out in the fields... they're in uniform fighting for our independence. Fewer farmers mean less food in our warehouses. I'd like to do more. Tell me how."

"Sit down, Colonel," Seddon said tersely. "We will do more. It's the Christmas season. Give me a miracle, Colonel."

Remaining on his feet, Northrop threw up his hands. "Miracles? I don't think there's a miracle left in Dixie."

Bill sighed. "We're going to need a miracle when our soldiers learn how much their wives and kids are suffering. We could be only days or weeks from mutiny in the ranks. For the moment the wives remain patriotic. They aren't letting their husbands know how bad it is on the homefront."

Northrop plopped down in the chair and leaned forward. "I fear the women are planting dangerous thoughts in darkey heads. I have nightmares thinking what could happen if the darkies rise up against us."

Bill looked heavenward. "So we don't help soldiers' wives feed their children because we're afraid darkies might stir up a slave rebellion? That's bizarre thinking."

"Lieutenant, you border on insolence," Northrop bristled. "You've impugned my honor. I'm inclined to demand—"

"Stop it, Colonel Northrop! We should be able to debate policy without someone threatening a duel." Seddon turned to Bill. "You were saying, Lieutenant Stamford?"

Lord, why can't you put a halo around a bastard like Northrop? Immediately, Bill felt guilty for the thought. Seddon had asked a question that needed answering. Mulling, Bill said, "The threat of a slave rebellion has become a bugaboo. It paralyzes us into making bad decisions. Soldiers' wives and widows are begging for help. I know the soldiers I served with at Fredericksburg and Chancellorsville would want us to help them."

Seddon rose from his chair. "I've made up my mind. I agree with Lieutenant Stamford. Our goal is to kill Yankees, not our children. I'm going to speak to the women. Colonel Northrop, I want you to prepare additional rations for them. Have the rations hauled to Capitol Square later this morning. Continue it on a daily basis through the holidays. Put an ad in the newspapers announcing the hours. We'll meet again on Monday, January 1, and see if we need to continue the supplemental ration program." He tore a sheet of paper from a notepad and scribbled some words. "An order to the city battalion: they're not to break up the protest until I have a chance to meet with the women." Note in hand, he walked Northrop to the open doorway. "Thank you for your cooperation, Colonel." Seddon handed his orders for the city battalion to Beardsley. "Captain, have the telegrapher send out these orders."

"Yessir. Glad that's your decision, Secretary." The captain folded the orders and sprinted for the telegrapher's office farther down the hallway.

Bill laughed silently. Northrop had been anything but cooperative. He wanted to forcibly shut down the protest.

Seddon motioned Bill to join him. "Let's go talk to some upset women."

~ * ~

The metal handrail on the portico steps didn't shine like it did on sunny mornings. Gray clouds had vanquished the sun as Bill and Seddon descended the steps. Flurries swirled like lightning bugs on a summer evening. None added to the melting snow cover. The symbolism wasn't lost on Bill. They were about to bring hope to despairing women on a day that had turned gloomy. As if his thoughts needed reinforcing, a snowflake landed on his nose.

They headed down the boardwalk toward the Capitol Square two blocks away. Four-story buildings kept the parkland concealed. They heard a female voice long before they saw the women, a strident voice leading cheers. A wagon filled with barrels wheeled by them, headed away from the square. The coat collar of the darkey teamster handling the horses lay up against his ears, covering the slave's neck, while a wool hat protected his head. A handful of pedestrians shared the boardwalk—an old man wearing a flour-smeared apron, a well-dressed middle-aged woman walking alongside a darkey pushing a baby carriage, and a twelvish boy toting a bag of marbles. That elicited a smile from Bill. He and Charlie loved playing marbles when they were kids.

"Marble kid's looking for his momma," Bill observed.

The boy had just scampered by Bill and Seddon. Wearing a thin jacket to hold back the cold wind, the lad walked a swift pace to keep his body warm.

"So you think he's on the way to Capitol Square, eh?" Seddon fastened his frock's top button.

"His momma's probably the woman leading the chants." Bill tugged his gloves from a coat pocket and donned them. "He wants to get there before the city battalion arrests her." He laughed sourly. There was truth in what he said.

The wind carried not just snowflakes, but the women's words over rooftops, streets and alleyways to Bill's ears.

"Bread!" the solitary woman's voice hollered. "What do we want?"

"Bread!" hundreds of women answered. "Give us bread! Bread! Bread!"

As the words faded, the solitary woman raised her voice again, "What won't we do?"

"Starve! We won't starve!

The shouted words refused to grow faint. They got louder as Bill and Secretary Seddon drew closer to the square. The upper half of the Executive Mansion and the Washington statue poked above the rooftops. They walked a farther half block, and like the opening of a theatre's stage curtain, the statue scene unfolded.

Wearing a mended mourning dress, the woman with the rowdy voice stood atop a soapbox in front of the statue, ensuring she towered above the hundreds of protesters who congregated around her waving their signs and empty food baskets.

On the boardwalk bordering the parkland, a detachment of the city battalion stopped the boy, who excitedly pointed to the statue. Bill heard the boy's plea, "Please don't hurt them."

"Damn! They must have marched before Captain Beardsley could send my order." Seddon increased his stride, his destination the detachment.

Bill picked up his pace. "What a mess!"

"It looks like they're just observing. I need to keep it that way."

Seddon went straight to the detachment's commander, a baby-faced captain in a neatly pressed gray uniform that looked to have been recently sewn by the Ladies' Aid Society. The captain had the kid corralled by his shirt collar.

"Let the boy go, Captain. He's harmless." Seddon clasped the youth's right arm.

The officer ignored Seddon. Tightening his grip on the boy's shoulder, he yanked him away from the Secretary of War. "Don't interfere, old man, or I'll have you arrested."

One of the detachment soldiers, a befuddled corporal, cleared his throat. "Captain, sir, he's Secretary Seddon." The corporal's voice quavered.

At the statue, one of the women had noticed the manhandling of the boy by the battalion detachment's commander. Alarmed, the woman darted toward the soldiers, the hem of her dress flapping above her ankles. Three companions ran alongside her.

Ballooning, the captain's eyes swung from Seddon to the onrushing women back to the war secretary. "My apologies, Secretary, I didn't recognize you."

"Apology accepted, Captain." Seddon eyed the approaching women. "I fear you're going to have more trouble with the boy's mother than me."

Reaching the soldiers, the mother slid to a stop on the slippery boardwalk. "Unhand my son!" She jerked the boy away from the captain. "You greenhorns are here to rough us up. Because we want to fill our babies' bellies, you think us not patriotic enough. Damn you all!"

Secretary Seddon bowed to the woman and her companions. "Ma'am, I'm the Secretary of War, and I know you and the other women who have gathered here this day have been suffering great deprivations. I assure you I have heard and will do what I can to help you." Seddon fixed his gaze on the captain. "These soldiers will not bother you, ma'am. I'm giving them new orders. Captain, you are to provide security for the women. If any ruffians harass them, you are to arrest them. Understood?"

"Yessir. I'm sorry, Secretary, for my slow brain. My men and I will keep the ladies safe."

"Good, sir." Although not an officer, Seddon still saluted the captain. "Soon, men from the Commissary General of Subsistence will arrive with rations for the women. You will help them hand out the rations."

"Yessir. We will do whatever we can to make the food distribution efficient. Again, I apologize for not recognizing you, Colonel."

Seddon gestured toward Washington's statue. "Ladies, let's go see your friends and give them the good news."

On the demonstration's periphery, dozens of protestors beamed curious looks at the advancing party. Some recognized Seddon. Perhaps they'd seen his woodcut mug in newspaper columns or observed him at a parade or ball. The crowd parted to let Seddon, Bill, the women and the boy pass. Two feminine voices pierced the crowd's loud murmurs.

"Lieutenant Stamford! Remember me!" Bill pinpointed the voice...the woman with the coal black hair and the We Are Starving sign he and Charlie had followed after leaving their brownstone.

"Hurrah! You did what you promised, Lieutenant Stamford," the other woman he'd met at the statue raved.

I told you I would, Bill thought as the demonstrators chanted "Don't let our babies starve!"

The strident-voiced woman on the soapbox, who turned out to be short and petite, raised her arms and motioned for the crowd to become quiet. "We have visitors, ladies. Thank the Lord it's not President Davis. He'd be threatening to shoot us. It's Secretary Seddon. Good news, sir?"

Mrs. Strident stepped off the soapbox and Seddon took her place. "Very good news, ma'am. Christmas rations are on the way. The distribution starts today and will continue through the Christmas season. Every day at the statue, the War Department will issue rations at noontime." Seddon nodded toward Bill. "That fellow there—Lieutenant Bill Stamford—saw your protest and came to me. He told me the promises made to you in April were forgotten, and that your babies are going to bed hungry." The chant "Don't Let Our Children Starve" resumed but soon petered out. "I promised him I would meet with you. I'm here. And I won't leave until I see rations in your baskets."

An anonymous woman cried out, "We've heard all this before. It never lasts."

Seddon let them shout their frustration. After a few minutes, the chants died out except for a few women who might have imbibed too much brandy. "I'm sorry. I will do my best to make sure it doesn't happen again. Chancellorsville and Gettysburg taxed our resources. We had emergencies. Lieutenant Stamford's door will be open to any woman with concerns. He will listen. And I will listen to him."

A new chant echoed through the parkland: "Seddon! Seddon! Seddon!"

As the Seddon chants reverberated around him, Bill formulated an idea that wouldn't wait until later in the day. He wanted to initiate it right away while the chants of the women were spurring him to do the impossible. With Seddon's permission, he turned and made his way through the crowd toward the edge of Capitol Square. Once on the boardwalk, he traipsed toward a well-heeled neighborhood where he hoped he could put his notion into action.

Sixteen

Bill and Franny Take on a Christmas Project

At first, a few flurries flitted around Bill as he zigzagged toward his destination, taking shortcuts through alleyways and yards. By the time he turned at the intersection and beheld the grand mansions, the flurries had turned to light snow that left a dusting on the boardwalk. He glided his way up to the most lavish mansion, the home of Secretary Seddon. The iron-rod fence gate squeaked as Bill opened it and navigated his way up the slick brick walkway. His boots made the only noise, a soft squish as the soles pressed into and out of the snow. No wagons, carriages or buggies plied Powhatan Street. Six empty buggies were parked along the curb in front of the gate, their passengers comfortably seated on couches and chairs barely beyond the foyer. Perched in front of a fireplace, the darkey drivers relaxed in the slave quarters thawing their bodies.

Inside the Seddon house and the others in the neighborhood, life during wartime wasn't as dire as in the ramshackle houses of the women protesting in the Capitol Square. Even the death of a husband or son in battle was different. A poor woman hoped for no more than a simple wood coffin. A rich woman's soldier went into the grave in an ornate metal casket. On Christmas Day in these mansions, families would manage to scrape together enough food for a feast the women in the square could only dream of as they slept in their cold beds.

His right hand fixed to the stoop railing, Bill ascended the steps onto the portico. He smacked the eagle-head doorknocker against the front door. The Seddons' darkey butler answered. "May I tell Mrs. Sarah who's calling, Lieutenant?"

"Bill Stamford, Franny's husband."

The darkey's black tailcoat and buttoned-up gray vest had been heavily mended. He'd obviously not been provided a new outfit since 1860, another casualty of the war suffered by the well-to-do. Bill chuckled at his boneyard humor.

"Here to see your wife, sir?"

"I'm here to see all the members of the Ladies' Aid Society."

This time the butler did the chuckling. "The ladies will be delighted to have such a handsome officer as a guest. Follow me, Lieutenant."

Framed paintings of western landscapes adorned the foyer walls. The home's grand stairway began just inside the main hallway. Bill's eyes wandered to an etched art-glass window of a peacock and a lake filled with sailboats. The butler stopped at a closed door and rapped softly. A cultured voice called out above the drone of voices, "Neeta Cunningham? Late as usual."

The butler opened the door. "No, ma'am. It's Lieutenant Bill Stamford. Here to see all you ladies."

Giggles broke out. They knew he belonged to Franny. They were prepared to embarrass her, a girlish game even matronly women sometimes played when gathered together and ready for some merriment.

Bill stepped into an exquisite music room filled with two pianos, a harp, harmonium, and eight women of varying ages including his wife, who bore a curious expression.

"Thank you, Gregory." A gray-haired woman's green day-dress rustled as she leaned forward in her chair and scrutinized Bill. "Lieutenant, I have heard good things about you from my husband. He has high hopes for you. At last, someone who can corral the newspaper editors."

"I've found they're willing to listen to reason when spoken by the son of a newspaper editor." Bill moseyed farther into the room and bowed to the women.

Franny hurried to Bill, clutched his hands and kissed him on the cheek. She murmured, "What are you up to, sweetie? It's the Christmas season and you show up when we're making plans for more projects. Planning to turn us into your elves?"

"No more lovers' whispers." Sarah Seddon giggled as if sixteen again. "Sit down, Bill. Lots of chairs and couches available. Tell us why you're here."

Franny scooted her chair beside Bill's and plopped into it. "I suspect I know the reason why he's here. Sometimes he surprises me, though. Surprise me, Bill."

"I'll try." He locked his fingers together just below his chin. "My apologies, ladies, for interrupting your meeting."

"I doubt you really want our apologies, good man." Sarah tucked the corners of her mouth into a wily smile. "I suspect you know what we've been doing for the last several hours."

"I do and I've the perfect project for you ladies to undertake." He dropped his hands to his lap. "And I promise to help you out."

A redheaded woman in a mourning dress—actually a girl who didn't look any older than sixteen—piped up, "Well, we've been doing the same humdrum projects since Christmas 1861. I'm ready to try something new."

"I concur, Agatha." Sarah returned her scrutiny to Bill. "Tell us why you barged into our meeting. I'm sitting on pins and needles."

Bill assumed a solemn look. "I've just come from the square where women who live far from this neighborhood are pleading for food for their young ones. Secretary Seddon is handing out extra rations to these long-suffering women and their kids. I want to help—"

"Balderdash!" A glowering brunette ran her fingers through her curls. "Shirkers! Fair-weather patriots! I wouldn't lift a hand to help them. They'd have their husbands fight for nothing. They don't know what sacrifice means."

Grimacing, Bill opened his mouth to speak, but Franny glared at him. Nodding, he waited for her to say her piece.

Instead of Franny, Sarah Seddon bristled, "Some of us need to learn how to listen to Jesus's words: 'One thing thou lackest...go thy way, sell whatsoever thou hast, and give to the poor, and thou shalt have treasure in heaven.'"

The gas-fired crystal chandelier above Sarah's head beamed glittery light down on the woman's head. In the shadowy room, the chandelier made her appear angelic.

Franny looked like she'd like to bolt from her chair and yank every last curly strand from the brunette's head. Thankfully, she didn't but patiently said, "A year ago, I nursed the wounded at Fredericksburg. Some of those wounded soldiers died in my arms. They were fighting for their loved ones, their mothers, their wives, their kiddies. Sacrifice should never mean the starvation deaths of our soldiers' children. I've heard many of us in this room complain over the loss of petty comforts—hats, gowns, stationery, books, magazines, dainty finger food." She swung her gaze from woman to woman until her eyes fixed on the bad-tempered brunette. "Sally Geary, none of us suffer like those poor women my husband wants to help."

"How dare you humiliate me, Franny Neale, I mean Stamford." Sally shot to her feet, and harrumphing her displeasure, flounced from the room. Her voice echoed from the hallway, "Gregory, get my driver. I'm leaving."

Franny started after Sally. "I guess I better apologize."

"No, Franny," Sarah countered, giving the others in the room a stern look before they started yakking. "Let her go. She'll seek me out later and try to get back in my good graces. Of course, I'll accept her non-apology, but not before I give her a stern lecture. Ladies, remember that these poor wives and their children are who we help during the Christmas season."

All the women nodded.

Franny returned to her cushioned chair. "A fine mess you've made, husband," she teased.

"Yes, a fine mess," Sarah echoed, 'but one I find intriguing. I'm going to help you, Bill. What can we do for you?"

"Wonderful." Bill heard the mansion's front door open and slam shut. "I do hope Sally will have a change of heart." He paused for a moment then continued, "Here's what has been rattling inside my head. On the afternoon of the day set for your Christmas Ball at the Spotswood, I'd love for you to hold a party for the children of Richmond. Cake, punch and Christmas presents for the little ones. Maybe the children can win Sally's heart. I can't imagine any woman not wanting to hug them."

"I think Sally will attend the party, Bill." Sarah stood and raised both hands. "Okay ladies, let's have a vote on Bill's party. All in favor say aye." Six feminine voices screeched aye. "Opposed, no." The room was silent. "The vote is unanimous. Bill. We'll do your Christmas party." Sarah took two steps toward Franny. "My dear, I know you have a lot on your plate for the ball, but since the party's your husband's idea, I would love for you to do the planning. Yes?"

Franny leaned toward Bill and patted his leg. "Of course." She chuckled. "As long as he agrees to help me."

Bill brought Franny's hand up to his mouth and kissed her fingers. "I agree." He spelled *love* on her palm.

The meeting of the Richmond Ladies' Aid Society soon broke up. Sally's buggy had long ago pulled away from the curbside when the remaining ladies piled into their buggies and carriages. Larger and more numerous, the swirling snowflakes looked like the inside of a snow globe. Bill expected to see Ernie's Hansom cab. "Ernie's on the way?"

"I decided to walk to Sarah's. Why hide from flurries?" She reached out for Bill's hand. "So it's snowing harder. It'll still be a romantic walk."

"You need to be more careful, sweetie." He jangled her purse before holding her hand. "Some of those bully boys would have no trouble cutting your throat to filch your purse."

"I'm a big girl. Besides, I'm not exactly defenseless." She reached down into the folds of her dress and revealed a hidden pocket. "It holds a derringer."

"So you're now my soldier-wife, eh?"

"We're all soldiers in this damned war. Except if I have to shoot someone, it won't be a Yankee. It'll be a Southern thug." Franny burrowed against him as they walked and sometimes slid along the snow-cloaked boardwalk. "The party's going to be easy to plan. Obtaining the gifts...that's going to be the rough spot."

"That's why I married the prettiest girl in Virginia. You're going to help me convince Richmond's toymakers to donate toys."

"You must think I'm a miracle worker. The party's only two weeks away."

"I've faith in you, Franny."

Seventeen

A Visit to a Toy Store

The late-afternoon December sun painted the cloud bellies muddy red above the waterfront's foundry buildings. Cocooned in their woolen winter coats, Bill and Franny sat on a park bench in the Capitol Square and watched the sunset. She nuzzled her head against his shoulder. Her whispers tickled his earlobe. "The sunset's spectacular, darling, but that's not why we're here. Let's do what we came out to do. Visit some toyshops."

Wisps of frost drifted from the mouths of passersby as they promenaded along the parkland's walkways. Winter and a light snow cloaking everything in the square couldn't stop Richmond's young lovers from enjoying their sunset strolls.

"See?" Bill pointed toward one of the couples sauntering past the Washington statue. "Charlie and Avis? Sure looks like them."

Franny squinted. "You're right. And they just noticed us."

Waving, Charlie and Avis diverted their path and headed toward Bill and Franny.

"I thought you two were going toy shopping," Charlie said.

"We decided to take in the sunset." Franny patted the bench beside her, inviting Avis to sit.

Once comfortably settled, Avis rearranged the scarf around her neck and pulled her hat down over her ears. "Almost too cold to walk let alone sit on a park bench. But I'm glad I let Charlie talk me into taking our stroll."

Franny squeezed Avis's knee. "I hear you've been spending most of your time caring for your granny."

"Yes. Momma and I take turns. I fear Granny Louisa will soon join Grandpa."

"I'm sorry to hear she's not getting better." Franny kissed her friend's shoulder. "I've missed you at the Ladies' Aid Society meetings. We need you. The Christmas dance is getting closer and the other ladies—let me say this delicately—are finding creative ways to avoid helping me."

Avis laughed half-heartedly. "I'll try to attend the next meeting." She swung her gaze to Charlie, standing near Bill watching three dogs frolic in the snow. "I've been neglecting my man as well, one of the reasons I agreed to go on his little excursion. I needed to get away from the sadness and Charlie always makes me laugh."

Bill leaned across Franny. "You and Charlie can join us on our toy expedition. We plan to scour the toyshops on Main, High and Olive streets."

"Sounds like fun?" Charlie eyed Avis for agreement.

Hesitating, Avis slowly shook her head. "Tonight's my night to sit with Granny Louisa."

"I understand." Franny winked at Avis. "Maybe you can bring Charlie along and let your granny meet him. He'll perk her up."

"She'd love to meet a legitimate Gettysburg war hero. What do you say, Charlie?" Avis grinned.

"I'd love to meet her." Charlie shifted several steps to the right so he stood before Avis. "You and your mother say Granny Louisa was a firecracker when she was our age. I want to meet that woman."

"Then it's done. I'm bringing my beau as my guest." Avis rose and kissed Charlie half on the chin, half on his lower lip. "Lordy your skin's cold. We'd better get you to Granny Louisa's so we can warm you up."

Charlie and his sweetheart meandered toward the streets that led to the genteel neighborhood of grand mansions. Bill stood and held out his hands to Franny. Strapping her handbag to her shoulder, she gripped his wrists and pushed herself to her feet. Holding hands, they went the opposite direction toward the downtown shops.

Christmas decorations prettified the storefront windows, at least the ones still open. Some had become casualties of the war, perhaps one in three stood vacant. Proprietors of two dress shops had fastened heads with wigs to mannequins and clothed them in red and green dresses, coats, scarves and Russian style hats. On either side of the mannequins were Christmas trees adorned with glass ornaments.

The next storefront, a men's clothing emporium, featured a wintertime tableau. Two mannequins dressed in Christmassy clothes sat in a sleigh with a just-cut tree in the back end. A small girl settled in near Bill and Franny and ogled the scene. The girl twisted around.

"Mommy, we're goin' to git a tree, ain't we?"

"Goin' to try, Mary Lou. Grandpa Bud's goin' out to the forest to look fer one. Say a little prayer he comes back with a tree in his wagon."

"I will, Mommy. You think he'll take me to the woods and let me swing the axe?"

"Maybe. Is seven old enough to help cut down a tree? You'll have to ask him when he and Granny come to the house to eat."

Bill glanced behind him. The girl's mother, a blonde like Franny, kept her hair in a conservative bun. A widow, she wore a coat over a mourning dress. Her only acknowledgement of Christmas? A green-and-red scarf tied around her neck.

"Hey, mister?" The girl, Mary Lou, tugged on Bill's coat sleeve. "You got a tree in your house?

"Are you trying to steal my husband?" Franny pretended to glare at the girl. She struggled to keep her face severe, but gave up and laughed. The girl's mother giggled.

"No, ma'am. I don't like boys."

"I'm joshing you, sweetie." Franny leaned down and hugged the youngster, then looked up at the mother who grinned. "Your momma's beautiful, which means you'll be a beautiful girl in a few years. You'll be winning the hearts of lots of boys."

"I don't like boys except for Jimmy Stone. He lives across the hall from us and we play marbles. He's nice." Mary Lou turned back to the store window. "Oh my! I think the fella in the sleigh just winked at me."

Bill patted the girl's wool hat. "You're right. I saw it too."

Mary Lou's momma grabbed her hand. "He's not a very good mannequin. Come, sweetie, let's look at more storefronts. I love the Christmas season." The mother and her daughter hurried across the street, slipping between a buggy and a wagon filled with crates and boxes, probably rifles and ammunition.

Their frosty breaths leading the way, Bill and Franny headed toward their destination, the Doodle Store, a longtime toyshop that had been the favorite of children for two generations. Bill curled his fingers around the shop's front-door knob.

"Stop! We need to discuss our tactics." Franny squeezed Bill's wrist, prompting him to release the doorknob. "Remember, we're going to ask these toymakers to go way beyond the call of duty. Many will balk. All these empty storefronts around us...the toymakers don't want to join them."

"I suppose you want to do the talking?" Grinning, Bill gave the toymaker's window display the once-over. Toy bag over his shoulder, a Clement Clark Moore-like Santa stood near a fireplace surveying the toys arrayed around a Christmas tree—dolls, a miniature fire engine, train, buggy, sailing ship, mechanical merry-go-round and a Jeff Davis coin bank.

"Of course, sweetie. And you know why."

"I do?" Bill rolled his eyes. "Of course, because you're prettier than me."

His chin beard neatly trimmed, a well-to-do grandfather cosseted in an Inverness coat and his preteen grandson exited the

Doodle store empty handed. The gentlemen tipped his topper hat to Bill and Franny.

Franny sighed. "The toymakers are up against sky-high prices. Even rich fellas can't afford toys except for the simple wooden ones. That's fine if your grandson's five years old. Not so fine if he's twelve or older."

"Then I'd say it really doesn't matter who does the talking." Bill slipped his arm around Franny's waist. "It's going to be difficult to get the toymaker to help us out. He needs to sell toys or this place will soon be vacant."

"You're so astute, darling." Franny rested her hand on the doorknob. "This evening we're not going to find any men under forty behind shop counters. The younger ones are all in the army." She batted her eyes at him. "Grandfatherly toymakers can't resist a lovely woman. I'm our only chance to get toy donations."

"And what if the man behind the counter turns out to be a woman?"

"I expect you to dazzle her with your wit, Bill."

"And remind them of their own men fighting with Lee?"

"Again, I married an astute man. No one can resist a handsome man in uniform."

"Open the door, Franny. Let's have a look inside. I'm not eight anymore, but I still love my tin soldiers."

Inside the toy shop, a coal-burning Oak Andes stove circulated welcoming heat. Bill and Franny hung their coats on a coat tree near the front door and browsed the toys. Just as Bill suspected, two-thirds of the toys were handcrafted wooden ones; the remaining third were clockwork tinplate toys ordered in 1860 and 1861 from the Philadelphia Tin Toy Manufactory and cast-iron toys made by J. & E. Stevens of Connecticut. On one side of the shop: toys for the boys; on the other, playthings for the girls. They had the shop to themselves except for the toymaker.

"Afternoon, folks." The gravelly voice clawed its way past a scraggly white beard that would have done Santa proud. "If I can help you with anything, please holler."

In his mid-forties, the toymaker looked like a jolly grandpa. Curly white hair cascaded to the middle of his back, the white beard concealed his chin and neck, and the red, blue and green paint splotches gave his leather apron a rainbow look. He probably got a plethora of invitations to don Santa Claus outfits for parties. He'd need some help with his belly, though. The toymaker was thin as a rail.

Franny tossed the older man a syrupy smile. "Oh, we'll definitely need your help, sir—after we've had a chance to look at your delightful toys."

Bill stroked one of the rocking horses lined up between the storefront window and the first shelf. The brightly painted horses were too large to become gifts at the Ladies' Aid Society's party for Richmond's children. The shelf looked more promising, packed with all sorts of wild animals—tigers, lions, long-necked giraffes, hippos, zebras, gorillas, monkeys.

Franny picked up a giraffe. "That's a perfect present for a boy dreaming of exploring Africa."

Something bright red caught Bill's eye, a fire engine with its shiny steam boiler and hose that could fling water across a kid's bedroom. Maybe Franny could convince the toymaker to donate the toy. No boy would unwrap that gift and be disappointed.

"Oh my word!" Franny rested her finger on a tiny buggy, one of the conveyances inside a livery stable. "A girl would like this. Wagons, carriages, hostlers and horses, a kid could spend hours playing with this toy."

The other shelves for the boys held grocery stores and restaurants, express wagons laden with boxes and barrels, locomotives and trains, canes, and riding whips, all miniature versions of the ones favored by grown folks, all wonderful gifts for boys.

Bill's gaze wandered to the girls' shelves and cases filled with dolls, miniature dinner sets of French china, oaken chests filled with glass goblets, silverware, bronze candelabras and table linen, everything a girl would need for a make-believe Christmas feast.

Franny reached into an oak chest and ran a finger along the lip of one of the goblets. "This could be a dream-come-true for a little girl. I just have to touch a toymaker's heart. Think I can?"

"You can open any man's heart."

"Look, Bill! I had a case just like this when I was a little girl."

Eyes fixed on a French-style makeup box complete with a mirror, she peeked inside and discovered a toilette set, brushes, combs, hand-glass and pomade jar.

"We've got to be careful with the makeup box. There'll be some mommas who won't want to see their daughter using such a vain thing."

"Hogwash!" Franny closed the makeup box's lid. "Combs and brushes, nothing wrong with them. And the pomade jar just makes your hair smell like apples. Look at the dollhouse, sweetheart. When I was eight, I spent hours playing with mine. I bet the toymaker made the furniture for it."

Leaning down, Bill scanned each room and marveled at the intricately crafted instruments in the music room and the library filled with teeny books. "It's a tiny version of the house we'll someday own."

Franny giggled. "Hopefully, there's a wall with ours. Unless you want to give the neighbors an eyeful."

So much on the shelves to fascinate girls and even boys with an artistic bent. Next to the makeup box, another box, this one furnished with worsteds, patterns, needles and simple directions. And next to the sewing box, a coloring kit filled with paints, pallet and brushes for a budding painter.

"Oddly, I'm considered a fairly good writer, but I've no talent with the paintbrush." Bill shrugged and turned to a Moss Rose Surprise Box. He stooped to smell the perfume of roses and buds. Suddenly, a concealed spring noisily opened the largest rose, and a doll fairy flew at his face. As if a dodging a mini ball, he nearly dove for the ground. An embarrassed smile creased his mouth.

Bill turned at the sound of heavy boots spanking the plank floor. The toymaker approached them, clapping quietly. "Quite a surprise, isn't it? That's one of my best sellers. Or was before inflation got really bad."

"Not many customers, eh?" Franny patted the toymaker's arm.

"Folks come in to browse, but they rarely buy. Don't see how I can stay open much longer." The toymaker lifted a clockwork toy from a shelf and wound its crank. A dappled clown began performing antics, whirling and flapping his arms as if attacked by a swarm of bumblebees. "I need a miracle, except miracles are in short supply in Richmond."

Surprisingly, Franny began singing, "Tis the song, the sigh of the weary. Hard times, hard times, come again no more. Many days you have lingered around my cabin door. Oh, hard times, come again no more." She wrote her name on a dusty glass case filled with dolls, many imported from overseas. "These belong in the arms of little girls or on pillows beside them."

They'd most likely stay unused in their case unless a shifty politician decided to spring the cash. Or a toymaker chose to donate them to a worthy cause—after Franny winked at him through her long lashes. *You'll not find a better moment to reel him in, Franny.*

The toymaker extracted one from the case, a French noblewoman wearing a skirt of cherry-colored satin. An opening in the front revealed a white silk petticoat ruffled with blond lace. A filigree necklace decorated the doll's ivory neck. A satin high-crowned hat sat atop her head. Exquisite doll, but not one for a little girl.

"Maybe I could raffle this one?" the toymaker mulled before returning the doll to the display case. "That way a girl can enjoy my French marchioness."

"Should you consider more than one doll for your raffle?" Franny fingered the blue glass eyes of the doll next to the marchioness. Not a baby doll, but virtually a diminutive version of Franny herself. Limbs and face molded of wax and golden curls of real hair, this Franny doll stood three feet tall arrayed in a dress of white poplin and a stylish white felt hat and blue veil. "Or maybe not a raffle at all. Instead, donations to a special cause, a Christmas party for the children of

Richmond." Taking the toymaker's arm, Franny led him to the next case, this one filled with baby dolls that could be burped, whose glass eyes would close when nestled in a tiny crib.

The toymaker's bushy brows arched. "I suspect I'm about to learn the reason for your visit, young lady." His cheeks quivered as he laughed.

"I've been thinking how nice some of your toys would be as Christmas gifts for war orphans." Franny moseyed to tables chockfull of puzzles, games and musical toys—gypsy oracles, squails and parlor lotto, Chinese billiards, croquet for the table, building blocks of wood, a kaleidoscope, and a miniature ballroom where gaily dressed couples danced to music whenever a boy or girl wound its clockwork mechanism.

The toymaker rolled his eyes. "Enough with the not-so-subtle mystery, ma'am. You're quite the plotter."

"Has anyone ever said you have an uncanny resemblance to Santa Claus?" She gestured to the toymaker's flat belly. "But only if you tuck a pillow or two between your shirt and your tummy."

"All the time." The toymaker bowed to her. "I do believe you want me to empty half my store."

"No, just what your heart tells you to donate." Franny took Bill's arm. "Your name, sir?"

"Leonardo Finkelstein. And you, dear lady?"

"Franny Stamford. And this fine soldier's my husband, Lieutenant Bill Stamford, veteran of Fredericksburg and Chancellorsville and now with the War Department."

Leonardo acknowledged Bill with a nod. "Ah, the silent one. Nice to meet you, Lieutenant. Two of my sons joined up with Lee. One's still with him. The other died at Gettysburg. Susan, my daughter-in-law, and her two children are staying with me and the missus."

Stepping forward, Franny kissed the toymaker on the cheek. "The war's hardest on our children."

"You're so right." Leonardo touched his cheek where moisture remained from Franny's kiss. "You're a very lucky man, Lieutenant."

"Indeed. I count my blessings every day." Bill looped his arm around Franny's waist and gently squeezed.

"Leonardo, I need your help." Disentangling herself from Bill's arm, Franny stepped up to the display case of baby dolls. "I'm with the Richmond Ladies' Aid Society, which is sponsoring the Christmas party for the city's children. I won't beat around the bush. I need toymakers to donate for the party."

"I'll make a donation in the memory of my son, Antonio Finkelstein." The toymaker wiped a sleeve across his face, drying an onrush of tears. "Do you have a toy preference?"

Franny finger-walked her hand along the glass of the baby doll display case. "Nothing fancy. Basic toys. I love your baby dolls for the girls. Maybe some play dishes and cups so they can pretend to have tea parties. Also, the sewing and the paint boxes. For the boys, toys that'll let them sprawl on the floor and use their imagination. Blocks for building a castle or a house. The livery stable and all the stuff that comes with it—wagons, buggies, carriages, horses and mules, the hostlers. And the miniature toy box with the jungle animals."

"For the older kids, brainy stuff." Bill pointed to the table of puzzles and board games. "Backgammon, Checkered Game of Life, Tiddledy Winks."

"When's the party—and where?" Leonardo scratched his forehead. "You may have already told me, but I do get forgetful."

"Christmas Eve at the Sportswood. In the afternoon before the evening's Christmas Ball." Franny lifted her hand and nestled it over her heart. "God bless your kind heart, Mr. Finkelstein. I hope the other toy store owners are as kindhearted."

"Would you like Saint Nicholas to swoop in and hand out presents?"

Franny pivoted her gaze from the toymaker to Bill. "I love the idea. How about you?"

"Yes. The little ones will love seeing Santa." Bill winked at the toymaker. "Please get a message to him. A Christmas Eve party needs him."

"I'll send a message bird out early in the morning." Leonardo escorted Bill and Franny to the front door. "I predict you won't have any trouble getting most of the other toymakers to donate. Like me, they know how brutal this war has been on the soldiers' kids. One or two, though, they love their money too much."

The young couple went to seven more toyshops. Only one proved intractable. The owner of The Lilliput said he'd only contribute cat family paper dolls. Franny accepted. Later, she complained to Bill, "What a Scrooge!"

Eighteen

A Children's Party for the War Weary

A booming voice echoed down the hallway inside St. John's Episcopal Church. "Ho! Ho! Ho! Merry Christmas to all and to all a hello." Saint Nicholas, actually toymaker Leonardo Finkelstein, waltzed through the doorway into the spacious room used as the adult Sunday school. Jam-packed bag slung over his shoulder, Santa Claus beelined straight for the ten-foot-high Christmas tree in the center of the room. "Out of the way, children. I've gifts to deliver. Got a busy night ahead. First, groom the reindeer. Then hitch them up to the sleigh and start flying. And I promise...no Yankee shells can streak fast enough to shoot me down. For this Christmas I've named my sleigh *The Lee Streak*."

The boys and girls hanging paper and glass ornaments on the tree leaped back when Santa's toy bag slid toward them. Their eyes ballooned when the bag's tie-swing loosened and they got a peek at the presents.

At a large trestle table, kids making paper ornaments pushed back their chairs, bolted to their feet and scurried to the half-open bag for a glimpse of the presents. One of the Richmond Ladies' Aid Society women, Avis Thompkins, Charlie's sweetheart, shooed the youngsters away from the bag and herded them back to their chairs. "Don't make Saint Nick late to his sleigh. Lots of houses to visit tonight. We don't want him to miss any, do we?"

The society didn't hold the Christmas party at the Spotswood after all, but at the Episcopal Church. All the festivities surrounding the ball left no room for the party. As Bill watched the kids plop down in their chairs, his thoughts darkened. It was in this church that Patrick Henry gave his famous "Give Me Liberty or Give Me Death" speech. *What irony. We're giving a party for the kids of Southern soldiers who are living examples of Patrick Henry's words. Sadly, many are growing up without their fathers.*

Back in his seat, a freckled, redheaded boy glared at his half-completed ornament and stamped his feet against the plank floor. "Saint Nick can't take presents to the young'uns of egg-suckin' Yankee scalawags. Their daddies kilt my pa." The boy's face got redder, tears blotting his cheeks.

His momma, her hair red as his, rushed over to him and murmured soothing words. Two toddlers, a boy and a girl, clung to her legs. "Your daddy's happy in Heaven, Alfonso. The Lord wipes away all tears. Your daddy doesn't want to see you cryin'."

Bill took two strides to the table. Leonardo raced past him and dropped to his knees between the ginger-headed boy and a brunette his age clad in her Sunday-best dress. Alarmed by the boy's eruption, she'd begun to weep.

"Alfonso, Saint Nick works for God," the toymaker told the boy, ruffling that strawberry-red hair. "And God hates war. When someone's daddy dies, we blame the war and the men on both sides who don't know how to find peace. God loves little children. He—and I—don't see blue and gray. Only innocent hearts." He turned to the little girl, her nose running. "I want you and Alfonso to help me with the presents. Okay?"

She nodded. "I'd like to help you. My name's Colleen."

Leonardo rose to his feet, straightened his fur-fringed nightcap, and holding the children's hands, led them to the toy bag. "I hear we'll soon have cake and punch." He handed a wrapped present to the girl.

In 1860, cake and punch at a Christmas party were not out of the ordinary. In 1863, they were miracles.

Under the supervision of their mothers, other children continued to hang cardboard ornaments—acorns, stars, snowflakes, reindeer, snowmen, bells, angels—along the lower portion of the tree. Older children took turns climbing two ladders to hang theirs higher up. For the highest branches, Avis assigned the task to Charlie, but he hadn't shown up.

More toymakers arrived with their donations. The wrapped ones went under the tree and the unwrapped to a table where mothers taught their older daughters how to giftwrap them. Franny helped a girl giftwrap a baby doll; the curly-haired near-teen had lost her mother to small pox and her father to a Yankee mini ball.

Franny summoned Bill. "Make yourself useful." She gestured to wrapped presents stacked at the end of the table. "Take them to the tree. Too many little ones with nothing to do."

Obeying his wife, Bill became a second Santa, distributing presents to toddlers for placement under the tree.

"So what did you end up donating, Saint Nick?" Bill eyed the nearly empty bag.

"Too many. But they're for our children. A dollhouse, a hurdy-gurdy music box, sailing ship, clockwork ballerina and a hot-air balloon. And lots of board games, puzzles, baby dolls, and my handmade push-and-pull toys." Leonardo shoveled the last present into Colleen's hands. "I'm not done, Lieutenant Bill. In my wagon are a rocking horse for a boy and a German doll for a girl. Santa's going to hold a drawing for these two gifts—if the Ladies' Aid Society approves."

Bill's brows arched. "That's a wonderful—"

"Billy boy, look who I brought to the party!" Charlie strolled into the room with the woman he and Bill had followed to the protest several weeks earlier. A gaggle of children flocked around the woman, her coal-black hair concealed under a man's fur hat.

The oldest child, a girl no older than twelve, shyly asked her momma, "Is this the soldier fella who came to your rescue?"

"All the women, Tina." The woman peeled off her oldest daughter's patched coat and draped it over her arm. "Lieutenant, let me apologize for not telling you my name. It's Callie, Callie Dampeer." She stripped off her other children's coats and headed for the coat closet.

Callie's youngest, a girl of about four or five, ogled the boys and girls decorating the tree, the presents beneath it, but especially Saint Nicholas. "May I?" The girl's pleading eyes swung to the table where ornaments were being made. "Please?" she begged her mother, newly returned from hanging up their coats.

Callie turned to Tina. "Take your sister over to the table and show her how to make an ornament."

Holding hands, the two girls meandered toward the table, but stopped so Tina could flirt with a boy. The two almost-teenagers floundered trying to find the right words and come-ons. They reminded Bill of his own starry-eyed, tongue-tied labors to woo twelve-year-old Kenansville girls.

Annoyed, the younger sister wandered to an empty chair and idly regarded a pair of scissors, watercolor paints, glue bottle and paper. The girl took a deep breath and sighed. Her mouth crinkled into a frown. "This is ridiculous!"

"Looks like someone needs rescuing," Bill told Callie, gesturing to her daughter.

"Thank you, Lieutenant Bill." Callie took the hands of her last kids, both boys and twins. "Yes, my youngest girl does look quite putout. Her name's Ruby." She reached out for the hands of her two boys. "Want to meet Saint Nick?"

"Yes, ma'am," one of the boys said eagerly. "He really has presents for us?"

"We get them tonight, little brother," the other said, bored.

"Little? Only by seven minutes." The so-called youngest twin stuck out his tongue.

"No arguing, boys!" their mother insisted. "Otherwise, I'll send you out to help the toymakers unload their wagons. It's getting nasty outside."

When Callie and her two boys were far enough away not to hear him, Charlie poked Bill in the ribs. "Remember, you're married, possum. Didn't take you for a cheek-ache boy."

"I only get cheek-aches for Franny."

"Charlie Kurtz!" Avis had grown impatient with her beau, who'd been in the room for a good ten minutes yet hadn't checked in with her for marching orders. Nestled in her arms were boxes of glass ornaments.

"My honey's calling." Charlie jumped to attention and saluted Avis. He slapped Bill on the shoulder and stepped smartly in her direction. "Got to keep the little woman happy, Billy Boy."

At the ornament table, Callie's youngest child, Ruby, struggled to make a paper trinket for the tree. Before Bill could help the girl, Franny sat beside her and watched as Ruby traced an angel pattern on cardboard. Franny slipped scissors into Ruby's hands. "Don't go fast. Cut carefully. Slow and steady. That's right. You're doing it perfectly."

Unable to find Ruby's big sister Tina, Bill combed the room. No Tina, no darling boy. Both were twelve, old enough to do some lip-to-lip exploring. Bill started toward Callie and her two boys, then saw a side door ajar on the tableau stage. Tina and the boy stumbled through the doorway, giggling, their mouths almost touching.

Rolling his eyes, Bill rushed up to the stage. The almost-teens were nearly to the steps when Bill reached the platform. Hands on hips, he muttered, "Where's Ruby?"

Reeling away from the boy, Tina looked around in near-panic. "Table, at the table with the pretty woman."

"That's my wife, who's doing the job your momma asked you to do." Bill waggled his finger, motioning her to descend the steps. "Not you, boy. I have other plans for you."

The boy gulped, legs wobbly.

"I'm sorry, sir," Tina choked out.

"Go give my wife some help."

"Yessir." She turned to the boy. "Bye, Connor. That was fun." She tittered.

Bill tapped the boy's nose. "See where the grannies are mixing the punch and cutting the cakes?" The boy nodded. "Get over there and help them. Say I sent you and you're not to leave their side." Again nodding, the lad looked at his boots as he made his way to the grannies.

Bill turned to the girl. "I'll escort you—in case you lack willpower. Your mouth's all red around your lips. I wonder what your momma will think."

"Please, Lieutenant. Don't say anything to her. I'll be good. I promise."

Bill hated being so hard on her. He'd kissed his first girl when just thirteen. Been sneaky just like Connor, but he had to be careful. Two twelve-year-olds caught kissing? Some mothers might never again bring their children to one of the Ladies' Aid Society parties.

"My lips are sealed, Tina, if you keep your sister happy. Agreed?"

She bobbed her head. "Yes, agreed."

At the table, Tina took the place of Franny and showed her sister how to paint her angel with a paintbrush and watercolors. Rising, Franny slipped her hand through the crook of Bill's arm and guided him to the anteroom that led to the sanctuary and front door. "Ruby says her big sister abandoned her. I'm glad you found her."

"Sneaked off with a boy for some kissing. They're only twelve."

Franny laughed heartily. "I admit twelve's a bit early. I had my first kiss in a neighbor's barn at thirteen. I knew a girl shouldn't kiss the neighbor boy. We were experimenting."

"I would've preferred they did their kissing in a barn, not in the church with all these mothers nearby."

"You're needlessly worrying, darling. Had they been caught, they would have turned every shade of red and their mothers would have been mortified. The rest of the mothers? They would've unmercifully teased the embarrassed mommas."

"I hope you're right, Franny. I want to hold another party next Christmas."

"You probably think I brought you out here for some kisses of my own." She smiled wickedly.

"Not really. I can get plenty of your kisses in our bed."

"The last two toymakers just pulled up to the curb. Make yourself useful. Help them unload the donations. We need to get the party going."

"By the way, Franny, Leonardo wants to hold a drawing at the end of the party and give away his two largest gifts, a rocking horse for a boy and a German doll for a girl. Could you take some of the cardboard, make tickets, and ensure each one has a kid's name, one stack for boys, one for girls?"

Franny clasped her hands around Bill's neck and planted a kiss on his lips. "I'll start on it right now."

Once both wagons were unloaded and the donations wrapped, Bill climbed a stepladder and helped Charlie hang glass ornaments at the tree's crown. With just a few branches still bare, Bill hooked an ornament to the end of a bough. As he withdrew his hand, the ornament slipped off the quivering branch, struck the floor and shattered. Charlie wisecracked, "Why are two-armed men so clumsy?"

"That's a church ornament or was," Franny shouted from across the room.

Some children were laughing, others crying, upset that a lovely ornament lay shattered on the floor. Mothers daubed the criers' eyes and whispered reassuring words. Waving her arms for silence, Franny pushed herself to her feet. "Santa will make another ornament in time for next year's Christmas party," she assured the weepy-eyed children.

The party went swimmingly well. Saint Nick sat with the children at their table and ate eggless cake and punch made with canned cherries. Later, the women of the Ladies' Aid Society scooped up presents from under the Christmas tree and distributed two each to the children, who sat on the floor arrayed around Santa. Shredded wrapping paper thick as the snowflakes falling outside filled the room as the boys and girls opened the presents. Eyes gleaming, they beheld their baby dolls, clockwork toys and board games. Later, Saint Nick drew names from two unused punch bowls. A five-year-old boy, Vernon Reeves, won the rocking horse; Callie's little girl Ruby, the German doll.

Far more children than Bill had anticipated turned out for the party. Franny estimated two hundred boys and girls. Bill paid for notices in all the Richmond newspapers. He even invited President Jeff Davis and his wife Varina as well as Mayor Mayo, but Davis and Mayo declined, citing another afternoon engagement. Paid by a donation from the War Department, cabs under snow-spitting clouds waited curbside and in the church parking lot, the cabmen ready to transport families back home. Bill watched the kids and their mothers tramp out into the snowy twilight. Inside the nearly empty room, the fires inside the two heating stoves were growing cold.

"Well, boys, time to clean up," Avis said, interrupting Bill's thoughts.

Charlie groaned. Bill tossed wrapping paper at Avis and Franny.

"We need to get this place tidy as soon as possible," Franny said, her voice good-humored. "We've got to get into our best duds. A gown in my case. We've a ball to attend."

Nineteen

A Ball Rings in Christmas Day

Hair coyly loose beneath a flower-adorned hat, Franny stood in the reception line beside Sarah Seddon and greeted couples who would soon be dancing at the Christmas Eve Ball. Bill feared his heart might just claw its way out of his chest and fly to her. *Escape, sweetheart! I need to dance with you.*

Just two hours since the kids' party ended, Bill was standing alongside Charlie and Avis near the band recruited from musicians ensconced in the defensive works encircling Richmond. The band members were all young, like Bill. They were starting out their lives. He whispered a prayer: *Please, Lord, don't let me see any halos around them. Let it be a Christmas gift to me.*

The musicians played "Prima Donna," one of French bandmaster Louis Antoine Jullien's dance tunes and a favorite of Franny's. Hopefully, the melody would provide her an excuse to bid adieu to the reception line and let Bill lead her onto the Spotswood Hotel's dance floor.

Couples waltzed as the light of fireplaces and gas sconces rebounded off the chandelier's crystals, spraying a kaleidoscope of colors across the floor and walls. Bill imagined Franny in his arms, the two waltzing beneath the chandelier.

"Bill? Billy Boy!" Charlie's voice pierced Bill's reverie, leaving his skin prickling.

"Damn it, Charlie! You scared me half out of my wits."

"How else am I to get your attention, possum?"

"A fine daydream should never be ruined." Bill veered his gaze to Franny who still greeted guests. "I was imagining us dancing. Franny loves 'Prima Donna.' When I'm sitting on the settee, I'll often look up from reading a book and find her dancing toward me. Wiggling an inviting finger, she'll waltz me to the bedroom."

"Well, I just wanted to let you know I'm going to waltz Avis onto the dance floor." He took her hand. "I'm going to prove a one-armed man can outdance two-armers."

Bill smirked. "Avis, watch your feet. He's known for stepping on toes. Charlie dances like he sings—atrocious."

Tittering, she did a jig, hips swaying within her gown emblazoned with Christmas berries and poinsettias. "My toes'll flit out of the way,"

Bill lost sight of Charlie and Avis among the dozens of Confederate officers and their ladies turning and twirling to the "Prima Donna" melody. A few politicians and Tredegar Ironworks bosses danced with their wives and sweethearts, their civilian suits looking peculiar in the sea of gray.

Bill heard the swish of a gown near him and detected the scent of Eau de Cologne. He turned to find a familiar young woman at his side.

"Lovely night for a ball, isn't it? I was going to stay home with my mother and father on this Christmas Eve, afraid your wife and others in the Ladies' Aid Society would ostracize me." The curly haired brunette offered a chagrined smile. "I see you're struggling to remember me. I'm the girl at the society meeting who left in a huff. I'm Sally Geary." She pivoted her gaze to Franny, who'd left the reception line and now approached. "I hope you and your wife can forgive me. I was wrong and I've said so to Sarah Seddon. I'm here to do the same with you, and of course Franny." Squaring her shoulders, she awaited Franny's arrival.

Bill couldn't read Franny's impassive expression. That meant Sally couldn't either. Still, Bill wondered if he should dive under a refreshment table to escape a coming hen melee. He hoped Sally's words were sincere, and she'd get to voice them to Franny before his wife said something she—and Bill—would regret.

At the entranceway, Sarah Seddon darted away from the reception line, chasing after Franny. She clearly intended to prevent a confrontation. Two girls of the Ladies' Aid Society brawling on the dance floor would become an above-the-fold headline in every Richmond newspaper.

Crystal chandelier light splattered a rainbow of colors across Franny's face when she stopped in front of Sally. Bill juxtaposed the two women, Sally in an exquisite satin gown tenderly cared for by a household darkey, Franny draped in a hoopless day dress with a daring décolletage. Likely, Sally dreamt of victory and a triumphant Confederacy. Franny clung to a less ambitious dream...that she and Bill would survive the war and get a chance to raise a child in a house not burnt to its foundations.

Arms folded against her chest, Franny said earnestly, "Sally, I'm so—"

"I was a fool, Franny. I'm so sorry. You were right." The words gushed from Sally's mouth. "Your party went well?" Her hand reached for Franny's wrist then jerked back.

"Yes, Sally, I've never seen so many children's eyes fill with tears of joy. The toymakers came through for us. The kids got a Christmas after all." Franny hugged the formerly obstinate woman.

Sarah joined them. "I wished you could have been at the church this afternoon, Sally. We missed you. It would have been an eye-opener."

Smiling hesitantly, Sally half-nodded. "I don't always agree with all the mothers of Richmond, but I don't want the little ones to suffer at Christmas."

A Confederate captain Bill didn't recognize stepped up smartly and bowed to Sally. "Ma'am, may I sign your dance card? My heart has been aflutter since I first set eyes on you."

Sharing a flirtatious smile with the officer, Sally grabbed the captain's hand and sashayed toward the military band.

Charlie and Avis passed them as they made their way to Bill, Franny and Sarah. "The captain didn't have to wait for a dance." Avis smirked. "Now that's a girl eager for a late-night walk to the Capitol Square."

"Sally has always been a bit of a wildling." Sarah glanced at the musicians as they played the opening notes of another waltz, the "Charming Waltz." She formed a half-smile. "A temper she sometimes fails to control. And a bit mad for the boys. I fear she may end up big in the belly before the war ends. It would devastate her invalid mother. There's my dear husband. I will have to steal James away from the politicians. They'll talk his ear off for the remainder of the night. Thank you for your help, Franny. The decorations are fizzing good." Gown swishing as she walked, Sarah made her way to her husband's side and soon they were waltzing.

Franny pinched Bill. "Remember my suggestion for tomorrow?"

"You have so many suggestions. Which one?" He tensed, expecting more pinching, perhaps painful.

No pinch came; instead, he heard an exasperated sigh. "What we talked about as you helped me into my ball dress."

Bill winked at Charlie and Avis. "I do believe Franny wants me to invite you to eat Christmas dinner with us."

"Was that so hard?" This time Franny elbowed him in the ribs.

And then Avis elbowed Charlie, prompting him to declare, "Sorry, Franny. I've been invited to eat with the Thompkins family."

"My granny's going to eat with us." Avis's mile-wide smile dissolved into a frown. "We don't know how much longer she'll be with us. She demanded we bring her to the mansion for Christmas dinner. I don't think father's going to let her return to her place. It'll upset her, but it's for the best. She needs to be looked after twenty-four hours a day."

"I'm glad the two of you can be with your granny on what could be her last Christmas on Earth." Franny kissed Avis's cheek.

"I'll miss you, chuckaboo," Bill told Charlie.

"Hell, I'm at your table most nights eating your grub. You'll be glad not to see my mug."

Franny gripped Bill's hands, tickled his palms. "You owe me a dance, Bill Stamford."

Bill withdrew his hands from hers and slipped his arm around her waist. "No need to sign your card. I intend to reserve every dance starting with this one." He pressed his palm against her back, urging her to move out and join the other dancers.

The dance song stopped mid-note. A moment later, the band struck up "Dixie." Franny stopped and pointed toward the hotel ballroom's double-door entrance crowded with Ladies' Aid Society women greeting Johnny-come-latelys. Led by an escort of Confederate soldiers, President Davis and his wife Varina strode into the room. Every few steps the president would stop, shake hands and share a few words with a friend or dignitary. Mayor Joseph Mayo ushered the Davises to a dais near the band. The crowd of several hundred clapped as the band grew quiet. Mayo pointed at the president and joined the clapping.

"I'd rather boo," Franny grumbled, her mouth against Bill's ear. "The man couldn't be bothered to make an appearance at our party. He's still angry over the bread protests."

"Act nice, sweetie. I want us to get home alive."

"Oh, I will. I'm quite good at placating politicians when necessary."

The mayor motioned for the cheering to stop. "I'm delighted to see so many brave officers tonight dancing on Christmas Eve." Mayo retrieved his watch from a vest pocket and checked the time. "Less than three hours and it will be Christmas Day. This is our third Christmas since the war began. I don't think any of us in the spring of 1861 thought we'd still be fighting as 1864 draws near." He returned the watch to its vest pocket. "But with such brave men as these fighting to ensure our independence, I have high hopes that

Christmas 1864 will see our Day of Jubilee. With us tonight are our president and his lovely wife. Sir, the podium is yours."

Davis squeezed his wife against his side. "I should let Varina do the talking. She's lovelier and much more articulate." Good-natured laughter greeted his words. Mrs. Davis dismissed her husband's efforts with a flip of her hand. "Ah, I see my Varina wants me to get on with my speech. I agree wholeheartedly with Mayor Mayo. We must and we will see the war through to victory and our independence. These fine men before me assure victory. The only Federals who will ever enter Richmond will be Lincoln's first ambassador and his staff." The room erupted in cheers then quickly died down. Davis didn't even have to call for silence. Instead, he took his wife's hand. "We're a bit late to the ball. The snow's snarling the streets. I know the band's been playing and folks dancing. Still, I'd love to do a waltz with Mrs. Davis. With your kind approval, of course."

"Yes! Have your dance, Mr. President," an officer shouted out.

Other soldiers echoed, "Yes! Yes! God bless President Davis and Mrs. Davis."

The president shouted out to the band, "I promised Mrs. Davis we'd dance to 'O Bird Of Paradise.'"

The band obliged. Alone on the floor, President Davis and his wife waltzed as hundreds watched. Halfway through the waltz, couples began trickling onto the dance floor, joining the Confederacy's First Couple.

"Should we?" Bill asked Franny, swinging his gaze to the dancing couples closest to them.

"No. Not as long as President Davis is out there. My little protest."

Bill leaned close and kissed Franny's ear. "The children of the poor deserve better than the treatment they got from President Davis and Mayor Mayo. We can have our dance later."

Afraid of the accumulating snow, the president and the mayor left early. *Fair-weather patriots*, Bill thought, inwardly laughing.

"Do you have a favorite tune you want played?" he queried Franny.

"Ah, you're so sweet, Bill. Let's dance to the 'Crystal Schottische.' I grow weary of the waltzes." She pinched his cheek. "We'll do our waltzing later tonight in our bed."

Ah, waltzing in bed...he'd definitely take her up on that invitation, Bill decided as he made his way to the band. At the end of the latest song, he submitted his request to the conductor. "'Crystal Schottische'? Fun dance," the conductor said, nodding to the musicians to make sure they heard. "We'll play it next, Lieutenant."

Finally out among the other dancing couples, Bill coordinated his steps with Franny. He enjoyed twirling her. He took a peek at the other couples, all dancing the same steps in a circle. Charlie and Avis had joined the circle with Bill's chuckaboo compensating nicely for the loss of his left arm.

Up to midnight the band played, not just waltzes and schottisches, but Virginia reels, polkas and even a square dance. Bill and Franny were sweating by the time the musicians stored their instruments inside their cases.

Bill and Charlie retrieved everyone's coats from the coatroom. "I asked Ernie the cabman to pick us up at midnight." Bill helped Franny into her coat. "We'll soon know if his cab's curbside or he's afraid of a little snow."

The four decided not to exit out the ballroom doors. Instead, they shuffled into the hotel's lobby, passing a grandfather clock. Bill noticed the location of the clock's hands—twelve o'clock.

"It's Christmas Day." Bill reached for Franny's waist, drew her up against his chest and shared a kiss as the clock chimed. "Merry Christmas, my love."

"Merry Christmas, Bill. Our first Christmas as husband and wife."

Near them, Charlie and Avis kissed passionately. They paused their kiss-fest until they found a divan near the hotel's outside double doors. Once seated, they kissed even more ardently.

Bill cleared his throat. "Merry Christmas, Charlie and Avis. Say hello to your grannie for me, Avis."

Avis shifted her mouth away from Charlie's lips. "I will, Bill. Merry Christmas to you both." She returned her attention to Charlie's lips—and not gently, giving him no chance to wish Bill and Franny a Merry Christmas. Bill figured it didn't bother Charlie in the least.

Ushering Franny out into the night lit only by a gas streetlamp, Bill stomped boot prints into the deep snow. "Not sure when our friends will get to the Thompson mansion. Poor Charlie, the great lover forced to sleep in a separate bedroom and Avis so close yet so far."

Franny laughed. "Poor Charlie. Only blankets to warm him on this night before Christmas."

Bill kicked snow playfully into the air. "I knew he'd come through! There's Ernie's cab. With the cold and all this snow, I've got to get you home before your toes freeze."

Franny patted Bill's buttocks. "I expect you to carry me to our bedroom, remove my soaked shoes and stockings, and initiate some Christmas cheer between the covers."

Bill winked. "Isn't that the best kind?"

Twenty

A Meager But Loving Christmas

Morning light filtered past the bedroom curtains, shining on Franny's face. Soft snores escaped her half-open mouth. Though deep in sleep, Franny seemed to sense the strong morning sun. She rolled on her side, face turned away from Bill and the window. He knew he should let her sleep. He didn't.

Sunlight played on her shoulder and upper back. Franny moaned, an indication she might soon awaken. Shifting closer, Bill turned on his side and draped a hand across her waist and caressed her belly. He finger-walked to a breast and fondled the nipple. He felt it harden. Her hand reached back and stroked his hip.

"You woke me, bad boy."

"It's Christmas. Time to kiss by the tree."

"We did good-cheer waltzing all night on this bed. I need my beauty sleep."

"I want more good cheer!"

Franny laughed. "You win. More good cheer."

Wiggling, she squirmed until her buttocks pressed against his groin. She purred, warm and inviting. Desire rolled through him. Engorged with blood, his penis hardened and reached full growth.

"Lordy, Franny, please tell me you're ready."

Maneuvering, she lay on her back, both legs drawn up. "Enjoy the bed waltz, Bill. It's my Christmas present to you."

Rising to a sitting position, he sprinkled kisses on her kneecaps, then worked his way along a thigh to her fruitful vine. She blocked him with her hand, preventing Bill from exploring the garden. Instead, she clutched the back of his neck and drew him down for a mouth-to-mouth kiss.

He brushed her lips then let his tongue mate with hers. "Can I count our bed play as my gift?"

"I think not. It's my gift. No duplicates."

"Then I don't have a gift for you, Franny." As he showered kisses over her mouth, chin and cheeks, Bill drew circles around a nipple.

"I expect five Christmas gifts from you on our first war-free Christmas."

"Done." He kissed then fondled both her breasts.

"I'm ready, sweetheart." Franny brushed her fingers against his cheek.

Bill glanced at his crotch. "I'm thoroughly ready." He skimmed his fingers along the tip of her toes, brushed his hand along her ankle and leg, leaned forward and kissed her thigh. "I'm on the verge of shattering into a thousand shards. A volcano's rumbling inside me."

"We share that volcano." Again, she caressed his cheek then reached into the bedside end table next to her and drew a rubber from the top drawer. "Yes, you are indeed ready." Franny drew the rubber over Bill's gaying instrument.

Her purrs an enticing invitation, he rolled on top of her and crooked a leg across her hips. Closing her arms around him, she drew him close against her breasts. He reached and guided his penis into her garden. The cast iron and brass bed shook and bounced, bedsprings squeaking loud as the mating howl of a tomcat. Passion spent, Bill collapsed. He lay sprawled atop Franny, his damp hair mingling with hers.

"Thank you for the last few minutes," he told her.

"My pleasure." Franny play-bit his earlobe. "Didn't you promise me breakfast Christmas morning?"

Rolling off her, he dropped his feet over the side of the bed and stared at the fireplace. Only embers burned in it. His first task must be warming up the bedroom. As he leaned forward, ready to rise to his feet, he felt fur graze his leg. A cat meowed. He looked down, met the gaze of Tessir.

"Hey, Tessir Boy. Were you watching us? You need to find a girl cat."

"Put him up on the bed so I can cuddle with him." Franny kissed Bill's back.

"I'm surprised he didn't jump up on the bed in the middle of our sexual congress."

"Tessir's always a gentleman." She laughed. "Don't forget to give him fresh water and some of whatever you make for us."

Bill fed new logs into the hearth and stoked the embers until flames erupted and warmed his skin. Donning longjohns, pants and a shirt, he guided his feet into slippers and padded into the water closet where he relieved himself. With hands washed and dried, he moseyed into the chilly kitchen and fired up the cooking oven. On cold mornings, it doubled proficiently as a furnace. Soon its heat snaked into the kitchen's corners and crannies. Bill unbuttoned his shirt's top two buttons and let the warmth caress his chest.

"How are you coming?" The shout came from Franny, still lounging on the bed. "Do you need my help?"

"I promised you breakfast. Let's say it's my Christmas gift to you."

"I must say my kissy good-cheer gift was better." Laughter rumbled from their bedroom.

Tessir rubbed against Bill's ankle. "I can get you fresh water, boy, but the oatmeal will have to wait. Still got to cook it."

The cat meowed, put his paw on the water dish and tapped it over and over, producing a racket.

Okay, I get it, cat, you want everything right now. I'll do what I can. Bill poured fresh well water into a bowl in front of the icebox. Tessir's bowl for food scraps remained empty.

Bill scooped oatmeal from a tin can and spooned it into a pot. He primed the sink pump and listened to the water spill into the pot. Soon flames licked the vessel's bottom. Cutting away four slices of bread from a loaf Franny had made two days before, Bill toasted them on a grill then buttered them. Franny had a sweet tooth, so he grabbed a Mason jar of strawberry jam from the pantry and placed it on the table.

"Almost ready," he shouted out to Franny.

Spooning oatmeal into two bowls, he added powdered milk, water and a couple of drops of molasses, and arranged the bowls, silverware and plates of toast on either side of a vase filled with paper roses. Just one more matter. Coffee. He emptied beechnuts and almonds into the grinder, ground them up, and then filtered hot water through them into a coffee pot.

Wearing a pink nightrobe speckled with blue and yellow flowers, Franny strolled into the kitchen holding a wrapped package in her hands. A smirk creased her face. "I don't care that I'm not getting a present. This year has been terrible for you. Your papa dying, you getting wounded at Chancellorsville. I found a way to get this for you, sweetheart." She waved the package in front of him, then pulled it back when he reached for it. "Not now. First it goes under the tree. We eat and then you can open it. By the way, breakfast smells wonderful."

Eyebrows knitted together, Bill watched his wife place the gift under their tiny evergreen tree that sat on a round end table near the parlor window. Franny fed fresh logs into the parlor fireplace and stoked them with a brass poker, reigniting the dying fire.

"It's a toasty Christmas morning in the Stamford residence," Bill joked, running his finger along the wrapping paper of Franny's present for him. "I really wish you hadn't bought this for me. Our Christmas cheer in our bed was enough."

She dismissed his concerns with a curt wave of her hand. "Who said I paid money for it? Maybe I made it for you?"

"I need to open it and find out. See if you're joshing."

"Not until we've eaten. The oatmeal and toast are getting cold." She jabbed her arm toward the kitchen archway and the table.

"Just a minute. I have something for you as well." Bill sidled over to the settee and reached down for the hatbox he'd left under the pedestal end table. Sitting down, he put the hatbox on his lap and lifted its lid. War Department documents lay inside, covering something at the bottom of the hatbox. Burrowing deeper, Bill clasped his objective and brought it out into the light—Franny's wrapped present.

"Darn! I'm so easily fooled. Not once did I think to look inside." She sighed. "Shame on you! I told you not to spend money we don't have." In spite of the voiced disapproval, Franny's face beamed with curiosity.

Bill treaded to the Christmas tree and nestled the present beside Franny's gift for him. "Let's open them."

"After breakfast. I don't want to eat ice-cold toast."

Shifting away from the tree and its paper decorations, Bill stopped at the window and looked down at the street scene. Flurries danced in a light breeze, so different from the night when blinding snow blanketed the sky like sand grains on a beach. No wheel tracks or footprints marred the snow shroud, except for tiny dog and cat prints that meandered among the bushes and trees. He felt the cold touch of the breeze slinking between the window and its frame.

Joining Bill at the window, Franny burrowed her head against his shoulder. He felt her fingers scratch his upper back. "Forget breakfast. I just want to feel those fingers for rest of the morning."

"My stomach's going to start growling. And it's my breakfast you made special for me. We can't go and ruin it." Pushing him away, Franny propped her forehead against the glass. "So cold, perfect for Christmas morning. Looks peaceful out there. No one out yet. That won't last. People will soon take their Christmas Day walks. The cabs and buggies will appear, carrying people to loved ones' houses."

They ate breakfast as Tessir perched on Franny's slippered feet and meowed raucously. "Should I give him some toast?" She dipped a knife into the jam.

"He won't eat it, especially if it has jam on it."

"Hear that, Tessir? Daddy doesn't think you'll eat this." She dropped a chunk of the toast—minus the jam—beside his tail. The cat tongued it into his mouth, chewed and meowed for more.

She dipped her spoon into the oatmeal. "Not bad. The molasses helps. I'm glad I picked up some dried milk. That's a good invention." She slipped her right foot out of the slipper and rubbed her big toe against Tessir's belly. He flopped onto his side and begged for more. "He acts like you, Bill, when we're bed romping."

"Yes, but I'm devoted to you. Tessir's wishy-washy. When you want to cuddle with the little guy, he's gone out the cat opening." Reaching across the table, Bill patted Franny's hand.

With approval from the landlord, Bill had cut a floor-level hole in the apartment's entryway door. A similar pet entry existed in the brownstone's portico door. Wanting to show unwavering support for the war effort, the landlord had agreed to the pet doors since nearly all the renters were War Department workers, mostly soldiers.

"Wish we had a bottle of wine stowed away." Franny pretended to pout. "We could drink a toast to our first Christmas as husband and wife."

Bill finished up breakfast with a cup of steaming-hot beechnut-and-almond coffee. He slid his chair away from the table and stretched. "I don't know about you, but I'm ready to open your present and see if I should kiss you or spank you."

"Naughty boy." Franny slipped her right foot back into its slipper and rose to her feet. Taking Bill's hand, she led him to the tree.

He handed her present to her. Tessir waddled back and forth against his legs. "Open it. I can't believe you didn't take a peek inside the hatbox."

Franny rolled her eyes. "Why should I? What do I care about your homework?" She pushed the gift away. "No. I want you to open yours first. No excuses, Bill! Open it."

"I should have learned I can't deny you." He returned Franny's gift to its spot beneath the tree.

"No, you can't." She laughed as she transferred the gift clenched in her arms into his hands. "When you see what I got you, you're going to want to carry me back to bed and join giblets." She blew him a kiss.

Franny had carefully wrapped the present in brown paper, drawn paper ornaments and glued them to the paper. Bill almost hated to tear it open.

Like a fastidious girl, he neatly removed the paper, folded it and set it aside. He blinked huge eyes, then steadied them and peered at the title of a book—*A Christmas Carol.* "This is a first-edition Dickens. We can't afford—"

"Look at the first page." Franny tapped the novel's cover.

He flipped open the cover and nearly dropped the book. Dickens had autographed it, even included a short note: Best of luck with your writing, Bill.

"It's wonderful, Franny. But the cost... did you sell your sixteenth birthday necklace?"

"Stop it, Bill!" Franny sighed, her exasperation palpable. "An anonymous friend gave it to me. The friend knows you love to write. Consider it a thank-you for saving me from a certain insufferable Tennessee officer. No cost, except for stamps. I mailed it to Dickens along with a letter asking him to autograph it. Wonderful man, he did it."

Bill pursed his lips. "Anonymous?"

"Yes, and the book's former owner will remain anonymous. Understand?"

Nodding, he drew his gift to her from under the tree. "Your turn."

Bill too had wrapped Franny's gift in plain brown paper provided free of charge by the neighborhood butcher. Unlike Franny, he'd not hand-decorated it with Christmas motifs and colored string.

With Tessir following her, Franny took the nondescript present to the settee, sat and let it dangle on her lap. The cat meowed. Petting

Tessir's head, Franny held the present out near the cat's nose and let him sniff it. "Do you love to tear open wrapping paper, Tessir Boy?"

The cat pawed the gift, sniffed, sank his sharp teeth into one side. A ripping sound out-shrieked the parlor clock's tic-toc... tic-toc... tic-toc. Using his front paws, Tessir clawed the paper, sending scraps flying, revealing a tattered shoebox.

"Be careful!" Bill warned. "If Tessir tears through the box, he could do damage."

"Damage? Let's see what's in the box." Franny flipped off the top. Tessir grabbed the lid and dragged it along the floor into the back hall, his destination their bedroom. "Oh, Bill! It's beautiful." She lifted the music box onto her lap and ran her fingers along the exquisitely painted ballerina affixed to the lid. As tears streamed down her cheeks, she turned the lever, and the ballerina began to dance to a waltz. "It's Swiss, isn't it?" She wiped the back of her hand across her face, soaking up tears. "I saw this in Leonardo's toyshop."

"Look inside the jewelry compartment."

When the song ended and the ballerina stopped her dance, Franny peered inside. Bill sat beside her, their hips touching. "Please read the letter first," he told her.

Plucking the note from the jewelry box, Franny unfolded the paper and scanned the words. "Oh, what a wonderful man!" She started crying again. "Leonardo donated more than any other toymaker—and he played Santa for us. I don't know what to say." She kissed the ballerina, then gave Bill a wet smooch. "We need to visit Leonardo and thank him."

"There's more." He slid his hand into the box and extracted a necklace of bright glass stones. "Sarah Davis made a bushel load of necklaces for War Department officers. Handed them out to us a few days ago. Made us promise to give them to our wives as Christmas presents."

"She sure kept it a secret." Franny twisted around, displaying the back of her neck. "Put it on me, sweetheart."

Fingers shaking, he fastened the necklace then kissed Franny's neck.

She set the jewelry box aside and stood. Her kneecap cracked, earning a laugh from Bill. "You're too young, Franny, to have popping bones."

Leaning over him, she pinched his cheek. "Cold weather, Bill. I crack like plank floors."

Franny scurried to the parlor mirror. Her eyes reflected in the mirror said she loved how the stones sparkled in the morning light.

"Well, what do you think?" he wondered.

"It's gorgeous. Please thank Sarah for me."

"When the war's over, I'll get you a necklace with real jewels."

"It won't be as nice as this one." Franny wiggled a finger, inviting Bill to join her. As soon as he smelled her familiar scent of perfume and not-long-ago lovemaking, he took her into his arms and shared a mouth-open, tongues-touching kiss. "Thank you for both gifts, Bill. This is the best Christmas of my life. After the war, when we can afford it, we need to pay Leonardo for the jewelry box."

"He'll be offended, darling. We can do something else for him. Honor him in some way. We'll put our heads together and do some brainstorming."

"Something that will bring tears to his eyes." She licked the end of Bill's nose.

Later in the afternoon, after changing into a green day dress with red lace sleeves, Franny cooked the Christmas meal—roast beef, turnips, carrots and cornbread washed down by sweet molasses water. The meat and vegetables had been a gift from a gentleman farmer living just beyond the outskirts of Richmond, the husband of a member of the Ladies' Aid Society. After eating, they played a game of tabletop croquet then enjoyed ginger cake sweetened with sorghum, also provided by the farmer. Bill stepped up to the parlor window and watched the setting sun spray dusk colors over the city's steeples and government buildings. Franny joined him.

"This sweet Christmas redeemed an awful year," he told her.

"I have one more secret to tell you, my darling." Franny caressed Bill's cheek and neck. "I'm taking you to St. John's Church to hear the choir sing Christmas carols and The Reverend Peterkin recite Luke's account of the birth of Jesus. It's the perfect way to end Christmas, isn't it?"

"I love your surprises." Bill glanced at his pocket watch. "I need to change clothes. Can't wear these to church. Did you say anything to our cabman?"

"Not snowing anymore. No need for a cab. We can walk the few blocks to church." She pressed her hands against her hips. "Get hopping or we'll be late."

Twenty-one

A Fiery Editorial

Just two months since Christmas and Richmond seethed with anger. Charlie had called the city a powder keg. The goodwill engendered by the Christmas party for the boys and girls of Richmond had faded away by late February, thanks to an inflammatory editorial in the *Daily Dispatch*. Disturbing rumors raced through the city. Women were planning an incendiary protest. They intended to ransack stores and shops and steal food and clothing. The palpable fear needed to be bottled up before President Davis and the governor ordered troops to shoot hungry, incensed women.

It was the reason Bill strode toward the *Daily Dispatch* office. He intended to meet with the editor, Michael Russell, for a heart-to-heart talk. Russell's latest editorial demanded the scalp of Colonel Lucius Northrop, commissary general of Subsistence. The editor's words could be the catalyst that would ignite the powder keg. One of the rabble-rousing women at December's protest had sent her son to Bill's office with a note: Lieutenant, I thought you would want to know. Some of the hotheads who read the *Dispatch's* editorial about bungling Northrop are hopping mad. They plan a repeat of April's bread riot. I fear there'll be bloodshed. Please do what you can to help us. Callie Dampeer.

Soldiers in the camps wanted to lynch someone. Bill didn't yet know who would feel the rope squeezing around their necks, the female hotheads or Northrop. Those women who didn't live in ritzy mansions staffed with a dozen darkies knew who to blame for their sorrows: Northrop who'd failed to supply nourishing food to their soldier-husbands and their children.

The *Dispatch* building took up a city block. Awnings covered two entrances, both alike except for a sign on a glass pane of the nearest door: Employee entrance only. Walking ahead of Bill, a laborer wearing an ink-stained, full-body leather apron turned to open the nearest door. He glanced back at Bill. "Mornin', Lieutenant." He laughed sourly. "Payin' a visit about yesterday's Northrop editorial?"

Bill nodded. "Russell disturbed a hornet's nest. Lots of angry soldiers, women and politicians."

"I think Russell's doin' a good thing. Northrop's in the pocket of the speculators. That's why soldiers, their wives and kiddies ain't gettin' the food they need."

Bill agreed, but didn't say so. He wouldn't last long at the War Department if he sided with the women and opposed Northrop. The politicians and generals were turning against Northrop, but that opposition would have to firm up more before he'd risk publicly damning the commissary general.

An old-fashioned sign hung down from the second door, squeaking as the breeze brushed against it. Bill walked underneath it, swung open the door and strolled into the atrium. Behind the counter, *Dispatch* ladies swathed in black from the neck down were listening to complaints from readers upset enough to make the trip to the newspaper office.

"So the editor won't see me?" stormed one of the complainers, a bald man in his forties. "Because of Russell's editorial, I'm goin' to have to hire private guards to protect my general store, money I can't afford to spend. My store got ransacked in April. I can't let that happen again."

The *Dispatch* lady listening to the grumbler appeared no older than sixteen, probably a new bride and widow in the same year. She gritted her teeth. "I told you the editor will see you, Mr. Stanfield. He has someone with him at the moment. Please be patient, sir."

"No, I won't be patient. I'm sorry for your loss, girl, but I don't have all day to stand here and wait." Stanfield spun on his heels and stomped to the exit. Hand on the doorknob, he twisted around. "This buildin's goin' to get burned before the war's over. I'm a hard-workin' shopkeeper, not a figgins or speculator. I deserve better than this." He slammed the door as he left. The bell above the door frame rang for a good minute.

At last seeing Bill, the teenage widow waved him into the newsroom. Another grumbler whined, "Why does the lieutenant get to go back?"

"He's War Department," the girl snapped.

The grouch rapped the countertop and grinned. "Give him hell, War Department."

Inside the newsroom, a cavernous space bulwarked by four whitewashed columns, dozens of reporters sat at table-like desks looking like medieval copyists inside a monastery. The editor's office, a small room enclosed by half-walls with windows, lay just beyond the atrium. A thirtyish reporter sat in a cushioned chair in front of Russell's roll-top desk. Arms flailing, the reporter growled at Russell, "You can't back down. We're right. That's our job, got to publicize ineptitude and corruption."

Bill knocked and waited.

"Come in," Russell shouted.

"Morning, Michael." Bill shut the door behind him and took a seat beside the reporter. "You've sure stirred up a hornets' nest."

Russell laughed then shared a knowing glance with his reporter. Bill had met the star reporter but couldn't recall his name. "Looks like the folks at the War Department read my editorial."

"Yep, Secretary Seddon thought a heart-to-heart would do you some good." Bill leaned back and slapped the armrests.

"Michael needs to keep the pressure on," the reporter injected. "Northrop has to go. He's hopeless. Probably corrupt; need more proof."

"Proof... that's the important word, Frank." Russell nodded toward the door. "Start pounding the streets, give me proof. You know I'll print it."

The reporter—Frank McBride—departed to do some investigative snooping. As soon as Russell mentioned the reporter's first name, Bill remembered. McBride was new, had been hired away from the *Charleston Daily Courier*.

Russell returned his gaze to Bill as soon as the door closed. "Northrop and his cronies coming with torches?"

"I think he's more worried about his own skin."

"It needed to be said." Russell picked up the latest edition of the *Dispatch* and circled his finger around the front-page editorial. "The man's a bungler. The Confederacy's the opposite of Joseph's Egypt. As the pharaoh's commissary general of Subsistence, Joseph filled granaries so when famine gripped the land, people would have enough to eat. Northrop's our Joseph and he failed us. If we lose the war, his blundering will be the chief culprit."

Bill crossed his legs, pretending to be more relaxed than he actually felt. "His fate should be decided by Congress and President Davis, not a mob looking for blood to spill. Thanks to you and the other newspaper editors, Northup can't walk around town like any normal person. He has to have two guards for protection."

"He needed protection long before my editorial. At least as far back as the Bread Riot."

"There's talk the women will be marching again, courtesy of your piece." Bill uncrossed his legs, scooted to the edge of the chair and rested his elbows on the desk. "If you keep it up, President Davis will call out the troops and they'll fire on the women—and God help us. Don't be the one that lights the match that burns down Richmond, including the *Dispatch* building."

"An order to fire on women? That will come from Davis or the governor, not me. The Northrop thing can be solved easily. President

Davis can sack Northrop and name a replacement. Congressmen have grown tired of Northrop's excuses. They'll gladly approve a competent replacement." Russell folded the newspaper and dropped it on a stack of older ones. "We're all tired of Northrop's excuses—bad weather that stops supply wagons, sabotaging darkies. Our soldiers march in their bare feet. Davis and the Congress have to show some backbone. I intend to use the *Dispatch* to help them grow some balls." He grinned.

"In the meantime, the women will march and you'll be running stories how Davis and the governor gave the okay to open fire." Bill drummed his fingers on the pile of newspapers. "You'll be running obituaries of soldiers' wives who only wanted food for their children and themselves. What do you think the privates in the armies will do when they hear their government shot their wives?"

Russell sighed, nodding. "I see your point, Bill. And I see no harm in giving President Davis and the Congress time to replace Northrop." He turned in his chair and scanned the newsroom. "I'll write a piece that calls for calm and advises folks to let the politicians do their jobs." He grimaced. "What I can't do is change President Davis's opinion of Northrop. He likes him."

"Time, Michael. Give them time. That's all I ask."

"You have it." Russell stood, signifying the meeting must end. "But you have to do your part, Bill. Convince Seddon to block President Davis and the governor from giving troops authorization to fire on the women."

Rising to his feet, Bill reached across the table and shook the editor's hand. "You have my word. Back in December, the war secretary backed the women. I will remind him only he stands between the women and ill-tempered politicians."

Russell opened his office door. "My wife says she might march with the working-class women. She went to that Christmas Eve party of yours and met some of them. They won her over." He laughed sourly. "We don't need soldiers pointing their guns at the women. My wife might be with them."

Bill understood...Franny might be with her.

Outside beneath a cloudless sky, Bill headed for the War Department building near the Capitol Square. Two freight wagons filled with corn and flour bags fresh from a James River granary rumbled along the brick street toward War Department warehouses. Bill agreed with the editor...President Davis and his congressional supporters could be so damned stubborn. The food trickled out of Richmond to the troops and civilians. The South won the battles, but couldn't supply its armies or the soldiers' families. Charlie called it a recipe for losing the war.

Bill's father had warned him. It didn't take much to incite a mob to burn down a newspaper office. Bill hoped Russell would follow through and call for President Davis and the Congress to find a replacement for Northrop, someone who could get the supply lines running efficiently, the speculators jailed, and prices down. Screaming for Northrop's head without a follow-up plan just invited mob violence and a deadly response from soldiers.

A captain skedaddled away from the War Department building as Bill made his way up the steps. The fellow acted guilty, not looking at Bill as he scurried by in a hurry. Way too early for a mid-day meal, he doubtless headed for a rendezvous with a lover in some out-of-the-way spot. Not the Capitol Square, the favorite spot for hand-holding walks. Bill figured the officer wanted to do more than hold hands with a woman claimed by another.

No sooner reaching his office, Bill heard Charlie exclaim, "The secretary has been looking for you."

Bill stopped at his friend's desk. "Odd. He must have overlooked my appointment with the *Dispatch* editor."

Charlie pushed away a pile of telegraph dispatches. "He's a bit forgetful, isn't he?"

"A lot on his mind lately. I better go find out what he wants."

Bill didn't hear any voices emanating from Seddon's office. He'd half-expected to find Northrop there, but the silence gave him hope the besieged bureaucrat had stayed away. Inside he discovered Captain Beardsley hunched over the heating stove feeding logs into its firebox. Beardsley spun around when he heard the thump-thump of Bill's boots. "He's been asking about you all morning, Stamford. He's quite put out."

"I told him I was going to see the *Dispatch* editor."

"Tarnation! I forgot," a voice sounded from inside the inner sanctum. "That's neither here nor there, Lieutenant Stamford. Not anymore. The president wants to see us as soon as possible."

Bill opened Seddon's inner door and stood in the doorway. "Me?"

"Yes, you."

Bill gulped. Nothing good could come from a meeting with President Jefferson Davis.

Twenty-two

A Meeting with President Davis

Seddon preferred not to walk the half-mile to the Executive Mansion on Clay Street, so they hopped aboard a Hansom cab. Ahead, the road and boardwalk held more piles of melting snow than folks. The only people along Ninth Street were two boys on their knees playing marbles in a cleared spot and an elderly grocer sweeping the stoop and boardwalk in front of his store. A snowbank at the Broad Street intersection towered over the boys' heads. If March brought warm weather and rain as many hoped, the snow would soon be gone.

"The president's feeling a bit under the weather today. He's doing his work at home." Seddon peered at the marbles-playing boys as the cab passed them. He shouted, "Why aren't you two scalawags in school?"

"Teacher's under the weather," one of the boys yelled back, "Just like President Davis."

"I guess he heard you, sir," Bill quipped.

Seddon avoided long walks whenever possible. In many ways, he'd become a near-invalid. Still, he always made it to work on time.

"Can you say why President Davis wants to see me?" Bill rested his hands on his kneecaps and let them dangle. "Russell's editorial?"

"I'm sure the president will talk about it." An enigmatic smile ghosted across Seddon's face. "I expect he'll bring up other matters as well. We'll know soon enough."

The war secretary pointed straight ahead as the cab turned right onto Clay Street, revealing the executive mansion, partially blocked by storefronts and skeletal trees. Just three more blocks and they'd be at Davis's home, an Italianate house that overlooked the Shockoe Valley.

"I never got a chance to tell you, sir. Russell has agreed to write an editorial calling on townspeople to be calm and let politicians solve the food crisis and Northrop."

The secretary shrugged. "The new editorial will calm President Davis some, but he'll still be mad. The president isn't ready to throw Northrop to the dogs, and he doesn't like newspaper editors who think they can force him into a decision he's not ready to make."

"So I've heard." The wind whistling into the Hansom nearly separated Bill's slouch hat from his head. The lieutenant barely saved the headwear from sailing out the cab. He dropped the hat into his lap and safeguarded it with a palm. "So President Davis works out of his home office most of the time, not the executive office building?"

"Yes, especially during the winter. He's like a lot of us older men. He doesn't want to venture into the cold and snow."

The cab stopped curbside in front of the executive mansion, guarded by two soldiers standing at ease on either side of the portico steps. Leaning on the wrought-iron fence in front of the mansion, foot-travelers eyed the mansion, hoping to get a glimpse of President Davis and his wife, Varina. The war secretary paid the cabman, and soon after the two were striding up the brick pathway to the portico.

Halfway to the mansion, Seddon led Bill to the back entrance. A lone guard snapped to attention when they approached. The soldier recognized Seddon and saluted. Atop the stoop, Seddon knocked on the door and leaned his frame against a wrought-iron railing.

"Are you okay, sir?"

"Taking a breather. The back's a bit stiff. Too much time sitting in the Hansom."

Seddon craned his neck. "The third story's new, built before the war."

"Impressive house." Bill swung his gaze from the third story back to Seddon. "Easily outshines the Yankee White House." A tiny lie, Bill acknowledged to himself. He still admired the one Lincoln called home.

The door opened with a fingers-across-a-chalkboard sound, revealing a butler dressed in black coattails and a chimney-pot hat. The darkey bowed to Seddon first then Bill. "The president's expectin' you'ums. Follow me, Mr. Secretary and Lieutenant."

The door to Davis's second-floor office stood open. The president loomed over a conference table covered by war maps. He turned leisurely as the butler led Seddon and Bill into the office. Davis poked his thumb against an ink mark on one of the maps. "General Lee's still in winter camp. I keep telling Northrop he's got to get more supplies to the soldiers. We need warm weather so the general can move the Army of Northern Virginia into the Shenandoah breadbasket and force Meade to chase him. I want the Yankee army away from Richmond." He nodded to the couch below an 1850s map of the world. "Have a seat, gentlemen. Help yourself to coffee." A coal-fired hot plate sat on Davis's desk, keeping a coffee pot warm. "Ben, I'm sure the gentlemen are famished. Please bring us a plate of honey cakes and cheese."

The darkey bowed. "The gentlemen will have their honey cakes faster than a beagle can run down a rabbit."

Davis sat at his desk and sipped a mug of coffee. He frowned; the coffee must be cold. Picking up the coffee pot, Bill filled mugs for Seddon and himself then offered to fill the president's Great Seal of the Confederacy mug. Davis held his palm over his mug, reconsidered, and allowed Bill to top it off. Bill joined Seddon on the leather couch.

"Lieutenant, I imagine you think I've called you here to grouse about the *Dispatch's* editorial." The president blew on the rim of his mug, lowering the heat before bringing it up to his lips. "Yes, I'm concerned about these galling editors who don't see the big picture. We're have to rein them in."

Seddon rested his mug on his thigh. "Lieutenant Stamford told me some good news on the way over to the executive mansion. The editor will be publishing a second editorial calling for the hotheads to calm down and let you and the Congress deal with Northrop and the supply-line hiccups." He took a sip and exclaimed, "That's real coffee!"

"Rank has its privileges. If the *Dispatch* editor does what he promises, that will perhaps keep the agitators off the streets. I really don't want to send in troops like Lincoln did in New York City back in July. That was an ugly riot." The president drummed his fingers on the edge of the desk and hummed "God Save The Queen," then pursed his lips. "But that's not why I called you here. Lieutenant, I want you to find Rose Greenhow."

Bill nearly spit out his coffee. Somehow, he managed to force it down his throat. "You mean sail to Europe?" His voice cracked as he spoke.

"You can't very well find Rose sitting at your desk at the War Department." Davis slapped his knees in merriment.

One of the last times Bill had seen Rose, a fiery halo silently flashed around her. That had been inside a Wilmington tavern. President Davis's words not only summoned memories of Rose, they also reminded Bill of the lover who rejected him—Becky Powell. The last he'd heard Becky worked as Rose's secretary. Finding Rose meant seeing Becky again, something Bill wanted to avoid almost as much as Yankee mini balls.

"I'm discombobulated, sir. Of course, I'll do it." Bill set his mug on a side table. He didn't trust himself to hold it.

"It may turn out to be the most important mission of the war." The rigid expression on the president's face left no doubts. He meant it.

The butler returned with two plates of honey cake and cheese, one plate for Davis's desk, the other on a table he set near the couch.

As soon as the darkey left the office, shutting the door behind him, Bill explained, "I did meet Rose in Wilmington. She took a shine to me, helped me recruit some fellows for the Eighteenth North Carolina." He tried one of the slices of honey cake, licked the crumbs from his lips. "Impressive woman."

"It shouldn't be too hard to find her. Rose does like the limelight." Seddon tried a honey cake and actually moaned, as if getting an under-the-covers kiss from his wife. "I see her name mentioned in the London newspapers every so often. But the news is already old by the time newspapers cross the ocean."

"Lieutenant, here's my dilemma." Davis dipped a new honey-cake slice in his coffee and took a bite. "I sent Rose to England and France to help secure official recognition for the Confederate States of America. Rose has a weakness—men. She assured me she could win the heart of one of England's ardent supporters of Lincoln and win him to our cause. Rose has gotten herself engaged while in Europe. Not one of Lincoln's staunch English allies, but a politician who's an aficionado of the Confederacy."

"Sounds like Rose." Bill washed down the last of his honey cake with a hearty swallow of lukewarm coffee. "She does like to flirt. Looks like her flirting got out of control."

"I gave her the mission because she possesses the wiles to win the heart of a Lincoln sympathizer. I didn't realize she's blessed with an abundance of wiles." Davis rolled his eyes.

"That's why she was eager to do the mission," Seddon opined. "She craves adventure, danger, men's attention. And she's a smart woman and knows it."

"We need to get her back on track. You're the man to do it, Lieutenant." Davis rose and returned to the map table. Lifting a flap of the topmost map, he extracted an envelope. "I've a coded message for you to deliver. Rose has the cypher."

"March can be quite damp and rainy in London." Seddon chuckled. "Better bring your overcoat, Bill."

"The department stores in London have some fizzing-good rain nappers." Rose's message in his hand, Davis approached the couch. "I've booked you passage aboard the blockade runner *Don*. Captain Roberts will be expecting you. She sails on March 12." The president handed the envelope to Bill. "You'll get a chance to see your family before you set sail from Wilmington."

"Yes, my momma and my brother and sister live in Kenansville."

Davis tacked a map of the Confederacy and the United States to an easel. "If I can get one of the British politicians who favor Lincoln to swing to our side, we can force Lincoln to come to his senses and accept a negotiated peace. Once we get British recognition, France will follow."

"I'll find Rose, sir. You have my word." Bill's belly churned at the thought of the massive change in his life that awaited him. A voyage aboard a blockade runner, undercover work in London and maybe Paris. *Rose's halo? Are you giving me a chance to save her, Lord, like I did the little girl?*

"You'll be undercover, Lieutenant," Davis explained as he returned the map to the table. "Union spies are everywhere in England and France. You'll masquerade as a blockade-runner sailor. When you go ashore in Liverpool, you're to enjoy the dockside delights, the taverns and whorehouses. When you feel it's safe, sneak away to London and look for Rose."

Bill grinned mischievously. "Don't tell my wife about the whorehouses. She'll scalp me."

"Pretend, Bill," Seddon emphasized, laughing.

"You'll not have much time to say goodbye to your wife, Lieutenant." Davis headed toward the door and opened it. "I've secured trains for you down to Wilmington. You leave in two days." He winked. "Make the next two nights glorious ones for her."

Davis ushered Bill and Seddon down to the back entrance.

"Thank you for your trust in me," Bill told the president.

"We've no time to spare, Lieutenant. Soon the battles will begin anew. My spies say Lincoln intends to name General Grant head of the Union's armies. We're running out of time."

Twenty-three

Franny Learns About Rose Greenhow

The intersections passed by quickly as Bill and Charlie made their late-evening walk from the War Department on the edge of the Capitol Square to the brownstone. Charlie hummed "Lorena" just before streaks of crimson sunlight dappled the low-floating clouds above Richmond's towers, chimneys and steeples. The same sun tinted the smoke clouds belching from Tredegar and the smaller foundries along the James River. Only a few hours had passed since Bill learned he'd be steaming to Europe to deliver a presidential message to Rose Greenhow.

"I know I should be thrilled," he told Charlie, a grimace vanquishing a half-hearted smile. "Damn, Charlie! I don't want to see Becky. She's in my past. I want her to stay there." Left unsaid: she might prove to be an irresistible temptation.

"I'm goin' to pop the question."

Obviously, Charlie hadn't heard a word spoken by Bill. "Huh?" *Pop the question? Like who's the sweetest night flower at Miss Jennie Craig's house of pleasure?* Bill felt guilty for thinking badly of his best possum, who now devotedly courted Avis, his first serious romance.

Charlie stopped in front of the Clayton Toy Emporium and pointed at the storefront display of dolls and windup trains. He gestured at a baby doll with button eyes. "I'm goin' to marry Avis and we're goin' to have a heap of babies."

Bill patted his possum's shoulder. "What makes you think she'll accept a crazy man's proposal?"

"No woman can resist my lovable personality."

Bill groaned. "I always thought it was your Sampson-sized nebuchadnezzar."

"Not this time. Avis's pure as snow. On our wedding night… that's when my kisses will wander down to her fruitful vine." Charlie resumed walking, forcing Bill to catch up.

"You can't get married until I get back from Europe. Understand?"

"Of course. You have to be my best man." Charlie chuckled. "It may take me that long to convince Avis's father to let me marry her."

"You're a war hero, Charlie. He can't refuse." Bill fixed his gaze on his friend's stump.

"That's what I figure, Billy Boy. Otherwise, why bother askin' for her hand? I ain't got the family connections or the moneybags."

"She loves you, Charlie. That's obvious, just like the way your eyes light up when you're looking at her." Bill scooped up icy snow from a dwindling snowbank and tossed it at Charlie, smacking him in the chest. They hurled snowballs at each other for maybe a minute, and panting, stopped. "Seriously, Charlie, you and Avis haven't joined giblets?"

"Heavens no! I can't take the risk. Her father might forbid our marriage." The snowball in Charlie's hand dropped to the boardwalk.

"Avis has been a civilizing influence on you, Charlie." Bill snickered.

Ignoring Bill's snigger, Charlie agreed, a solemn tone in his voice. "Best thing to ever happen to me."

"When are you going to pop the question?"

"Tonight." Charlie's voice sounded almost somber. "I'm going to go to her house and win her father's permission. She's been hinting how she thinks it's time for a wedding ring." His mouth sagged. "But I don't know how I'm going to afford one. Damn Yanks! And damn our politicians for stumbling into this confounded war. She wants to get married in St. John's, but we can't do it there if I can't put a ring on her finger."

"We've friends in high places. You'll get your ring."

The stroll past the final few blocks went quickly. With the sun below the horizon and lamplighters out igniting mantles, Bill fastened his top-coat button and turned up the collar. No longer warmed by the sun, the breeze had turned cold and pricked at his skin. Bill gritted his teeth. Soon he would have to tell Franny he must set sail for Europe.

At the sight of their brownstone, Bill quipped, "My bed's going to be cold tonight."

"She'll be glad to be rid of you for several months." Charlie kicked an empty food can into a snowbank. "If you're worried another man will catch her eye, don't worry, chuckaboo. Avis and I will keep watch on her."

"I know Franny will stay true, but she knows Becky's traveling with Rose."

"Ah, I see your point." Charlie grinned acerbically.

They climbed the portico stoop, checked their mailboxes in the foyer, and tramped up the stairs to the fourth-floor landing. Outside Charlie's apartment, Bill joked, "Let's tip the glasses at Old Tom Griffin's Tavern. It's just two blocks away."

Charlie rolled his eyes. "No putting it off, chuckaboo. Face your wife like a man."

"Bad idea, eh? I guess you're right, Charlie." Bill watched Charlie unlock and open his door. "Good luck with Avis."

The smell of Hoppin' John Stew greeted Bill when he stepped into the parlor. In the kitchen, Franny tap-danced to a song—"Liza Jane"—as she stirred the pot of stew. "Where's Tessir?" Bill was surprised at the cat's absence. "I thought he'd be pestering you."

"I fed him. He's under the settee napping."

Bill swept Franny away from the stove and planted a wet kiss on her mouth.

Pushing him away, Franny patted his cheek. "That kiss had extra oomph to it."

"All my kisses do, all the way back to our night at the overseer's cottage."

Franny traced her finger along Bill's lower lip. "I better change the subject or we'll soon be shedding our clothes. I do want to eat a bowl of stew. So how was your day, sweetheart?"

Bill blurted, "I'm going to Europe." He smacked his forehead. *Damn! Way too abrupt. What was I thinking?* He scowled. *Or not thinking.*

Franny's eyes ballooned. She grabbed the countertop to steady herself. "Europe? You're kidding, right?" Staggering to the kitchen table, she plopped down in a chair.

He joined her at the table, stretching his legs out toward the stove. "No, I wish I was. President Davis ordered me to deliver a message to Rose."

Franny buried her face in her hands. "Am I asleep and having a nightmare?" Head raised, eyes fixed on Bill, she gripped the edge of the table. "Franny, wake up!"

"No one refuses the president of the Confederacy." He reached out and clasped Franny's hand. "More bad news, sweetheart. I'll be leaving in a few days."

"So soon?" Franny dabbed her eyes. "I hate President Davis." She tried to smile and gave up. "First my father. Now you." She began to cry.

"Your father?"

"President Davis is sending him to the Texas border with Mexico. Something about keeping an eye on the French troops. So far away. Mother's in a dither."

"It's an order, Franny. For him and for me. I love your mother, maybe she can stay with you while I'm gone. I'll be heading down to Wilmington to board a blockade runner. I can't say anything else."

"I'll ask her. We can help each other. It could be months before you return, right?"

Bobbing his head, Bill clenched his teeth. "I'll return to you as soon as humanly possible. President Davis has promised to keep my pay coming to you. And he'll get you a job at the Treasury—if you want it."

Starring at his hand that still gripped hers, she raised it to her mouth and kissed his fingers. "I want you in bed beside me. This is crazy—chasing down Rose Greenhow. Is Rose even alive? The halo?"

Hearing her bring up Rose's halo left his belly knotted. "Nothing in the papers about her death. Remember, she's famous over there."

"Damn it, Bill!" She jerked her hand away from him. "Your Becky's with Rose, right?"

"I don't know. She's not my Becky. I love you. She was an infatuation. I needed solace knowing you were in Tennessee with your fiancé."

Her hands shot upward, then slammed down on the table, rocking it. "I don't trust her. She didn't reject you. She rejected the war, ran away from the war."

Bill took deep breaths, calming himself. His nose twitched. He swung his gaze to the stove. "The stew's burning."

Franny bolted from her seat. "See what you made me do, Bill Stamford!" Darting to the stove, she damped the burner and transferred the pot to a trivet. Chewing her lower lip, Franny shoveled the stew onto two plates and set them on the table alongside glasses of molasses water. Seated once more, she barked, "I'll be marching up to the executive mansion to give President Davis a piece of my mind."

"It won't do any good, Franny." Bill spooned stew into his mouth and swallowed. "The president has made up his mind. I guess I talk too much. Seddon knew I'd become friends with Rose in Wilmington. Seddon's impressed with what I've done with the newspaper editors, keeping them from lighting the powder keg. He has convinced the president I'm the best choice to find Rose. You know I can't say no. And neither can you."

Franny planted both elbows on the table and stared at him. "If Secretary Seddon and President Davis think you're doing such a fabulous job, why the hell are they sending you to Europe? Who's going to keep the newspaper editors in line? Who's going to keep the powder keg from blowing?"

"I'm going to recommend Charlie."

Franny's laugh sounded more like a man's—a belly gusher that roared out her mouth. "He'll blow up the keg. Charlie can't keep his temper in check."

"Losing his arm at Gettysburg taught him to control it. He'll make a good politician after the war. Before we joined the Eighteenth, Charlie told me he wanted to help bind the wounds after the war—win or lose."

"Charlie?" Franny reached across the table and pinched Bill. "Sounds like a fairytale."

"You're too hard on him, Franny. He told me he's going to ask Avis to marry him. Said so on the way home this evening."

Franny clapped. "She'd be mad to marry the miscreant, but she's crazy in love so she'll accept."

"That's lukewarm praise for Charlie." Bill glanced at the red mark on his wrist where Franny had pinched him. "Do you like him, Franny?"

"Yes. Of course. It took time for me to get used to his ornery ways. At first, I thought he was a bad egg who only knew how to think with his plugtail. I do have a higher opinion of him now. He's not a lemming like so many of us. And Avis will make a fine politician's wife."

"He has struggled since Gettysburg, but Avis saved him. I just hope her father doesn't oppose the marriage." Bill squinted at the nearly empty bowl. Two spoonfuls finished off the stew. He leaned back in the chair and burped.

"Oppose a war hero?" Franny picked up Bill's empty bowl and glass, and along with hers toted them to the sink. "Her father will be glad to marry her off to one of the Confederacy's finest." She offered Bill a lopsided smile. "Charlie better never let slip his disillusionment with the war. Franny's father believes the Lord favors the Confederacy and won't allow Richmond to fall." She tossed a dishtowel to Bill. "Help me wash these."

Bill pumped the kitchen pump, drawing water Franny relied on to scrub the pot, bowls and glasses. Drying the tableware, he returned them to the cupboard then playfully slapped the towel against Franny's rump.

"Stop it! That hurt."

"Let's go to the bedroom. You can show me how much you're going to miss me."

"Later. We never play games."

"That's what I'm talking about—some bed-play games." Bill reached for Franny's waist, but she danced away from him.

"Real games, Bill. How about indoor croquet? We've only played it once. I thought you liked the game. Your eyes lit up when we got the package from mother." She sidled past his grasping hands and grabbed the game stored on a pantry shelf.

"Okay, Franny. Get ready to lose."

"Lose? Never!" She placed the game on the settee. Tessir meowed, but immediately resumed his heavy breathing through his nose. "We'll set the hoops in the parlor, kitchen and the hallway." Franny grinned naughtily. "The last hoop will be in our bedroom."

Franny knocked her ball through the first hoop near the fireplace a turn before Bill. She continued her winning ways, her ball rolling first through all the hoops until it recoiled off the bedroom wall after spinning through the last hoop.

"Yep, you won the game," Bill conceded. "But I'm about to set a new record. How fast I'm going to take off your clothes."

Soon, they were naked and enjoying another favorite game of theirs—bed wrestling. Eager hands exploring, Bill and Franny relearned all the delightful nooks and crannies on their bodies. When sated, they fell asleep in each other's arms, their breaths tickling their flushed faces.

Twenty-four

A Stormy Encounter

Ship masts and smokestacks stippled the Wilmington waterfront on both sides of the Cape Fear River. Foundries along the east bank belched smoke into the gray sky pregnant with rainwater. A miasma of smells—tar, foundry grit and foul water—permeated the soggy evening air. The sounds of hammering and sawing echoed from the west bank where slaves were repairing a blockade runner dinged by Union cannonballs. Just a few feet from Bill Stamford, another blockade runner bobbed beside the dock at the foot of Market Street. The sleek ship with its two masts and two smokestacks would soon become Bill's home.

"Look out, lady!" a clean-shaven stevedore shouted, his voice guttural. "Don't get knocked into the river."

Bill's mother Icie Belle and his siblings, Mark and Laura, jumped out of the way of a dozen stevedores rolling barrels onto the ship's gangway. Bill danced back as a barrel clattered toward his boot tips.

"What's inside?" Bill addressed a stevedore who sported a ragged beard. "I know it's not cotton."

"Lid's hammered shut, sir. I ain't sure." The stevedore wiped sweat from his forehead with a bandana. "But I heard a rumor. Toys made by darkies. They sell like hotcakes in London."

"Who'd have thought?" Icie Belle mused. "Slave toys for London's rich folks."

"Yep, we can't supply 'em fast enough." The stevedore resumed rolling the barrel up the gangplank.

The talk of toys made by slaves turned Bill's thoughts to Wilson and Malinda, the family's household slaves. They'd made a dash for freedom during the Kenansville cavalry raid back in July 1863. Bill knew nothing of their fate. They might be in New Bern working for the Yankee occupiers—or rotting in shallow graves.

Eyeing Bill, the stevedores rolling the barrels of toys up the gangplank were not seeing a Confederate lieutenant but a young businessman garbed in a frayed tailcoat and high-waist trousers. Bill knew many had a jaundiced view of him. That's what he wanted. Since leaving Richmond by train, Bill had worked undercover.

Small fingers reached out for his hand. "I'm not going to let you board the ship," Laura whined. "I want you to stay longer. Momma needs your help at the newspaper."

Icie Belle rested her head on her son's shoulder. "I feel the same way, Laura. I wish I could grow wings and fly to Richmond. I'd give Jeff Davis a tongue lashing."

Bill patted the straw hat atop Laura's head. "Franny threatened to storm the executive mansion and read him the riot act."

"Good for her," Icie Belle retorted. "We women rarely get a say in this war."

"Yes, no one listens to us," Laura agreed enthusiastically.

The others laughed. "Bill's going to Europe to look for a woman who has the ear of the president," Mark pointed out.

"True. President Davis listens to at least one woman besides his wife." Icie Belle gestured up at the gangplank. "I think it's time for you to board, Bill. They're about to draw up the gangway."

Frowning, Bill held a finger up to his lips. "Not so loud. Could be Yank spies lurking on the docks."

Bill shook Mark's hand and kissed Laura and his momma on their cheeks. "Wish me luck."

Sniffing, Icie Belle wiped a sleeve along her runny nose. "Deep down I know it's going to be a grand adventure for you." She eyed the blockade runner, a schooner bearing the name *Don*. "Beginning with this sleek ship."

Put bird wings on the *Don* and it might just rise from the water and fly like an eagle, Bill thought. The ship looked fast—and it was moored to one of the seaport's bollards.

Carpetbag in hand, Bill rearranged his pouch's shoulder strap, stepped onto the gangplank and headed up to the deck. From the top of the gangway, Bill could see the upper deck contained three tiers of bales. He figured the *Don* likely carried twelve hundred steam-pressed bales, each weighing five hundred. His father had once told him the profit was so great owners could afford to lose a vessel after two successful trips.

When a child, Bill loved models of sailing ships almost as much as toy locomotives. His papa helped him build them. They sat proudly on a bookshelf in his room until his later teen years when books replaced them. Malinda relocated the models to a chest in the attic.

None of his models looked anything like the *Don*. She was a long, low side-wheeler of six hundred tons with a slight frame, sharp and narrow. The *Don's* length ran nine times her beam. The British-built blockade runner sported feathering paddles and two raking telescopic funnels that could be lowered close to the deck. Her hull rose only a few feet out of the water. Gray paint made the *Don* hard to see at two hundred yards during the daylight. At night under a thick cloud cover...impossible. Even if a Yankee warship stumbled across her, the *Don's* turtle-back forward deck enabled the steamer to fly though a heavy sea. Not one ship in the U.S. Navy could catch her at full speed.

Noticing the carpetbag, a deckhand waved Bill aboard. Glancing back at the foot of Market Street, Bill waved to his momma, Mark and Laura. "Love you all. Momma, you're doing a wonderful job with the *Gazette*. Papa would be proud of you."

Sprinkles spattered his nose and cheeks. His momma, Mark and Laura were unfolding umbrellas. Inside his carpetbag, Bill's umbrella remained beyond his reach.

"Lieutenant Stamford I presume?"

"Captain Roberts?"

The *Don's* captain nodded. "Welcome aboard, Stamford." Roberts spoke in a refined British accent. "The rain has finally arrived. Splendid for us, a miserable inconvenience for the Yankees. We'll be cloaked by it when we make our dash."

As the sprinkles intensified, Bill dropped the carpetbag to the deck and reached into the pouch. "I hope my papers are in order." He handed the orders to the captain.

Roberts scrutinized them. "Your president speaks highly of you, Lieutenant. I'm to give you an alias for your time on the *Don* and in Liverpool and London. I've prepared identity papers for you." The captain reached into his jacket pocket and produced the folded documents. "Your name's Monty Keynton. You're a British merchant sailor. I've given you a hometown, parents and siblings—a life story that should satisfy curious bureaucrats. No one will bother you in Nassau or England." He handed President Davis's orders and the forged documents to Bill, who slipped them into the pouch. "Let me show you to your cabin. You're a lucky man, sir. No other passengers are on this run so you get the VIP cabin."

"I'm a bit jittery, Captain. Never tested my sea legs until now." Bill picked up the carpetbag.

Roberts took off his cap and shook it, scattering water droplets. "The Atlantic's a big ocean. It can handle some Stamford puke. Follow me. I'll show you to your cabin."

Crouched over, Roberts led Bill through the ship's bowels, maneuvering through a maze of cotton bales and crew and officer quarters. The captain stopped at a cabin door. Opening it, Roberts stepped into a tiny parlor furnished with a settee, chair and a table. He hurried through the parlor into a sleeping compartment. A sailor's outfit lay atop the bed.

Bill chuckled. "A sailing I will go."

"Change into your new duds, Seaman Keynton. Come up onto the deck and I'll have First Officer Witten show you some chores you can do while we get underway."

Unbuttoning his tailcoat, Bill draped it across the foot of the bed then unfastened his vest. "There were two jobs I wanted to try when I was a kid—locomotive engineer and seaman. Thanks to you, Captain, one's off the list."

"When we sprint for the open sea, we could come under the scrutiny of a telescope. They're looking for Confederate officers and civilians so they can pass on the information to their superiors. All we want them to see are sailors."

The *Don's* engines rumbled to life, shaking the vessel as Bill followed the captain onto the deck. "Witten!" Roberts shouted to the first officer. "Put our new sailor to work. Something he can master quickly."

Panting as a light rain peppered the deck, Bill helped draw in mooring rope. Sailors laughed as he struggled to coil the rope around a becket. "We've got ourselves a virgin flower boy," one hollered.

"Don't pay them mind," Witten told Bill. "They're just funning you." The ship shuddered. "Feel that? We're getting underway. Tug's taking us out into the river."

Bill took a last glance at the dock. Under their umbrellas, his momma and siblings were blowing kisses to him.

Under its own paddlewheel power, the *Don* steamed up the Cape Fear River past the big guns of Fort Fisher. Swaying on the unruly deck, Witten and Bill stood at the railing gazing at the east-side bank. Nothing could be seen, no lamp-lit windows of farmhouses, no lanterns bobbing from the doors of moving buggies. The rain-cloaked night was darker than the inside of a closed armoire.

Topped by a floppy slouch hat that did a decent job of holding off the raindrops, Witten sported the shaven look that left his cheeks pink. His owl eyes could be seen in lantern light that would be extinguished when the *Don* drew close to the mouth of the Cape Fear.

"It's so quiet," Bill observed. "I expected more of a racket from the engines."

"We've worked hard to make the *Don* invisible to Yankee eyes and ears." The wind muffled Witten's voice. It had picked up over the last minute or so. "Mostly it's ill luck that gets us into trouble. We keep records of the comings and goings of Union warships, but sometimes they cross us up. Like I said, can't do anything about bad luck."

Up in the crow's nest, a sailor kept his eyes fixed on the horizon looking for any telltale stacks and masts of Union gunships cruising off the mouth of the Cape Fear, beyond the guns of Fort Fisher. They were about to cruise out into the Atlantic.

Bill tightened his grip on the railing. Waiting to see if a Union gunboat had spotted them proved more nerve-wracking than huddling behind a breastwork on the night before battle. "They don't detect a runner often, eh?"

"Nope. Especially on a night like this." Witten signaled for the lanterns to go dark. "Into the breach." He cupped Bill's ear and put his mouth close. "Now it's a cat-and-mouse game."

"I don't smell smoke from the stacks." Mouth full of phlegm, Bill spit into the water.

"We're burning semi-bituminous Welsh coal. No lights and the binnacle and fireroom hatch are covered. Steam's being blown off under water."

The *Don* didn't steam straight out into the Atlantic. The pilot guided the vessel north along the seashore, hugging the beach. Although low in the water, the *Don* sliced effortlessly through the choppy sea. The ship kicked up spray that doused Bill, drenched already in pelting rain.

"I'm nervous as a farmer who sees a funnel cloud off in the distance." Bill felt the first mate's hand patting him on the back.

As a gust of wind prickled his face with rain, Bill sensed the *Don* tacking eastward into the Atlantic. He gritted his teeth to keep them from chattering.

"Well, we'll soon know if the *Don* and her crew are lucky this night."

"The Union fleet could be out there about to blow us to smithereens." Bill looked up at the crow's nest lookout, but couldn't see him.

"Are you a lucky man, Keynton?" Witten winked. "If we're seen and cornered, the boys will blame their bad luck on you. They'll toss you into the drink."

Bill sputtered, "You're kidding, right?"

"Aye, kidding. Even if a gunboat sees us, we'll outsprint them. No one can keep pace with the *Don*." Witten held up his right hand and let the wind-driven rain slap his palm. "It's letting up. Going to be only sprinkles soon."

The darkness along with the misty drizzle combined to get Bill's heart thumping. Anything could lurk inside the night shroud. His imagination ran amuck—sea monsters waiting to swallow the *Don*, half a dozen Lincoln warships ready to pummel the blockade runner until it settled on the ocean floor. Grimacing, Bill tamed his imagination. *Not nearly as bad as hearing Yankee guns in our rear.*

"I've been told you'll be pretending to be one of us when you reach our shore." Witten's words calmed Bill. "Let's hear your Limey accent."

"Damn the torpedoes! Full speed ahead!" Bill cringed at the sound of his atrocious accent.

"You're going to need more practice, lots of it. But we'll have you sounding like an Englishman before we dock at Nassau and you transfer to a merchantman."

"An Englishman worked for my father in his print shop when I was a boy. I pestered him until he agreed to teach me how to sound like a Tommy. I got quite good at it. He said I had a knack. I think I can get it back."

In the crow's nest high above Bill and Witten, the barrelman's voice emerged from the mist, "Enemy ship bearin' down. Two points abaft the port beam. Closin' fast."

Squinting, Bill scanned around the ship, trying to peel back the opaque sky. Nothing. Maybe the barrelman could see better through the drizzle.

"Damn bad luck!" Witten grumbled. "The game begins."

A Union ship emerged out of the gloom, a steam-powered gunboat plowing through the choppy seas. The enemy ship pitched and rolled through the rough water. Maybe two hundred yards. Way too close, and Bill said so. "He's got us!"

Witten offered up a sidesplitting laugh. "You're a nervous Nellie!"

Aboard the enemy ship, an officer with a telescope took a bead on them. Witten waved, then a swell washed over the Yankee officer, knocking him to the deck.

"Poor fella," Bill quipped, trying to act as nonchalant as Witten.

"Got to have some fun." Witten again slapped Bill on the back.

Smoke and fire belched from the barrel of a cannon aboard the gunboat. A boom echoed across the water's surface. An invisible shell whined through the night. Saltwater fountained twenty yards short of the *Don's* railing, splashing Bill and soaking the deck.

In the pilothouse, Captain Roberts screamed into his voicepipe, "Engine room, more steam!"

On the Yankee ship, another cannon roared. Its shell fell short too, the splash spraying Bill a second time. Bill tongued his lips and tasted the saltwater. The cannon fire took his thoughts back to the opening moments of the battle of Fredericksburg. "Sure different from a battlefield." The *Don* shuddered and picked up speed.

"You've seen the elephant, eh?" Witten stared straight ahead.

"Chancellorsville and Fredericksburg." Bill didn't mention his shrapnel wound.

"Steam! I need more steam!" Roberts pressed his mouth against the voicepipe. "Give me speed!"

Another shell plunged into the water, just ten yards from the railing.

Down in the ship's belly, the engines whined, pistons shrieking. The side paddle wheel groaned then screeched as it spun faster and faster, its blades pushing into the cold Atlantic. The drizzle tickled Bill's face; the wind rustled his hair as the *Don* raced through the water, outdistancing her pursuer.

"Be glad you're up here on deck and not down in the engine room," Witten said, his voice animated. "Hot work down there." One last cannonball, a parting shot, splashed well short of the *Don*. "We've won this one. Luck's on our side this night."

"Close call," Bill replied.

"Never in doubt. Maybe if the Union gunboat had been blocking us. But chasing us? Impossible."

"Not even a lucky cannon shot?"

"Not on this night. Three shots, three misses. They'll say we were a ghost ship."

"Instead of the *Don*, the *Gray Ghost*?"

"Changing names would bring bad luck. I'll tell you what…I'll work with you on that atrocious accent of yours. When we dock in Nassau, you'll be spouting British slang with the best of us."

"Thank you." With his elation and fear tucked away in the past, Bill felt flutters in his belly. He leaned over the railing and puked.

"Queasy, eh?"

"A little."

"Most times we breeze to Nassau without any troubles. I guess the Yanks wanted to make your first blockade run memorable."

"I don't think I've the makings of a sailor." Bill offered a crooked smile.

"For the men down in the engine room, shoveling coal into the boilers is as close as they're ever going to get to being a sailor." Witten pushed himself away from the railing. "I've got to leave you. My advice for rest of the voyage to Nassau? Let your wanderlust take over. See how the *Don* works then get some sleep. Hopefully, there'll be blue sky when you wake up."

Bill liked Witten's advice. Making his way along the topsy-turvy deck, he wobbled past sailors working on ropes. Once below deck, he peeked into the engine room. The bare-chested men shoveling coal into the boilers reminded Bill of the firemen keeping locomotive boilers stoked. On the way to his cabin, Bill craned his neck for a look at the sailors' berths, bunks and hammocks crammed together. The hut he called home during the winter at Fredericksburg was more spacious.

Self-guided tour finished, Bill trudged bent over to his own cabin. He sidled to his carpetbag and drew out a Charles Dickens' novel, *A Tale of Two Cities*. Sprawling on the bed, he lit a wall lamp and read the first page before letting the novel fall to his belly. He couldn't concentrate. Bill's first sea voyage had nearly been a catastrophe in spite of Witten's reassurances. Maybe the first mate was right. Blockade running was a matter of luck. Hopefully, the luck would hold up for rest of the voyage to Nassau, the capital of the British Bahamas. Bill corrected himself. The luck would need to continue through the loading of cotton, toys and whatnot aboard the British merchantman and during the trip from Nassau to Liverpool.

In the morning, he intended to rise early and help with mopping the deck and maybe some painting. He picked up the Dickens novel and tried to read the second page. He never got past the third paragraph. Sleep proved more tempting.

Twenty-five

A Train Ride to London

Dressed as a British merchant sailor, Bill Stamford leaned on the railing of the *S.S. Sirius* and watched stevedores unload the first of hundreds of pressed bales of cotton and transport them to a Manchester New Quay Company warehouse just off the Georges Dock. Nearby, Liverpool's domed custom house rose above the four-story warehouses. At the south end of Prince's Dock, sailors from the *Sirius* made their way up a pier into a large ship that sported a steeple, not a foremast.

A merchant sailor Bill had come to know during the voyage from Nassau, Trevor Norman, joined him at the railing. "It's not a ship. It's the Seaman's Church. Sailors go aboard ter praise the Lord and fank him for a safe voyage across the Atlantic."

"I should pay the church a visit." Bill felt the sun caress his face. First time in days. But at least no rain, not like the *Don's* sprint from Wilmington. While hectic, the blockade runner managed to outrace the Union gunboats and steamed on to Nassau without incident. "The Lord has been good ter me. Pro'ected me durin' two battles and now this voyage." He didn't tell Trevor the Lord hadn't protected him from a shell fragment that burned its way into his lower back. Or told him about the Lord's unwanted halo gift. At least he'd not seen one since a manifestation around that little girl back in Richmond.

"Ya're a strange fellow, Keynton. Traveled ter America ter fight with the rebels. Now ya're a merchant sailor. Ya've had a life'ime of adven'urin' for one so young." Trevor stared at the Liverpool skyline.

"I con'racted for just this voyage, so I'll soon be a chap again." Bill followed Trevor's gaze to a magnificent Roman-style building that outshone any building found in Richmond or Washington, D.C. "Goin' ter look for a bookstore job in London. It'll tide me over while I wri'e a book about me adven'ures as a Confederate soldier."

He'd taken some liberties with the persona Captain Roberts had prepared for him. Now Bill intended to discard his sailor outfit and rely on the sack suit tucked in the carpetbag. He'd take a train to London and secure a job with a bookshop that sold Rose's book on her spy adventures. *My Imprisonment and the First Year of Abolition Rule at Washington* was a big seller in London. The sailor persona got Bill across the Atlantic. Now it was time for another guise.

Trevor rapped the railing as he laughed. "What a coincidence. That buildin' with the Roman columns, that's the Free Library on William Brown Street. Funny I should be eyein' the library just as ya tell me ya want a book job."

"If a man were ter believe in signs, that would be a for'uitous one, wouldn't ya say?" With halos in his mind again, Bill allowed himself a private chuckle. *Are you, Lord, telling me I'm free of them?*

"The rail sta'ion for London's out near the library," Trevor spoke up after Bill sent his query heavenward. "Ya'll pass the new Duke of Welling'on Monument on the way. The hero's still bound up in scaffoldin'. Must feel a mite cooped up." The Englishman shifted his gaze back to the chapel ship. "I'm goin' ter do some prayin'. Care ter join me?"

"Than's for the invite, Trevor, but I want ter get ter the train sta'ion and check the schedule. I'm eagah to get ter London and start wri'in' me book. Goin' ter be a dinger."

Trevor shook Bill's hand. "Good luck, sailuh and soldier. Later, I'll be gettin' a room at the Adelphi Ho'el and then quaffin' a few mugs of ale. I'd love for ya ter join me, if the train schedule allows."

"Is that likely?"

"Probably not. Trains are runnin' all the time. Any case, the invi'ation's open, mate."

"If I see I've a two-hour or longer wait, I might snare a Hansom and pay ya a visit. Not a promise. A possibility."

Dozens of Hansom cabs waited dockside ready to take packet passengers and merchant sailors to taverns, dramshops, pubs, inns, flophouses, hotels and brothels. Bill had never seen so many in his life. The street along the piers teemed with them. Hailing one, he climbed aboard. The cabman opened the trapdoor, emitting an odor of tobacco and beer. "Des'ination, mate?"

"The Liverpool ter London Rail Sta'ion." Bill let his back settle comfortably against the backrest. Last spring and summer such a simple body maneuver was unthinkable. The wound in his back, now a scar, would have howled.

On the boardwalk near Bill's cab, two stevedores in suspiciously clean clothes gave him the onceover before they stumbled through the doorway of the Old Roan pub. Bill wondered: *Yankee spies*? Had they heard him and questioned the authenticity of his accent? He must have passed their critique or they wouldn't have entered the pub. Then again, maybe he was imagining things.

Bill's cab shared the roads with other Hansoms, coaches and carriages, so many they clogged the streets and brought traffic to a near-stop. Near the Adelphi Hotel, Bill's cabman diverted his Hansom away from a horsecar tram rolling along its tracks.

The London and North Western Railway Station on Lime Street lay six blocks beyond the grand library and the other majestic buildings, all five- and six-stories that dwarfed anything in Richmond. Bill expected the rail station to look similar to the ones in Richmond. He was wrong. The station lay under a huge curved roof of iron that offered rain and snow protection to boarding and departing passengers. All the Richmond depots would fit easily under it.

Bill paid the fare, and carpetbag in hand, strolled through the station's front entryway. Although he knew what to expect, Bill still found himself stunned by the sheer size of the station, a wait area ten times the size of any in Richmond, a wing of offices, a schedule board that took up a wall, even a restaurant.

At the schedule board, he learned the next train wouldn't leave for London for an hour. Not enough time to meet up with Trevor, but sufficient to eat a meal in the restaurant. Bill bought a ticket to London, dipping into his stash of British money he'd been carrying in his wallet since leaving Richmond. A waitress was still scrubbing the restaurant's only vacant table when Bill sat in one of the chairs.

"I'll be back with a spot of tea for ya, gent." She closed her wrinkled hands around the damp washrag. "Our special today is our world-famous s'eak and ale pie." She was obviously a transplant from London.

"World famous, eh?" Bill said in the London cockney accent he'd been working on diligently since leaving Richmond. "How can I say no? I must have a bite." He patted his carpetbag, making sure it still sat beside his foot.

"I've served it ter the Prince of Wales and Sir John Lawrence, viceroy of India." The woman winked.

"Want some company?" The voice with a New England accent belonged to a gentleman passing near Bill's table.

The New Englander plopped down in the seat across from Bill before he could answer. Bill's eyes ballooned at the sight of the fellow, a well-dressed, thirtyish man with wild curls and a thin mustache. Those two stevedores eyeing him as he stepped into the Hansom? This chap had been one of them, no longer in his work clothes but in a sack suit. Bill's mind shrieked: *Yankee spy! Be careful.* Bill brushed his sailor jacket where a concealed holster held a derringer.

"Please do." Bill acted nonchalant outwardly. *Don't foul up your accent! Make Witten proud.*

"I saw you step off the *Sirius*. One of the crew told me you'd been a deckhand aboard the blockade runner *Don*."

Bill had practiced his story over and over. Now he had to make it real to this New Englander. "Tryin' ter get back to me home. Figured I'd help out on the *Don* and the *Sirius*. Instead of gettin' shanghaied, I volunteered and worked for me passage."

"The *Don* makes runs to Wilmington, right?" The New Englander paused when the waitress returned to Bill's table with the tea and steak pie. "I'll have what my friend ordered."

"Aye, ter and from Wilmington. The *Don's* British built and manned by British sailors." Bill tasted the meat pie. "Aye, righ'ly world renowned," he told the waitress.

"Before the war I did business in Wilmington. Hear the conditions are frightful nowadays."

The New Englander was trawling, seeing what could be learned about conditions in Wilmington and the rest of the Tar Heel state. Maybe the chap believed Bill to be a British subject. Bill hoped so. Witten had near-tortured him to strip all the imperfections from his London accent. Bill didn't want to end up dead in some back alley, victim of a dreadful accent.

Bill ogled the waitress as she returned to the kitchen, then jibed, "I don't know about frigh'ful. The whorehouses were fine. Yellow fever's over, and the bro'hel doves were fightin' over me. It's a fizzin' town for givin' a man's nebuchadnezzar a spor'in' workout."

"Name's Sydney Shane from Stockbridge, Massachusetts. I'm in Liverpool doing some scouting for a Bay State steamship company. From what I read in the *Boston Evening Transcript*, the blockade's strangling the South's economy. Except for the brothels." Sydney grinned. "The London papers say the same. The war can't last much longer unless the South gets help from foreign governments."

"Me sen'iments as well." Not a lie, Bill acknowledged to himself. The war was no longer winnable.

"What brought you to these fair shores?"

"The war. Volun'eered for a ninety-day enlis'ment with a Tar Heel regiment. Wanted ter see the war close-up. I plan ter write a book about the men doin' the fightin'. Too much written about the generals and colonels, not enough about the sergean's, corporals and priva'es."

"You're crazy...I don't even know your name."

"Monty Keynton."

"Well, Monty, I'm sitting out the war. Never felt strong enough for Lincoln and the Yankee cause to fight in the ranks. What do I care about emancipating ignorant darkies down in Richmond, Wilmington, Charleston and New Orleans? I'm over here making my company and myself rich. Gonna to be sitting pretty when Lincoln finally wins the war."

Sydney's story sounded plausible. Bill didn't believe a word. Sydney was a Yankee spy curious about a sailor getting into a Hansom and going to the London and North Western Railway Station. Hopefully, Sydney bought Bill's story. He'd know soon enough—if Bill saw the fellow or his companion in London. Sadly, the derringer might become necessary.

"Ya goin' ter London?" Bill wondered if he would have to listen to the New Englander's rambling all the way to the capital city.

"Nope. Heading up to Edinburgh. Don't know when I'll get back to the New World. It'll be after the war, whatever the outcome. I do like being an expatriate. No discombobulating issues like slavery to ruin people's lives here."

The train to London—the *Fair Maid*—arrived on time, something unheard in the Confederacy. Bill's passenger carriage looked new, no peeling paint or frayed seat cushions. He slid his carpetbag under the seat in front of him and gazed out the window at folks waving goodbye to loved ones. No goodbyes sent his way and it made him sad. He missed Franny.

After the locomotive chugged away from the rail station, there was no stopping for work crews repairing track. Bill had to admit it was comforting not to see wounded soldiers or Home Guard militiamen armed with flintlocks aboard the passenger carriage. Children ran up and down the aisle, dolls and toy locomotives clasped in their hands. A mother screeched, "Tommy and Sally, sit down!"

The *Fair Maid* rode the rails past majestic buildings. Beyond the city center, the cottages of Everton swarmed up the hillsides. In the countryside, the *Fair Maid* passed alongside the gardens of

Knowsley Park. No longer running amuck in the aisle, children sat on their fathers' laps and gaped out the windows.

Just a few decades earlier, folks went no faster than a horse could pull a buggy. Now the *Fair Maid* traveled at an amazing speed of sixty miles per hour, racing by villages that were old in the Thirteenth Century and manor houses that made Virginia plantations look like cottages. And not one sign of war. Young men were out in the fields, not in winter camps. Bill didn't see one meadow or woods shredded by cannon fire and no hastily dug graves.

The London and North Western Railway symbolized British power. There was nothing like it in the United States or the Confederacy. Britain stood atop the world, Europe's greatest power. If the Confederacy gained its independence, both the CSA and the USA might come to regret dividing the country, Bill suspected. Britain would dominate the two nations, especially with Canada to the north. Rather than become the pawns of Britain and France, the Confederacy and the United States might very well decide to reunite sometime in the early twentieth century—if and when the CSA discarded slavery.

Closing his eyes as sunlight burned away the last of the cloud cover and bathed his window seat, Bill had almost fallen asleep when a ginger-haired girl no more than ten plopped into the seat beside him. "Hey, sailuh, do ya live in Liverpool?"

In the row directly behind Bill, the girl's momma rebuked her, "Don't bother the bloke, Shirley. Can't ya see he's tryin' ter sleep?"

"Just bein' friendly, Mum. A girl can fiddle with her dolls only so long."

"No problem, ma'am," Bill told the girl's mother. "I've a sister her age."

The girl leaned closer. "Really? What's her name?"

"Laura. She's younger than ya. Two years maybe. Your name?"

"Shirley. We're on the way ter London ter see Granny and Gramps. He's a carriage maker. He built one for the queen."

"A fairytale carriage?"

Shirley jumped up and down in the middle seat. "Gold all over it. I haven't seen it in person, though. Gramps showed me a daguerreo'ype. Queen Victoria sat in it."

"Before he went ter Heaven, me gramps built sailin' ships," Bill lied.

"That's why ya're a sailuh?"

"Aye, matey."

She giggled at his pirate phrasing. "Me gramps built a ship in a bottle fer me. Where did your ship come from, mister?"

"America."

Her eyes lit up. "I've cousins who live in New York City. In a tenement. They want ter move ter Iowa and live on a farm. But there's a war goin' on, and they can't do anyfing until their daddy comes home. He's a Union soldier."

Bill hoped the man would get back to his family alive and in one piece. And he hoped and prayed they'd take that journey to Iowa.

"Me ship brought cotton ter Liverpool. Very dangerous work, Shirley. The Yanks tried ter stop us. Our brave cap'ain outfoxed fem, though."

The girl's momma joined them in the aisle seat. "I hope Shirley's not causin' ya any grief. She's a prattler."

"He just came from the war in America," Shirley explained.

"In my sister's last letter, she blames the blockade runners for lettin' the war drag on." Shirley's mom grimaced. "I pity everyone in America."

"I'm just tryin' ter make some smackers, ma'am. A couple of runs and I'll be set for life."

"Unless Lincoln's Navy sinks your ship. Then what? Way too many people have died in that awful war." Crossing her arms, she pressed them against her chest.

Shirley made a sourpuss face. "I like the sailuh. He's nice."

The woman ruffled her daughter's hair. "I know, darlin'." She tapped Bill's arm. "I'm sorry, sir. I'm blamin' ya for that war. That's not right."

There were too many British families with loved ones living in Yankee country who opposed slavery and supported Lincoln's war aims. "The war can't last much longer," Bill predicted. "The Confederacy's worn out. Mothers don't want their sons drafted."

The rest of Bill's ride went smoothly with Shirley mostly leaving him alone so he could window watch as the train approached London. The *Fair Maid* steamed into the Great Hall, the terminal of the London and North Western Railway. Architects throughout Europe considered the station one of the world's magnificent buildings. Bill couldn't believe the size of the station—at least four times larger than the one in Liverpool. He'd not taken a train to New York City, but he imagined this Great Hall had to be at least twice the size of the New York & Harlem's railroad station at Tryon Row. The crowds inside the terminal moved briskly along the track platforms, husbands in the lead, wives holding their children's hands, businessmen reading newspapers. Bill noticed a few sailors. Nonetheless, he couldn't wait to change into his sack suit.

"I'll be prayin' for ya, sir, if ya decide to make another blockade run." Shirley's momma grabbed her daughter's hand and pulled her toward the passenger carriage's exit. Once away from the rail station, Bill craned his neck, counting the stories of a nearby hotel—seven of them. He decided he'd secure a room and rethink his strategy for locating Rose. He started with a purchase of the *Daily Telegraph*. Maybe the society section had something about her. Newspaper in one hand, carpetbag in the other, Bill headed for the Great Hall Hotel.

Twenty-six

The Search for Rose Begins

Clad only in longjohns, Bill moseyed from his bed to a walnut rocking chair where he sat and wiggled his toes. He stretched his arms above his head and sighed, happy with his accommodations in the Great Hall Hotel. Bill reached for the day-old newspaper on a side table between the bed and the rocking chair. He let it settle on his lap, the front page above the fold visible. The date of the *Daily Telegraph* caught his eye—Thursday, March 31, 1864. After a long and arduous journey by sea and rail, Bill had reached his destination. Now his detective work would begin. *Rose, where are you?*

Even with his room's window closed, Bill could hear train whistles blaring. The hotel stood a stone's throw from the Great Hall railway station, one of the busiest in Europe. A cold draught from the window prickled his exposed skin in goosebumps. Standing, he stepped to the stove, fed a log into its firebox and stoked the flames with a poker. When warm, Bill trod to the window. Just eight in the morning, and people already flocked into and out of the station's double-door entrance. The sight made him think of Shirley, the young girl who talked his ear off on the train trip from Liverpool to London.

May you have a grand time visiting your gramps. And may your aunt in New York City not become a widow. May she and her Union veteran husband celebrate many Iowa Fourths of July. If spoken aloud back in Richmond, such sentiments would get angry retorts from many fellow officers. Bill didn't care. Too many men had died on both sides.

Bill settled his gaze on an alleyway between two four-story railroad office buildings. He squinted, trying to pierce through the morning gloom, looking for those who might lurk in the alley. Had the New Englander, Sydney Shane, followed him to London and now skulked in the alley hoping to spy on Bill's doings? Bill squinted, but the gloom stayed impenetrable. No doubt Yankee and Confederate spies fought the war in the alleys of London and Paris, their weapons pistols and daggers.

He turned away from the window. Bill needed to stay focused on President Davis's orders—find Rose. His gaze wandered back to the *Telegraph* on the rocking chair. The night before he'd dissected the society pages and found one reference to Rose in a *London After Dark* column. She'd been seen on the hand of a pro-Lincoln English politician at the Alhambra music hall on Leicester Square— three days before. Nothing from the columnist on where Rose might appear in the next day or two. It would take more detective work to get the coded message to Rose. Even so, he had a lead: Rose liked the theatre.

Suddenly, a front-page headline jumped out at him, one he had stupidly skipped over, instead going to the society pages. Even standing at the window, he couldn't miss the words: Lincoln Names Grant General-In-Chief. Racing back to the rocking chair, he scooped up the newspaper and scanned the lead and follow-up paragraphs. Although General Meade would stay in command of the Army of the Potomac, Grant would make his headquarters with Lincoln's eastern army.

Bill plunked down in the rocking chair and let the newspaper slide off his knees to the floor. *Grant's with the Army of the Potomac?* Frowning, Bill picked up the newspaper and tossed it onto the bed. *That man refuses to retreat. God help the South.* And here stood Bill in London, not Richmond where he might be able to do some good. *Help Rose gain British support for the South? Too late, damn it!*

What choice did Bill have? The president wanted him to find Rose, so he would. First, though, he dressed in his sack suit for the first time since Wilmington and went downstairs to taste the hotel restaurant's morning fare. He bought the standard breakfast. When the plate arrived, Bill gulped in astonishment at the sight of bacon, eggs, sausage, baked beans, fried tomatoes and mushrooms, toasted bread and black pudding. A mug of ale accompanied the meal.

This time no one with a Yankee accent joined him. Maybe the alley hadn't concealed a Lincoln man sneaking peeks at the rail-station courtyard. For most of the war Bill had been a lowly private. He didn't come from one of the South's patrician families. The Union spies had given him the once-over and dismissed him from their thoughts—or so he hoped.

As he ate the meal, Bill couldn't help but think of Franny, his mother, Mark and Laura. Across the Atlantic, they were eating cornbread and salt pork. The breakfast feast taught Bill a fundamental truth about human nature. He could come to immensely enjoy life in London far from the deprivations of war. And he realized something else—London's allure would only get more seductive the longer he stayed. As Franny knew, he could easily be seduced.

Before returning to his room, Bill bought the latest edition of the *Telegraph* and planted himself on a sofa in the hotel's lobby. He'd intended to take a look at the *London After Dark* column, but a strawberry blonde beauty in the latest French-style gown usurped his attention. Draped on the arm of a British Army officer sporting a musketeer mustache, the young lady purred to her gentleman, "You must tell me all about your time in India." Her accent surprised Bill. French, spoken in a coquettish manner. Her dress shocked him even more.

Designed to allow its wearer to laugh at priggish mothers and fathers and pompous preachers, the peach-and-white-striped linen dress clung scandalously to the woman's hips and legs. The décolletage featured a plunging neckline that revealed the upper portion of the woman's breasts. He'd only seen such décolletages pictured on risqué playing cards some soldiers had purchased in a New Orleans curio shop.

A dandified gent stopped next to Bill's sofa and admired the French woman. "I've read of this new French style, but it's the first time I've actually seen a lass wearing one," he told Bill as he took a seat. "The *Telegraph* calls it a tea dress. It's meant to be anti-fashion. No crinoline. No machine sewing. All hand embroidered. It's the rage in literary and artistic circles."

"So the French lass's an author or painter?" Bill nearly fell back into his Tar Heel accent, but caught his mistake before doing any damage. *Damn, that was close.*

"She wants us to think so. Maybe she is, maybe she isn't. I don't recognize her. She's wearing the tea dress to shock wives—and to let the officer know she's willing to let him tip the velvet."

"I'm just back from America. Went over ter see what the war's all about. The prudes overseein' Richmond balls would faint dead away if they saw their daugh'ers wearin' that dress."

"Aye, tea dresses are a full-out assault on the guardians of vir'ue." The gent grinned. "She probably dinks she should have the right to vote." The Englishman had worked hard to surmount his childhood cockney accent, but once in a while it crept back into his speech.

"My wife knows more about politics than most of me mates." Bill watched the French woman and her beau leave the hotel. The officer hooked his arm around her waist and enjoyed the benefits of no crinoline interfering with hip-to-hip joining. "I favor grantin' the vote ter the fairer sex."

"I predict they'll get the vote when the hemlines rise above their knees." He rose to his feet. "Nice meeting someone else who favors tea dresses." The dandy bowed then headed up the stairway.

No longer inundated with distractions, Bill opened the latest *Telegraph* and scanned the front page headlines. Prussian forces were fighting Danish troops in the Duchy of Schleswig. *Where in tarnation is the Duchy of Schleswig?* He rolled his eyes and turned to the society pages.

Finally, some good news. A copyeditor had included Rose's name in a headline about a garden party held by Queen Victoria. One news item drew extra curiosity: "Famed Confederate spy Rose Greenhow, the toast of London, has recently been seen on the arm of John Arthur Roebuck, the Liberal MP from Sheffield. The lovebirds are quite the couple. They've been seen eating dessert at the Albemarle restaurant in the Brown Hotel, sharing the same spoon. Later, the sweethearts held hands in the Charing Cross Theatre watching *Lady Audley's Secret*. Those in the know say that over the last two months Rose has been seen at Roebuck's townhouse more often than at the Brown Hotel where she has her place of residence, not just during daylight but at night as well. Can an engagement be far off for the beautiful Rose and London's most handsome bachelor?"

Roebuck? Bill knew that name. His father had run a *Charleston Mercury* article in the *Gazette,* and had caught an embarrassing misspelling during proofing. Somehow the Englishman's last name had become Robuck. "Damned embarrassing," Bill's papa had said, slapping the side of his noggin. "Roebuck's the Confederacy best friend in the House of Commons. He spearheaded a push to get the British government to recognize the Confederacy." Those were his father's exact words. Odd that Bill remembered them so clearly.

No wonder President Davis sent Bill across the Atlantic to find Rose. She was romancing the wrong Englishman. Her job was to cozy up to one of Lincoln's allies, not someone already in Davis's pocket. In harsher terms, Rose was seducing the wrong man. The president's coded message must be a blistering rebuke. With Grant commanding the Union armies, time was running out for the Confederacy, and Rose was warming the bed of a CSA sympathizer, not a man who could induce Lincoln to accept a negotiated peace treaty.

Roebuck's motion to officially recognize the independence of the Confederacy had failed. Roebuck might be good in bed, but he couldn't overcome Britain's reluctance to recognize the CSA. Too much to lose...the U.S. grain supply, potential loss of Canada, a rise in tariffs, angering pro-Union working class Brits—and maybe a war with the United States.

Bill understood his mission. He must set Rose Greenhow straight. She needed to win the heart and arbor vitae of a Lincoln man. Her beano times were about to end.

He'd pick a theatre premiering a new play and lurk there for the next several nights, anticipating Rose would want to see the performance. He flipped through more pages until he found the theatre listings. Bill settled on the Haymarket Theatre, unveiling a new play with the title *A Virginia Slave Seeks the North Star*. The provocative title would prove irresistible to Rose.

His stomach filled with the best breakfast since before the war, his heart yearning to experience adventure, Bill needed to decide how he would spend the rest of the morning and the afternoon. His theatre escapades wouldn't happen until the evening. Putting aside the *Telegraph*, Bill moseyed over to one of the lobby's windows and eyed a line of Hansoms alongside the hotel. He'd flag down one of them and tell the cabman to take him to the nearest bookstore. Later he'd walk back to the hotel, and if he noticed a gentlemen's emporium, he'd step inside and purchase a light-colored dapper suit and a bowler hat. At the Haymarket Theatre, he'd be one of the swells, a gentleman who'd be noticed by all the ladies with follow-me-lads curls hanging over their shoulders.

A thought intruded as Bill made his way to the hotel lobby: Rose might be in a heap of trouble with President Davis, but at least the reviled halo hadn't claimed her.

Twenty-seven

An Old Friend Greets Bill

Bill had serious misgivings. He decided his pouch might prove too tempting for any Union spies who might be tailing him—or even a run-of-the-mill bag snatcher. The president's letter to Rose lay tucked inside his suit pocket, enveloped and neatly folded. The letter felt safe next to his heart.

Out near the cherub fountain in front of the Great Hall Hotel, Bill waved to a Hansom cabman. "Take me ter a bookshop?" he shouted over the din of locomotive whistles blaring from the nearby rail station.

"Aye. Climb aboard," the cabman yelled back.

Under the mostly clear sky, sweat trickled down Bill's chest as he hurried to the Hansom. "I'm not familiar with the area. Any within five or six blocks?"

"Author Attic's closest. No train whistles. Just a doorbell tinklin' when people come and go. Me Gertie loves the place."

"Your wife?"

"Aye, best cook in London."

"Well, if your Gertie likes Author Attic, then let's go see it." Bill clambered aboard the passenger compartment.

The trapdoor opened above Bill's head. "There's the quick way and the pic'uresque way," the cabman said. "The lengthier one costs a bit more, but it's worth it."

"Worth it? Why?" Bill loved how easily he now slipped into the London accent.

"I'll take ya through Vic'oria Park. It has some splendid carriage paths."

Leaning forward, Bill craned his neck and looked skyward. "Grand day, not cold, not hot, perfect for a ride through Vic'oria Park."

The Hansom jerked into motion. The cab shared the congested street with horse-drawn buses, carriages, freight wagons and other Hansoms. Bill's cab crawled along...he swore a snail passed them. Working-class women strolled the pavements along both sides of the cobbled road, some pushing wicker baby carriages, others carrying baskets filled with foodstuffs. Not one nanny in sight. Although plain bonnets encased their hair, the women were obviously pretty, clothed in practical cotton dresses dyed light blue or green. A few added embellishments like wide pagoda sleeves. One noticed Bill eyeing her and stuck out her tongue.

The street curved slightly. Ahead, where it straightened once more, Bill could make out parkland. The trapdoor opened. "Vic'oria Park."

The Hansom wheeled onto a gravel carriage road that meandered through the park, passing through a copse of chestnuts, elms and maples. Strollers hugged the pathway edge. A dandy and his sweetheart, riding two-wheeled boneshakers, pedaled past the cab. Bill found the park charming except for the low-floating coal clouds drifting over the grounds. Most Londoners, he guessed, cooked and heated their homes with coal fires, the wealthy affording the luxury of gas-lit lamps.

The cabman kept the trapdoor open and gave Bill a running commentary. "The park's officially Vic'oria Park, but East-Side blokes call it the People's Park. It's for folks like me and Gertie. No 'oity-toity types...they keep ter Hyde Park. They think we'll sully them."

"I've no patience for bighead toffs. Name's Monty Keynton." Bill maneuvered his arm up through the trapdoor, and the cabman shook it.

"I'm Jack. Jack Longbottom. Ya like our park?"

Something back among the trees snared Bill's gaze, delaying his response. He squinted, getting a look at what appeared to be an alcove for strollers. "Aye, Jack. There's somethin' in the trees. See it?"

The cabman laughed. "Indeed. It's a place ter escape the rain. It was built from fragments of the old London Bridge, demolished thirty years ago. Popular with the fillies and foals."

The Hansom skirted around a lake. Bill's eyes widened in surprise at what dominated an island in the body of water—a Chinese pagoda. "Sure didn't expect ter see that thing."

"I thought ya were a Londoner." Jack's voice was tinged with suspicion. "Ya sure don't know nuttin' about Vic'oria Park."

Bill silently cursed his stupidity. He needed a credible explanation for his ignorance. "I've lived in Canada since age ten. When the war broke out, I became a war correspondent with the *Montreal Gazette* and traveled with General Lee's Army of Northern Virginia. Now I'm back in London hopin' ter find a publisher for a book on the war. I don't have many memories of London. Been gone too many years."

"Canada, eh? I'd like ter go there or maybe even New England once the war's over. Fancy a fresh start, I do."

Jack wheeled his cab back onto the street, slipping in behind a horse-drawn bus overflowing with working men. Bill heard the trapdoor shut. Jack's commentary had ended. With the parkland far behind him, Bill abruptly felt overwhelmed by the sights, sounds and smells of London. At the rail station and hotel, he'd contended with the familiar smells and sounds of locomotives. This was different. Even with the contraptions for catching horse droppings, the street smells were horrendous. Drunks lay in alleys, the smell of puke strong on their coats and shirts. The pavement stank of chamber pots and the sour riverbank mud of the Thames.

The Hansom lurched to the right, flinging Bill against the cab's wall. By the time he scooted back to the center, the cab had stopped in front of the Author Attic. The trapdoor opened. "Sorry for the rough stop. Needed ter get the spot ahead of a carriage. That will be twelve pence. Good luck on that war book of yours. Should I wait for ya?"

"No, Jack. I'm goin' ter walk back to the hotel."

Bill went to the display window and let his eyes feast on the books showcased. They were mostly British, but there were a few Americans, all Yanks except for Poe. The cover of one—knights battling on horseback—reminded him of how much he'd changed since donning Confederate gray. Sir Walter Scott's *Ivanhoe* no longer was a favorite. The one next to it, Mary Shelley's *Frankenstein,* was the book he must purchase. The unending war stalked him like a relentless monster eager to rip apart what little remained of his innocence. Yes, he'd buy the novel and read a few pages every night before extinguishing the oil lamp.

So many fine books, but he could afford only one more besides *Frankenstein.* Jane Austen's *Emma*? That one didn't tug at his heartstrings. Or Anthony Trollope's *Barchester Towers* and Charlotte Bronte's *The Professor.* Bill almost decided on Dickens' *Great Expectations*, but then noticed George Eliot's *The Mill on the Floss.* Franny adored Eliot and her novels. Bill had never read one. Eliot, born Mary Anne Evans, shocked society. A radical and agitator, she flaunted society's suffocating courtship rules. Eliot slept with married men. No doubt Eliot prowled inside Franny's mind when she lured Bill to the Yerby Plantation overseer cottage for a night of lovemaking. Franny had been engaged to another at the time. Bill would buy *The Mill on the Floss* and see why Franny yearned to pattern her life after Eliot.

His hand on the doorknob, Bill almost opened the bookshop's door, but let go and sidled closer to two American books that had escaped his attention. Both dealt with the bugaboo Confederate politicians were loath to even debate—permitting slaves to serve in Southern armies. The most famous—Harriet Beecher Stowe's *Uncle Tom's Cabin*. The other featured a bright red front cover and the title *Incidents in the Life of a Slave Girl*. Tempted to buy them, Bill shook his head, sighing at his cowardice. He'd have to leave them behind when he returned to Richmond. His disillusionment with the war would have to remain a secret shared only with Franny.

Avoiding further distraction, Bill entered the bookshop. He edged past two women, a fortyish mother and her twenty-something daughter who held the hand of a toddler. Hovering over a round table, the ladies were debating whether or not to buy London's latest bestseller.

"It's a good adventure story," the younger one insisted.

"If ya buy it, then I'll buy *Incidents in the Life of a Slave Girl*," the older woman snapped. "I don't approve of her or her support for slavery."

The toddler tugged on his grandmother's dress. "Granny, Momma says the Yanks put the lovely lady in prison."

Bill joined the women at the table, getting a closer look at the subject of their disagreement. Thickheaded again, he should have known. A dozen books lay on the table, all having the same title, *My Imprisonment and The First Year of Abolition Rule at Washington*. Rose was the bestselling author.

He picked up a copy and thumbed through the pages. "I understand Rose Greenhow's in London gallivantin' from theater ter theater and music hall ter music hall." Bill handed Rose's book to the young mother. "I overhead ya, ma'am. So ya're goin' ter buy the book and help Rose raise money for the Confederate war effort?"

The middle-aged woman groaned. "My daughter's headstrong. The more I complain, the more determined she becomes ter add it to our library."

"Aye, I'm going to buy the book." A wicked smile creased the young mother's mouth.

"Bill! Bill Stamford!"

Hearing his name jarred him. Bill knew that voice. His legs turned rubbery. He gripped the table with both hands. His breathing rapid, Bill swung his gaze to the woman who'd shouted out his name.

Becky Powell, her brown hair cropped short in a boy's haircut, clad in a man's blue plaid pants and a gold vest, tore toward him. "Good Lord! It's you!" Launching herself, she leaped into Bill's arms and spattered kisses on his lips, chin, cheeks, even the end of his nose.

He tried hard to resist her charms, but weakened and returned the kisses. Overcome by guilt, Bill pushed her away. "I'm married, Becky."

In shock, he realized he'd lost his cockney accent.

"I know. But who cares, Bill. I'm a bohemian."

Frowning, he nodded toward the two women and the toddler. "Becky! Remember where we're at."

An amused look on her face, Becky glanced at the younger woman. "Better cover your child's ears." She regarded Bill. "I dress as I like. I make love whenever I like and I've missed you. I left my fiancé at home." She ran her fingers along his lips and grinned lasciviously.

He damned himself for letting her fingers caress his lips. He felt his penis engorge and press against his pants. Gritting his teeth, he tamped down his desire for her.

The older woman and her daughter were gaping.

"An old friend," he told them.

"I can see." The older woman skewed her face into a disapproving look.

Bill hadn't seen Becky since the night in the Wilmington hotel room where they'd made love. He'd asked her to marry him and she'd refused. They went their separate ways, he into the arms of Franny, and Becky to Europe as Rose's private secretary. Becky hated the war, hated all the killing, hated the deprivations, hated how the fighting had corrupted the South's soul. So she fled the war and Bill.

"I will not deceive Franny." Crossing his arms against his chest, he returned to the cockney accent, hoping Becky would put two-and-two together.

"Your loss." She laughed at the sight of his rigid pose. "I'll always think of you as my first bosom sweetheart."

"Stop it. No doubt your fiancé is devoted to ya. Make him your puppy dog."

She frowned. "Why are you dressed like this? And why the accent?" Her eyes scanned him from his hat down to his brogans. Understanding dawned on her face. "I see."

"We need ter talk…in private." He swung his gaze from Becky to the front door.

"I parked my horse in the back." She pointed to a doorway behind the bookshop clerk who stood at the counter going through a box of books. "Follow me."

"I still have a couple of books I need ter buy."

He quickly located *Frankenstein* and *The Mill on the Floss* and headed up to the counter.

"I would never have thought you'd be a fan of George Eliot." She caressed the book in his hand, then his fingers.

He twitched at her touch. "I like to stay unpredic'able." Still in the cockney guise, he gave her clothes the once-over. "I can see why ya like her books."

"Indeed. I like her philosophy on life and love." Becky glanced back at the table full of copies of Rose's book. "You're not going to buy *My Imprisonment and The First Year of Abolition Rule at Washington*?"

"Later. It gives me an excuse for a return trip."

This time Bill did follow Becky out to the loading platform in back of the building.

"That's your horse?" He chuckled, not bothering with the faux accent. They were alone.

"A horse made of metal. My beau bought it for me. He's sweet that way. It's the rage."

"I've heard people call them hobbyhorses. Or a dandyhorse."

"I have a different kind of dandyhorse. He sleeps beside me at night." Becky winked. "I prefer to call it a velocipede."

"Sounds like an insect."

"Insect or hobbyhorse, I just know it's a great way to move through London traffic. I ride right past the stopped Hansoms and carriages and wave at everyone. And it's much easier to pedal in pants."

"You're not the Becky I knew back in Duplin." Bill scratched the stubble on his chin. He'd been lax. He'd need to get out the straight razor.

"I got a taste of real freedom. I like being a bohemian. Someday you're going to see my book in print. It's about the journey of a young woman who frees herself from silly manmade rules." She opened the lock chaining the boneshaker to the loading dock. "Why are you in London and using the accent? And why aren't you in uniform?"

"President Davis sent me to find Rose. I'm to give her a message." Bill patted his coat pocket where he'd stored the dispatch. "I'm undercover."

"I'd offer to take it to her, but I'd have a devil of a time getting it to her. I hate that man…I'd tear it up."

"That's why I'm keeping it." Again, Bill patted his coat at the inside pocket. "By the way, from now on refer to me as Monty Keynton. Monty's an English merchant sailor."

Becky climbed atop the velocipede. "She's been staying with John at his house, so if you investigated any of the hotels, you left frustrated." She leaned on the handlebars.

"John?"

"John Arthur Roebuck, the Liberal MP from Sheffield. He adores Rose." Becky groaned. "I can't stand him. He's fiery for the Confederacy. For Rose, all that matters is that he's good in bed and Davis's strongest British ally."

"I need to see her without Roebuck present."

"You'll not see Rose tonight, Mr. Keynton." Becky grinned. "See? I can play the part. Anyway, Rose and John normally take in a playhouse performance once or twice a week. They were planning to go to the Adelphi tonight to see one of Dickens' plays, but John's feeling under the weather. They intend to see the play tomorrow evening. Come by the Adelphi and I'll introduce Mr. Keynton to her."

Bill tucked his new books against his side. He pointed to the empty book bag tied to her boneshaker. "Decided not to buy any books?"

"You ruined my plans. I'll buy a couple later in the week. Maybe another George Eliot book."

"When do I get to meet your beau?"

"Tomorrow at the Adelphi. No way around it. My two lovers face to face." She kissed her hand and pressed it against Bill's mouth.

"Stop that, Becky!"

She laughed as she rode off on her dandyhorse, turning into an alley running behind the bookshop. Bill found Gabe's Clothing Emporium just one block from Author Attic. He emerged from the men's store with vivid plaid pants, a gold vest brighter than the sun, and a maroon tailcoat that would have made a carnival barker envious. Bill had planned on two sets of dandy suits, but found the cost too exorbitant. Living the dandy lifestyle could drive a rogue into the poorhouse.

Bill felt eyes on him as he ambled back to the hotel. He sneaked glances over his shoulder, but saw nothing suspicious, just fellow walkers returning from Victoria Park. There were plenty of freight wagons in alleyways that could conceal a Yankee agent. He wondered if the two ladies in the bookshop had said something to someone. Even in normal times rumormongering spread like wildfire. With the war seeping into London alleyways at night, and daylight revealing corpses with slit throats, Bill could trust no one. Not even Becky Powell. Yet he'd shared vital information with her. He hoped he hadn't made a mistake.

Twenty-eight

A Night at the Alhambra

Bill closed the door behind him and dropped his dandyman suit on the bed. Just nineteen, tired of wearing military uniforms and now a sack suit, he looked forward to donning his fancy new clothes. He only wished he'd be going out later with Franny at his side.

As he tugged off his boots and slithered out of his sack-suit pants, Bill caught a glimpse of a headline on the front page of the *Daily Telegraph*. A Welshman had lost his balance and fallen into the path of a train in the London underground. Bill had seen too much killing at Fredericksburg and Chancellorsville for the death to upset him. Maybe his heart had turned cold, but he found himself fascinated by the revelation of a steam locomotive in an underground railway. As soon as he changed into his dandyman getup, Bill intended to find the subterranean railroad and take a ride. The newspaper said its first segment had opened the year before.

When he finished dressing, he admired himself in the mirror hanging above the rocking chair. He reached for a comb, but before he could run its teeth through his unkempt hair, his belly rumbled.

Barefoot, his pants' crotch unbuttoned, Bill raced out the door to the men's water closet down the hallway. The Great Hall Hotel had been one of the first London hotels to install Thomas Crapper's pull-chain toilets. Bill could testify…it worked perfectly. He flushed, and Crapper's water system sent Bill's excrement down into the city's new sewer lines. The hotel's desk clerk was quite proud of Crapper's toilets and the city's sewer system. "It took three cholera epidemics and the Great Stink before the government built the sewer system," the man had said when Bill checked into the hotel.

Back in his room, Bill hung his sack suit's pants in the armoire and started to fold the shirt and vest when someone knocked on the door. Before he answered, Bill hurried to the armoire and dug out the president's message from the inside suit pocket. He slipped it into a pocket inside his new maroon tailcoat, then scurried to the door as the anonymous caller rapped for the tenth time. Bill answered as the eleventh knock vibrated the door.

He caught a whiff of perfume, then beheld Becky Powell standing before him still dressed in her velocipede duds, pants and a vest. "Well, are you going to invite me in, Mr. Keynton?"

"A married man takin' a single lass into his 'otel room? That wouldn't be proper." He easily slid back into the cockney accent.

"I'm through being proper." Becky sidled past him and plopped down in the rocking chair.

"Ya're tryin' me pa'ience."

"Enough with the irritating accent." She picked up the Eliot novel, *The Mill on the Floss*. "Have you started reading it?"

"No. Leavin' it for me bed'ime readin'."

"Bedtime reading? Up for reading aloud to me?"

He dropped the accent. "No. You need to return to your fiancé."

"I'm a free-love woman." She offered Bill a naughty smile. "Percy understands."

"So Percy's your lover's name? He doesn't get mad as hops over your antics?"

"He likes my wildness. I can see I was right to turn down your marriage offer. You're such a dull man."

"I like dull. Franny likes dull." Bill smiled at the canard. Franny could never be described as dull. And dull men don't cross the sea looking for Confederate spies.

"One more chance, Mr. Keynton, for some bed-play. Franny's across the Atlantic. No reason for her to ever know we engaged in sexual congress."

"Never. I love my wife." And he'd be unable to hide his guilt. "You coming here has probably blown my cover. Everyone in London knows you're Rose's private secretary."

"Yes, and they know I delight in dalliances. To them, you're just one more swell I seduced." She stood and kissed him on his chin, brushing his lower lip. "I do vividly recall our night together in Wilmington...you enjoyed yourself."

"I wouldn't enjoy myself this time."

"Then Percy will get all my love." She patted Bill's cheek. "Well, let's not make this a wasted night. I came here to take you to the Alhambra music hall. Lena Ring will do acrobatics on the flying trapeze, dance and sing. I need a man's arm and Percy's not available. His momma's having a tea party—and I'm not proper enough to be seen. Rather than sulk, I'm aiming to have nanty-narking fun with you. Yes?"

"I'm planning to take a ride on the London Underground Railway."

"We could do the railway first then the Alhambra?"

Bill agreed without arguing. He decided to scour Becky's brain for more information on Rose and her doings. "A warning, though."

Headed to the door, she stopped and regarded Bill. "A warning?"

"Always refer to me as Monty Keynton and remember I speak with a cockney drawl. I'm a merchant sailor by profession. I used to live in Canada, became a war correspondent with a Canadian newspaper covering the war. Now I'm back in Britain with plans to write a book about the war."

"Monty Keynton, Monty Keynton, Monty Keynton. Never Bill." Becky closed the gap between her and Bill, then drew back a step when Bill raised his arms to push her away. "I know you play a dangerous game. Rose plays one too. I suspect Yankee spies try to keep close to her, yet they probably think she's harmless. She loves the Confederacy's best friend in Britain, and he has already proven he can't win recognition. Rose doesn't fear Lincoln's spies. She says, 'Becky, Yankees are beasts, but they haven't sunken so low they'll murder a woman.'"

"And you think she's right?"

"No. When they bombarded Fredericksburg, they didn't care it was full of women and children."

"That's why you mustn't ever slip up and use my name." He shifted from Kenansville brogue to London cockney. "If asked, ya're ter say ya met me in Wilmington. I was in the Tar Heel state's largest city talkin' to folks about morale, the bloc'ade runners and the yellow fever scourge."

"Monty Keynton. Came down from Canada to cover the war for a Canadian newspaper. I met you in Wilmington where you were getting a firsthand look at life in a wartime city. Satisfied?"

Bill nodded. "Let's go see that subterranean train."

Cabman Jack Longbottom drove them to the underground railway. Bill found the steam train noisy and smoky inside the subterranean tube. Glad to be above ground after climbing the stairs to street level, he hailed one of the Hansoms parked curbside. Once seated, Bill asked Becky, "What did ya fink of the below-ground train?"

"So many people down there. It's a hit with Londoners for sure. Can you imagine what it's going to be like when it's finished? There'll be tubes running all over the city. People will get to places faster than by cab."

The trapdoor opened above them. "I 'ope the underground railway don't put me out of business."

Squinting her eyes, Becky looked up through the trapdoor. "There'll always be work for Hansoms, cabman. It's a new opportunity for you. The fast underground trains will allow people to live farther away from work. Cabs will do the short hauling."

"I hope ya're right," the cabman said, his words gruff. "Where do ya want ter go?"

"The Alhambra. Fast so we don't miss any of the show." Becky's voice shifted from a matter-of-fact tone to coy.

"Fast I promise, ma'am. The Alhambra's me favorite music hall. I'm spoony for Lena Ring. Nightingale voice and so lovely on the trapeze." The trapdoor closed and the cab juddered into motion.

"Smoke's terrible down there." Bill didn't like how close Becky sat. He eased himself further away. "There'll be plenty of folks who'll choose a Hansom or hackney rather than breathe in the train smoke."

Hatless, Becky ran her fingers through her clipped tresses. "My hair must smell like a smokestack. Probably seeped into my clothes too."

The cabman dropped them off on the west side of Leicester Square away from the Alhambra. It meant a warm April walk through the small park. The music hall lay on the park's east side. Bill escorted Becky through the west gate and past the century-old statue of King George I. Ahead of them, the ten-year-old Alhambra sparkled in the clear night sky, its front façade lit up by arc lamps.

"I love Leicester especially at sunset." Becky gaped at Bill's arm hanging at his side, but made no move to reach for his hand. "The square used to be surrounded by private residences. The Alhambra has brought a renaissance to Leicester—shops, museums and the Hotel Sablonière et de Provence."

A couple walking toward Becky and Bill let their clutched hands slide free. The girl, wearing a bohemian getup similar to Becky's, waved her arms. "Becky Powell! Who's this darling fellow? Tired of Percy's shenanigans?"

"Darla, this is Monty Keynton, a friend I met in North Carolina last year. Just this afternoon I ran into him at the Author Attic." Becky palmed Bill playfully on his shoulder. "I'll never grow tired of Percy. He tickles my fancy, did from the moment I set eyes on him. He's at his mother's tonight; otherwise, he'd be seeing Lena Ring with us."

Darla laughed. "I don't believe a word, Becky. Monty's far too fetching to be a chuckaboo."

"I admit he's fetching. If I wanted Monty as a lover, I'd not have him out here where jams like you can ogle him."

"I wonder what Percy would say if I asked him about Monty?" Darla smirked as she slipped her fingers around her beau's hand.

"Ask him, dearie. Percy knows he's first in my heart." Becky turned her gaze on Bill. "Monty's a war correspondent and covered the American war for a Canadian newspaper. I have a rule. I don't let men who love the smell of gunpowder and blood court me. Monty's a sweet man, but he loves the sounds of war more than the bedroom moans of a lover."

Once Darla and her beau bid adieu and continued west on the brick walkway, Bill regarded Becky thoughtfully. "Ya've dared that woman. Ya know she'll seek out Percy as soon as possible."

"Not before I see him. You worry too much, Monty. I'll mention you to Percy during our bedroom talk tonight. He'll be fine. He has learned to accept my chummy male chuckaboos."

"Don't know if I believe ya." At the eastside fence, Bill stopped near the gate to stare in wonder at the Alhambra. In his nineteen years, he'd never seen a building quite like it. Built in the Moorish style, the Alhambra breathed lavishness that included two ornate minaret towers and a dome.

Becky appeared to have read Bill's mind. "Wait until you see the inside. Three thousand people, many drunk and looking for kisses, cheering wildly whenever a woman on stage flings her leg higher than the others. Nothing like that in Wilmington."

At the fence gate to the Alhambra, Bill grabbed Becky's arm, keeping her from leading him across the street and into the music hall's ticket boxes. "Sweet Lord above! It's bedlam."

"Indeed. That's why our cabman dropped us off on the other side of the square." She fixed her gaze on Bill's hand, still clenching her forearm. "You keep holding my arm like that, Mr. Keynton, and I'm going to start cuddling with you."

Relaxing his fingers, Bill wrenched his hand away from her. "The Wilmington Opera House never looked like this!"

"It's typical for the Alhambra—and it's ladies night."

Dozens of hackneys and Hansoms were entangled in front of the music hall, their horses champing and biting. Music hall goers spilled from the cabs and joined the long queues of men and women lined up to buy tickets. Near Bill and Becky, a Hansom passenger and his sweetheart argued with the cabman over the fare. "Highway robbery! I won't pay it!" the well-dressed man thundered.

"Ya'll pay it or I'll summon that copper." The wiry cabman pointed to a helmeted policeman eavesdropping.

Hand on his billy club, the peeler trod over to the Hansom. "Trouble, cabman?"

Before the cabman could answer, his male passenger, a red-faced gentleman, flung the fare up through the trapdoor. "See, I've paid!"

"Tyrone, you're ruining the night for us," the man's sweetheart pouted. "Quarreling like a common gonoph. I'm mortified!" The cabman unlocked the door, and the woman flounced from the Hansom.

"I'm sorry, darling," the fellow said, his voice contrite. "I didn't mean to make such a fuss."

"I don't want to hear another sour word from you tonight." The gent's sweetheart didn't offer her hand to him.

Another couple stepping down from a hackney tried to ignore a beggar boy who'd opened the coach's door and pleaded for a penny tip. The lad, his face smeared with grime, dogged them until they rewarded him with a coin from the woman's handbag. "Tank ya, lady." The boy kissed the coin.

Bill and Becky crossed the street, meandering between cabs, buggies and carriages before reaching the ticketing boxes beneath the Alhambra's marquee. Around them, single-minded ladybirds promised a good time to indolent swells high on opium.

Bill gawked at a freckled, redheaded prostitute who leaned provocatively against a swell. The dollymop bent over, revealing the cleavage between her ample breasts.

"The swell's feeling merry," Becky said off-handedly. "I'd say he's been spending the afternoon in an east-side den enjoying laudanum.

Swells love to drink it in wine. She knows her boy will be carefree with his money."

"The swell's pa must be at the end of his pa'ience." Bill watched the couple doing the bear.

"Just like my father," Becky rejoined, laughing.

Becky and Bill reached the front of the ticket-buying line far quicker than anticipated. Under the glare of the gas-jet above his head, a young man dispensed tickets. At Becky's urging, Bill handed the ticket clerk two shillings and received two circular tin pieces with holes and letters punched into their surfaces.

Bill surrendered the tickets to a red-uniformed porter who wore a black cap trimmed with scarlet bands. Once beyond the wooden barrier, Bill glimpsed the stage sheathed in gas-lit lights. He caught a glimpse of ballet girls' shapely legs before the press of bodies in the promenade blocked his view.

Ahead, boisterous voices turned out to belong to a half dozen young ladies smoking cigarettes. The lasses stepped out of the way, allowing Bill and Becky to pass, and Bill found himself inside the Alhambra's raucous promenade. The strolling space encircled the ground floor, leaving the railed-in seating area for gentlemen's respectable wives who wanted to hear the band music and see the dancing, pantomime, singing and acrobatics.

Becky guided Bill to a bar just off the promenade. A barmaid noticed Bill uncertainty. "Ya look like ya could use a drink, sir."

"He could," Becky answered. "It's all a bit overwhelming for Monty. It's his first visit to the Alhambra. He's been living across the Atlantic telling Canadians about the war south of their border." Becky gestured to alcohol bottles on the countertop. "I'll have a sloe berry gin. My friend will have a gin sling."

"Don't go wanderin', ya two. I don't want to chase ya into the promenade." The barmaid glanced at the stage. "I do believe I see Lena Ring climbin' the trapeze ladder. Over there"—she jabbed at spot just outside the bar—"is a luscious spot for watchin' Miss Lena."

Bill and Becky had nearly reached the recommended viewing spot when a feminine voice rose above the earsplitting noise in the bar and the promenade, "Becky? Is that ya, Becky Powell?" A delicate woman in a wicked French gown scurried up to Becky and kissed her full on the mouth. She turned to Bill, scrutinized him from his head to his shoe tips, then threw her arms around his shoulders and pressed her lips against his. "Where did ya find this delicious man, Becky me love?"

"In a bookshop, Amy. And no, he hasn't replaced Percy. He's a friend from America. London born, but Monty hasn't lived here since a boy."

"He still looks like a boy. That's why I want him." The miniature blonde, no taller than five feet, caressed Bill's chin with the tips of her fingers.

"Monty promises to stay true to his sweetheart in Canada. I don't think there's a woman in London who can sway him otherwise." Becky regarded Bill. "Isn't that true, Monty dear?"

Bill decided to let a morsel of truth creep into his undercover tale. "Me heart will always belong ter Franny."

"Ya've got to give a London girl a chance, Monty. We need our bellies and breasts kissed too." The tiny blonde fingered her cleavage revealed by the low-cut dress. "I know I can change your mind."

Bill didn't want to know Amy better. She was stunning in the way a thunderstorm is stunning: Something to be admired from miles away, not close up where a bolt of lightning can kill.

"I didn't fink there were any men left in London like Monty," Amy told Becky. "In his chest beats an unsullied heart." The blonde kissed Bill lightly on the mouth then disappeared into the mob cajoling one another in the promenade.

Two full glasses in her hands, the barmaid found Bill and Becky, and soon they were sipping the gin drinks. "Anything else, me darlin's? We've belly-satisfyin' pies, sandwiches, and all kinds of lunches."

"Later, at intermission." Becky slid a coin into the barmaid's cleavage.

They sat in the railed-off section on red-cushioned chairs that looked more comfortable than they actually were. "Amy friends with

Percy?" Bill wondered as he watched Lena Ring perform her trapeze routine fifty feet above the stage.

"Don't worry. I'm going to tell Percy about you later tonight at his flat. I'll assure him the two of you are destined to be best possums." Becky stroked Bill's arm, earning a glare. "You'll get to meet him tomorrow night when you see Rose."

"I can't wait," Bill said with a weary sigh.

Around Bill, the music hall's aficionadas began pounding pewter pots and plates on tabletops. The noise came in response to Lena Ring's latest maneuver—hanging upside down on the trapeze bar, displaying willowy legs and thighs.

Soon, Lena slid down the trapeze rope to the stage. The band in the pit struck up "The Cigar Girl," a ditty aficionadas loved to sing aloud, and that's what they did while Lena Ring kicked her legs high and exposed her derriere. As the last notes of "The Cigar Girl" faded in the smoky air, Lena sang the first of the songs that made her famous—"Fishing for a Sweetheart." When she flipped up her short costume for a brief glimpse of her corset's ruffled bottom, the crowd again hollered and pounded their pewter plates and pots.

The song ended with Lena jumping down into the pit to kiss the conductor, then clambering back onto the stage, again giving her fans a peek at her underthings. When the plate pounding subsided, she shouted out to the conductor, his face smeared with rouge, "Maestro, time for "Popsy Wopsy!" The crowd joined in, singing "I shall dream about you all night tonight. You're the sweetest girl I've seen. I could kiss you, my Popsy, but there's one thing that stops me...those footlights in between."

Later, Bill found himself humming "Popsy Wopsy" as he and Becky made their way outdoors into the Leicester Square. Passing the decrepit George I statue, Bill directed Becky to take a side walkway through a gateway to a half-dozen waiting Hansoms.

"Did you have a good time, Monty?" Her back against the door of a Hansom cab, Becky reached out as if she intended to hug Bill, but made due with patting his vest. "I hope you did. I did."

"It was quite flashy. I loved Lena Ring. I loved every minute inside the Alhambra." He helped her climb inside the Hansom.

She waved goodbye. "I'll see you at The Britannia tomorrow night. Be rest assured...Rose will know you're coming."

The cabman reined the horse into a trot. Becky's Hansom wheeled away and was soon lost in the traffic. Gesturing for a ride, Bill headed for another cab. He yawned and yearned for the comfort of his hotel-room bed.

Twenty-nine

Rose Makes a Decision

Fare paid, cab door open, Bill sprang down to the boardwalk in front of the Britannia Theatre. Compared to the Alhambra and its twin minaret towers and central dome, the Britannia seemed commonplace. If not for the marquee, passers-by might not realize a magnificent theatre lay inside. Bill scanned the raucous crowd milling in front of the foyer, searching for Becky and Rose. Maybe he got to the theatre too early. His inspection of the throng of theatre-goers didn't turn up the two women. He mulled his next move.

The night before he'd gone straight from the Alhambra to his hotel room. He'd slept in the nude, too tired to slip into a clean pair of longjohns. A vivid memory of the night remained fixed in his brain hours later. Bill had dreamed he'd crawled into bed beside Franny in their Richmond apartment. Hugging and kissing had escalated into bed-squeaking, full-steam-ahead lovemaking. Bill smiled as he recalled the sweet dream and then mumbled, "Just a dream, but the prigging left me exhausted for real."

He wondered about the timing of the dream—Becky back in his life and playing seductive games. Percy should be with her. He wanted to see those two holding hands. This new bohemian Becky... Bill wanted nothing to do with her.

Frustrated, he started at the back of the line and walked along the boardwalk toward the ticket booths under the marquee, looking for the Tar Heel woman he wanted out of his life. Well, that wasn't entirely true. He needed Becky in his life until she took him to Rose. Then he could deliver the president's missive and return to Richmond and Franny's arms.

Bill scrutinized oodles of women, some stone-cold serious as if their husbands had forced them into the long line, others staggering-drunk bangtails fishy about the gills. None, though, looked remotely like Becky.

Maybe he should buy a ticket and head inside. Becky and her beau Percy might be waiting in the auditorium. Grinding his teeth, Bill took his place at the end of the line behind a bobtail who had spent most of the afternoon imbibing in one of Hoxton's innumerable pubs and saloons. She stank of sweat and hours-old-beer.

"Lookin' for companionship, handsome boy?" The woman cupped her breasts. "Me diddeys want kissed. They're winkin' at ya."

The tottering woman looked at least twenty years older than Bill. A few gray hairs peeked out from her rumpled bonnet. Yes, he wanted to kiss some bubbies—Franny's.

"Sorry. They're not me type. I like me wife's. They're jaunty."

She snapped a retort then turned her attention to a tommy clad in his redcoat uniform. "He don't appreciate pretty bubbies. How about ya, tommy?"

Bill ignored their prattle. Instead, he eyeballed the massive jam on High Street in front of the Britannia. Under a crimson sun sinking behind four- and five-story buildings, Hansom cabs shared the brick street with middle-class buggies, aristocratic carriages, wagons toting furniture and lumber, and omnibuses crammed full of sweaty factory workers. He even saw a dandyhorse. Instinctively, he checked its rider, just in case it turned out to be Becky. Not this time. A foppish gentleman wearing a feathered hat and brilliant blue coat pedaled the contraption.

Romantic couples in spring finery, businessmen in starched sack suits, working-class girls in unadorned gray dresses, bumpkin farmers ogling gilded buildings… all squeezed into line behind Bill.

At his place in the slowly moving line, Bill got a peek at the Britannia's lobby, brightly lit by gas lamps in the windows of the attached tavern, the Pimlico. A corridor covered by glass linked the Pimlico to the Britannia. Their silhouettes floodlit by more gas lamps, men and women who'd been drinking in the tavern made their way into the theatre through the glass enclosure.

"See anyone you know inside the tunnel?" The impish female voice came from behind Bill.

He turned and regarded Becky and a man with her—Percy, Bill supposed.

"I was hopin' to see ya or Rose." Bill altered his voice so he'd sound almost bored.

"Well, I'm here, Monty. And I brought Percy with me. I think it's time you two met."

Becky had bathed; her damp hair simmered beneath the gas lights. She wore different clothes, yet still the style of bohemian girls rebelling against straightlaced rules—dark wine-red pants, peasant blouse cut low to reveal cleavage, and Roman-style sandals. Bill had kissed those toes nearly a year before. He drove the thought from his head.

Percy cleared his throat. "I wish she'd wear a dress now and then. I do get tired of watching men gawping."

Face reddening, Bill swallowed hard. "Ladies in pants? Shockin', ain't it?" Bill forced a laugh he hoped sounded sincere. "Men can't peel their eyes away. It's like seein' a steam-powered carousel for the first time."

"Becky tells me you have a wife." Percy wound his arm around Becky's waist and drew her against his side. He ran his fingers through her hair. "You must be desperate to get back to her."

In Percy's view, the clothes made the man, Bill decided. Percy's flamboyant dandyman suit and beret looked flawlessly correct for a wooing tryst in a rowboat on one of London's parkland streams. Not a wrinkle, not a stain or a spot of dirt, no lint or pet hair, impeccable proof of Percy's superiority of mind. Of course, a dandyman needed to prove himself worthy in the literary sphere, both as a writer and a target of scandalous gossip. Bill came to a realization... Becky and Percy were perfect for each other.

"I'd do it now, but I have to wri'e me book about the war," Bill explained to Percy. "I'm hopin' Rose can set me up with her publisher. I won't go back until I've gold janglin' in me moneybag."

Bill had feared Becky would reveal his true name and true mission—not write a book, but deliver a letter to Rose from the Confederate president. Percy looked like the type of man who'd chinwag relentlessly when three or four cups of wine or gin sloshed in his belly. Bill had breathed a sigh of relief when Percy addressed him as Monty. Of course, once Rose had the missive, the charade would end. Bill sure hoped Becky's words wouldn't be: *This is Bill Stamford. I tipped the velvet with him before I knew you, Percy.*

"Why are you in line, Monty?" Becky turned her gaze on Percy. "Monty may have been born in London and raised in Canada, but he sometimes acts like a dull-witted Yankee." She seized Bill's arm. "You're a guest of tonight's star actress—Marie Wilton. Follow us, silly man."

They didn't lead him into the theatre as Bill expected or through the front door into the Pimlico. Instead, Becky and Percy directed him down an alleyway. A helmeted bobby with his hand resting on his holstered nightstick stood guard at the alley entrance. "Oh, it's ya, Becky. Miss Wilton and Miss Rose told me to be on the lookout for ya."

Near the back of the tavern, they turned right into the rear alleyway and stopped at a stage door. Becky rapped twice. An aging doorman answered. Gaslight revealed him to be Indian. His thick Punjabi accent confirmed it. "Marie's expecting you, Miss Becky. And your albelaa as well as this new man." He squinted at Bill.

"Thank you, Kabir." Becky squeezed the Indian's hand.

The doorman grinned. "My pleasure, Miss Becky. I love your odd American accent."

"It's a North Carolina accent, Kabir. I'm from Wilmington." We all talk this way." Becky giggled as she moved toward a narrow, winding stairway half-hidden in the shadows.

Bill trailed Becky and Percy as he climbed the metal steps. "So this Wilton woman's famous?"

"Famous? Quite the rage," Percy said, a sneer in his voice.

Bill heard the smirk, but ignored it. Once he put the president's letter in Rose's hand, he'd not see Becky or Percy again. He'd step aboard a merchant ship, steam to Nassau and catch a blockade runner into Wilmington.

"Monty, you're about to meet one of the most famous actresses in Europe." Becky's voice rose, its manner animated. "Marie has performed on stages in Paris, Berlin, Vienna and Rome, and of course London. Marie's taken a liking to Rose. They're bosom buddies."

"You're pretty famous too, Becky darling." Percy stepped up onto the top floor and swept her into his arms, his hands settling on her derriere.

"Oh, Percy my love, you're such a cad." Becky giggled again.

To Bill, it appeared the two lovers were much like Marie Wilton, playing their favorite roles, literary free spirits. He wondered if either one actually possessed the talent to write a publishable poem or novel.

Pushing Percy away, Becky sidled to a door with the name Marie Wilton painted across it. She knocked.

The door creaked open. At the last step, Bill caught a glimpse of the man who'd opened the actress's door. A thick strand of gray hair fell across the right eye of the ancient fellow. "Ah, Becky, I see ya and Percy have arrived with another of Rose's admirers. Please come in. The draft's quite cold. I need ter get the door closed before Miss Wilton freezes."

The old man's circulation must be terrible. It was a warm April night.

Bill entered Marie Wilton's dressing room last. Rising from a red velvet chair next to a wood-burning stove, Rose Greenhow strode toward Bill, squeezing past Becky and Percy. He thought back to that summer day nearly a year before when a halo flared around Rose as she left Wilmington's Worth Tavern. Bill scrutinized her, searching for a remnant of divine fire, something that would tell him he'd actually seen a halo. It didn't matter. Rose might still be alive, but Bill knew he'd seen that halo flare. Always before a halo meant death—and soon, unless Bill managed to thwart it. Charlie Kurtz saved but at the cost of General Jackson's life—a melancholy outcome. The little girl, Tonya, rescued from the crushing wheels of a speeding Hansom, a gift from God who obviously loved little girls. Again, Bill faced a dilemma: intervene and warn Rose or let fate claim her at its appointed time? He'd been wholly successful with little Tonya. Bill decided he must warn Rose before he returned to Richmond.

Rose kissed Bill on the cheek. "Becky told me I'd be having a visit tonight from an admirer, a would-be author hoping for some help." Backing away from Bill, she wheeled around and regarded a fiftyish gentleman sitting in an upholstered rocking chair. Blessed with a full head of dark hair mixed with white and gray specks and bushy sideburns down to his chin, the fellow fidgeted with his coat lapel while giving Bill a skeptical inspection. "This is my beau—John Arthur Roebuck, the Confederacy's most spirited champion in the House of Commons."

A fortyish woman, Rose hardly looked the part assigned to her by Lincoln's politicians and generals—a seductress. She seemed little changed from the woman Bill had shared drinks with inside the Worth Tavern. Same austere hair parted in the middle and tied in a bun. Same olive skin flushed with a touch of a suntan, thanks to London's spring sun. One difference...Rose wore a vibrant dress speckled with rose and morning glory patterns. A new colorful dress to complement a new lover.

Roebuck stood and offered his hand to Bill. "Nice to meet you, Monty. We've something in common—our love for Canada. Later you must tell me about your plans for a book on the war."

"Gladly, sir." Bill shook the politician's hand. "No book on the American Civil War would be complete without an account from the Confederacy's no'orious spy, Rose Greenhow. She has captured the hearts from all—"

"Rose, sweetheart, it's so easy to get the cheekache over this beautiful boy." In her scanty performance costume, Marie Wilton emerged from behind the changing screen.

"Marie, you're not the first woman to make that claim." Rose swung her gaze back to Bill. "How's that back wound coming, Monty? Or should I say Bill?"

"Oh, Rose, you're no fun," Becky complained. "Bill worked so hard to perfect his disguise and you just ruined it for him." Becky's expression showed she wasn't a bit upset. More amused.

Roebuck raised an eyebrow. "So all isn't as it—"

"Who the hell is he?" Percy growled, hands fisted, eyes spitting fire.

"Behave yourself, Percy," Becky chastised.

"Whatever his name, he's very handsome and a splendid dresser. I'm glad you brought him, Becky. I'm already spinning romantic tales in my head and he stars in every one." Marie looped her arm around Rose's shoulders. "Bill, you say?"

Rose nodded as Bill reached into his coat pocket and slipped his fingers around President Davis's message. Revealing the letter, Bill held out the paper for Rose, who eyed the presidential seal with misgiving. "You came all this way to hand me this letter, Bill Stamford?"

Bill went from face to face, letting them absorb the new information. He fixed his eyes longest on Percy. "I'm Lieutenant Bill Stamford, attached to the War Department in Richmond. President Davis personally charged me with delivering this letter to Rose. As soon as she takes it out of my hand, mission accomplished."

"How do you know Becky?" Percy's eyes burned holes through Bill's skull.

Bill shrugged. Fake accent gone, he explained, "We're from the same county, Duplin. She went to my church's picnics." He waved the letter in front of Rose's nose. "Here, take it. I'm tired of carrying it."

"You're a slippery one, Bill." Rose took the letter. Unfolding it, she gave the paper a cursory glance. "It's in code."

"President Davis wanted Lincoln's spies to work hard to decipher the letter—if they managed to relieve me of it." Bill sidled to a curtain, opened it and looked down on the back alley. A shadow moved and vanished.

Percy laughed. "Codes are always broken. Your president is a fool."

Rose growled, "Everybody out!"

"Everybody?" Roebuck took Rose's free hand and kissed her fingers. "You can't mean me. You and I need to read this together, Rose."

"I love you, John Arthur, but I must do this alone." Rose walked him to the dressing room door. "I'll meet you later in the Pimlico."

"Please reconsider—"

"Later, John Arthur."

"Should I stay?" Marie rested a hand on her changing screen.

"So sorry, Marie. It feels wrong tossing you out of your own dressing room. I have to do this alone. The president expects the letter to be read in private."

Marie glided behind the screen and emerged clad in a day-robe that partly concealed her underthings. "I think I'll pop into John Anson's dressing room and pester him. He'll think I want him to seduce me. It'll be fun breaking his heart."

Roebuck led Becky, Percy, Marie and even the doorman out into the corridor and down the staircase. Bill started to follow them.

"Not you, Bill." Rose seated herself in the chair near the stove and stared at the creased letter in her hand.

Bill shut the door and stood frozen, unsure what to do. "I've carried this letter for weeks. I feel peculiar now that I no longer have it in my coat pocket."

"Be a gentleman, Bill. Close your eyes. I keep the cipher key in an intimate place only a lover sees." Rose undid the first button of her dress as she made her way behind Marie's changing screen.

As he regarded the letter left on the chair, he heard her unclasping her dress. Standing before the stove, he let its heat caress his face and hands. "I wish we were getting together under better circumstances."

Rose sighed. "So the president told you why he's sending the letter?"

"Better to read it, Rose. Get it directly from him."

"I've clumsy fingers. Oh, there I have it—the key. Let me get back together and we'll see what the letter says."

"In my experience, it never turns out to be as bad as your imagination fears."

"I'm going to sit at Marie's makeup table. Bring the letter to me."

Rose sat as Bill handed the message to her. The cipher key on the table in front of her, she placed the letter next to it. Eyes pivoting between the letter and the cipher, Rose scribbled like a frenetic Moses writing the Ten Commandments atop Mount Sinai as words thundered from God's mouth. She said nothing, not even when she finished reading her translation.

"Are you okay, Rose?" Standing behind her, Bill rested his hands on her shoulders and squeezed. "I hope the president wasn't too harsh."

She turned the chair toward him. "The president thinks he can decide who I can and cannot love. I'm not sixteen years old and he's not my father."

"No, he's not your father. He's the leader of your country. He sent me overseas to find you because you're romancing the wrong man. Rose. John Arthur's already a sympathizer to our cause."

Rose crumpled the letter, both her new translation and the coded one from President Davis. "You'll find no one more dedicated to the South than me. No one. I'd gladly give up my life to gain our freedom from the tyrant Lincoln."

"They're orders, Rose."

Bill found himself wondering if the delivery of the letter finally set Rose's halo into motion. He needed to be forthright with her about the halo, but now seemed the wrong time. Rose appeared genuinely distraught over the president's chastising words.

"I hear you have a new bride. How would you feel if you were told you had to divorce the woman you love and marry another for political reasons?"

"I would have to decide—choose love or choose my nation?"

She swept her hand across the makeup table, brushing the scrunched paper into a metal trash can. "I've been so lonely since my husband died ten years ago. Little Rose is going to school in Paris. Her older sisters live in Ohio, enemy country, Leila with her big sister Florence. Florence's husband is a captain in the Union army. I'm alone, Bill." She fisted her right hand and smacked the makeup table. "Please don't think I'm an ingrate. I gladly chose prison rather than betray my country. Don't I deserve a little happiness? I want to be able to marry the man of my choice."

"Can I see the letter?" Bill held out his hand.

"Of course. That's why I had you stay. You carried it for weeks. You deserve to read it." She retrieved the transcribed copy from the basket, unscrunched it and slipped it into Bill's hand.

He read the letter, not surprised at all by the words. President Davis considered Rose's mission to Europe a last-ditch attempt to gain British and maybe French recognition. The Dixie-loving aristocrat politicians were flocking around her, seduced by her notoriety and her alluring personality. Lonely, her daughters far away from her, Rose had let her heart guide her, not President Davis's wishes. "You must do what your conscience decrees," Bill said softly.

"The thousands of dollars in gold I've gotten from the sale of my book should be enough. Not for President Davis! He wants me to marry someone I will detest."

"And win recognition for the Confederacy. Maybe you can learn to love a Lincoln sympathizer?" Bill dropped Rose's translation into the trash basket, joining President Davis's coded one.

Sighing, Rose extracted a friction match from its box beside a packet of Cuban cigars, lit it, and dropped it into the can. The smell of burning paper soon permeated the dressing room. "Perhaps. My oldest daughter's the wife of a Yankee officer." Swiveling the chair, Rose rested her elbows on the makeup desk. "I understand the president's reasoning. If I marry a Yankee man, I can turn him, and he can turn the Parliament and Prime Minister Palmerston to our cause. And I'll go into the history books as the woman who saved the Confederacy."

Would that be such a bad thing? Of course, he couldn't say that to her. Instead, he told her, "If you choose to follow your heart and marry John Arthur, I will back you up. I really believe the president is asking you to something he'd not do."

"Thank you, Bill." Rose rested her hands in her lap and leaned against the backrest. "I know the perfect candidate. Granville George Leveson-Gower, a Lincoln man." She stuck a finger into her mouth as if she wanted to make herself throw up. "Before my courtship with John Arthur turned serious, Granville kept calling on me. I'd make up excuses. The more I ignored him, the more determined he became." Gripping the armrests, she pushed herself to her feet. "I think he'd love to chase me again. This time I'll let him catch me. I've no doubt he'll want to put a ring on my finger. He likes to play with fire."

Rose's abrupt change of mind surprised Bill. "What about Roebuck?"

She bit her lower lip. "He's an inconvenience, isn't he? I'll just have to break his heart."

"I'm sorry I'm the bearer of bad news."

"Not so bad. I get to play one of my favorite roles—siren. Through Granville I get to bring Yankeedom to ruin." She took his arm. "Let's join our friends in the Pimlico."

Thirty

An Unpleasant Surprise

The inside of the Pimlico tavern looked like an Elizabethan hunting lodge—wood panels with wainscoting, a bar made of oak, and a cedar hammer-beam roof. Bill closed his eyes and saw barmaids, sailors, shopkeepers, thief-takers and soldiers dressed in Elizabethan clothes.

Enough daydreams. Bill opened his eyes. Instead of Elizabethan patrons, Becky, Percy and Roebuck lounged at the bar, sitting on stools, sipping mugs of warm ale. Noticing Bill, Percy draped his arm around across Becky's shoulders and whispered in her ear. Rising from his barstool, Percy cupped Becky's chin and kissed her hard on the lips, then exited the Pimlico through a side doorway near a fireplace. He spared one last withering glance at Bill.

"You've made an enemy, Bill," Rose said sourly. "Did you see the look Percy gave you? He's acting like a five year old. All because Becky left him in the dark."

"Do you think Percy believes I'm more to Becky than a friend?" Bill frowned as he waited for Rose's opinion.

"Yes. Becky likes making him jealous. She'll tell Percy you've not kissed her, yet say it in a manner that leaves doubts in his mind. Becky's a schemer."

"She's not the woman I remember. Not by a long shot." Bill placed his arm against Rose's back and urged her toward the countertop.

"I don't understand what Becky sees in him. Especially when she could've had you."

"I'm a happily married man."

"Back in Wilmington I could've sworn you and Becky were in love."

"She wanted the life over here—with the Percy types." Bill forced a half-smile. "Thank God I'll be heading home soon."

"I'll miss you." Rose squeezed Bill's arm.

"Thank you, Rose. I'm glad I got to see you again."

Roebuck waved at Rose and Bill before maneuvering his way to his sweetheart's side, squeezing past other patrons and their irritated looks when ale splashed out of their mugs. Rubbing his cheek against hers, he snaked his way to her mouth and kissed her.

Rose let the kiss linger then gently pushed him away. "We'll be hearing 'pull down the blind' if you don't stop spooning."

She looked past Roebuck's shoulder at Bill and scowled. Bill could read Rose's mind. She dreaded telling her lover their romance must end.

"Who cares what others think! I like showing how much I love you, Rose." Roebuck brushed his hand along Rose's chin.

"Bill, Becky just ran after Percy. Looks like she's upset." Rose nodded toward the side door.

Bill rolled his eyes. "They're a very melodramatic couple."

Roebuck swung his gaze to the bar then palmed Bill's back. "Be careful with those two, Mr. Stamford. He's jealous and she's doing nothing to tame it. She likes the attention."

"My guess? Becky's trying to repair the damage." Rose shook her head, the derisive expression on her face plain to see.

A familiar voice coming from behind Bill intruded on his

thoughts before he could turn them into a spoken response to Rose's observation. "Bill, darling, I'll make you forget Becky and Percy." Clad in an Ottoman kaftan that covered her underthings, Marie grabbed Bill's arm and dragged him toward the bar. "I insist you buy me a glass of sherry."

"He's happily married, Marie," Rose reminded her actress friend.

"Maybe he'll decide to live dangerously." Marie slid her hand along Bill's sleeve, found skin and stroked the hairs.

"I do live dangerously except when it comes to the fairer sex." Bill removed Marie's hand from his wrist. "I won't risk Franny's love."

"I'm just keeping you company for a spell." Marie brushed her hip against the bar counter. "Becky's an old friend. New friends like me are much more beano."

"You'll have to prove it to me." Bill leaned against the counter, his elbow propped on the bar close to Marie's.

"Oh, I intend to, my new friend." Marie waved a bartender over to her and Bill.

"Evening, Miss Marie." The mustached bartender glanced at his pocket watch. "Surprised to see you here, ma'am. The show starts in less than thirty minutes."

"I'm an old pro, Douglas. Sherry droplets on my lips will inspire me when I'm on stage. Glasses of sherry for me and my friend Bill. Do hurry. Like you said, I mustn't be late to my show."

Rose and Roebuck joined them at the counter. Bill felt a twinge of pity for the aristocrat who'd soon learn Rose had set her sights on another. Roebuck would no doubt question Rose's decision to end the romance, coming so soon after reading President Davis's message.

"So what did your President Davis have to say?" Roebuck asked in a contemplative voice.

"Just a warning, John Arthur." Rose removed his bowler hat and mussed his hair. She left the hat on the countertop. "Some agents in France believe there's a plot to harm me. Balderdash! But I'll be extra careful when I go there in a few days."

What a suave liar. At least she didn't say the president wants her engaged to a politician who supports Lincoln and the Republicans.

Roebuck rubbed his lower lip. "The Froggies want a friend on Mexico's border, so I don't see why they'd not immediately quench any plot to do harm to the Confederacy's most enchanting spy. At Napoleon the Third's instigation, Maximilian just declared himself emperor of Mexico. If Lincoln defeats the South, he'll send his troops across the border to chase Maximilian out of Mexico."

"So you think we're going to lose the war?" Rose huffed her displeasure.

"I didn't say that, darling."

"Yes you did, John Arthur. You insinuated the beast Lincoln will stomp his heel on our necks and crush us. I guess I don't know you at all." Rose turned away from her aristocrat lover. "I'm sorry for this nastiness, Bill. We have brave soldiers. The South won't lose this war."

"Forgive me, sweetheart. I didn't mean it." Roebuck kissed the back of Rose's neck.

Rose stiffened her spine. "We'll talk when we get home. I want to hear no more about Lincoln and Maximilian."

"My wishes as well." Roebuck gritted his teeth.

"You must join us in John Arthur's box for Marie's performance," Rose told Bill, her voice curt.

"Thank you. I've love to see Marie's performance." Turning to Marie, Bill beamed a moon-bright smile.

Marie stood. "I wish I could stay longer, Bill. I so do enjoy your company. Not often do I get to spend time with a genuine war hero. Someday soon I will insist you let me count your scars." She winked.

Rose laughed. "Count his scars? How scandalous!"

"I've made scandal a new art form. Joanna Hiffernan loves the company of painters. I do as well, but I much prefer war heroes. I dedicate tonight's performance of "The Maid and the Magpie" to you, Bill." Marie pinched Bill's earlobe then hurried into the glass tunnel leading to the theatre.

With Marie beyond hearing distance, Rose warned, "Be careful of that one, Bill. She's a nice woman, but collects men the way Virginia Tidewater children collect seashells. If you want to stay true to your wife, avoid Marie."

"No more than playful smiles." Bill glanced at the glass breezeway and Marie's back.

A short jaunt through the glass breezeway and under a wide archway brought Bill, Rose and Roebuck into the horseshoe-shaped theatre. Bill's first view of the interior took his breath away. They made their way along the promenade, passing along the back of the orchestra pit. At the first staircase, Roebuck led them up the steps to the first of three tiers of boxes at the sides of the house before ushering them into his box. In Wilmington's Opera House, Bill never had a view of the stage like the one from Roebuck's box. Once ensconced in his seat next to Rose, Bill rested his fidgeting hands in his lap and waited for Marie to make her appearance on stage.

Roebuck leaned across Rose. "Bill, the Britannia's one of Dickens' favorite theatres. He once told me he likes how easily all the classes can mix."

Bill propped his elbows on the front railing and looked down at the audience in the first few rows near the promenade and the pit. Sure enough he could see factory workers sitting next to shopkeepers and the sons of dukes. He even saw some darkies sitting next to whites. "That's something you'd never see in Charleston or New Orleans."

"What?" Rose fanned herself as she glanced down at the seats in front of the floodlights.

"I think Bill's referring to our black colonials," Roebuck inserted.

"Disgraceful!" Rose scowled. "If one sat next to me, I'd slap her—or him."

"It's the young aristocrats I find amusing." Roebuck nestled his hands against the back of his head. "They like to sit out with the commoners and hunt for a willing jam tart. If you tell them they'll soon be pissing pins and needles, they mutter: 'Not me. I'm invincible.' My youngest son exhibits the same—"

Her fan whirling even faster, roiling air near her face, Rose abruptly cut Roebuck off. "You must tell me how you went from being a wounded private to an undercover Confederate agent, Bill."

"It's quite remarkable, isn't it?" Bill replied, stunned with how much his life had changed since he chatted with Rose inside the Wilmington saloon.

"The letter from the president isn't unexpected," Rose acknowledged. "You being its bearer...that's startling."

"My wife Franny did some strategic maneuvering on my behalf. Her father works at the War Department. He wrangled me a job helping Secretary Seddon work with newspaper and magazine editors."

"Franny Neale, right? I've met her a few times. A spirited young woman who has bohemian tendencies as well. A bit like Becky, but not muddle-headed like your former sweetheart." Rose swiveled in her seat and looked back at the box's exit. "Odd that Becky and Percy never returned."

"Percy gets on my nerves, so it's fine with me." Roebuck sprawled his long legs out from his chair.

"My nerves as well," Rose concurred. "Tell me, Bill, what do you think of Secretary Seddon and President Davis?"

Bill mulled Rose's question before answering. "Secretary Seddon wants to be liked. When the Virginia governor and some generals were threatening to shoot the bread-riot women, Seddon called for calm and showed a generous heart. He listened to the women. President Davis has a hard row to hoe. He reminds me of General Jackson. Jackson carried on unnecessary feuds with subordinates. The president does the same." Bill wanted to be honest yet not be overly censorious. "He needs to be more like Secretary Seddon."

The proscenium grand drape swished open, a sound heard when theatre-goers' voices hushed. Bill looked down on the first scene of "The Maid and the Magpie." On the stage, a young boy sat on a stool milking a cow while two goats, a calf and a dog looked through a split-rail fence. A magpie perched on a branch flapped its wings and flew over the head of a bearded man carving a piece of wood.

Rose pinched Bill's arm. "Don't you recognize her? That's Marie dressed as the milk-boy Pippo."

"Lordy! I didn't expect to find Marie playing a boy." Shaking his head, Bill smiled sheepishly.

"Marie's famous for her boy roles," Rose pivoted her head between Bill and the stage. "Her fans can't get enough of her dressed as a boy. The English love burlesque. The playwright, Henry Byron, wrote the Pippo part for Marie." Rose leaned on the railing and waved to Marie. "I don't think she can see much from the stage. The gas floodlights are really blinding. Boys from ten to eighty are madly in love with Marie. Bill, she has her eye on you. I can't warn you enough. Be careful."

"Don't worry, Rose. I can't be tempted by Marie—or Becky."

The comedy ended too soon. Bill had never laughed so hard through all five acts. If he'd never met Franny, Bill could envision himself falling prey to Marie's charms. But that New Year's Eve night in the Yerby Plantation's overseer cottage with Franny in Bill's arms left him immune to other women's wiles. He wanted to grow old with Franny beside him, the two of them holding hands as their grandchildren played at their feet.

~ * ~

Bill could hardly keep his eyes open. Strain gnawed at his belly and made his eyelids heavy. He wanted to snag a Hansom cab and wheel back to the hotel and his cold, lonely bed. Bill's memories of Franny's spoony ways would soon warm him up.

Yawning incessantly, Bill nevertheless agreed to drink a gin and tonic in the Pimlico with Rose and Roebuck. Later, dressed in her Ottoman kaftan, Marie joined them. The actress kept returning the conversation to her favorite subject—Bill's strong hands, "Perfect for a girl seeking caresses." Marie invited him to her dressing room, even kissed his earlobe as a final enticement. "Two glasses of sherry, the clink of glasses touching, a harbinger of bodies someday touching."

Bill begged off, saying the gin drink had made him so tired he wanted to do nothing more than dash for his hotel room bed. "I can't do this to Franny, even though I know she'd never learn of my weakness." He could feel his groin responding to Marie's amorous invite, prompting him to say goodnight and make his escape.

Relieved to be away from Marie, Bill stepped through the Pimlico's front doorway onto High Street along with a dozen more theatre-goers, all eager to clamber into hackneys and Hansoms for journeys home. For some men and women clinging to each other like limpets cleaving to rocks, the cab ride meant a short trip to a secret apartment for a night of tipping-the-velvet bed play. Bill wondered: had he allowed himself to be maneuvered into Marie's dressing room, would the night have ended with a tryst?

He sniggered at the maddening scene in front of him. Folks were pushing and shoving, racing to hop aboard cabs before their foes. Arguments erupted; men in sack suits and dandyman outfits raising fists to brawl in the gutter next to cabs. Near Bill, two sloshed dollymops squabbled over who would ride with a young nobleman who wanted to take both to his hideaway. Eager to be the only one to ride the rantipole with the swell, the birds dug their fingers into each other's hair and kicked at their shins. Tumbling onto the boardwalk, the comely women rolled toward Bill, fists flailing, teeth searching for enemy skin. Bill jumped out of their way as the two screeching females scuffled past him.

The nobleman grinned. "Winner wins a night at my lair. Hope it's the redhead. I simply love freckles on glistening skin."

Bill deadpanned, "Both will be too bruised and battered to enjoy a night with your nebuchadnezzar."

The swell found Bill's remark amusing and roared laughter.

Leaving the tussling women and swell behind, Bill shadowed the long line of cabs, searching for one he could climb into without first outdueling a rival. Two blocks from the Britannia, Bill angled toward one of the last cabs. He stopped abruptly, his hand on the Hansom's door, and wrenched his head toward a convulsive sound coming from an alley. A gas streetlight cast enough light to show the faint shape of a man sprawled in the alley moaning for help. An older couple dressed in latest fashion walked past, ignoring the pleas. Unlike them, Bill sprinted under the streetlight and into the alley.

Squatting beside the groaning man, Bill probed for broken bones. Except for a bleeding lip and a bruise beneath his left eye, he looked remarkably well. "Where do you hurt?" The man's clothing might conceal a broken bone, Bill feared.

The injured man reared up and slammed his fist into Bill's face. "Actually, nowhere."

Straddling Bill, he rained blows down onto his face, shoulders and chest.

Arms raised above his face, Bill managed to block some punches before bucking and tossing his attacker over his head. Scrambling to his knees, Bill reached for his concealed derringer holstered between his coat and vest. A previous unseen door squeaked and shadows shifted along a wall.

The shadows became clear...two masked men brandishing knives. One launched his foot toward Bill and knocked the derringer from his hand. The gun bounced along the ground. As a boom rattled Bill's ears, a bullet erupted from the derringer's barrel. The man pretending to be hurt yelped out in pain as the bullet struck him in the leg. One of the goons smashed Bill in the face with his boot. Curling into the fetal position, Bill prepared for an onslaught of kicks and punches.

The goon dropped beside Bill, produced a stiletto knife, then raised the blade above his head. A round-pea whistle shrieked along the alleyway, muffling the wounded goon's screams. Nightstick raised, whistle bouncing against his chest, a burly constable tore down the alley toward them. The bobby let the nightstick fly. The truncheon struck the knife-wielding goon in the shoulder, ruining his aim as the stiletto plunged toward Bill's chest. Instead, it sliced through cloth and grazed Bill's side.

His companion ripped off his mask. "Stay away from Becky!"

Bill squinted at the unmasked man, taming his pain as his blurred eyesight came into focus. Percy, grim satisfaction distorting his mouth.

Becky's sweetheart and his two hired thugs skedaddled, fleeing the copper. The goon with the gunshot wound limped badly, but managed not to fall. Obscured by a building, Bill's attackers disappeared down a back alley.

Bill touched his side, felt the torn coat, vest and shirt—and warm blood.

Retrieving his nightstick, the copper knelt at Bill's side. "Bastards! Let me check your wound, sir."

"Just a flesh wound. I'll survive." Grimacing, Bill laughed acridly.

"Bill! Bill! Please be all right." Rose scurried toward him. Roebuck ran alongside her.

"He's been wounded," the copper told them.

"Knifed," Bill wheezed. "In the side. Flesh wound. Hurts like the dickens."

Bill's thoughts drifted. Rose and Roebuck had arrived not long after Percy and his goons bolted. A happenstance? Or deliberate?

"We'd just come out of the Pimlico and saw you dart into the alley." Roebuck palmed Bill's shoulder as Rose ruffled his hair. "You were running like a madman. I knew something was wrong."

"Damn them!" Rose squawked. "Probably Lincoln's agents."

"No! Not Lincoln." Bill struggled to rise to his knees and gasping, succeeded. "Percy! Told me to stay away from Becky."

"Percy's a bastard," Roebuck growled. "I'll have Scotland Yard go after him for this and won't let Percy's father stop me."

"No! Leave him alone." Bill tried to get to his feet, but collapsed to his knees. "I don't want to stay here and testify at a trial. I just want to board a ship and steam back home to Franny."

"Damn Becky and her bohemian ways!" Rose crossed her arms and pressed them against her bosom.

"Please, Rose, don't punish Becky. Let her stay your secretary. She never came to John Arthur's box. Percy and Becky just had a terrible fight—enough of one to make him go after me. She helped nurse me after Chancellorsville"—Bill managed a crooked smile—"or at least tried. Becky would never want to see me wounded."

Rose nodded. "I will accede to your wishes."

The copper eyed Roebuck. "Do your best, sir, to stem his bleeding. I'm going to get a carriage that can get him to the hospital."

"A carriage? I'm fine." Again, Bill struggled to get to his feet, and again he collapsed. "Well, maybe I do need that carriage."

Thirty-one

A Frustrating Hospital Stay

Bill sat in a comfy chair next to his hospital room's third-floor window looking at the blue-sky scene beyond the glass. St. Thomas Hospital patients on the mend, many with canes or crutches, hobbled along a brick pathway through a small park as nurses monitored their progress. When they reached a pond, some settled onto benches and watched ducks swimming in the water, gliding toward a fountain in the center. He turned away from the window to mull the half-eaten food on the attached tray. Bill felt like a baby in a high chair. The eggs, beans and black pudding tasted fine, but he lacked an appetite. Although a flesh wound, the stitched cut still throbbed every time he moved.

A middle-aged nurse with a gray-haired chignon scurried into the room. Bill combed his mind, trying to recall her name—Emily. "Are you going to chastise me, Emily, for not finishing breakfast?"

"Heavens no!" Her eyes gleamed in the morning light, a sign she enjoyed flirting with a man young enough to be a grandson. "Pain'll smother an appetite. Ya did fine, considerin' ya were just sti'ched a few hours ago."

"How long do you think I'll be here?" Bill lifted his hands out of the way as the nurse scooped up the food tray.

Tray cradled in her arms, Emily quipped, "Gettin' fidge'y, eh? Ya're young and rugged, tough as old boots. Ya'll be out of here in no time and on a ship back to America."

"I'll put up with the pain to be on my way to Richmond. My soul shrinks each day I can't kiss my wife. It'll disappear if I don't get back to her soon. We're newlyweds."

"Ah, that's so sweet." She turned at the sound of someone knocking on the door. "Looks like ya've company."

Rose and Roebuck stood in the doorway. No Becky, though. Not unexpected. *She runs from trouble and worrisome matters.*

"I'm so glad to see you in the chair, Bill." Rose made her way to the window, leaned down and kissed him on the cheek. "Were you able to move from the bed by yourself?"

"Got some help from Emily." Bill gestured to the nurse standing in the doorway alongside Roebuck.

"Humbug! Ya did it all on yar own." The nurse turned and disappeared down the corridor.

"I want to thank you for paying for my hospital stay," Bill said as the politician joined Rose beside the chair.

"It's the least I can do for one of Rose's dear friends." Roebuck squeezed Bill's shoulder.

Guilt bubbled up from inside Bill. Soon Rose would manufacture a breakup with Roebuck so she could do President Davis's bidding and pursue a Lincoln-leaning politician.

Bill shifted his gaze to Rose. "Becky pay you a visit?" Beyond the window, a child's laughter made Bill smile. A duck from the pond had approached a boy, his mother and a bandaged man, probably his father. The boy tossed oats into the air and the duck ate them as soon as they landed on the grass.

"I gave that girl a piece of my mind." Rose's face paled as she sidled to the bed and sat. "I told her to stay away from you, Bill.

It's only because of your words that I didn't fire her on the spot. Unbelievably, she kept making excuses for Percy."

"Excuses?" Bill tensed and pain shot from his wound to rest of his body. "He warned me to stay away from Becky. Obviously, he paid those goons to beat me up and knife me. He sees me as a prigstar, probably wanted me dead." As the pain subsided, Bill slouched in the chair and squirmed to get more comfortable.

"Percy denies he was even there." Rose dug her fingers into the bedsheets, her agitation self-evident. "He says your stabbing had you so chumpy you were seeing things that weren't real."

"Hogwash! She really believes him?" Bill harrumphed his frustration.

"I've never seen a girl so crushed over a man. Goes to show a woman can have perfect vision and yet be blind." Rose rubbed her eyes for emphasis.

"I know I saw him. Jealousy gone amok."

Roebuck settled into a chair near the bed and crossed his legs. His fingers tapped incessantly on the armrests. "I hate that Percy's going to get off scot-free. I'll do what you say, Bill. I won't push Scotland Yard to arrest him. I won't push for a trial. But I can't let him get away with this outrage. I'll do all in my power to see him ruined financially. His father won't be able to save him this time."

Holding his breath to forestall pain, Bill shifted his chair toward the bed. "That's better. Now I won't get a stiff neck. I've no problem with your plan. Still can't believe Becky swallowed Percy's explanation hook, line and sinker."

A human storm blew into the room—Marie Wilton. "You're not in bed? I thought you were on death's door, Bill." She sauntered to his chair, leaned forward and kissed him lightly on the mouth.

"Barely got nicked, Marie."

"Let me see the wound. I'll be the judge."

Bill snorted. "I know your game, Marie. No, I won't lift my hospital gown so you can see my stitches. I'll say this...I'm getting stitched up way too often."

"A soldier's life." Marie settled onto the bed beside Rose. "Hear you once loved Becky. You're a fool, Bill Stamford! Before I came to St. Thomas, I went to Percy's townhouse to slap his face. Almost knocked, but I heard squealing and grunts coming from the parlor. Here you are in the hospital and Becky's prigging the fellow who almost killed you. I turned my back on them and came straight here." She regarded Rose. "The bitch better never step into my dressing room. She'll get a bloody dewskitch—both eyes blackened, hair yanked bald."

"I'll tell her." Rose chuckled.

Bill's nurse, Emily, returned to the room, this time toting a medicine bottle. "Pain the same? Or gettin' worse?"

"A little worse. Nothing I can't handle."

The nurse frowned. "I know ya can handle it. I saw yar battle scar. But I want to make the pain go away for ya."

"Listen to her, Bill!" Marie waggled her finger at him.

"Absolutely. Be honest with the nurse." Rose's eyes flamed with impatience. "If you're hurting, tell her."

Bill surrendered. "I could use something for it."

"Laudanum comin' up." The nurse uncapped the bottle and poured the painkiller into a small cup. She held it up to Bill's mouth. "Drink all of it."

Bill cringed as the bitter brew swished down his throat. "Lordy, I hate that demon-spawned stuff."

The nurse smirked. "Better say yar goodbyes to yar friends. Ya'll soon be asleep." She capped the bottle and retreated from the room.

Roebuck rose to his feet and glanced out the window. "Going to be a beautiful spring day. Terrible to waste it in here. Oh well, I'll book you passage on a merchantman to Nassau as soon as I know what day you'll be released." The aristocrat offered his hands to Bill. "Want help back into bed?"

"No, I think I'll stay in the chair and enjoy the view out the window until I fall asleep."

Roebuck scooted the women out the doorway. Unable to resist one more flirtatious moment, Marie whirled. "Are you sure I can't talk you into staying longer? I want us to become better friends." Not giving him a chance to answer, she blew him a kiss and gamboled down the corridor.

Rose ducked her head back into the doorway. "Bill, race back to your wife. You belong in her arms." She lowered her voice conspiratorially. "If your willpower weakens, I might have to pay Franny a visit when I get back to Dixie."

"I won't weaken. And you're more than welcome to pay us a visit."

"Bye. Have a nice sleep." And then Rose was gone, her fading footsteps marking her progress down the corridor.

Damn! Did it again. Let her go without telling her about the halo.

He closed his eyes. The laudanum stole thoughts before they could fully form. Something about Marie, but the thought flew away to a distant nest. Nest? That made no sense—until he heard the bird twittering outside the window.

Bill opened his eyes, his eyelids flitting. He caught a hazy glimpse of Emily hurrying down the corridor. "Nurse! Emily!"

The nurse craned her head around the doorframe. "Aye, Bill?"

"You busy?"

"Ya sound like ya're plottin' somethin', my American friend." Emily leaned against the doorframe.

"I'd like to go down to the pond. I know I can't do it myself."

"Ya just took laudanum. Ya'll fall asleep mid-step."

"Not with you along. You'll punch me in the arm if I doze off. Besides, I walked a lot farther with hot shrapnel in my back."

"Ya win." Years disappeared from Emily's face as she smiled. "Let me check with the other nurses and see if one will fill in while I take ya down to the pond. I'll be back in a second."

The walk might prove to the hospital people that Bill could be released the next morning. Outside his window, a goldfinch landed on a sagging branch and eyed him. Maybe this very bird did the chirping that kept Bill from falling asleep. "Thank you, goldfinch."

"Okay, let's take that walk." Emily strode into Bill's room. "Need help gettin' up?"

Gritting his teeth, Bill stood. "Nope. Me and the laudanum can conquer the world."

She helped him into a housecoat Rose had left for him, slipping it over his thin cotton hospital robe. Her right hand never left his forearm as they made their way along the corridor and down the stairwell to the ground-level lobby. He initially wobbled, his legs rickety, but soon walked with a steadiness that surprised him. Sheer willpower, he thought. The steady pace kept the effects of laudanum at bay. Lightheaded, but nothing he couldn't handle.

Outside, the warm sunlight caressed his face and arms. Bill didn't mind that he wore a housecoat, not his dandyman suit. Then again the fancy outfit had a knife slit running down the coat, vest and shirt. Only his for a few days, the suit was headed for the trash heap. Flower beds bordered both sides of the pathway. The fragrances of hollyhocks, marigolds, lilies and peonies tickled his nose as Emily led him to an unused bench.

A bird—a goldfinch—settled on a limb of a sycamore near the bench. *The same bird at the window?* He decided it was highly unlikely. The ducks were paddling in the pond, except for some pestering patients and their families for handouts.

Emily broke a long silence. "I'm amazed ya know Marie Wilton. She seems quite fond of ya."

"Much to my detriment."

"I hear she's also quite fond of an actor, Squire Bancroft. Fond's too puny of a word for their affair. Passionate, hot-blooded, fiery... those are the words that come to mind. She'll not risk havin' Bancroft seek out the company of another actress. He does get offers."

"Thanks for the warning, but I've no intention of courting her."

"Courtin'? Sweet word." Emily gazed at the goldfinch on the branch near Bill's shoulder. "Marie Wilton doesn't get courted. Her men go straight to her bed." She brushed his shoulder. "Ya have a friend. See?" She pointed to the bird.

"I know. It's odd. I saw a similar bird outside my window. Think it could be the same?"

She shrugged. "I've no idea. Maybe it's bringin' ya good luck."

"Good luck? I need it. Would you speak up for me? I want to get out of the hospital tomorrow. It's time to go home."

"Ya do seem quite robust fer someone who just got stabbed. Yes, I'll speak up for ya. But ya'll need the laudanum. Now let's head back to yar room."

Thirty-two

A Warning for a Dear Friend

Bill dipped his finger into his gin sling and stirred the drink, his third since coming into the Great Hall Hotel's Walpole Saloon. Raising the glass, he took a sip. Since leaving St. Thomas Hospital the day before, he'd been cooped up in his hotel room reading Rose's book, trying not to make any jerky movements that would irritate his stitched wound. Laudanum tamed the pain, but it also made him sleepy so he tried to get by without it—except at night when he needed to sleep. Book finished, Bill swore he'd not spend his last full day in London imprisoned in his room. So he chose the Walpole and gin slings at a table with no one but himself.

For the best. His actress friend, Marie Wilton, would love to while away a few hours with him, but gin slings and a beautiful woman could lead to unintended consequences—the two of them naked on his hotel bed. Bill shook his head. He wouldn't fall prey to that temptation at least.

A woman's voice from behind his shoulder jolted him out of his gin-sling musings. "I suspected I'd find you here, Bill."

Brain dulled by alcohol, he unthinkingly whirled around in his seat. Pain seared through his body. Hand shaking, he closed his fingers around the half-drunk glass and finished off the gin sling. "Lordy, Rose, you scared me half to death. My body's screaming at me for forgetting about the wound."

"Sorry." Removing his bowler, Rose kissed the top of Bill's head, then seated herself next to him. "I thought I'd better be with you—in case Marie gets any ideas in her head."

Bill ignored the comment. "Rose, so glad to see you. Please sit. Where's John Arthur?"

"Holed up writing a speech for Parliament. The man thinks he's a great orator. He's a big bag of gas. Nonetheless, I love him. Bill, I'm having trouble ending the courtship."

"I knew you would." He waved to a barmaid who sauntered to the table. "Another gin sling for me and one for the lady."

"Done." The barmaid dashed away, her eighteenth-century tapstress costume swirling about her ankles.

"He's such a kind man and fervent for the Confederacy. We belong together." Rose cracked a sad smile. "I honestly tried at the Britannia the other night. You heard. I treated him miserably. But he's been so good to you, Bill. Paid your hospital-room bill. Booked passage for you on the freight steamer *Lora Lee*. I can't hurt him."

"I just finished your book, Rose." Bill knew she'd understand his meaning without him coming right out and growling, "Do your duty." Besides, he liked John Arthur. But the Rose depicted in her book would never defy President Davis's orders. Had Rose changed so much she would mutiny?

"I'll end our relationship—at a time of my choosing. But it will be ended."

"I expected no less from the woman who wouldn't lose hope inside Lincoln's prison." Bill straightened the look of his bowler on his head. Rose had placed it at a cockeyed angle.

Her ginger curls set off by the saloon's gas lights, the barmaid returned with the two gin slings. Bill paid and slipped a tip into the redhead's fingers. The coins dropped between her breasts. "Fank ya, kind sir." Grinning, she eyed Rose. "He's certainly a fine, toileted gent, ain't he?"

"Best dandyman in London." Rose chuckled. "Normally, he's in a Confederate officer's uniform, so he goes hog wild when he gets to play a toff."

The barmaid nodded eagerly. "He's the best looking swell in the Walpole." Winking at Bill, she flounced away.

"Marie's got some competition. Back to more serious matters. John Arthur says he's going to France with me and get the Frogs to recognize the Confederacy. More likely he'll make recognition impossible. I can do better with Napoleon by myself. Anyway, I'm mainly going to Paris to see how Little Rose is doing. I enrolled her in the Sacred Heart Convent School." She sipped the gin sling. "An excellent choice, Bill. We ship them cotton; they give us gin slings."

"Only the best for Rose Greenhow and her beloved Dixie." He raised his glass to his mouth and tongued the liquor against his lips.

"I know you must be tired of my warnings, Bill." She gestured to a gray-haired gentleman at a table near them, a newspaper in his hands. "If you're not careful with Marie, you could end up in the newspapers. She may plot a tryst since tonight's your last night in London. I hear her understudy will be taking over her role this evening. I think you're in her sights."

"I've been told Marie has an actor beau who adores her. Why would she risk losing him?"

"Because the woman loves scandal." She tapped his wrist, let her nails graze skin.

"Ouch!"

"Listen to me!"

"Two women I intend to avoid like the pox. Marie and Becky."

Her sigh breathed exasperation. "If you hear a knock on your door, remember it could be Marie with schemes to get you to help her out of her clothes. I know for a fact she plans to be at the docks tomorrow to see you off. Don't let her kiss you. You'll end up in all the London newspapers. Those papers will eventually reach Richmond and Franny will see the gossip—and your goose will be cooked."

"No kisses, I promise." He took a swig of the gin sling and let it burn its way down his throat.

"She loves seeing her name in the society journals. Push her away if she won't take no for an answer. Be rough. Make her stumble. Society journalists will write you rejected her. Franny will know she married a faithful husband." Rose ran a finger along the rim of her glass. "I want to drink a toast to a safe voyage home, Bill. Not the gin sling, though. A proper drink for a toast should be a sherry cobbler."

Again, Bill signaled the barmaid for service. When the teenage girl pranced to their table, Bill inquired, "Ever hear of a sherry cobbler?" She looked puzzled.

"It's a New Orleans drink. It's bang-up in the Confederacy." Rose listed the ingredients.

"Ya're Rose Greenhow," the girl gushed. "I read all about ya in the *Morning Star*. Ya were so brave the way ya outfoxed them Yankees. Ya've lived such a beano life."

"Too much beano sometimes," Rose reflected. "Remember the sherry cobbler ingredients?"

The girl nodded. "Comin' right up. For both of ya or just the lady?"

"Both," Bill and Rose said simultaneously.

"I may try one meself." Chuckling, the barmaid sashayed to the bartender.

"The girl looks like she just stepped out of *Tom Jones*," Bill remarked.

"You'd not catch me dead in that outfit of hers."

"Of course not. Many girls in Europe and the South picture you in a short dress and bloomers, a six-gun strapped to your waist." Bill hummed a few notes of the "Bonnie Blue Flag." "To them, you're dead-eye Rose."

"Dead-eye Rose, eh? I should have put that in my book." Her smile lit up the saloon.

The barmaid returned with the two sherry cobblers. Sweat beaded her forehead and cheeks, and as she leant over, Bill caught a whiff of armpit and salt. "I'd love to visit the Confederacy after the war," she enthused. "Don't want to be anywhere near gunfire, cannons or rifles."

If the South didn't soon get European recognition and some help breaking the Yankee blockade, the Confederacy might not be around for the barmaid to visit. The South's misery could very well be God's judgment on Southerners for the Peculiar Institution. Even in late April 1864, the Confederate Congress and President Davis couldn't bring themselves to offer freedom to darkies if they served in Southern armies.

Bill left the barmaid another sizable tip, which she promptly deposited in her favorite spot. Once the girl had made her way across the room to three gentlemen competing to ply her with roguish compliments, Rose exclaimed, "Good Lord, Bill! I haven't asked how you're doing. The pain? Not too bad I hope. Better not be any rot."

"Don't need laudanum like I feared I might. I've been watching for infection. Nothing so far. I'm not worried about the sea voyage. I'll have the stitches removed in Wilmington." Bill steepled his fingers beneath his chin. "It's you I'm worried about, Rose."

Can't keep making excuses. If Rose and her daughter can survive a Union prison, you can summon the mettle to tell her about the halo. Then it's between Rose and the Lord.

"Me? For heaven's sake, why?" Her brows furrowed.

"You're going to think I'm nuttier than a fruitcake." He held up both hands, signaling Rose to stay quiet. "I won't be able to live with myself if I don't warn you. You're a woman of faith, right? You believe in miracles and messages from God, right?" His heart beat like the pistons of a steam engine. He hadn't tripped over his words nor said anything to make her run out of the saloon screaming—so far.

"Of course. I'm a God-fearing woman." She looked heavenward. "Lord, help this man make sense."

Tell her, damn it! Just say it and be done with it! "Rose, I see halos around men and women just before they die."

"Why are you telling me this?" She fisted her hands so tight they turned wax white.

"In Wilmington I saw one around you."

"That's months ago, and you said the halos appear just before the people die. I'm alive." Rose laughed nervously. Men at nearby tables gave her odd looks.

"I don't understand either. But they've never been wrong—until you." He decided not to tell her about Charlie and General Jackson. That would only confuse her. "I think the Lord's giving you extra time. And why would He give me this gift unless to allow me to save you? I'm warning you, Rose. Don't laugh away the halo. Be careful. Don't give it an opening."

She shuddered, as if a ghost had passed through her. "So He's giving me extra time? That must mean He wants me to help the Confederacy. He backs us, backs my mission." She seized Bill's hands, tugged them up to her mouth and kissed them. "This time your halo's a false one. The Lord changed His mind. I'm His instrument to bring down Lincoln and his evil war."

I don't think so, Rose. I fear we're the evil ones. We refuse to acknowledge the evil of slavery. Bill left that thought unsaid. "Maybe you're right, Rose. Maybe after the halo, he decided to make you His instrument. The halo has weighed heavy on my mind since the day it flared around you. I had to tell you."

"I'm glad you did, Bill. I can feel the Holy Spirit inside me. It's telling me I'm right." Sighing, she set his hands on the table. "I'll work even harder to gain more European friends for the Confederacy."

"Well, that's off my chest. Now I can board the merchantman tomorrow without regrets and return to Franny."

"Tell me all about her."

"Where do I start?"

"I suppose the beginning."

Bill stared at the two drinks in front of him, the sherry cobbler, full; the gin sling, almost empty. "During the Fredericksburg battle, I took a dying friend to the field hospital at the Yerby Plantation."

"Yes, I'm familiar with the place."

"They enlisted me to help look after the wounded and the dying." He finished off the gin sling. "Turned me over to a girl my age. Her bloody apron, the unkempt blond hair, sunburned face couldn't hide her beauty. That's how I met Franny amid so much death and destruction."

"I can see how you two ended up married. It was foreordained."

Bill pursed his lips. "It wasn't so clear to me."

"You impressed her. Not many privates impress Fredericksburg girls." Rose straightened her straw hat before tightening the chin strap.

"I never expected to see her again. She stunned me, though. Franny invited me to the town's New Year's Eve ball. I nearly didn't go."

"Ah, fate intervened."

Bill brought his hands together as if in prayer. "More like a chaplain who wouldn't take no for an answer. He cleaned me up, gave me a Zouave uniform and drove me to the Forrest Hills plantation for the ball."

"Like a contrarian halo. Figures a romantic gooseberry picker would be a man of God."

"I never thought of it that way." Bill feared Rose had just taunted her halo. *Not wise.*

Rose held her hand over her heart. "I'm a strong believer that quixotic love can fly into our hearts directly from God's throne."

"Franny looked like an angel. Or a Greek goddess. Hair more golden than Queen Victoria's crown. Azure eyes fixed only on me. I had trouble understanding why this divine creature would like a printer's son. I'm still stunned at my good luck."

"I never took you for a humble man, Bill."

"Around women like Franny, I am."

"I bet she describes you differently, my friend."

"Not at first, Rose. I never thought I'd win her. Not long after the New Year's ball, Franny went to Tennessee to nurse her fiancé."

"A fiancé?" Rose giggled. "You romanced another man's betrothed? Bill, you're a rake, a Don Juan."

Bill disagreed. He didn't consider himself a Don Juan. "He never loved his conquests, Rose. He just wanted the chase and the seduction. I loved and still love Franny. When she left, I was devastated."

Rose leaned back in her chair and pretended to clap. "Sorry. I know what happens next. You looked for solace in Becky's arms."

"Yep, my most foolish move. Wanted to marry her, but she ran off to Europe with you."

"Your tale ended well, didn't it?" Rose grinned broadly.

"Indeed. At the lowest point of my life, with Yankee Cavalry raiding my hometown, I rode to a neighboring town to get help from a detachment of regulars. A miracle happened. Franny broke the engagement, headed back to Fredericksburg, and then went south into North Carolina to find me. You know what she told me?"

Rose shrugged her shoulders. "That she planned to smack Becky in the nose?"

"Not quite. But close enough. She said she loved me and intended to win me back."

"I appreciate a love tale that ends well." Rose glanced at her untouched sherry cobbler. "Don't forget our toast to a fast, safe voyage back into Franny's arms. And many nights of passionate kisses and Franny's bosoms for pillows."

"Naughty, Rose." He held up his sherry cobbler glass. It clinked against Rose's glass. "And another toast, this time for a safe voyage for you back to Wilmington, but not before you get to spend some sweet time with your daughter."

They drank to the bottom of their cups and then Rose stood. "I'll see you and Franny back in Richmond in a few months. I've some errands to run." She hugged him tightly. "You're a good friend, Bill Stamford."

Thirty-three

Homeward Bound

Toting his carpetbag and pouch, Bill jumped aboard a horse-drawn tram whose final destination was the Wapping docks. A hangover pounded his head as he took a seat. The night before he'd returned to the Walpole for more gin slings. Too many it turned out. All night Bill kept a wary eye on the saloon's entrance, expecting to see Marie. Rose's warning proved groundless. The actress never showed up.

On the seat opposite, someone had left a paper behind. Just one day left in April, Bill thought as he glanced at the front page. Italian Giuseppe Garibaldi had just departed London after meeting with Prime Minister Palmerston and exiled revolutionaries. The column described how Londoners had greeted him with applause.

"Move over, dearie."

The woman's voice barely penetrated Bill's consciousness. Without looking up, he slid over to the window and returned his gaze to the front page.

"Bill Stamford, pay attention to me!"

He swung his gaze in time to see Marie Wilton plop down beside him.

"What a pleasant surprise, Marie," he lied. "I expected to see you at the port, not here."

"I wanted to spend more time with you. A streetcar ride will be beano." A coquettish smile formed on Marie's lips. "I'm sorry to hear that Rose won't be able to say goodbye."

"What!" Bill let the newspaper slip from his fingers and slide to the floor. "She told me she'd meet me at the dock."

"Rose twisted her ankle last night. This morning it was too tender for much walking."

"I just saw her yesterday. We shared some gin slings and sherry cobblers in the hotel's saloon."

"I wanted to surprise you last night, Bill. Have a drink with you too." She stroked his dandyman sleeve. "An old lover—Squire Bancroft—showed up on my doorstep and ruined my plans." A scowl obscured her dimples.

Bill gave Marie a curious look, like he did one time when Charlie claimed to be a virgin. "I've heard you two have a filly-and-foal courtship." He grinned. "I'd not want to risk your or Squire's happiness."

"We're sometimes hot, sometimes cold. Right now we're frigid." Her dimples returned as Marie showered him with a come-hither smile. "I caught Squire doing the bear with another actress."

Bill didn't believe a word coming out of her mouth. He remembered Rose's warning not to fall prey to this seductress. No kisses, no hugs, no caresses—a reporter could be in the seat behind them. Bill removed her hand from his sleeve.

"You're trying to get me into a heap of trouble with my wife."

"Really? I'm just here to give you an affectionate farewell." Marie tweaked Bill's earlobe.

Bill said nothing more, letting Marie chat away with just nods and harrumphs in answer to her natter. Every three blocks, the tram stopped to unload passengers and pick up new ones. Ahead, Hansoms and omnibuses squeezing close to the rails darted out of the way as the tram approached. Often foot-travelers would race across the rails, barely outpacing the looming vehicle. At the docks, the trolley company's tracks did a U-turn. The tram stopped at the end of the U near the wharves and riders poured from it like flood waters over a spillway. Toting his carpetbag and pouch, Bill pushed past the crowd waiting to board the tram.

"Better not be any journalists lurking about," Bill warned Marie.

"Ah, you were doing more than drinking sherry cobblers with Rose." Hand above her eyes to shade them from the sun, Marie gazed at Bill's ship, the *Lora Lee,* one of dozens of steamers and sailing ships moored to the docks. Their boiler stacks and masts projected up toward the white-marble clouds.

"Rose keeps me safe."

"Her sherry cobblers are little too sweet for me. You should stick to gin slings, Bill. Don't be a safe, cherry-cobbler guy. Live dangerously, be a gin-sling guy."

At the pier, children clung to their parents' legs as husbands hugged their wives. Bill figured the men in their sack suits were headed to Nassau to board ships for Philadelphia, Boston or New York to conduct business. Only one young couple headed up the *Lora Lee's* gangplank, a toddler holding her mother's hand. There were a few passenger berths available on the steamer, one reserved for Bill by John Arthur.

Bill and Marie played a tag-you're-it game. Her tag foretold a bear hug and kiss had he not backed up rather hastily. "I'm actually a lemonade guy, like that father with his wife and daughter." Bill gestured to the man, his wife and the toddler, stepping aboard the steamer. "I want to get home to Franny and make babies."

"Well, Bill, you leave me speechless. I can't compete with your homey desires—a wife in an apron, a baby in her arms." Marie made a sourpuss face. "I'm not ready to leave the stage and push a baby carriage. I guess it's Squire for me." She leaned against a railing, the river water lapping the bottoms of the posts. "Americans fascinate me, especially those with Southern accents. I find them—I find you— irresistible."

"Squire's the perfect man for you."

Marie stuck out her tongue. "Perfect maybe. Fun? Not so much. You're a real live Confederate soldier. You've been wounded, shot at, killed Yankees. You're a much more adventurous man than Squire. That's why I'm attracted to you. People think that because I'm an actress I'm adventurous. I'm not. I can sing, dance, repeat memorized lines with great emotion. The characters I play are adventurous, not me."

"Not adventurous?" Bill shook his head, a skeptical look on his face. "You've met the queen, great nobles. You mentioned my soldiering...you've been courted by generals. I wager you've been to the pyramids and the Roman colosseum."

"That's run-of-the-mill sightseeing." She did her own head shaking.

Two thirtyish men, one a dandy wearing a russet derby hat atop his head and an indigo bowtie secured to his neck, the other smothered in a banker's gray sack suit crowned with a top hat of raffia and silk, strolled to the railing and perched their forearms on the top balustrade. They said nothing, just contemplated the *Lora Lee* docked in front of them. They lacked carpetbags, which made Bill suspicious. He wondered if he'd seen them on the streetcar. They looked familiar; then again, most men nowadays dressed like them.

Bill jabbed his thumb toward the two men. "Reporters?"

Marie shrugged. "With all the society journals in London, there's way too many reporters to remember faces. I long ago gave—"

The gent with the derby hat spoke up, "Mornin', Miss Wil'on. Plannin' a trip to Nassau or perhaps New York City?" He nodded at Bill's carpetbag, big enough for two people.

"No, just seeing off one of Rose Greenhow's friends." Marie smiled prettily for Mister Derby Hat. "Bill here wonders if you're a reporter out to ruin his marriage."

The two men laughed then Mister Derby Hat responded, "Aye, a reporter." He didn't deny the bit about ruining Bill's conjugal bliss.

"Where I come from reporters don't have time to cover the mischief of stage actresses." Bill said his words with cold disdain. "They're too busy covering a war."

"I expect I'll cover a war or two before they nail me coffin shut," Mister Top Hat opined. "We Bri'ish always have a colonial war goin' on somewhere."

"The London newspapers can't get enough of the war on the other side of the Atlantic." Bill swiveled his gaze to the *Lora Lee*. "I'll share my berth with you if you want to see the war from a Confederate grayback's point of view."

Marie flipped her hand dismissively. "Why cover a war when they can cover my antics? I sell more papers than any old war."

"She's right ya know," Mister Top Hat informed Bill.

"Of course I'm right. You two must be here to see me kiss this Confederate officer before he boards the *Lora Lee*." Marie caressed Bill's coat collar. One finger tickled his neck before she drew her hand to her side. Her face turned sad. "He won't let me."

"I don't blame him," Mister Derby Hat admitted. "We do have a talent for exaggeration. And the papers do make it over to New York and Wilmington."

"Exaggeration? Naw." Mister Top Hat scratched one end of his waxed mustache. "I overheard Squire Bancroft complain ter a friend that Miss Wil'on has been showin' a heap of attention ter our Confederate officer."

"He may be an officer, but he's also a spy." Mister Derby Hat sported a mischievous smile. "It's quite understandable why Miss Wilton is all filly-and-foal over him. I expect a kiss any moment."

"The ques'ion remains…will he resist?" Mister Top Hat fixed his gaze on Bill.

"I kind of promised not to kiss him." She held out her arms toward Bill. "He's very good at resisting me. I'll always think of him as the one who got away. He's so lovable." She sighed. "They really want me to kiss you, spoilsport. What do you say, Johnny Reb? Should I?"

Bill shook his head vigorously. "No, no, no."

"I know what you're thinking, Bill Stamford, just as these reporters know as well." Marie sighed again. "Deep down you do want to be my lover, but you're terrified these reporters' gossip will be read by your wife. I don't think it's likely. The politicians and the generals read the London newspapers, not wives with pretty little hands."

Bill harrumphed, rolling his eyes. "Of course Franny will read it. That's how fate works."

Marie did her own version of a harrumph. "I think this Franny of yours is kissing someone else at this very moment. You've been gone for quite a while. No doubt she's feeling the need for a man's embrace."

Stepping back from the railing, Bill braced both hands on his hips. "I trust her."

"Let's ask the reporters." Marie gave Bill an impish smile. "Do you think his wife's staying true to him?"

"No way I'm answerin' that ques'ion," Mister Top Hat shot back.

"Agreed," Mister Derby Hat said.

"I would never break your heart." Marie reached out to tickle Bill's earlobe. He slapped her hand away.

"Ouch! I like rough men."

"Stop it, Marie!" Bill grabbed her arm. "You don't weigh much. It would be easy to toss you into the water."

"Even wet I'd never break your heart." Marie removed Bill's hand from her arm. "Can you be sure about your wife? Remember what Becky did? You loved her once, right?"

"Becky fled from me. Franny fled to me."

Puckering her mouth as if she meant to kiss him, Marie didn't carry through with the threat. Instead, she eyed the reporters. "You won't get your story, boys. I've lost my touch. I tried, but I can't wrap this boy around my little finger."

Mister Derby Hat smacked the upper rail with delight. "But we did get our story, Miss Wilton. It'll be the top item in the *Telegraph's London After Dark*."

"And top billin' in the *London Times* too," Mister Top Hat said, smirking.

Marie's brows knitted together, her forehead furrowed. "I don't understand."

"Ya've been refused, Miss Marie." Top Hat gave Bill a gold-piece smile. "That's never happened."

"Had I really wanted to seduce him, I would have, boys."

"True or not, Miss Marie, the readers will love how your seduction game came up short with this handsome American." Mister Derby Hat shook Bill's hand. "Tell your wife hello for me."

"I sure will. You've made my day. I'll be sure to grab both the *Telegraph* and the *Times* when I get back to Richmond."

As Bill reached to pick up his carpetbag, Marie seized his face and planted a wet kiss on his mouth. "Don't be surprised if I show up in Richmond and make your life a living hell."

Bill pinched her cheek. "Please come. I'll introduce you to Franny."

"Now you've dared me, Bill Stamford. A big mistake."

Pouch and carpetbag in hand, Bill headed up the gangplank. He turned and waved goodbye to Marie and the reporters. He yelled out to the reporters, "Are you going to tell your readers about Marie's shifty kiss?"

"Aye," Mister Derby Hat shouted back.

Thirty-four

Trouble on the Tar Heel Coast

Belly grumbling, Bill stood alone at the deck railing of the blockade runner *CSS Lady Stirling* staring into the night-time fog. He searched for distant landmarks—Federal Point, Dish Pan Shoals, twinkling lamplights of Fort Fisher, its guns aimed at the Union fleet lurking offshore. He'd felt that stomach-churning feeling before— during the tense hours leading up to the battle of Fredericksburg.

Almost two weeks had passed since Marie underhandedly kissed Bill goodbye under the snooping eyes of two London gossip reporters. In stormy waters below clouds laced with lightning, the British steamer *Lora Lee* had safely transported him from London to Nassau. Safe, but seasick most of the way. With the *Lora Lee* bucking in the Atlantic waters, Bill spent most of the trip retching in his cabin's piss bowl or on deck puking over the railing. Once moored in Nassau, Bill had enjoyed May's Caribbean heat as he watched stevedores transfer the *North Star's* cargo of war supplies into the *Lady Stirling's* hold. Perversely, he wished the Atlantic swells were as choppy now as they were on the way to Nassau. When making a night-time dash into the Cape Fear River and Wilmington, Bill preferred squally weather over fog.

Looking up past the masts and smokestacks, Bill saw a starry sky above the ocean-hugging fog. As he stared upward, he felt the deck vibrate. At the captain's orders, the *Lady Stirling's* engines cranked into an ear-thumping hum, propelling the blockade runner toward the Cape Fear River. Ahead lay the safe waters below Fort Fisher's guns. Dozens of Yankee ships awaited the *Lady Stirling*, her crew and passengers somewhere in the fog, their deadly goal to send the blockade runner to the sea bottom.

"This is my first time," a youthful voice said nervously.

Lulled by the sounds of seawater thumping the hull and the wind slapping the Confederate flag flying from a mast, Bill hadn't heard fourteen-year-old Timothy Donavan's approach.

"Don't worry," Bill reassured him. "Most runs are successful. I've dodged Yankee mini balls. What's a few Federal ships belching off-target shells?"

Stanley, the boy's father, joined them at the railing. He gestured to where fog-cloaked Union cruisers patrolled the waters. "In my younger days, I was in the U.S. Navy. It's a hard, tedious job running down a ship trying to sneak into a harbor. Frustrating work. One moment of napping and your prey escapes." He gazed up at the star-studded sky. "The fog's good, but an overcast night would be even better. You'd not think so, but a clear night filled with stars can reveal a ship—even without a moon."

A Coston flare lit up in the dark sky like a rocket on the Fourth of July.

Bill cursed. He knew what the flare meant.

"What's happening?" Timothy rasped, his voice trembling.

"Some really rotten luck, that's what's happening." Stanley groaned. "We've been spotted."

"We've been seen by a fast cruiser, Timothy." Bill punched the railing in frustration. Months earlier, the *Don* had escaped the Union dragnet without a problem. Well, there were two off-target shells, but the *Don* easily outran the blockaders. The *Lady Stirling* would face a harder task.

Stanley put Bill's thoughts into words. "The fast cruisers are Lincoln's first line of defense. The captain's going to have to outrun them and two interior lines of ships, especially the bar-tenders just off the shoals."

"But the fog's so thick." Timothy shook like a tree in a spring thunderstorm.

"Like I said, son, rotten luck. It happens." Stanley put his arm around Timothy. He kissed the teenager's wind-mussed hair. "It's going to be a great adventure, like those in the books you read. 'Once more into the breach, dear friends.'"

"Shakespeare?" Timothy still quivered. At least he proffered a half-formed smile.

"Yep, the great bard. I see you remember your lessons." Stanley pointed into the fog. "Watch closely. See if you can spot the first smoothbore that fires at us."

Timothy craned forward and squinted.

"We'll outrun them," Bill predicted. "Speed wins these blockade battles. Before you know it we'll be safe in the Cape Fear River, protected by Fort Fisher's guns."

"We're fast. Listen to those engines growl. Without the shielding, they'd be much louder." Stanley chose silence for a few seconds then continued, "They've nothing as fast. But our captain's young without much experience. Never served in the British Navy."

Bill trusted Stanley Donavan. The man served as an aide in the North Carolina governor's office, one of the Tar Heel experts who made sure Wilmington stayed a secure port for blockade runners. He, his French wife Juliet and their son were returning to North Carolina after visiting Juliet's parents in Marseille.

"Never? Where did Holdren get his experience?" Like Timothy, Bill maintained a steely gaze on the foggy horizon, waiting to see the first hint of fire erupting from a smoothbore cannon.

Turning toward the pilothouse, Stanley regarded one of the men inside—Captain Dudley Holdren. "He captained merchant ships for his father's shipping line of cargo steamers. First yachts, now merchant ships. My theory? Holdren and his father think this one trip by the *Lady Stirling* can net them a thousand percent profit. Holdren's an adventurer. He considers himself a Don Juan." Stanley rolled his eyes. "He's been sweet talking Juliet."

"Ogling your wife in front of you, eh? Foolish man. Sea captains don't need to be making enemies in the governor's office, almost as bad as angering President Davis. I hope Holdren has better sailing skills than romance talent." Bill leaned over the railing and spit into the frothing water.

"Yes, better at this than wife-stealing." Stanley nodded as if agreeing with his own words. "Holdren's got fire in his heart. He's going to love the challenge."

Bill scrutinized the captain. Holdren held a speaking tube to his mouth. Bill could feel the *Lady Stirling* speeding up, sprinting through the Atlantic at maybe fifteen knots. The side-wheel paddles were spinning faster, churning the water. Down in the engine room, stokers were shoveling coal into the boilers, getting extra steam to support the swift speed.

Far behind the *Lady Stirling's* stern, smoothbores roared fire and cannonballs ripped through the fog. Timothy yelped, his voice as high as a girl's.

"Calm down, boy!" Stanley urged as the ship's engines purred and cannonballs whirred through the damp air then splashed into the water well short of the ship. "We've outrun the cruisers."

Ahead, three Coston flares blazed, chasing away the night.

"What the hell!" Timothy croaked.

Stanley slapped his son beside the head. "No profanity!"

"The second line's seen us." Bill couldn't keep the fatalism in his heart from creeping into his voice. He felt like a fly snared in a spider's web.

Timothy summoned sudden courage. "They won't get us. We're faster than lightning."

Even with the raucous sounds of the engines and swells crashing against the hull, Bill still heard Holdren's voice. "More steam! More steam! Give her more steam!"

The engine-room sailors responded. The deck shook like a mini-quake beneath Bill's feet, and the *Lady Stirling* raced even faster.

With excellent closing angles, two blockaders narrowed the distance between themselves and the *Lady Stirling*. Lit lanterns dangled from the bowsprits, a message from Union captains: we don't fear you.

Fire burst from the two ships' cannons, bright red against the night and the lanterns' amber light. Booms echoed off the water followed by the whir of round shot and shells knifing through the misty air. They ploughed ocean all around the *Lady Stirling*. Water geysers fountained upward, splashing against Bill's face. Next time the Yankees would do better, he knew.

Timothy howled frenzied laughter. "It's the Devil's rain." Soaked strands of black hair trickled water drops down his face. He shrieked a child's rhyme: "Rain, rain, go away, come again another day."

Heralded by a deep buzzing sound, a hundred-pound bolt passed over the ship, barely missing the bridge and pilothouse.

"God save us!" Wailing, Timothy slumped to his knees.

His father knelt beside the boy. "Remember what you said, Timothy? We're faster than lightning. The Yanks will never catch us!"

Bill raised his arms, hands fisted. "Before you know it, we'll be seeing Wilmington's church steeples in the morning light. Captain Holdren will outfox them."

Timothy looked up at Bill. The teenager's eyes reflected starlight. "You think so?"

Bill helped Stanley bring the boy to his feet. "The Yankees won't get a prize this night." Bill hoped his assessment proved correct.

Engines groaning, the *Lady Stirling* steamed toward the protection of Fort Fisher's guns. Out on the bridge, the captain hissed, "Damn it!"

Next to Holdren, the first officer groaned, "Hemmed in! Ships all around us."

A cannonball split the foremast, sending the sailor in the crow's nest plunging into the ocean. A shell seared into the hull at the waterline, dislodging an iron plate. Water plunged into the ship's guts.

Timothy's panicky eyes fixed on Bill. "You lied! Damned Yanks got us."

This time Timothy's father didn't chastise him for cursing.

At the bow, a cannonball rocketed over their heads and demolished the pilothouse. The first officer's head bounced down the splintered ladder then rolled along the deck, leaving a bloody trail. It smacked against Timothy's ankle and stopped. The boy leaned over the railing and puked. His father kicked the severed head toward the wrecked pilothouse.

Groaning, spitting blood, Holdren crawled from the wreckage and shouted out an order, "Beach her!" He tried to stand, revealing a wood shard in his chest, pitched forward and jammed the fragment further into his body. The captain lay on his belly, unmoving.

Somehow, the ship's wheel remained intact. Reaching up and gripping the wheel, the pilot heaved himself to his feet. The *Lady Stirling* steamed toward the shoreline as water gushed into the hull breach. Cannonballs and shells continued to splash around the fast-moving ship. As the ship plowed through a shoal, a cannonball smashed the paddlewheel, crushing several paddles. Crippled, the *Lady Stirling* ran aground between Fort Fisher and the mouth of the Cape Fear River. As if dying, the ship groaned.

Bill and Timothy clambered over the railing and dropped to the sand. Bill gritted his teeth as pain surged out from his side. *Damn the wound! Damn Percy!* Looking back, Bill didn't see Timothy's father. "Your papa's not with us."

"He's gone back for Ma. She's still in the cabin."

"Those cannon hits and the rough beaching hopefully goaded your mother to come up on deck." Bill swung his worried gaze from the boy to the hull's railing, then aimed it out to where a Union bartender drew in close as if meaning to steam through the surf and onto the shore. Federal sailors dropped a rowboat full of Marines into the water. Fort Fisher batteries opened fire, dropping shells near the tender.

"Good Lord! They're trying to capture us!" Timothy stared at Bill as if expecting him to have a miracle in his pocket.

"We need to get your papa and your ma before we do anything more." Bill leapt upward, hoping to snag the *Lady Stirling's* deck railing and flip-flop onto the deck. He failed, falling back onto the beach.

Mounted troops and two field pieces dashed out of Fort Fisher's sally port, churning up sand as they raced for the *Lady Stirling*. At the ship's railing, Stanley cradled his wife in his arms then tossed her over the balustrade. His boots buried in the sand near the ship, Bill reached out and caught her. Stanley hurdled the railing and landed on his knees. Panting, climbing to his feet, the governor's aide opened his arms and welcomed his wife's passionate hugs and kisses.

"When they get this way, they always embarrass me." Timothy curved his mouth into a sheepish smile.

"Hey, it's my favorite pursuit." Bill shrugged, ignoring a twinge of pain in his side, another reminder of the knife wound.

The rowboat made land as the Fort Fisher detachment reached the ship. The U.S. Marines took cover behind their boat and opened fire with their Springfields. Bill grabbed Timothy and sprawled atop him next to the hull. Mini balls whizzed by their heads, striking the hull's plating with a tuning-fork clang.

"You're hurting me," Timothy wheezed.

"Shut up," Bill snapped. "Keep your noggin down. Don't become a target."

To their front, Stanley and Juliet lay prone against the hull. "Timothy? Where's Timothy?" Juliet shrieked.

"I'm here, Ma. Behind you." Timothy dug his hand through the sand and tapped his ma's shoe.

Fort Fisher's soldiers opened fire. The Marines ducked their heads behind the rowboat. Unlimbering the field pieces, the artillerymen fired at the rowboat, showering the Marines with an avalanche of sand. Turning their attention to the tender, the gunners reloaded and hurled shells at the small ship, striking a mast. The tender withdrew. Behind the rowboat a Marine shouted, "We surrender. Don't fire."

Rolling away from the fourteen year old, Bill came to his knees. His stitches howled, but he refused to surrender to the agony. "Now the U.S. Navy has the rotten luck."

Thirty-five

Bill relaxed as the Hansom cab bounced along the tree-lined brick roadway that wound through the Richmond neighborhood of apartment buildings. His feet rested atop the carpetbag as he tried to read the mid-July *Richmond Dispatch* front page. The read wasn't easy, not with the bumpy ride. One headline caught his eye…STALEMATE. No longer behind fortifications around Fredericksburg, General Lee's Army of Northern Virginia lay pinned in defensive earthworks around Richmond and Petersburg. *What the hell happened?* In the morning, he'd have Charlie give him an update. His chum wouldn't sugarcoat the war, not like Secretary Seddon might do.

So much had happened since Bill left London for Wilmington. Even with him back in the Confederacy, the pace still seemed dizzying since the Union dragnet had forced the *Lady Stirling* to run aground near Fort Fisher. That had been two months ago. Bill had planned to hop a train for Virginia, but a telegraph missive from Seddon ordered him to recuperate at his momma's until his wound healed. He'd gone to Doctor Iuppenlatz in Wilmington and had the stitchings removed. The wound had festered. The *Lady Stirling's* beaching hadn't helped—sand and dirt trickled into the wound. The good doctor cleaned out the decay then re-stitched the wound.

In Kenansville, Bill had wanted to take a buggy ride up to Warsaw and begin his train journey into Franny's arms, but his momma insisted he sit on the front porch and enjoy the Tar Heel weather, be it sunshine or a thunderstorm. She'd even forbid him to read about the war; said she didn't want to see him fretting about a lost battle or the worsening economy. At least she'd let him send Franny a telegram alerting her that he was back in the Confederacy. He'd wanted to tell her about his troubles with Becky and Marie, not have her read about them in a Richmond newspaper's gossip columns, but decided to say nothing in the telegram. Bill feared he'd have heaps of explaining to do. He'd soon know. Bill recognized the block of apartments—home.

"Whoa!" The buggy driver reined the horse to a stop. With fare paid, the cab door opened and Bill climbed down onto the boardwalk in front of his apartment building. He sighed. He hadn't seen this building since the spring. The façade looked worn compared to the apartments and townhouses in London. The war was wearing down more than men, women and children.

He brushed a wind-snipped leaf from his sleeve. Not a sleeve to a uniform, but one sewed to his last remaining London dandyman suit. Tomorrow he'd wear his officer's uniform again. The suit would go into the armoire until the end of the war. When Bill took the train, he hadn't telegraphed anyone in Richmond, not even Franny, so no one knew he'd left Kenansville. Taking a deep breath to calm his nerves, he stepped up the stairs to his apartment building's portico porch and front door. A blue-sky day allowed the sun to kiss his face. The thought gave birth to another thought: *A fizzing day to kiss Franny and carry her to their bed.*

Bill swore under his breath. He'd forgotten. Franny's mother had been staying with her since her father had been transferred to Texas to keep an eye on Maximilian and his French troops stirring up mischief in Mexico. No way could Bill tip the velvet with Franny, not with his mother-in-law in the apartment. Fisting his hands, he tried and failed to sigh away his exasperation.

Bill felt something brush against his pants leg. A loud meow revealed the source—Tessir. "Howdy, cat. Your momma home?" Tessir slithered through the cat door into the atrium, the tiny entryway Bill had made with permission from the landlord. Bill followed, opening the front door. His heart beat fiercely. He couldn't wait to hug the wife he'd missed so much—even if her momma stood beside her.

Once in the atrium, Bill glanced at the mail slots and his apartment number—thirty. He could see envelopes on the other side of the glass. Franny had yet to pick up the mail. *Of course not.* She and her momma were probably at a Ladies' Aid Society meeting. Or maybe Franny had accepted President Davis's offer and was working as a clerk at the Treasury Department.

Rolling his eyes at his forgetful mind, Bill climbed the stairs and beelined down the hallway to his apartment. Out of nowhere came a terrifying thought: what if she wasn't at the Treasury Department but in bed with another man? He smacked his forehead. *Stop it!* With her momma staying with her, starting an affair would be nigh impossible. At number thirty, Tessir slinked between Bill's legs and darted through the cat door. "I know what you want, Tessir."

The gray-furred cat scurried into the kitchen and meowed next to the stove and pantry. Barely home and Bill found himself answering to a damn cat. "Let's see what we can feed you, big boy."

Tessir always ate well, getting dinner-plate scraps. Bill fired up the coal stove, dug out some desiccated vegetables and salt pork. "We'll both eat, buddy. Like Franny's always saying, the best way to become a cat's bosom buddy is through its belly."

Later, after Bill ate his meal, he put down a bowl of scraps for the cat who gobbled it up before Bill could clean his plate, utensils and cup. He resumed sitting then lowered his hand. Tessir sniffed his fingers and meowed insistently. "Ah, you want to be petted." He scratched the cat around the ears and on the underside of the critter's chin. With Tessir's purrs loud in his ears, Bill hung his dandyman coat and vest on the back of the kitchen chair.

As the late-afternoon sun beckoned evening shadows, Bill settled on the parlor's settee and picked up a Holmes stereoscope from the end table. He plucked a two-image photo card from its case, slipped it into the slots, and slid the picture along the rail until it came into focus, an image of tourists sightseeing at India's Taj Mahal. The case held dozens of two-image photos of famous foreign sites most Confederates would never see. A couple of hours of daylight remained, but Bill still lit the oil lamp beside the photo box. He intended to do some reading.

At the sound of a key slipping into the door latch, Bill jerked his head toward the front door. He heard the lock flip open. "Scat, Tessir." The cat leaped from his lap and darted for the door. The door squeaked. Franny and maybe her mother would soon step into the parlor.

"I've got a derringer," Franny shouted. "So don't do anything funny, whoever you are."

Bill hadn't expected that response. Franny must have seen the light from the oil lamp, and knew she'd left it unlit when she headed to the Treasury Department or the Ladies' Aid Society. With Richmond's population soaring to nearly one hundred and fifty thousand, the city teemed with ruffians, including pickpockets, burglars, and murderers. Two women living by themselves needed to be extremely careful.

"Franny, it's me. Back from Europe." Bill hoped he got out the words in time—before she put a bullet in his chest.

"Bill? Good God!" Franny sidled away from the door, eyeing him as if beholding the ghost of her Grandmother Adelia. In the lamplight, her azure eyes filled with love for him, dazzling his heart. She stood as if stuck in deep mud. She couldn't take her eyes off him. "Shame on you! I nearly died of fright."

"I decided not to send a telegram. More romantic this way." He rose from the settee. Even in the drab work dress, Franny looked lovelier, more stunning than in her gown on the night of the

Fredericksburg ball. He reached out his arms, inviting her into his embrace.

She dropped the derringer. The tiny gun slapped the hardwood floor and bounced onto the parlor rug. Thankfully, it didn't discharge. Dancing on her toes for a few seconds, Franny sprinted into his arms. Her arms wrapped around his waist. Her mouth sought his lips.

Pain shot through Bill's body. His muscles tensed, became rigid. A yelp escaped his mouth, the air blowing against Franny's cheek.

Her hands flying to her face, she leaped back out of Bill's arms. "Oh God! I'm sorry. I should have remembered you'd been hurt in London. How could I forget? I read your telegram a hundred times."

Pain subsiding, he managed a lopsided grain. "Passion overwhelms everything but our immediate desires." He looked past to the door. "I expected your sweet momma to be with you. Been a worry actually."

"Worry?" Franny smiled naughtily. "So you thought mother would put out the fire in your trousers?" She snorted. "Momma hated the apartment. Too small, too humdrum. She left a month ago for her cousin's place just outside Hicksford."

"Hicksford?" He'd never heard of it. Probably a village of no more than ten families.

"A railroad town near the North Carolina border. Momma's a mansion girl, and her cousin Josephine has the most imposing house in Hicksford. Jo married a railroad baron. And I think momma didn't want to be here when you returned. As you know, she loves you dearly, but she realizes we need our privacy." Franny stroked his cheek. "Let me kiss you—gently." On her tiptoes, Franny rested her hands on Bill's shoulders and delivered wet, messy kisses—five minutes' worth, he estimated. Withdrawing her lips, Franny stepped back and admired him. "You've lost weight."

"Because of this." Lifting his shirt, he showed her the re-stitched wound.

"Oh Bill, what kind of mess did you get yourself in?"

He gestured to the settee and she sat. Immediately, the cat jumped into her lap.

"Did Tessir miss you?" She petted the fellow around his ears, earning a purr nearly as loud as a locomotive engine.

"He did—until I fed him. Then he disappeared until you came through the door. He's obviously your cat."

She patted the cushion beside her. "Sit. Tell me how you got the wound."

Bill settled beside Franny and rubbed Tessir's back. "I hope you haven't read any of the London newspapers. I want you to have the truth straight from me, not in a gossip column."

"I read them while you were in London." She scratched her chin then scratched Tessir's belly and laughed when all four paws twitched at steamboat speed. "Even saw a few items about an American Southerner paying Rose a visit. I wondered if he was you—especially after the reporter said the fella had been set upon by thugs and wounded." She gently touched his shirt near Bill's wound. "So you were the fella?"

He leaned against her, earning a rancorous meow from Tessir. "I'm going to kiss my wife whether you like it or not, cat." Bill cupped Franny's chin and staccato kissed her mouth. He drew back and said coolly, "Becky's beau hired some thugs to rough me up. One decided fists weren't enough. He carved me with a knife."

"So did he have a reason to be jealous?" Her eyes drilled into Bill's heart.

"I told her I love you. She told me she loves Percy and her bohemian life in London. Franny, she wears pants." Bill shook his head in wonderment.

"No doubt she's writing a novel that'll never get published." Franny's mouth bent into a sneer.

"London changed Becky in a bad way, Franny. She used me to make Percy insanely jealous. That's why I have this knife wound."

"What did she have to say for herself?"

"I never saw her again. Rose told her to stay away."

"Bitch! Sounds like this Percy and Becky deserve each other." Franny sighed, her disgust self-evident. "Once I got the telegraph message saying you were back in North Carolina and safe, I stopped reading the London newspapers."

Bill chewed his lower lip, all the time wondering if he should reveal Marie Wilton. If he chose silence and Franny got a look at a London newspaper, he could do terrible damage to his marriage. "Rose has some interesting characters who flock around her including a flighty actress, Marie Wilton."

"Uh oh…you're worrying me again, Bill. So why are you bringing up this woman's name?" Frowning, Franny fidgeted. Not liking Franny's nervy lap, Tessir jumped to the floor and scurried under the settee.

"Marie has one irritating foible. She loves to see her name in the headlines." He crossed his arms and rested them against his belly. "She constantly flirted with me. At the docks to bid me farewell, with gossip reporters present, Marie tried to give them a show. I pushed her away, refused her kisses."

"No man should go through such torture." Franny exhaled an unlady-like snort. "So you've been a nervous Nellie worrying I read about Marie in the newspapers?"

"Not really, not after the reporters laughed at her antics and revealed what their headlines would say: 'Actress fails to seduce adventurer.'"

"I never heard such a cockamamie story, which means it's true. Too bad about your wound. Otherwise, I'd finish her job and seduce you."

Bill took her hands. "With some imagination employed, we can tip the velvet." He winked.

They held hands on the way to the bedroom since carrying her was out of the question, not with the wound ready to complain at the slightest pressure. They failed to see Tessir stalking them.

For the first time in months, he undressed her, kissing her breasts after her underthings puddled around her toes. As she undid his shirt buttons, she kissed each spot of revealed skin. When his dandyman pants lay on the floor, she pushed him onto the bed and lay beside him.

Entangling his legs with hers, he kissed the tips of her breasts and then worked his way to her belly and down to her fruitful vine. He wanted to mount her, but knew his wound would have conniptions. Instead, she rose to her knees and purred, "Ready?"

"Lordy yes!"

She looked at his tallywag. "You're definitely ready."

Her saucy eyes dancing, Franny crooked a leg over his hip and mounted him. Desire rolled through Bill. He gaped at her firm breasts, her ivory skin. She moved her hand in a slow circle across his chest then thrust her fingers into her hair and unbound the curls. The blonde strands rippled as she moved, maneuvering so the tresses stroked his chest. She took his tallywag in her hand and guided it into her fruitful vine. Drenched in sweat, she writhed passionately atop him. When both were spent, she collapsed against his chest, breathing heavily. Once, the wound feigned ethereal pain, but Franny took care not to let her hand get close to the stitches.

Bill caressed the edge of a breast. "I love you, Franny. Every night in London I dreamt of this moment."

"I missed you terribly, Bill."

Not expected, Tessir leaped onto the bed and landed on Bill's belly. Claws extended, he jumped to the edge of the bed and stared at the two of them as if wondering: What are you humans doing?

The cat's machinations hurt more than Franny's frantic lovemaking.

Bill scooted Tessir closer to Franny's hip. "Bad timing, cat."

"For us, but not for him. He's a little devil."

Thirty-six

Bill Gets New Orders

Bill's uniform chafed his neck and armpits as he and Franny strolled toward the Capitol Square. On Main Street between Tenth and Eleventh streets, they stopped, and standing face to face, held hands. "Last night and this morning are the best moments of my life," he told her. "Sleeping beside you and now walking to work with you...I'm the happiest man alive. This far outranks every Hansom ride to London theatres."

Laughing lightly, Franny swung her hands to Bill's cheeks and kissed him. "It will be old hat soon enough. Maybe we can walk home after work?"

"I'll stop by the Customs House and see if you're ready." He kissed her again, his passion not curbed by people passing by. Bill stopped long ago worrying about what the moral police thought about all their public kissing and cuddling.

They hugged as if in their bedroom, and then he watched her go into the former U.S. Customs House, now Treasury Department quarters and President Davis's executive office. With the taste of her kiss still on his lips, Bill walked on to the Mechanics Building that housed the War Department. Ten minutes before, the sky had been cloud free except for a smattering of dark ones on the horizon. Now the smidgeon had become thunderheads. Bolts of lightning flashed one after another, followed by rumbles. Bill regretted he'd left his umbrella back at the apartment.

As Bill headed up the War Department's portico steps, Corporal Craig Skinner sidled next to him. "Welcome back, Lieutenant Stamford. I'm surprised to see you. Charlie said nothing."

Bill returned the corporal's salute. "Charlie doesn't know. Not even Secretary Seddon. I'm supposed to be back in North Carolina recuperating from an injury, but I got tired of sitting on my momma's porch. I decided to come back without sending a telegram. Surprises can be fun, especially when you play them on your wife."

"Really? You didn't let Franny know? Sleep in a cold bed?"

"On the contrary. The hottest it's ever been." Bill whistled the first few notes of "Lilly's Pale White Thighs." He figured the corporal often heard the song sung in Richmond's saloons.

"Marriage night all over again, eh? Did a Richmond fire pumper have to put out the bed flames?" Corporal Skinner opened the portico door with a flourish and stood aside so Bill could enter.

"How did you know?"

"I've had it happen a few times myself." The corporal escorted Bill to the office he hadn't seen in months. The door was closed.

"My chuckaboo must be up to no good." Bill gripped the door handle. "He probably has a Treasury Department girl in there."

"I've gotten to know Charlie—a scoundrel." The corporal laughed. "But a splendid scoundrel and fine drinking partner at all the saloons. But a dark cully? No way. Not since Avis Thompkins came into his life."

"We'll soon know." Bill opened the door and stepped into his office.

Charlie wasn't at his reception desk, his normal spot. Bill peeked through the open doorway into his private office. As lamplight fluttered on the back wall, he detected two legs propped up on his desk.

"That will be all, Corporal." Bill nodded toward the hallway door. Skinner saluted and withdrew. "Take mercy on your chuckaboo."

Stepping toward his office, Bill raised his voice. "Charlie Kurtz, take your damned boots off my desk."

Charlie jerked backward, nearly overturning the chair. His eyes grew large as he came to his feet and fastidiously straightened overturned pencils, pen-holder, pen and inkwell, newspapers, and memos from Secretary Seddon. "I could do all the business at my reception desk, but sometimes I just like sittin' in a comfy chair." He stopped his chatter and stared at Bill. "I should be mad at you, Billy Boy. I'm the one no good at writin' letters, not you. A telegram would have been nice. Secretary Seddon knows, right?"

A smug look on his face, Bill shook his head. "Nope, told no one, not even Franny. I wanted to surprise everyone. Momma didn't think it was a good notion, but I told her to hush up. Quite a surprise, eh?"

"Billy Boy, I helped you to the field hospital at Chancellorsville, so don't do any complainin' when I give you a hug. Hear me? No grumpiness."

"Hell, we're chuckaboos." Bill held out his arms. "Give me that hug. Won't be like Franny's, but it will be the second-best one I'll get today. Be careful, though. The knife wound's a tad touchy." So they hugged the way friends for life do. Bill stepped back. "Now out of the way, possum. I want to sit in that chair. I've missed it almost as much as I missed your silly mug."

Charlie sprawled in a chair at the front of the desk while Bill settled into his cozy one, a stranger to his buttocks after all those months away from Richmond. Bill glanced at Seddon's memos and whistled.

"I miss somethin' rib-ticklin'?"

"No. Looks like you've been doing a competent job." Bill tapped his index finger on the top memo. "The secretary let you do the work while I was gone. He trusted you, Charlie. He didn't call in a bugger with chicken guts on his cuffs. That air of responsibility clinging to you must be due to Avis's influence."

"Yep, nothin' escapes your superior spyin' talents, Billy Boy. Avis's kisses have turned me into a proper soldier. Guess what? She agreed to marry me, but we've not set a date yet." Charlie crossed his legs and propped his right kneecap up against the edge of the desk. "I'm dyin' to hear about your escapades in London, especially how you got that new wound. Shell slivers and knives seem to like your flesh."

"Congratulations. I knew Avis was a keeper. As to my new wound...the simple answer: Becky. You should have kept me away from her, Charlie."

Charlie's chortle turned into a wholehearted laugh, one seldom heard by Bill since his friend lost his arm. "That girl has been nothin' but trouble for you since that church picnic. You tip the velvet with her in that Wilmington hotel, and she thanks you by turnin' down your marriage proposal and runnin' off to England. So what's Becky's role in your woundin'?"

"Becky fancies herself a bohemian, complete with pants and a hunger for men. Live life as fast and as wild as George Sands. That's Becky's philosophy. That way she'll have the makings for a novel. I think she envisioned me and her beau Percy brawling over her. I couldn't get her to tamp down her flirting. Percy saw me as a gal sneaker out to bed his girl. He hired thugs to put me in the hospital. He accompanied them so I'd know who ordered the knifing. Bastard told me to stay away from Becky—and that's what I'd been trying my best to do. Those two deserve each other."

"There's somethin' not right with that girl. Her refusal was the best thing to ever happen to you...next to marryin' Franny, of course." Charlie set his elbows flat against the desktop and regarded Bill the way a virgin girl ogles a fortune teller, eager to hear the story her palm foretells. "So how did your mission turn out?"

"Rose has the letter from President Davis." Bill noticed an errant pencil on the desk that had escaped Charlie's notice. He returned it to the pencil cup. "The president's words left her gloomy. Nevertheless, she's going to obey him. She's a patriot after all."

Charlie snorted. It was a look Bill was familiar with going back to the heady days of 1861 when school chums brawled with Charlie over the Peculiar Institution, the enslavement of black men and women. Charlie thought the war a mistake, a belief being borne out by the Confederacy's economic collapse.

"Poor Rose Greenhow!" Charlie laughed bitterly. "Her great Southern crusade ain't much of a crusade anymore, eh?"

"Can't marry the man she loves."

"Let's shed a tear for Rose. Yes, she spent some time in a Yankee prison, but look at her now. She's far from the war and all its misery, and lettin' English and French aristocrats show her a good time."

"There's a place in warfare for flirting and dallying, especially when it comes to Union and Confederate generals and British and Frog politicians." He shifted the subject away from Rose. "I bought a newspaper at the railroad depot yesterday. Instead of our troops fighting Yanks up at Fredericksburg or in the Shenandoah, they're backed up against Richmond and Petersburg. What the hell happened, Charlie?"

Charlie rose and shut the inner door then returned to his seat. "I don't want anyone else hearin' this, Bill. The Confederacy's runnin' out of steam. The Army of Northern Virginia's runnin' out of steam. The western armies are runnin' out of steam. In 1862 and 1863, we made the blue bellies fight battles in Maryland and Pennsylvania. No offensive operations in 1864...runnin' out of steam. I predict it all ends in early '65. And deservedly so. The South's got to pay for the sin of slavery."

"I can see why you closed the door." Bill swung his gaze from the door to age lines in Charlie's face. Those lines didn't belong on a man just nineteen years old. "Men like the president and Secretary Seddon need a miracle—European recognition and aid. From what you just told me, it may be too late for a Rose miracle." Bill tapped his fingers on the war secretary's stack of memos. "If the war can no longer be won on the battlefield, the president and war secretary will seek other avenues, one in particular—a negotiated treaty with Lincoln that secures a future for the Confederacy. Again, desperate men look for miracles, eh?"

"You make sense, Billy Boy. The North's war weary as well. In the months ahead, there'll be plenty of Southern prayers sent to Heaven askin' for Lincoln to lose the November election."

"A Lincoln defeat will show a loss of resolve in the North for the war. I can see President Davis sending out feelers for peace-treaty talks. Will it work?"

Charlie shook his head. "I don't see the Yanks givin' us a victory we didn't earn on the battlefield. Sounds like the president and the war secretary are graspin' for yet another miracle."

Bill nodded. "And Lincoln could confound us and win the election."

"Think General Lee has a battlefield miracle up his sleeve?"

"What do you think, Charlie? I've been in London these past few months. Here in Richmond you've been in the thick of things."

"I know Seddon's worried. After the casualties we took in the Wilderness, Spotsylvania and Cold Harbor, General Lee's limited in what he can do. The Yanks in May and June suffered terrible casualties, yet fill their ranks with new recruits and draftees. We're out of recruits. I don't think God wants us to win, so no, I don't see General Lee winnin' a great victory. He's out of miracles too. It's just a matter of—"

The inner door opened, revealing Secretary Seddon, a frown stamped on his fussy mouth. "I thought I heard a familiar voice."

Bill wondered how much the war secretary might have heard. The door had been closed, muffling voices. Yet even with the frown, Secretary Seddon sounded jolly, not the mood he'd be in had he heard Charlie's defeatist views.

Bill stood, ignoring the sudden jab of pain in his side. "I sneaked back to Richmond. Got tired of sitting on momma's porch. Wanted to surprise Franny and all of you. Now it's time to get back to work."

Charlie cleared his throat. "I've been tellin' Bill about the spring campaign here in the East, Mr. Secretary."

"Not the outcome I had hoped to see." Seddon rested his hand on the doorknob. "Grant has his army entrenched around Richmond and Petersburg. Can't let that stand. We've got to bloody the

Yanks and send them scurrying back to Washington. This siege is intolerable." The secretary motioned for Bill to follow him. "Since you're full of surprises, Lieutenant Stamford, let's pay a surprise visit to the Executive Mansion. President Davis will want to hear about your adventures in London."

~ * ~

At President Davis' urging, Bill and Secretary Seddon settled into chairs in front of the presidential desk. Davis reached into the upper desk drawer and produced a newspaper. "It's the *Daily Telegraph* fresh off a blockade runner. The July eighteenth edition. Thanks to this newspaper, I probably know more about Rose than you do, Lieutenant Stamford. I know you were successful. Why? Rose has a new beau, George Leveson-Gower, a staunch supporter of Lincoln and the Northern States. You may know him better as Lord Granville. He's handling the dispute over the *Alabama* and seems willing to pay compensation to Lincoln."

Bill struggled to remember the significance of the *Alabama*. Then clarity: The *Alabama* had been a warship built in Britain for the Confederacy. The ship and her crew enjoyed a glorious career raiding Northern ships until sunk by a Union cruiser off Cherbourg. "Good news for us then. Rose followed her patriotic soul, not her romantic heart."

"I hope this *Alabama* thing is the last good deed Lord Granville does for Lincoln." The president thumbed through the newspaper and stopped at the society pages. "Hopefully, the *Telegraph* will soon have news of an engagement. Then we'll know for sure Rose's bedroom diplomacy has been successful and Lord Granville has become a friend of the Confederacy."

"Looks like your London mission could lead to British recognition of the Confederacy, Bill," Seddon echoed.

A darkey servant appeared holding a platter filled with bowls of corn chowder. "Ben, bring a bottle of Brunello di Montalcino and three glasses," Davis said off-handedly. Returning with the wine and glasses, the slave filled the goblets and departed.

"The news in the *Telegraph* calls for a toast." Davis raised his glass. "To Rose's success in snaring Lord Granville. And to a General Lee battlefield success that will see Lincoln defeated in the November election. And to a fortuitous decision by the new U.S. president to seek a negotiated peace that guarantees our independence."

Bill downed the wine. "I'm glad to have had a small part in Rose's success. I even did some bleeding on the night I gave her your letter, Mister President." Laughing sourly, Bill wondered if his action would end up prolonging a war the South was destined to lose. Blue-belly troops lurked just outside the gates of Richmond. For the citizens of Richmond, it would be a dreary fall and winter.

"My apologies for not asking about your wound, Lieutenant." Davis held off taking another sip of wine. "Getting sand and grit in a wound is bad news, but I hear the doctor in Wilmington did a bang-up job cleaning it."

"I'm as good as new, sir, thanks to Dr. Iuppenlatz." Bill got antsy in the chair, trying to find a position that lessened the niggling pain. The wound hadn't hurt until the president mentioned it.

"I'm getting good news after good news." Davis finished off his wine and refilled the glass. "Your successful mission, Lieutenant. Rose winning the heart of Lord Granville. And a likely battlefield success as I speak." He produced a newspaper clipping from the desk drawer. "It's from the District of Columbia's *Evening Star*. Good news for the South. Jubal Early has taken the Army of Northern Virginia's Second Corps into Maryland and is threatening to capture Washington City. His daring movement caught Lincoln and his generals sleeping."

Seddon regarded Bill. "Your old corps. Stonewall Jackson's foot cavalry."

Bill took off his hat and ran his hand through his hair. "Abe must be having some fearful frights."

"Foulmouthed, tobacco-chewing Jubal Early stands at the gates of the Federal capital." Davis beamed an ornery smile. "I dreamt last night that Early brought Lincoln to me in chains. Best dream I've had since 1860. Even if the dream doesn't come true and Jubal can only hold the outskirts of Washington City for a brief time, it'll be enough to bring European recognition. With Rose soon to marry Granville and General Early firing shells into Washington City, how can we not soon celebrate the war's end and our independence?"

There were so many more damned Yanks compared to Graybacks. Grant would send some up to Washington City and stop Early. Maybe it had already happened. The president's hopes were mirages. He, Seddon and all the other politicians were too late. Richmond faced siege warfare. Of course, Bill couldn't voice his thoughts. He said simply, "I hope we'll soon hear cheering in the streets."

At Seddon's urging, they made another toast. "To a Jubal Early victory and an honorable peace."

"To Southern independence," the president said solemnly.

"To no more tears." Bill downed all the wine in his glass.

"No more tears," Davis concurred, finishing off his wine. "I've a new mission for you, Lieutenant. I want you to go up to the front lines and talk to our brave boys. I want you to write their stories and send them to the newspapers. You're to buy ads in the Richmond newspapers to ensure the stories get good play." Davis directed them to dig into their corn chowder.

Seddon spooned the last of his chowder into his mouth and swallowed. "Wives will love reading about their husbands."

"Charlie and I will go to the trenches together." Bill didn't need to explain further, not with Charlie's arm buried somewhere on the Gettysburg battlefield. Finishing off the chowder, he held the bowl up to his lips and swallowed the last of the broth.

Davis signaled an end to the meeting. "Welcome home, Lieutenant. I'm sure Franny's delighted to have you back." The president grinned. "And away from that actress."

Bill grunted. "So you saw the society journals?"

"In this edition of the *Telegraph*." Davis stuffed the stopper back into the wine bottle and handed it to Bill. "Marie Wilton is quite the firecracker, isn't she? Give the bottle to Franny. Maybe it will quench her temper when she learns about Miss Wilton."

"I told Franny about Marie and her games. She didn't get upset."

"You're the first man to ever resist her charms according to the *Telegraph*." Davis's brows arched. "Maybe I should give you a medal." Chuckling, the president slapped Bill on the back then ushered Bill and Seddon downstairs to the front entrance.

Outside, a light rain splashed the executive mansion steps and the boardwalk, forcing Bill and Seddon to unfurl their rain-nappers. Ensconced in the Hansom cab and on the way back to the War Department, Seddon pointed to a painted bangtail swaying her hips as she made her way along the boardwalk. "Let's hope for your sake Marie Wilton never buys passage on a blockade runner. God forbid the actress and your wife should ever meet." The war secretary's lips quivered with amusement.

"Won't happen." Bill took a final look at the bangtail and returned his gaze to the war secretary. "Marie likes the bustle of London too much."

"Sounds like the London newspapers are saying she's losing her touch with men. What if she decides to prove the gossip journalists wrong and comes to Richmond to renew her flirtation games?"

Bill squirmed in his seat. "If Franny and Marie ever met, people would call it the Third Battle of Manassas. It's an impossibility, though. Marie has already forgotten me. Too many handsome actors and noble admirers in London to snag her amorous attention."

Thirty-seven

A Visit to the Breastworks

The corporal lay against the breastwork wall, his rifle perched beside him, a tin cup of ersatz coffee pressed against his lips. The soldier looked maybe twenty-one, his face smeared with grime, a faraway gaze in his eyes. "Huh?"

Colonel Larry DeVoe took a deep breath. "These two soldiers are from the War Department—Lieutenant Bill Stamford and Sergeant Charlie Kurtz. They want to give you a chance to tell your family how you're doing."

"Your words will be in the newspaper, so your family and friends will read them." Bill settled beside the coffee-drinking private and extracted a small notebook and pencil from his haversack.

"I really don't have anything to say." Coffee cold, the corporal dumped it against the breastwork. "I write letters home a couple of times a week. They do my talking."

"Wouldn't your momma love to see you in the newspaper?" Bill turned the notebook to the first page without any scribbles.

The corporal eyed Charlie's stump. "Name's Terry Scott. How did you lose your arm, Sergeant?"

Secretary Seddon had promoted Charlie a week before, rewarding him for outstanding service in Bill's absence. The War Department's newest sergeant patted his stump. "Gettysburg. Third day. Pickett's Charge." Charlie turned his gaze on Bill. "My chuckaboo may look like a greenhorn. He ain't. A shell fragment tore up his body at Chancellorsville."

"Volunteers, eh?" Scott scratched his neck and shoulder. "Damned lice! Bragg's bodyguards!"

"Joined up in 1862 in time for the sleet march and Fredericksburg." Bill hugged himself as he thought back to those times.

"I got conscripted. Who were you guys with?" Scott sprawled his legs.

"Eighteenth North Carolina Regiment." In his notebook, Bill wrote down the corporal's name, confident the soldier would agree to an interview. "They're up in Maryland visiting the Capitol dome and scaring the living daylights out of Lincoln."

"I've been hearing some chin music about General Early puttin' the fear of God in Yankee Sunday soldiers." Scott seemed to be warming up to the interview. His easy-going expression seemed to indicate so. "Too good to be true, I say."

"We'll know soon enough. The Yankee newspapers will be full of Jubal Early news." Bill pointed to his notebook.

"Write away, Lieutenant. So what do you want to know about me?"

Men like Scott were rare. Most Bill approached wanted nothing to do with him and his notebook. The 1864 fighting had lasted for weeks and weeks, not days. There had been no time to lick wounds before the Yanks were again attacking. Buddies were dead or maimed. The regiments were skeletal remnants of what they'd been in 1862 when Bill and Charlie joined up. But President Davis and Secretary Seddon wanted interviews done to prop up homefront morale. Bill sat cross-legged, pencil in hand. "Your friends in the Twenty-First Mississippi say you're a hero, Corporal."

Scott's expression took on a stoic mien. "I'm no hero. Just a soldier doing his best not to let his buddies down."

"I know some artillery fellers who think you're a hero. Tell us about the gun crew at Spotsylvania who wheeled up behind the Twenty-first." Perspiration dripped into Charlie's eyes, causing him to blink incessantly.

"Any one of my possums would've done the same." The corporal shrugged.

Removing his hat, Charlie wiped a handkerchief along his forehead, soaking up the sweat driblets. "What happened?"

"Okay. Just don't make it sound hunky-dory. The Yanks struck us at the Muleshoe. Terrible fighting. They breached our line. One of their shells exploded over an artillery piece behind the Twenty-first. Killed or wounded half the crew. I took some of my possums and ran to the crew's aid."

While Bill scribbled notes, Charlie continued to coax the story from the corporal, "So you manned the gun?"

"We *helped* man the gun." Scott grimaced as he mulled his next words. "We poured shot into the charging blue bellies. Closed the breach, sent the Yanks retreating."

Sweat ran down Bill's back and sides. He looked down at his right hand and wished it held a church fan. He'd be waving it furiously, churning the air around his face. Later in the afternoon, Bill and Charlie would take their Hansom cab back to Richmond. The soldiers in the trenches would get no relief from the heat until October. The graybacks would welcome the colder temperatures—until the ice and snow came. That meant building winter huts and makeshift fireplaces. Still, the field hospitals would fill with sickly soldiers who often never left the beds alive. And wives would get the dreaded news—the war had claimed their men. Bill looked up into the brilliantly blue sky. No late-afternoon storms to cool temperatures.

Charlie butted in on Bill's thoughts. "I've been told you saved Humphreys' Brigade."

"As I said, doing my duty."

Bill scribbled the corporal's response in his notepad. He looked up from his scrawls. "Where's home in Mississippi?"

"Tunica. It's an Indian name. Cotton town of one hundred and thirty hard-working souls."

The trickling sweat continued to bedevil Bill, but he didn't let it confound his thoughts. "And your mother and father?"

"Rachael and Theodore Scott. Will they see the story about me?"

"I'll make sure they get a copy." Bill smiled. "Expect they'll be sharing the newspaper with their neighbors and friends. 'Look what Terry has been up to. The story says he's a hero.'"

"So you're goin' to call me a hero? I'm not. But Momma and Pa will like the story, so okay."

"The homefront needs heroes." Bill closed up his notepad and slipped it and the pencil into a coat pocket.

"I guess you're right, Lieutenant," Scott allowed. "It's just... General Lee's a hero, General Jackson was a hero. Me? Not so much. But you say it's important, so I'm goin' along with your plans."

Standing stiffly, Bill felt a twinge of pain in his side. He gently rubbed around the new scar then patted the corporal's shoulder. "It's not as bad as drill, is it?"

Scott laughed. "Nothin's as bad as drill. The next fella you interview...do it just before drill so he gets out of it. He'll be glad to talk to you, Lieutenant."

~ * ~

"No more interviews today, Lieutenant Stamford?" Colonel DeVoe walked Bill and Charlie to their Hansom.

"No, Colonel. I need to get back to my office and write the story. Need to get it to the newspapers in the morning."

"I sure hope this story and future ones do some good." DeVoe sounded dubious. "Never good when soldiers' wives riot over food."

"Agreed," Bill and Charlie echoed.

Atop the Hansom, cabman Ernie fretfully eyed the distant Union lines. "Hurry! Get in!"

"Hold your horses." Laughing, Charlie slapped a kneecap.

"More like one horse." Bill grinned.

"If the Yanks start firing cannonballs, I just know one of 'em goin' to take off my head." The cabman gestured animatedly, signaling for Bill and Charlie to pile into the cab.

The captain bid adieu as Bill and Charlie settled against the cab's backrest. Craning his neck, Bill looked up through the open payment door. "Back to the War Department, Ernie. And stop worrying. Yank artillerymen aren't going to waste ammunition on a cab."

"I hope you're right, Lieutenant. I don't want to become the headless cabman of Richmond."

Charlie looked out at the summer greenery and flowers as the cabman raced them back to the streets of Richmond. "It won't be long until all this becomes a battlefield," he told Bill. "In the fall or maybe next spring, the Yanks are going to put an end to this decrepit nation. Yet we've been ordered to improve homefront morale. How much good can we do?"

"You're wondering if we're banging our heads against the proverbial wall. Probably. But if the stories help wives and mothers get through these next few months, it'll be worthwhile." Bill glanced at the wildflowers bordering the plank road. Men and flowers never did well in battles. "I wish more soldiers were eager to tell their stories. Too many feel forced when there's a colonel with us."

"I fear Secretary Seddon's goin' to want to see fairytales from you, not true heroism. Sometimes a soldier's heroic when his regiment gets flanked and he doesn't panic like so many fellas around him."

Bill understood the meaning of Charlie's words. At Fredericksburg, Charlie had panicked and fled to the rear. He hadn't been around to offer aid to a dying friend. The loss of an arm hadn't been enough to end his guilt. He'd learned to live with it—barely.

"I'm not going to let the stories drift into pretentiousness." Bill chose silence for a few moments then added, "Each soldier's heroism will come out without embellishment. If the president and the war secretary don't like my approach, they can fire me."

"So you're okay with going back to the breastworks?" Charlie arched an eyebrow.

"A figure of speech, Charlie. Seddon and the president will love my stories. There are so many tales of bravery that need telling. I don't need to make them heroes. They're already heroes."

Charlie chuckled. "Seddon won't order you out to the breastworks. He'd face Franny's ire. No one wants to be on the receiving end of that woman's anger."

Thirty-eight

Plans Made for the Future

A Raparlier vacuum coffee pot brewing on a stove in Bill's office grew quiet, signifying the morning's coffee could soon be sipped. Charley moseyed over, filled two mugs and handed one to Bill who took a swallow.

"Damn! It's the real stuff." Bill inhaled the aroma. "You're full of surprises this morning, Charlie."

"You can get anythin' in this God-forsaken city if you know the right people." Charlie raised his mug up to his nose and took in the fresh-brewed aroma. "Some black marketers are makin' a killin'."

"So how did you afford it?" Bill swished the coffee inside his mug. "Sneak something expensive out of Avis's office?"

"Avis gave me a trinket from her jewelry box. It paid for this and coffee for Avis and her family. Paper money's worthless. Gold necklaces and diamond rings are the new currency."

"Please thank her for me, Charlie. I wonder if she'll have anything left in her jewelry box when the war ends."

"Probably not. She likes helpin' out folks. This mornin' Avis took some of the coffee to the treasury girls."

"No wonder Franny just pecked me on the cheek outside the War Department and hurried on to the customs house." Bill laughed and scratched the left edge of his mustache. "My wife chose a cup of real coffee over canoodling with me."

Many from the Ladies' Aid Society were scandalized that Franny and Avis had chosen to work as treasury girls, signing and cutting Confederate currency. The job required excellent penmanship, a skill they shared due to upper-class schooling. When Franny told Bill what she made per month, he'd gasped in disbelief—sixty-five dollars a month. "Soldiers get a miserly eleven dollars—when they're paid," he'd said.

"Lieutenant Stamford! You inside? I got the newspapers you asked for!" The unexpected voice booming from the hallway sounded amplified by a speaking trumpet. Charlie hooted as Bill slid off his chair and dropped to his knees, startled by the sound, like a shell shrieking overhead.

"Not so loud!" Charlie shouted, his voice nearly as loud as the one incoming from the hallway.

"Lordy, Charlie, you're going to burst my eardrums." Cussing under his breath, Bill climbed back into his chair.

"Sorry, chuckaboo."

"I'm back here," Bill told the hallway voice. "No need to scream. You've newspapers?"

Wheel cap atop his head crowned with curly hair, ink-stained leather apron tied around his waist, a boy no older than twelve ambled through the inner doorway. He carried a stack of newspapers. "I've got your copies of the *Daily Examiner*."

Bill cleared a spot for them on the edge of his desk. When the boy drew close to put down the newspapers, he exuded a most unpleasant odor. The chatty damfino needed a hot-bath scrub. "Tell the staff at the *Examiner* thank you." Bill's belly churned as the boy's stink assaulted him.

The youth appeared oblivious of the smell clinging to him like feces on a cat. He set the stack down on the desk. "Just a two-block walk, but it felt like fifty blocks. By the time I reached your office I thought I held a hundred-pound dumbbell."

"Thank you!" Bill hoped his clipped tone would get the boy moving toward the building's front entrance.

It didn't. The youngster clasped his hands on his hips. "So what's so important in the *Examiner*?"

"Sergeant Kurtz?" Bill gestured toward the hallway.

Charlie stood and took the boy by the arm. "You'll have to read the newspaper later and figure it out."

"Time to go, eh? I get it. You're about to tell General Lee how to win the war and you think I might be a spy for Abe Lincoln." Snorting, pleased with his humor, the twelve-year-old brushed aside Charley's hand. "I know the way out. And don't tell me I need a bath!" The kid swaggered out into the hallway.

Bill heard the boy's footsteps long after the kid disappeared from view. He reached into the desk drawer and withdrew a half-written story for the Richmond newspapers. He'd resume writing the piece after Charlie returned to his reception desk. Bill prepared to slip the story back into the drawer when he noticed a misspelling. Annoyed, he picked up a quill pen, dipped it in an inkwell, and circled the mistake.

Charlie plopped into his favorite chair in Bill's office. A second later, he slapped the side of his head. "That stack of newspapers reminds me I forgot to show you somethin'." Bolting to his feet, he rushed to his reception desk.

Stack of newspapers? Bill was intrigued. Charlie obviously wanted him to see one in particular.

Charlie held up a paper, just as Bill expected. "Notice the name?"

"No. You have the banner covered." Bill motioned Charlie to return to the inner sanctum. "You sure like drumming up suspense."

Once seated in front of Bill's desk, Charlie ended the suspense. "It's the *Baltimore Sun* with more on the Fort Stevens battle of July eleven."

Bill whistled. "How do you do it, Charlie? A Yankee newspaper... you've still got the magical touch. What did you have to trade to get it?"

"Some North Carolina tobaccy. The Yank sailed a toy boat across a brook. It contained the newspaper. I put the tobacco in it and sent the boat back to him. It's good old American enterprise."

"Well, what does it say?" Exasperation crept into Bill's voice.

"Yankee reinforcements—more Sixth Corps troops sent up from here—forced Early to call off his attempt to capture Washington City." Charlie flipped the newspaper across the desk. "Read the paragraphs about Lincoln."

Bill scanned the columns until he found the account of Lincoln's visit to Fort Stevens. He read the short piece and choked on spit. "So our boys recognized him in his stovepipe hat and started shooting. Somehow they missed. I can't help but wonder: God's doing?" Bill rolled up the newspaper and slapped it against his kneecap. "The Yanks around him shouted, 'Get your damned head down, fool.'" Bill lowered his voice and leaned toward Charlie. "The war's lost. But if Lincoln had been killed, that would have turned things topsy-turvy."

"I guess God doesn't want him dead. You know what that means, Bill?"

"These are the Confederacy's last days." *No halo for Lincoln.*

"Billy boy, you look the way you did on the march to Chancellorsville. Always tellin' me to be vigilant."

Bill ignored Charlie. Instead, he read another paragraph from the Jubal Early article. "The *Sun* says Early's retreating back into the Shenandoah Valley. Want to take a horseback ride to the Shenandoah? It'll be just like old times." Bill stacked the *Sun* on top of the *Examiners*.

"You're not joshin', are you?" Charlie studied Bill's eyes. "Nope, you're not. I'm not too fond of the Shenandoah. That was a nightmare march back in '62. Nearly froze my toes off."

"We won't be marching. On horses, remember? I want to interview some of Early's soldiers. Good for homefront morale. These boys were taking potshots at Lincoln. Lincoln! They didn't capture Washington City, but Lincoln and Grant were in a near-panic. Readers will love this stuff."

"This may be one of your really bad ideas, Billy Boy. Long ride with high risk of an encounter with blue belly cavalry."

"I'm my papa's son. Anything to get a good story." Bill meant it as a jest, but realized he spoke the truth.

"That must mean when the war ends you'll be takin' over the *Gazette's* reins from your momma." Charlie smirked. "I wonder what Franny will say."

"I haven't thought much about it. Maybe I will—for a time. As for Franny, if she's against it, I won't." Bill glanced at his watch. Nearly ten o'clock. "I nearly missed my meeting with Secretary Seddon. Hold down the fort, Charlie. Seddon hates not being punctual."

~ * ~

Seddon still confabbed with his assistant secretaries, reviewing the day's schedule, when Bill arrived. Captain Beardsley gestured for him to sit in the anteroom. Mr. Punctuality would be late giving Bill his day's marching orders.

Bill had grabbed two of the *Examiners* and brought them to Seddon's office. One he handed to Beardsley. The other he placed on his lap and waited for an update from the captain. Bill didn't have to wait long.

"They've been talking about shoes and winter coats," Beardsley informed Bill. "Hard to believe we're only a few months from October."

"It'll take a miracle to see any of the boys in new shoes and coats. The only ones they ever get come off Yankee corpses." Bill scowled, unable to conceal his irritation.

"Maybe this time it'll be different. General Lee's troops are backed up to our doorstep." Beardsley tried to sound optimistic, but by the last few words his voice turned monotone.

"Like you said, Captain, they're only a hop, skip and a jump from here." Bill laughed sourly. "But the shoes and coats aren't getting from the shoe factories and textile mills to Richmond's warehouses. If they haven't fixed the problems by now, I don't think they ever will."

"We'll muddle through. We always do." Beardsley looked away from Bill as men, both officers and civilians, exited Seddon's inner sanctum. "As soon as they're out the door, go on in. The secretary's been eager to talk to you about your soldier stories." He whispered, "He likes them."

Bill didn't mince words as he stepped into the inner sanctum. He wanted to get his two-cents in before Seddon gave him different marching orders. "Sir, I want to visit Jubal Early's troops. Sergeant Kurtz will travel with me." Bill hadn't even sat down.

"Terrible idea. I want you in Richmond." Seddon gestured for Bill to sit in one of the chairs arrayed around his desk. "The Second Corps is fighting almost every day in the valley. You can get your soldier interviews in the bombproofs around Richmond."

"If necessary, Charlie and I will fight alongside them, and at night do interviews by candlelight," Bill said, a human whirligig. "I want to know how the boys felt being so close to Washington City, especially the fellows who took potshots at Lincoln. The home folks need some good news."

"You're right in that, Lieutenant. The home folks do need some good news. They know Lincoln's eastern army is besieging Richmond and Petersburg. They keep expecting a miracle from General Lee. I pray every night the Lord grants General Lee the victory that gives us peace and independence. But until that day comes, I want you here bulwarking the home folks, not out getting yourself shot somewhere between Richmond and the Shenandoah."

"Sadly, I concur, Secretary." Bill grimaced, unable to hide his disappointment. "But I'll always see it as a lost opportunity."

"Perhaps. General Early's a cuss. He'll scream bloody murder if you show up during a battle. He'll grumble to General Lee, and Lee will carp to President Davis. Not worth battling the politics."

Bill nodded reluctantly, then handed the other *Examiner* to Seddon. "Not sure if you've seen this, sir."

"Someone mentioned it at the earlier meeting, but this is the first I've seen it." Seddon glanced at the front page then eyed Bill over the top of the paper. "Look at this! The editor put your interview on the front page."

Bill grinned. "I hoped you'd notice the story placement."

"It reinforces my decision to keep you here in Richmond." Folding the *Examiner*, Seddon dropped the newspaper on the desk. "You can do more good here."

Admitting defeat, Bill returned to his own office and broke the news to Charlie who took it indifferently. "Now I don't have to worry about a saddle chafing my butt."

At the end of the day, Bill returned to the apartment in a melancholy mood. After a trip to a nearby market, Franny cooked a pork stew over the coal stove. With Shenandoah farmers tending their fields, Richmond folks ate a tiny bit better than during the wintertime. But the North's Phil Sheridan hard pressed Jubal Early and his men. Soon the Confederacy could lose Virginia's breadbasket.

Franny could see the glum look on his face. "What's wrong, darling?" She hugged him, dripping stew from her stirring spoon onto his jacket collar.

"Jubal Early's back in the Shenandoah Valley. I wanted to go there and interview some of his men. Secretary Seddon vetoed my plan, thought I was mad."

Franny's pretty face twisted into a scowl. "Deservedly so. There's almost constant fighting there. I don't want to be a widow."

He read the thoughts churning in her mind. "The last time I saw you look like this we were soon visiting every toyshop in Richmond."

She pushed him away. "Oh, it's boiling over." The kettle sizzled, and meat bits and vegetables leapt above the pot and pelleted the floor like raindrops. After Franny lowered the flame, she noticed the spoon's droppings on Bill's jacket and brushed them off his shoulder. "I do have a suggestion that won't see you gallivanting all over Northern Virginia, dodging Yankees, not to mention Confederate patrols who think you're a deserter."

Franny's ideas were always worth considering. "Yes?"

Drawing two bowls from a cabinet, she dished out the stew. "Why not interview some of the pleb mothers who work at the Treasury helping their new nation while supplementing their soldier husbands' meager wages? Let them tell you how they're surviving inflation and shortages. It seems we only hear from them when they take their anger to the streets."

Bill mulled her suggestion. Putting his arms around her waist, he kissed the back of her neck. "We'll do it—if you can find the girls willing to talk to me. The secretary will love your idea. The editors too. Patriotic girls making great sacrifices for their men and children."

Twirling around, Franny jumped into Bill's arms and smothered his face with kisses. She motioned for him to sit at their small kitchen table. Once they finished eating, they both eyed the hallway leading to their bedroom. Next to their bed, he carried out one of his favorite past-times—kissing Franny's skin from her forehead to her toes while he playfully undressed her. Lying naked beside her, Bill cupped her cheeks and tongue-caressed her from her lips down to her breasts.

Rolling away, Bill reached for the end-table drawer. "A rubber, sweetheart?" He knew Franny's answer. She'd not bring a baby into the world until after the war.

"No, not tonight." Her straightforward answer shocked him.

He jerked his hand away from the drawer knob. "I don't know what to say."

"I feel it in my bones, Bill. The war's going to soon end. We won't be raising a baby in a land where children go hungry. Children will have their daddies in their lives, not dead on battlefields."

"Or in field hospitals losing their limbs."

"Yes, no more war." Smiling lasciviously, she scooted into position as he mounted her. "I'm ready."

When they were spent and he lay beside her once more, she moved her hand in a slow circle across his chest. He brought her hand up to his mouth and kissed her fingers. "A baby born next May?"

"Only God knows at the moment." Franny patted her belly.

Thirty-nine

Treasury Girls Tell Their Stories

The brunette fidgeted in the chair next to Bill and Franny, kneading her ink-stained leather apron. Tonya Cook was obviously tense. Bill hoped having Franny in the room with him would make the treasury girl less nervous. Maybe once he spoke for a few minutes, Tonya would grow more comfortable in George Trenholm's office. Trenholm was Secretary of the Treasury—on the job for less than a month. The secretary wanted to snag some good publicity for the Confederate Treasury Department and so had been more than happy to accommodate Seddon's request for Bill to conduct interviews.

"Relax, Tonya," Franny reassured her friend. "My husband doesn't bite."

A mischievous grin spread across the girl's face. "That's not what you told me."

Franny returned the grin. "Shame on you, Tonya. That was just between you and me."

A slave in a fancy butler uniform toted a steaming-hot pot of ersatz coffee and set it on a potholder on Trenholm's desk. Bill had chosen not to sit behind the desk, but out in the open and close to Tonya and Franny.

When the slave handed a mug to Tonya, her hand trembled as she gripped the handle. "I've never done anything like this. Never seen my name in the newspaper. Well, that's not true. A couple of times when I got engaged and married and when we went on a trip to France in 1859. Got a big write-up for that."

"No different," Bill inserted. "I just want you to tell me how you're coping with the war's hardships."

Tonya grimaced. "Where do I start? Everything's so expensive. That's why I wanted this wonderful job. My husband sends me his pay. He knows it isn't enough for me and our three kids. He's the one who told me to apply. Thank God he did. I can afford to do nice things for the girls and the boy. Better food, a trip to the New Richmond Theatre, new clothes for the kids." Tonya fiddled with her hands, still on her lap. "And at the same time I'm helping out our fledging nation. I'm doing my duty, working in this fabulous building."

Bill nodded. "Do you know President Davis has an office tucked away in one corner?"

Tonya's face lit up like a streetlamp in the early evening. "Indeed, I do. I've seen him on a couple of occasions, even exchanged pleasantries."

Bill mulled his next question then simply said, "What do you do in this busy building, Tonya?"

"Let me take you out on the floor and show you. Franny does the same thing." Tonya took them to where girls were scrupulously signing notes. "I'm a signer. Other girls are note clippers. They trim the bills. We really have to be meticulous."

"I hear you girls do a better job than men." Bill offered her a crafty grin.

Tonya held her right forefinger up to her mouth. "Shush. We don't talk about such things." She laughed lightly.

"I used to set type in my father's print shop. Comparable work, I think." Bill observed a redhead as she carefully signed a note.

"We make sixty-five dollars a month," Tonya told Bill. "And work from nine in the morning to three in the afternoon five days a week. Less money and fewer hours than the boys, but that's okay."

"Not for me," Franny interjected, patting the redhead's shoulder.

The redhead twitched, looked up at Franny. "Or me." She returned to her work.

His peg leg spanking the wood floor, an illustrator for the Treasury Department, Sergeant Simon Tidwell, made his way toward Bill, Franny and Tonya. He'd lost his leg at Chancellorsville in the same charge that left Bill wounded. In Augusta, Georgia, he'd done woodcut illustrations for the *Chronicle and Sentinel*. Simon's skills proved compatible with treasury work. Trenholm assigned him to Bill to do woodcut engravings of the girls Bill interviewed.

Darting into a feminine sea of tables, desks and chairs, Franny soon returned with a comfy rocking chair. Simon settled into its seat and produced a sketchbook from inside his jacket. "Sit down where you usually sit. I'm going to do charcoal sketches as you work."

Once seated, Tonya began signing bills. "We have quotas—three thousand bills a day without any errors. We're docked ten cents for every damaged bill, imperfect signature or blotted spot of ink. Being careless can be costly." She chuckled. "But we girls don't make as many errors as the boys."

Simon worked for a good twenty minutes then eyed Tonya. "Done."

Tonya turned to Bill. "Finished with me?"

"Almost. Your kids' names? And your husband's?"

"Jennifer, eight; Cecilia, six, and Michael, three. My momma lives with us and looks after the kids when I'm at work. My husband: Captain Gary Porter with the Third Virginia Cavalry. He's in the Shenandoah Valley with General Early. I got a letter from him saying they almost captured Washington City, but Army of the Potomac regulars showed up and saved Lincoln's goose."

Bill considered Tonya's words. Too bad he couldn't ride out to the Shenandoah and interview her husband. The two stories together would make for a wonderful tale. But Seddon had been adamant. No

Shenandoah Valley, no Jubal Early. "Thank you, Tonya," Bill said, signaling the end of the interview. "Keep your eyes out for the story. It'll be in the Richmond papers soon."

Franny kissed Tonya on the cheek. "See? It wasn't so bad. You're going to be more famous than Rose Greenhow." Franny turned to Bill. "I'll go get Lizzie. Meet you back in Secretary Trenholm's office."

Ensconced in Trenholm's office once again, Bill heard his wife's voice as Franny and her friend Lizzie Matzner approached. "You'll love Bill. I fell in love with him the moment I laid eyes on him. Such a kind heart. I can't wait to tell him about our plans, okay?"

"I'm doing this only because you're my friend." Lizzie didn't sound happy.

Franny lowered her voice, preventing Bill from hearing her plotting.

Lizzie squealed, "That's wonderful."

Simon sat in Trenholm's seat, his sketchpad on the secretary's desk. Bill uncrossed his legs and rose from his chair to greet his wife and Lizzie. "So what have you two cooked up?"

"I have no idea what you're talking about." A smug look settled on Franny's face.

Bill swung his gaze to the open doorway. "I heard you two talking outside the office."

"We've been found out, Franny." Lizzie wore a mourning dress that contrasted with her mischievous smile.

"So it seems." Franny settled into the chair next to Bill. "Secretary Trenholm says it's fine with him if we do the interview at Lizzie's house. You can meet her two kids and her mother and father."

"Go to her apartment? And the secretary approves?" Considering Franny's words, Bill saw the possibilities. Lizzie would be more comfortable there, away from supervisors. "Well, it's getting closer to three o'clock. Why not? If it's not too far, we'll walk."

Simon pointed to the office's single window. "The clouds look threatening. We might want to take a cab."

~ * ~

Muddy sprinkles fell as Bill and his group hurried to the four-seat hack. The factories along the James spewed gritty smoke from their chimneys, and on damp days the rain fell as water and soot. No longer requiring Franny's umbrella, the two women clambered into the front seats and waited on Bill and Simon. With Simon's peg leg slapping the brick walkway, the men slowly made their way to the cab, Bill's umbrella held above their heads. The air felt warm as the drizzle peppered the rain-napper. Once Bill and Simon slipped into the backseat, the cabman took them to Lizzie's brownstone townhouse, just two blocks beyond where Bill and Franny lived.

"We're almost neighbors." Bill looked out the window.

As soon as the cab wheeled to a stop and Bill paid the fare, they piled out of the vehicle. "We won't be long," Bill told the cabman. "Please wait. The sergeant will need a ride to his home."

Lizzie barely cleared the front stoop before two youngsters dashed out the front door and hugged their momma's waist. "Got hard candy?" the older boy, no more than six or seven, blurted.

His younger sister shouted out, "Peppermint. My favorite."

"These two rambunctious young'uns are Basil—he's seven—and Arianna, five." Lizzie tousled the boy's hair.

An older gentleman stood in the doorway, his hands inside his overalls. "Ah, I see you've brought guests."

"Yes, Daddy, they're here to interview me about how we're coping with the war's hardships." Lizzie directed her gaze to Bill and Simon. "Bill's with the War Department and he's going to write a story for the newspapers. Simon draws. The woman's Franny, Bill's wife and my friend."

"Nice to meet you fellows. Name's Frederick Stephens. Please call me Fredo." By the time Fredo finished speaking, a timeworn woman attired in a mourning dress had joined him in the doorway. "This is Lizzie's momma."

"I'm Celia." The older woman leaned wearily against her husband. "All this rain has my bones complaining."

"For goodness sake, get your bodies out of the dampness." Stepping back, Fredo hustled Celia away from the doorway. "We promise you hospitality."

"We don't have much, but I'll put out some extra plates for supper." Celia patted the wizened hand draped over her shoulder.

Based on Fredo's words, Bill expected Lizzie's townhouse to be spartan. Instead, he found the parlor filled with couches, chairs, tables, even a grandfather clock.

Lizzie noticed Bill's confused look. "After my husband died in the war, I had trouble making ends meet and the county stipend wasn't enough. Pa sold the farm, packed the furniture in the wagon and moved in with me and the kids. Lots of widows need their parents' help."

Fredo helped Simon to the nearest couch, a red walnut settee. "We had too much furniture, so we sold some of Lizzie's and some of ours to give us a financial cushion. Add in the sale of the farm and Lizzie's salary as a treasury girl, and we're able to keep our heads above water—barely."

Celia limped to a larger couch and settled into it gently as possible for a fifty-something woman. "So many families are doing what we're doing. With Lizzie's husband shot dead by a Yank and Lizzie struggling, we couldn't let our grandkids starve."

Lizzie sat beside Simon who began sketching her portrait. "Things were so bad I joined the bread riot last year." Her voice cracked, indicating embarrassment "Broke into a general store and butcher's shop and stole food. I'm not proud of my behavior back then, but what choice did I have? People shouldn't be profiteering off widows and kiddies."

Lizzie's mother patted the couch cushion beside her, motioning for her husband to sit. "Things are better now. The kids got nice Christmas presents at a party put on by the Ladies' Aid Society."

Bill winked at Franny as the kids hightailed it to their bedrooms. Seconds later, they re-entered the parlor with their Christmas toys in their hands, a doll for the girl and play locomotive for the boy.

Finished with his portrait of Lizzie, Simon moved the family to the kitchen table where everyone—even the children—played checkers as the artist sketched them. Nodding his approval, Simon showed the family his completed sketch. "Like it?"

"I do." Fredo's eyes brimmed with admiration. "I can grow about anything, but if I try to draw I end up with stick figures."

The kids sang out, "So we're going to be in the papers?"

"That's the plan," Bill told them. "I'm going to make you famous."

The boy and girl clapped. "I'm good at reading," Basil claimed. "I promise I'll read every word." He gawked at Simon's peg leg. "How did you lose your leg?"

Simon tucked away his sketchbook. "A Yankee mini ball hit it, and a Confederate surgeon cut it off."

"You walk on your peg leg real good." Arianna crinkled a lopsided smile.

"I do, don't I?" Simon confirmed, beaming.

Bill looked at the scribbles he'd made while Lizzie, her father and mother chitchatted in the parlor and kitchen. "I've done the interview without interviewing anyone. Just wrote down what you said. Your words will look great in the newspapers." He eyed Fredo and Celia. "Can I use your quotes?"

Fredo answered for both. "Sure. Anything to help women like my daughter."

Knowing the family's hard circumstances, Franny and Bill begged off eating with them. They and Simon let Lizzie walk them to the front door. "I'd be destitute without my dear parents and the wonderful treasury job. God bless Momma, Pa and President Davis."

Forty

Time for a Funeral

For Bill and Franny, summertime became the days of autumn as trees along the boardwalks between their apartment building and the Capitol Square turned from leafy green to riotous red and yellow. Since late July and early August they'd been producing the occasional soldier or treasury-girl story with Simon tagging along to provide the artwork. The editors of the Richmond newspapers liked the stories. Some even assigned their own reporters and sketch artists to do similar features.

The second day of October started out like most days since Bill's return from London. Waking early and feeling frisky, he kissed Franny's belly—sadly not yet the home of a baby—and made his way up to her lips, stopping to lick-kiss both breasts and their hardened nipples. Soon spirited as Bill, Franny teased him into making love to her. Glistening muscles slid and shimmied against sinuous flesh. A cool wind drifted through the open window and prickled their skin. When finished and exhausted, Franny sucked in air and let it out with a soft moan. Bill draped a hand across her long legs and hips then rose from bed. His heels rested on the rug; his toes, the chilly plank floor. He involuntarily shivered.

Franny joined him on the side of the bed, her feet dangling above the floor. "We forgot the rubber." Her silk hair rippled down onto her shoulders.

"Forgot?" Bill rolled his eyes. "Sure."

Together, they brushed their teeth with a horrible-tasting chalk-paste so that their teeth wouldn't rot and their kisses would smell sweet. Once dressed and their hair prepped, they intended to eat oatmeal and head out the door for a Sunday walk to the Capitol Square. While Bill perched on the edge of the bed and tugged on his boots, someone knocked on the front door. In the parlor, the cat Tessir meowed at the insistent thwacks.

"Answer it, Bill. I'm doing my hair." Franny's tone indicated annoyance that Bill hadn't answered the door, allowing the knocks to continue.

"On my way." Bill beelined down the hallway and through the kitchen where the oatmeal cooked on the stove. He darted around the still-meowing Tessir. The cat could slither out the cat entry and inspect the visitor, but showed no inclination to do so.

Opening the door, Bill expected to see Charlie or one of his other neighbors looking to borrow some foodstuffs. Not his possum after all, it turned out. He'd be calling on Avis, bending her ear on wedding plans and how many babies they'd have. But nuptial day still lay months in the future.

Bill's brows scrambled up his forehead. One of the War Department's telegraphers waited at the door. "This just came in, sir. I knew you'd want to see it since you were a friend." The bearded soldier wept as he put the tear-stained paper into Bill's right hand.

Bill read slowly. Just like the telegrapher, tears seeped down Bill's cheeks. A runny nose triggered more problems, forcing him to run a sleeve over his mustache.

"Who is it, darling?" Franny called out from the bedroom.

"Rose's dead."

"I'm sorry, sir." The telegrapher's voice quivered. "Sweet Lord above…I knew this would upset you. At least you got to visit with her in London, right?"

"Yes, a gift from God." Bill remembered another unwanted gift from God—a halo flaring around Rose as she departed a Wilmington dockside tavern. "And no need to say you're sorry. Not your fault." He squeezed the man's shoulder. "Fate can't be denied."

"Yessir," the telegrapher mumbled, not taking in the full import of Bill's words.

Franny hurried into the parlor. "Rose dead? What happened?"
Bill sniffled, "Drowned."

The telegrapher wiped his eyes with a handkerchief. "Fell out of a rowboat fleeing a blockade runner on the Wilmington coastline—near Fort Fisher, it was."

"Lord, take care of her soul." Franny pressed her palms together. Light splashed past the parlor window overlooking the street, lighting up her blonde hair. The display looked like a halo in a medieval painting. Bill shuddered.

He couldn't resist combing a hand through Franny's freshly brushed curls. "Want to take a train trip to Wilmington?"

"Way too many funerals." She frowned. "I'm really tired of them. It's a cruel obligation."

"I'm not sure you gave me an answer."

"Yes, I'm going with you. I'm sure I can get Trenholm's permission."

Quiet until then, the telegrapher spoke up, "Secretary Seddon has secured a train for the War Department. It'll be going to Wilmington. It's departing at eleven o'clock."

Bill looked at his watch. Eight o'clock. He hoped the telegrapher meant tomorrow. "Tomorrow morning at eleven, right?"

"No, this morning. Funeral's tomorrow." The telegrapher shrugged. "Sorry for the short notice."

"Franny, better get out the carpetbags. We don't have much time."

Again apologizing for the bad news, the telegrapher bid farewell and headed to the front boardwalk and street. Later, as Bill and

Franny packed their carpetbags for a short stay in Wilmington, Bill let his mind transport him back to the summer of '63 and the moment the halo enveloped Rose. He took out a handkerchief and blew his nose. "Well, the halo won. That's not so bad, is it? To be in the arms of the Lord?"

"No, my love. Not at all." Franny did the bear with him, then stepped back and wiped tears from his face with the tips of her fingers.

"In London, I told Rose about the halo and its meaning." Tessir brushed against Bill's legs, prompting him to stoop and pet the cat. "She said the Lord had decided not to take her…He had a role for her to play in securing the South's independence."

"Rose was wrong."

"We really should eat before we leave for the depot." Bill nodded toward the kitchen and the stovetop where the oatmeal simmered. "Not sure when we'll get another chance to grab a bite."

"And I need to check with our neighbors, find one willing to feed scraps to Tessir." Franny spooned oatmeal into a bowl and sat at the kitchen table. "Need to catch them before they head to church." She shoveled the cereal into her mouth then stood and bolted for the front door.

Tessir lay beside Bill's feet, expecting oatmeal would soon magically appear next to his nose.

"Charlie and the little girl outside the depot remain the only ones the Lord has spared," Bill told the cat. "But Charlie's life came at a hefty price—General Jackson's life." Bill put his bowl on the floor so that Tessir could lap up the remnants. "I wish I knew the answer to the halos. I don't. Expect I never will. God's unfathomable. I know he believes in free will, so I'll do what I believe is right on a case-by-case basis." Bill scratched Tessir's chin, earning some purring. "It's a heavy burden, Tessir, one I don't think the Lord intends to lift—ever." He managed a pained smile. "I'll muddle through."

~ * ~

Yawning, Bill held out his hand and helped Franny step down onto the freight platform. After a slowpoke ride over failing track that covered two hundred and sixty miles, the War Department train arrived in Wilmington at eight in the morning, a straight-through, twenty-hour trip with little sleep. The locomotive and its passenger car had only stopped to take on coal and water whenever necessary. Its lantern light had shone on a worn-out land sapped by three and a half years of war. Before darkness cloaked the Virginia countryside, Bill had seen threadbare towns, faded paint peeling from schoolhouses, banks, stores and depots. Out in the farm fields, dog-tired women clad in bloomer dresses and adolescent boys toiled alone, their darkies commandeered by Richmond and state governments for work in factories, shipyards, mines and railroads.

At least Franny had found a neighbor to feed scraps to Tessir, Bill thought as he joined his wife on the platform. "My kingdom for some sleep."

The train's other dignitaries—John Archibald Campbell, Assistant Secretary of War, and Stephen Mallory, Secretary of the Navy—had already dumped their carpetbags on the freight cart and were shuffling toward a cab.

"Leave your luggage on the cart, sir," a Wilmington and Weldon slave instructed Bill. "I be takin' it to the Purcell House. A room's been reserved fer ya."

Carpetbags dropped on the cart, Bill and Franny followed Campbell and Mallory to the cab. Mallory held the door open for them.

"No thanks." Bill grinned in a perfunctory manner. "It's a nice morning. I think we'll walk."

Mallory nodded, and the cab's horses trotted down Water Street toward the Dock Street intersection and the St. Thomas the Apostle Roman Catholic Church. A biting wind nipped at Bill's exposed skin as he and Franny made their way along the boardwalk. Above them, sunrays occasionally bolted through the overcast, brief but welcome warmth on an otherwise cold morning. A nippy wind portended rain. Cider-making weather.

"That might not have been your smartest idea, darling." Franny squeezed her fingers into gloves."

"After that inferno ride, a walk will do both of us some good." Bill doubted his wind-scoured face looked as positive as his voice sounded.

"You're loony, Bill. I hope we get to the church before it pours."

Bill scrutinized the sky. "Later in the day, sweetheart."

"I was hoping to see your momma, Mark and Laura at the depot." Franny took his arm.

"I got the telegraph message off to Momma before we left Richmond. We'll just have to wait and see."

Franny suddenly scowled as she eyed the early morning strollers. "How sad! All but one of the women are wearing black. Rose didn't take a mini ball, but she's a victim of this war too."

"I can't see the war lasting much longer." Bill yawned. "Grant has Lee pinned in. Frankly, people have sacrificed for so long they can no longer see what's real and what's lost hope. Who wants to admit it's been for nothing? The Confederacy's in its death throes. Soon, it'll exist only in history books."

Franny laughed caustically. "If anyone hears our talk, we'll get tarred and feathered."

"Here we are late in 1864, and Davis and the Congress still won't give darkies an opportunity to serve in the army and earn their freedom. Too many folks are still living in the past, afraid of the Nat Turner bogeyman."

Two young women, both in mourning attire, passed them. "Our national flag should be all black," Franny whispered.

"I'll pass your recommendation on to President Davis." Bill rolled his eyes.

"He'll not like the graveyard humor."

At the Dock Street intersection, Bill and Franny turned east and proceeded toward Third Street. Saint Thomas dominated the skyline. Instead of a tower like other Wilmington churches, the church sported a massive central gable and lancet-arched windows. At least thirty buggies lined Dock Street in front of the church. Folks in black suits and dresses were exiting them and heading up the stairs into the church. Bill recognized a Wilmington-based soldier standing on the bottom step, Lieutenant Leroy Sieffenbach, an officer who had helped him recruit men for the Eighteenth North Carolina more than a year earlier. Leroy too had fallen under the spell of Rose Greenhow.

"The lieutenant must know you, Bill." Franny nodded toward the lieutenant. "He's eyeing you."

"Indeed, we became friends when I set up a recruiting desk at district headquarters. Took over when I needed to—" Bill didn't finish the sentence. He'd gone to the depot to pick up Becky. That night they'd made love, their first and only time they tipped the velvet.

"Ah, Becky," Franny said, her laugh acerbic.

Bill didn't need to answer. Leroy yelled out a greeting. "Captain's bars? You've shot up in rank as fast as a shooting star streaks through the night sky."

"Got the promotion last month. "For London. Not really deserving in my opinion. It's all a bit of a whirlwind to—"

"Bill! Bill! It's Nelly from the Worth Tavern." Bill remembered the tavernkeeper's wife, a friend of Rose's. Clad in a black dress, the middle-aged woman hugged him as if she'd just found her long-lost son. "Oh Bill, poor Rose. Too young and brave to die. What's to happen to Little Rose?"

Bill had not seen Little Rose while in London. Her momma had enrolled the girl in a French religious school. She must have sailed back to Wilmington with her momma. His imagination ran wild, visualizing Little Rose draped over her mother's coffin weeping copiously. "Little Rose inside? I want to talk to her. She needs to hear kind words from someone who knew her mother, like you, Nelly, and me. So many at this funeral hardly knew her."

Nelly's handkerchief couldn't keep up with the stream of salty tears. "Little Rose is still in Paris going to school. I don't know if the girl knows her momma's gone."

"Left her behind?" Nelly's words had stupefied Bill. "Rose must have been planning to return to Europe as soon as possible."

Franny cleared her throat. "Bill darling, please introduce me to your friends."

"Yes, introduce us to this beautiful creature." Nelly ogled Franny.

"You've chosen a different course in life, my friend." Leroy spread his devilish smile, encompassing Bill, Franny and Nelly.

"I've found a far better woman. This is my wife Franny." Bill kissed Franny's gloved hand.

The curious, along with those wanting to pay their respects to a genuine Confederate heroine, filed past. Hardly any had ever spoken a word to Rose. Maybe a handful passed her on one of Wilmington's boardwalks.

"You must stop by the Worth Tavern before you return to Richmond," Nelly insisted. "Beers on the house for both of you."

Bowing to Franny, Leroy raised an eyebrow then gave Bill a smirk. "I'm surprised Franny agreed to marry a rascal like you."

The start of organ music drowned out Bill's reply. Just as well. The conversation had become too jovial considering the circumstances. Franny clinging to his arm, Bill climbed the steps and advanced into the vestibule. Leroy and Nelly followed.

The four sat in a back pew where Nelly's husband listened to the organist play a hymn that had all the ladies sniffling and blowing their noses. Campbell and Mallory sat in the second pew at the front, just one row back from where a solitary woman sat.

Becky!

Where was Percy? Had she left him behind?

Bill continued to stare, his heart growing cold.

Becky...no longer the girl who'd once infatuated him, but harder, more brazen since living in London.

Rose's flag-draped casket rested in the sanctuary between the railing and the altar. She'd thought God had grand plans for her, but it turned out otherwise. She'd not save the Confederacy, not turned her pro-Union fiancé against Lincoln.

The organist, an elderly man in undertaker-style clothes, began playing "Jesu Dulcis Memoria." The music induced Bill to look upward at the sanctuary's rafters. The faces of the disciples and apostles were carved into the thick beams. Just below them along the walls, stained-glass windows told the story of Christ from birth through the resurrection. According to Bill's father, the artists who crafted the windows were glass masters from New York City, but the actual builders of the church were darkies, shipbuilders both slaves and freemen. Bill could see how the intricate carvings aboard ships could be adapted for churches.

Franny leaned against Bill. "Who's the woman in the front pew? One of Rose's daughters?"

"No. Rose has two daughters in Ohio." Bill took a measured breath. "The oldest, Florence, is married to a Union officer. Rose sent the middle daughter, Leila, to stay with Florence. Rose has a family with divided loyalties, like many of us."

"Yes, you've told me about your family." Franny patted Bill's kneecap. "Then who's the woman?"

Bill cleared his throat. "I think you know. Becky."

Swallowing hard, Franny squirmed in her seat. On her lap, her fingers curled into claws. "So she returned with Rose. Odd she didn't drown too."

Bill coughed fretfully. "Franny! You shouldn't wish harm on anyone."

"I'm not. I'm asking a simple question. Was she in the rowboat with Rose when it capsized?"

"I'll ask her after the service. If she'll talk to me." Near them, people were staring, censorious looks on their faces. "And please keep your voice down, Franny."

"Sorry. Still, her antics got you stabbed," Franny cupped her mouth against Bill's ear. "She probably pushed Rose's head under the water." She tugged on his lobe as she drew away from his face.

The organist played the last few notes of the hymn, then Dr. James Corcoran began the funeral Mass. The words were meaningless to Bill, phony platitudes Corcoran probably said at every soldier's funeral. He rubbed his eyes when tears dribbled down his cheeks. *Dead words for a dead woman.*

Men and women sitting in Bill's pew shifted in their seats, making room for Bill's mother to sit on the aisle. Their eyes met and she blew him a kiss. No Mark or Laura, though. Probably for the best. *They're too young for a funeral.*

Dr. Corcoran stopped speaking. Becky rose and stood in front of the casket. As the organist played a seventeenth-century hymn set to the words of the Twenty-Third Psalm, Becky began to sing. She stared out into the pews, her eyes fixing on Bill. Her sorrowful expression turned tense, and she stumbled over "I will fear no evil" before continuing with the hymn.

At the song's conclusion, with Becky once again seated, Colonel William Lamb, commander of Fort Fisher, one of the few mourners in the church who had actually spoken to Rose, shared the eighth chapter of Romans. Every muscle in Bill's body twitched at the words, "As it is written, for thy sake we are killed all day long; we are accounted as sheep for the slaughter."

"Describes this war, doesn't it?" Bill's murmur caressed Franny's cheek.

When Lamb closed his Bible, the colonel and other officers of the Wilmington Military District as well as Campbell and Mallory borne the flag-draped coffin to a horse-drawn hearse. Becky trailed them, her gaze fixed on nothing until she neared Bill's momma. "Hello, Mrs. Stamford. I'm so sorry about Mr. Stamford."

Late for the funeral, Becky's coat-bundled parents waited outside near the hearse. Before stepping up beside the hearse driver, Becky spoke a few brief words to her father and mother, words Bill couldn't make out. The two horses pulled the hearse away from the curb and trotted toward Oakdale Cemetery, a sad journey of a mile and a half. Deacons handed out umbrellas to mourners as they departed the church. Raindrops splattered the footpath between the church and the boardwalk.

Only eight buggies made the trip to the cemetery. Most people surrendered to the inclement weather and returned to their homes. Bill hugged his mother then quietly accepted her scolding for not staying longer in Kenansville after his return from London. Icie Belle kissed Franny on both cheeks and patted her daughter-in-law's belly. "I'd love to have a grandchild."

"Someday." Franny pinched Bill's cheek. "I don't see the war lasting too much longer."

Following in the wake of townspeople willing to brave the cold drizzle, Bill, Franny and Icie Belle scrambled into a military ambulance and followed the hearse and buggies. Once in Oakdale, they unfolded their umbrellas and pushed through the rain to a grassy slope dappled with magnolias, oaks, gravestones and a recently dug hole. The coffin lay on a bier beside the hole. Dr. Corcoran and Becky stood near it, shivering in the drizzle. Arrayed around the open grave were Campbell, Mallory, Colonel Lamb and other district officers, a dismal ending for Rose Greenhow, heroine of the Confederacy.

As darkies lowered the coffin into the ground, gray clouds parted and sunlight sprayed down on the mourners. A rainbow spanned the horizon beyond the Cape Fear River.

Dr. Corcoran said a few final words, and then everyone prepared to return to their buggies and carriages. Becky, accompanied by a mustached man in a seaman's uniform, approached Bill and the two women. He introduced himself as William Murray, captain of the blockade runner *Condor*. Bill knew his real name, Captain William Hewitt of the British Navy, but let the ruse stand.

"Rose spoke much of you, Captain Stamford." Hewitt turned his gaze to the hole and the darkies shoveling damp dirt into it. Each time the dirt splattered on the coffin lid, it made a dull thud sound. "She couldn't wait to get to Richmond—and not just to confer with President Davis. She wanted to buy you a sherry cobbler. She claimed to have introduced you to the drink."

Bill grinned, a smile he didn't have to force. "Indeed, she did."

Before Bill could elaborate, Hewitt interrupted. "The sailor who rowed Rose ashore blames himself for her death."

Becky spoke up, her voice barely above a mouse's squeak, "I begged her not to enter the rowboat."

Behind Becky, nearly camouflaged by an old oak, her parents lurked, saying nothing, just observing. No doubt her father wanted to castigate Bill for deflowering his sweet girl, starting her down the path that transformed her into a hellion proud of her bohemian ways. With important Confederate officers present, he didn't dare.

"We all tried to stop Rose." Hewitt gazed skyward. The break in the clouds that allowed the sun to kindle a rainbow had disappeared.

Drizzle wet Hewitt's face. "Weather wasn't good nor visibility. Blockaders were as plentiful as honeybees around a hive, and I had to race the *Condor* to the Cape Fear River to escape them. The *Condor* ran aground. Rose, along with a couple of gentlemen"—he pointed to where two men were taking a final look down at Rose's coffin—"chose to board a rowboat against my advice and go ashore. It capsized. She didn't surface."

"I begged her not to go." Becky refused to acknowledge Franny's harsh stare, eyeing Icie Belle instead. "She'd sewn gold from the sale of her book into her underclothes. Its weight doomed her, all for a lost cause. How can anyone still believe the South can escape Lincoln's stranglehold?" The girl who'd traded the Southern Belle façade for European bohemian ways daubed her nose with a scented handkerchief. "I need to watch my words, don't I? Too many zealous Confederate officers all around me." She shrugged. "What does it matter? The zealots can hate me all they want. I'm returning to London as soon as possible. They found a letter on Rose's body addressed to her youngest daughter she left in Paris. I'll be taking the letter with me and will see that she gets it."

Becky's gaze lingered on Bill, as if she wanted to say something. If so, the words never left her mouth. *Not one word about my knifing.* Anger roiled in his gut. *Obviously still sodden over Percy. She's lost her soul.*

Bidding farewell, Becky walked away, still not meeting eyes with Franny. The ersatz bohemian girl didn't even acknowledge her parents, walking in the opposite direction. Bill made small talk with Hewitt for a few minutes. He turned to talk to Franny and discovered her gone as well. He looked around. No sign of his wife—or Becky.

"You see Franny leave, Momma?"

"She followed Becky. Probably decided to give her a tongue lashing for what her beau did to you."

Bill grimaced. "I could have handled it. Don't need Franny's temper on display."

Hewitt looked puzzled. "Miss Powell's beau?"

"Yes. He hired thugs to stab me in London. At the start of the war, I'd courted Becky."

Bill swiveled his head, searching for Franny. He shivered as a markedly cold breeze slithered through openings in his uniform and numbed his chest. Over the banter percolating around the gravesite, Bill heard feminine squeals then shouts. Sharing a worried glance with his momma, he scanned the rainy mist where he'd heard the unlady-like voices, a copse of skeletal oaks with gloomy red leaves still clinging to their limbs.

He sprinted toward the oaks. His momma and Hewitt were doing the same. The mist hid everything. Women in black are not easily seen inside a mist.

The wind shifted swirls of mist, revealing Franny and Becky. Their hats on the ground, their hair disheveled, Bill's wife and his ex-girlfriend stood face to face near a low-lying limb, so close they could have been mistaken for conjoined twins. Franny's black lace shawl lay swaddled around Becky's forehead, an improvised bandage.

Blood stained the shawl. Mud coated Becky's dress as if she'd fallen. Her shawl lay on muddy grass. The red vestiges of a palm print blighted one of Becky's cheeks.

Franny whirled away from Becky, revealing a palm print as well. She wore an innocent expression. "Becky took a nasty fall. We'd been having a spirited talk. She turned to leave and ran smack dab into the tree limb. Right, Becky?"

Becky raked strands of tawny hair away from Franny's rigged bandage with an unsteady hand. "I'm so clumsy. I'm shocked I didn't knock the oak down."

Hurrying to Becky's side, the sea captain slipped an arm around her and fixed the fit of Franny's shawl. "I'll look after her."

Any thugs Percy hired to stab the sea captain would find it no easy task, Bill thought.

As Hewitt and Becky shuffled toward his buggy, chased by her parents, she looked back at Bill. "I'm sorry for what Percy did to you."

Franny crossed her arms against her chest. "See, Becky, dear, that wasn't so hard."

Bill opened his umbrella as the drizzle intensified, and Franny moved closer and snuggled against him. As they walked to the Oakdale archway gate, she gripped his hands. Strands of tawny hair dropped from her fingers.

Trailing them, Icie Bell remarked, "I don't think I've ever seen such a spectacle. I'm thinking I should write it up as a sporting event."

"Please do." Franny sighed then breathed out a most unladylike hoot. "As your son will attest, I don't have much of a reputation left, especially since starting work as a treasury girl."

Forty-one

A Sumptuous Turkey Dinner

Bill thought everything had been worked out beforehand. Peace could lurk just beyond the bend if the Yankee soldiers barring the three buggies, including the one containing Bill, would move aside and allow the Confederate peace commissioners to proceed. Except the buggies were stuck in no-man's land between Confederate and Union entrenchments outside Petersburg. Bill sensed he stood on a dangerously swaying rope bridge, peace waiting on the far side if he could just get there.

In January 1865, nearly four years into the war, Richmond women were scrambling to put enough food on plates for their children. A lit powder keg burned in Richmond, ready to explode. Even at the most recent Ladies' Aid Society Christmas party, an undercurrent of frustration and growing rage permeated the Episcopal Church. Richmond's wealthy had ways to secure food. The desperate poor made do with prayers that weren't answered.

A Union Cavalry colonel rode up to Vice President Stephens' buggy and spoke words loud enough for everyone to hear. "Major

General Ord has an answer from Washington City, sir. You can proceed to General Grant's headquarters at City Point."

"Not to Washington City?" The voice belonged to Stephens. "Can you tell me why, Colonel?"

"The orders came directly from President Lincoln, sir. The *River Queen's* taking him down to City Point. You'll meet aboard the boat." The colonel saluted smartly.

The Yankee cavalrymen moved aside, unblocking the road through the Union lines. The colonel waved the convoy forward, and buggies lurched into motion. As the conveyances rolled along River Road, Union troops encamped behind their entrenchments cheered, screaming out huzzahs as the buggies drew away from Union lines. Beyond no-man's land, Confederates cheered, mingling their rebel yells with the Union huzzahs.

Led by an escort of Confederate cavalrymen, the Rebel negotiators—Stephens, Assistant Secretary of War John Campbell and Senator Robert Hunter of Virginia—–wheeled deep into Union territory, Bill praying they'd succeed in their aim, some kind of armistice. Whether it involved independence or re-admittance into the Union, Bill no longer cared.

Blue-belly cavalrymen broke into a gallop and passed the convoy and its Confederate escort. They took the lead, ensuring no trigger-happy soldiers would take shots at the Confederate dignitaries. The Confederate national flag and a white pennant flew from the three buggies, each borne by two bone-skinny horses.

Partly melted snow dappled the countryside scarred by trenches and bombproofs. Just two days left in January, more than a month since the dreary Christmas party and almost four months since Rose's funeral. The war in Virginia had settled into trench fighting. General Grant appeared willing to wait for the cold and snow to disappear before launching yet another spring offensive. Bill feared this assault would prove too devastating, and the Confederate trenches and bombproofs would break. Then again maybe the peace conference would succeed and no men need die in a spring offensive.

Campbell put down the report he'd been reading. "How's your delightful wife doing?"

"Franny quit the Treasury Department to do the planning for her toy party."

"She couldn't do both?" Campbell scratched at his knitted brow.

"My wife does charity work at one hundred and ten percent. The party's a full-time job for her."

"Your Franny's a firecracker." Campbell chuckled.

"She sure is," Charlie agreed. "Franny loves to scandalize the granmaws of Richmond and Fredericksburg."

"I heard she and another woman brawled like sailors at Rose's burial? I'd left the cemetery before all the shenanigans." Campbell kept his face blank.

Bill rolled his eyes. "Exaggeration. Becky turned to leave and smacked a low-lying limb. Franny helped stem the bleeding."

"Becky? The woman in the front pew at the Wilmington church?" Campbell folded his report and slipped it into a satchel at his feet.

"Rose's secretary. Someone I once courted. Her English beau got insanely jealous and hired some thugs to knife me. Becky never said a thing to me afterwards. Franny took umbrage."

"Helped stem the bleeding, eh?" Campbell mused, again chuckling. "Hope our peace conference succeeds as well."

"Lincoln will demand we rejoin the Union," Charlie opined. "I can't see how the conference can go well for us."

Bill stifled a laugh. Charlie held a secret close to his gray Confederate vest. He wanted the Union restored and slavery gone. He dreamed he'd someday win election to the Tar Heel General Assembly and then to the U.S. Congress where he could help the South rebuild its fortunes.

"The sergeant voices little hope for peace," Campbell told Bill. "What's your thoughts, Captain?"

Bill needed to be careful with his answer. He couldn't say what he'd like to say: free the slaves, lay down arms, and seek to reunite with the North without any retribution for secession. Instead, he said, "I'm amazed Lincoln's willing to meet with us. I figured he'd unleash Grant and play his fiddle as Richmond burns."

Campbell glanced at the bleak countryside, trees bare and the occasional farmhouse looking tumbledown. "Vice President Stephens knows Lincoln well from their Whig Party days and says he's a kind man. We'll soon find out."

Bill thought back to November and Lincoln's shocking election win. Southerners overwhelmingly hoped Yankees would rebuff Lincoln and his war. "Nearly three months ago, folks up north voted to keep the war going and make us surrender unconditionally. It hardly seems realistic for him to let the CSA survive."

"This convoy's an amazing sight." Campbell pointed ahead. "We're led by Yankee and Confederate cavalry. Some politicians in Richmond think we should offer an armistice to Lincoln that includes a combined military mission against Mexico. The armies of the CSA and the USA marching together to send Maximilian skedaddling back to France."

"Crazy idea." Charlie's expression mirrored his words.

"We need some crazy ideas if we're to hang on to our independence." Campbell nuzzled a thumb under his chin. "It's actually a Union idea—from the brain of Major General Francis Blair."

The passengers chose silence as the convoy pushed deeper into Yankee-occupied Virginia. Beyond the buggy windows, the towns and farms looked drab and used up. Courthouses, churches, general stores, banks, apothecaries, dress shops and schoolhouses looked worn and in need of a lick of new paint. Only old men and women— and the occasional young boy—were seen in the fields. The darkies were gone...working for Yankee money. The countryside looked as depleted as General Lee's army.

Near City Point, the horses drawing Campbell's buggy came to a shuddering stop. Up ahead, a band of blue-belly cavalry troopers trotted up to the convoy. The two Yankee Cavalry companies conferred for a few minutes, then the commander of the new cavalrymen greeted each buggy. At Campbell's buggy, the young captain waited for Campbell to open the window. "Morning. I've orders from General Grant to escort you to Hampton Roads. First, though, the general and his wife Julia have invited you to dine at his headquarters in City Point."

Campbell rested his elbow on the windowsill. "I look forward to meeting General Grant. Your accent, Captain? Pennsylvania man? Pittsburgh?"

"Ohio, sir. Wayne County."

"Near Akron, right?" Campbell's face beamed with recognition.

"Yessir. From Apple Creek."

As the buggy bounced along the rutted road toward City Point, Charlie quipped, "Nice to be wanted."

"Well, we'll know soon enough just how wanted we are. If the peace conference ends after a day…" Campbell shrugged.

"We all want the Day of Jubilee." Bill cleared his throat. "We just don't seem to know how to get there."

City Point breathed military might—dozens of cargo ships full of war supplies, troop transports and warships, all moored at the docks. Bill wondered what Campbell thought as the convoy wheeled through the port. Grant obviously wanted the Confederate politicians to see the North's power. The display reinforced the obvious. The South couldn't last much longer. Bill and Charlie exchanged knowing glances.

Appomattox Manor, Grant's headquarters for the Petersburg Campaign, sat on a bluff overlooking the confluence of the James and Appomattox rivers. Surrounded by waterside farm fields, the eighteenth century manor house dominated the countryside around City Point. Up ahead, near a bend in the plank road, the house's circular driveway beckoned. The Yankee escorts turned onto the private road and led the three-buggy convoy past outbuildings up to the wraparound porch where a contingent of stablehand darkies awaited them.

"Lordy be! Git me some smellin' salts." Eyes like two full moons, Wilson, his father's darkey gardener, approached Campbell's buggy as Bill stepped down to the gravel carriageway. "If it ain't my soldier boy. Ya're a sight for sore eyes, Bill Stamford. And a captain now!"

Wilson picked up Bill as if he weighed a feather and hugged him. "I be thinkin' I'd never see ya again."

"Put me down, Wilson, and tell me how you got these muscles." Bill patted his friend's arm.

The tall, stringbean man set Bill down and kissed him on the forehead, not once but three times. "Workin' my behind in the stables, that' how, young Bill. Shoein', feedin', waterin', muckin' out, groomin', ruggin' and exercisin' the horses. I'm a free man and I git a decent wage." Wilson mussed the hair below Bill's slouch hat. "Wait 'til Malinda sees ya. She'll do some dead faintin' too."

"Malinda's nearby?" Bill sported a smile wide enough to swallow Kenansville.

"Please don't say Malinda's helpin' you take care of Grant's horses." Charlie hopped down from the buggy.

"Master Charlie, ya're lookin' fine." Wilson swung his gaze up to the grand house. "She's in there. One of the cooks. And makin' a decent wage too."

As soon as Bill got back to Richmond, he intended to send a telegram to his momma telling her Wilson and Malinda were safe at City Point.

Bill followed Wilson's gaze past the stoop to where a seedy-looking Union officer and his wife, a petite woman with dark, glossy hair, made their way out the door onto the porch. Bill figured him no more than a captain until he saw the four stars on his shoulders— General Grant, the man pounding the Confederacy into the dust.

"That short fella's Grant," Charlie whispered, hesitation in his voice. "He don't look like a general, not like Lee or Longstreet. He's wearin' a private's coat and they say he likes his liquor."

"Hush!" Bill hissed.

The woman, her bright coloring presaging a cheerful personality, approached Bill, Charlie and Wilson. Grant went in another direction, greeting Vice President Stephens, Campbell and Hunter. "Good evening, gentlemen. I'm Julia Grant."

"Pleasure to meet you, ma'am. I'm Captain Bill Stamford." Bill tipped his hat as others introduced themselves.

The sun dipped behind the house, spraying the countryside—and Julia Grant—in sunset colors. The mottled light painted her chignon-style hair, giving the curls a reddish glow.

"My husband's taking the commissioners on a fancy tour of the plantation. You're stuck with me." She grinned, a smile so sweet Bill couldn't help but immediately like her.

Another Union general joined her. "They're getting the gold dollar tour."

"This is General Rawlins, my husband's aide-de-camp." Julia squinted, a habit that camouflaged an almost imperceptible cross-eyed disorder. Bill might not have noticed if not for the squinting.

"I'm your entertainment for tonight," Rawlins deadpanned, turning to Julia. "Darts, Mrs. Grant?"

"Scintillating conversation, that's our entertainment." Julia scrutinized Wilson, who lingered in the vicinity of the aides. "A homecoming?" she asked Bill and Wilson.

Grant's wife must have seen Wilson hugging him. But why inquire? Of course, she deserved an honest answer. "My papa owned Wilson and his wife Malinda. He helped them escape to freedom. It's the first time I've seen Wilson since the summer of '63."

Julia's eyebrows scrambled up to her forehead. "How wonderful! You want to hear a secret?"

"A secret?" Bill swung his gaze back and forth between Julia and Wilson.

"I grew up in St. Louis. My father owned slaves. In some ways, I miss that way of life. But I do understand your joy."

"Thank you, Mrs. Grant." Bill fidgeted.

Julia and General Rawlins ushered the aides up onto the porch and into the manor house. The ostentatiousness reminded Bill of the Yerby house in Fredericksburg where he'd met Franny after the December 1862 battle. The furnishings reeked of planter-class wealth—eighteenth century French settees, tables, armchairs, secretaries, cabinets, pianos, all gilded or intricately hand painted. Landscapes and portraits by Dutch masters hung on the walls. Bill reconsidered his earlier thoughts. The ornate furnishings easily outshone the Yerby house.

"My husband refuses to stay here." Julia and Rawlins led them past the parlor, music room, and the library. "It's in use as the offices of U.S. Quartermaster Ingalls and his staff. We're staying in one of the outbuildings—a cabin. Sam's not one for gaudy display. That's why to me he's Sam, not The General."

"I'm from the mountains of North Carolina, ma'am. We're not much for display either," Charlie's mouth curved into a lopsided smile.

"Mountain people never are. My husband's keen on peace. He knows the war's nearly over and, like President Lincoln, wants the South and the North to reunite on fair, amicable terms. If we don't do this right, the damage will reverberate for decades." Julia led them into what she called the cigar abode, a room filled with game tables. She produced a cigar box from a drawer and handed out cigars to the Confederate aides. "You must be famished. I'll have a snack prepared, but I don't want to ruin your appetite. My husband has a banquet planned for later." She turned to Rawlins. "I turn our new friends over to you, John."

Once Julia left the cigar room, Rawlins crossed his legs then inspected the chess pieces on a game board before lighting a cigar. "So what do you fellas think? Can we end the war without another spring of fighting?"

Charlie tapped his stump. "This may surprise you, General Rawlins, but I'm not bitter. So many like me are, though. They'll not agree to any peace treaty without a guarantee of independence. Yes, a Yankee mini ball shattered my left arm, but that's part of war's cost." Charlie eyed the other Confederate aides including Bill. "I can't speak for these men, but if President Lincoln offers us somethin' better than unconditional surrender, we'd better take it."

Bill laid his cigar aside. "My momma's from Ohio. I've cousins serving out west and with the Army of the Potomac. I love them and don't want to be separated from them for the rest of my life. It's important this war ends with healing, not acrimony."

Behind Bill, Julia swept into the room followed by darkey servers carrying plates of delicacies—cheese and crackers, lemon gingerbread, sugar cookies, Pennsylvania pudding and lemonade. The smells took Bill back to before the war to church socials. A clanking crash—ceramic plates shattering, glass breaking—jolted Bill from his thoughts. A feminine voice shrieked, "Young Bill! Lordy, it can't be! Satan, don't deceive me!"

Bill whirled in his seat just in time for Malinda to wrap her arms around his shoulders and smother him with forehead kisses. "Easy on me, Malinda. You're going to crush me." As Malinda drew back, Bill rose and embraced the former slave who'd helped raise him.

"Oh, another homecoming," Julia trilled. "You must be overjoyed, Captain."

An odd thought crept into Bill's mind. He wondered if Grant and Julia had bitter arguments over the slavery issue. He bottled up that thought. "I am, ma'am. This woman is like a second momma." Bill did the kissing this time, planting several on Malinda's forehead.

"Another homecoming?" Malinda made a face. "Wilson's in a heap of trouble."

"I'm sure he wanted to tell you, Malinda, but he had to help get our buggies into the stables." Charlie lit his cigar with his one hand and puffed.

Malinda settled her gaze on Charlie for the first time. "Oh young'un, your poor arm! Sweet Lord I'm sorry, child."

"I'm fine, Malinda. Goin' to soon be married to a wonderful woman. I may be missin' an arm, but I'm still a whole man." Charlie winked at her.

"Did I hear someone say earlier he has cousins in Ohio?" Julia sat at a card table and nibbled on a sugar cookie.

"I did, ma'am," Bill acknowledged. "On my momma's side."

"I can sympathize with you, Captain. My father's a zealous supporter of the Confederacy. He wanted my husband to join the Confederate military." She grimaced, undoubtedly remembering bad times. "When Sam refused, my father wanted me to leave him. I'm here now beside Sam, providing the love he needs during these terrible times when men die at his command. You and I, Captain, we have to heal not only our nation but our families as well."

The other Confederate aides continued to say nothing except for Charlie, never one to avoid difficult conversations. "Let's hope Mr. Lincoln and our commissioners keep your family, Bill's and thousands of others in their prayers when negotiations begin."

"I suspect you'll find that President Lincoln will turn out to be your friend," Julia predicted. "As to your President Davis? I'll let you decide."

An aide attached to Stephen's staff spoke up, "I think we can all agree there are too many empty seats at dinner tables. God have mercy on our souls if thousands more die unnecessarily in the weeks and months ahead."

"Please eat." Julia continued to nibble the cookie. "The servants have been cooking like Henry the Eighth's chefs since we learned you'd be paying us a visit." Nearby, Malinda stooped and picked up the broken ceramics and glass.

Charlie sampled the pudding. "Yummy. I almost hate to go back to Richmond." Everyone in the cigar room knew what he meant.

"Remember, leave some room in your belly for dinner." Julia patted her stomach. "My husband wants it to be a feast you soon won't forget. We're having turkey with scalloped potatoes, sage dressing, creamed onions, mashed turnips, cranberries and pumpkin pudding."

In the trenches, skeletal Confederate soldiers ate measly rations that barely kept them alive. How could the Confederacy hope to defeat a people that fed its soldiers like this? Bill grimaced. Treasonous thoughts.

~ * ~

The Confederate peace commissioners were famished when they returned to the manor house and sat down in the dining room, lit only by candlelight. While the aides ate tidbits in the cigar room, their bosses had drunk beer with Grant and his generals at a City Point tavern, then were given the tour of the stables and Grant's horses including Cincinnati, son of Lexington, the fastest four-mile thoroughbred in the Western Hemisphere. By the time President Davis's representatives unfolded their napkins, the three men were ready to dig into the turkey and scalloped potatoes. If the politicians thought about the hungry children back in Richmond, they were careful to keep their thoughts to themselves. Grant's feast stated the obvious: the North had the South in an anaconda death grip.

Grant didn't look the part of a conqueror. Delicate hands with long, slim fingers tucked his napkin into his shirt collar. Soft blue eyes scrutinized everyone at the large table. Thin lips hiding behind a full beard and mustache distributed a smile all around as Grant introduced guests who'd joined the Confederates at the table. "Our son Jesse will be eating with us this evening as well as John's wife Mary Emma and their daughter Emily."

"Delighted." Stephens nodded at the Grants' boy and Rawlins' wife and daughter. "We thank you for your hospitality and hope our talks with President Lincoln bring peace to our two nations."

Bill groaned silently. Stephens lived in a fantasy world. No table in the South would eat a feast like the one set before the vice president. That Lincoln was willing to meet with the peace commissioners was a miracle of sorts. Bill hoped the three Southern politicians would put peace ahead of gossamer dreams of independence.

"When you board President Lincoln's *River Queen*, if you remember that the flag it flies has your stars emblazoned on it, you'll realize you've nothing to fear from him." Grant mussed his son's hair. "I do believe Jesse wants to say grace so he can begin eating turkey. Jesse?"

"Lord, bless this food we're about to eat. And please bring peace so no more soldiers die."

Beyond the window nearest Bill, the moon shone in the night sky. The dinnertime chitchat made Bill feel the war had happened on another world, perhaps the moon. Grant amused the Confederates with tales of his boyhood hijinks in Georgetown, Ohio, where his pa ran a tannery—pole fishing on a local pond, wintertime ice skating, horseback riding, playing hooky and sneaking away to the county fair.

"I pole fish from the bank of the Appomattox." Jesse straightened his spine.

At meal's end, Grant rose stiffly from his chair and told the Confederates, "Get a good night's sleep. You'll need to be on River Road just after first light. Seventy miles away, Hampton Roads is where President Lincoln awaits you on the *River Queen.*"

Bill invited Wilson and Malinda to join him in the bedroom assigned to him so they could catch up on family news. On the way up the stairs, he overheard Grant speaking to Rawlins. "Tell Julia I'll be late to bed. I'm going to mosey over to the telegraph office and tell the president that Stephens, Hunter and Campbell are reasonable men and will give peace a chance."

Once inside his bedroom, Bill told Malinda and Wilson about Clarence's death. Malinda gasped; legs wobbly, she collapsed and would have hit the floor if Wilson hadn't caught her. "Poor Icie Belle," she wailed.

Forty-two

Peace Talks

His gloved hands gripping the ship's railing, Bill tallied the Union vessels steaming into and out of the harbor at Hampton Roads, so many he soon lost count. Warships, merchantmen and troop carriers plied the waters at the mouth of the James River. For every Yankee soldier killed or wounded, Lincoln could send two replacements. For every blockading cruiser sunk, Lincoln's shipyards could build two new ones. The spectacle reinforced Bill's long-held sentiment...the Confederacy faced extinction.

Behind Bill, inside a stateroom on the *River Queen*, Abraham Lincoln, president of the United States, listened to the Confederate peace commissioners make their case for peace—one favored by Jefferson Davis. With the door closed and sounds muffled, Bill couldn't hear their pitch to Lincoln. Davis needed to be aboard the *River Queen*, needed to see the North's military might. Then maybe the politicians could negotiate the best deal possible—and end the war before more men needlessly died.

Bill swung his gaze to the *River Queen's* pier. Charlie paced between the gangplank and the buggies where Confederate and Union cavalrymen mingled. Taking a last look at the stateroom's closed door, Bill headed for the gangplank.

"Hey, Billy Boy, Lincoln ask for your advice yet?" As Charlie walked up to Bill, he chortled, pleased with his wisecrack.

"Lincoln's a wise man, He knows better than to seek my advice."

"Care to join me? I'm wearin' a hole into the pier." Charlie ground his boot heel into a plank as if extinguishing a cigar.

"Why not? You and Avis set a date for your marriage?"

"Thinkin' about sometime in early April. Flowers will be bloomin' and winter long in the past." Flurries falling from a bleak overcast sky twirled around Charlie's head, some landing on his hat and shoulders. "Of course, it has to snow on an important day like this. Good or bad omen?"

Bill sighed. "In literature often sadness or death."

"Not what I wanted to hear, Billy Boy."

At the buggies, a Yankee sergeant shouted, "Hey, rebs, hear any news?"

"Too early," Bill opined. "Been less than four hours."

"The longer they talk, the better for us soldiers, eh?" Charlie quipped.

"Sure hope so," The cavalryman braced an arm on a buggy wheel.

More snowflakes gamboled in the air as Bill and Charlie made their way back to the gangplank. Just as they reached the narrow passageway up to the one-stack paddlewheeler, the stateroom's door flew open and the three peace commissioners hastened out onto the deck. Bill and Charlie stared at each other, uncertainty stamped on their faces.

Shoulders slumped, Stephens, Campbell and Hunter rushed down the gangway and stomped to the buggies. "We failed," Campbell told Bill and Charlie. "Nothing to negotiate." The swirling snow coated Campbell's thick eyebrows.

"Sadness, eh?" Charlie stared at Campbell's encrusted eyebrows. "Confounded snow!"

Union Secretary of State William Seward emerged through the doorway, followed by Lincoln draped in his knee-length overcoat. Snow glazed Lincoln's tophat as he watched the Confederate politicians trudge away from his boat. The beginnings of a halo flamed into existence above the tophat and flared along both sides of Lincoln. Seen by no one but Bill, the aureola didn't melt the snowflakes. Swirling through it, they landed softly on the deck and joined the growing white blanket.

~ * ~

Huffing and puffing, Bill started up the steps to his apartment building's lobby. He couldn't wait to see Franny's expression when he walked into the kitchen. She didn't expect him until later in the week. As he reached for the door, Bill jumped as it flew open and a neighbor woman bolted through the entryway.

"Welcome home, Captain," Mrs. Mitchell puffed, sliding to a stop. "You just missed Franny. She left for the Ladies' Aid Society meeting at Margaret Goodwin's house."

Thanking his neighbor, he watched her head for the general merchandise store a block away. Debating whether to go upstairs to the apartment or walk to the Goodwin house, Bill chose the latter.

He tightened the collar of his frockcoat and tramped away from the brownstone. The afternoon had turned cloudy, but not completely so. The sunbeams bussing his face helped make the near-freezing cold tolerable. Elms between the boardwalk and the street had yet to sprout leaves on this day in mid-February. The first buds wouldn't appear for another month. Earlier in February, a light dusting of snow along the Virginia seaboard slowed the peace commissioners' journey away from Hampton Roads. The return trip to Richmond turned out to be a dismal one with no one talkative. Now, though, the prospect of soon seeing Franny brightened Bill's mood.

The neighborhood looked deserted except for a great horned owl perched high up on a limb a block from the brownstone. Bill didn't notice the owl until it screeched, spread its two-foot-long wings and launched into the air in search of a woodchuck or rabbit. A one-horse wagon rumbled along the brick roadway over deep grooves that had once contained trolley rails confiscated for the war effort. An old white man with gray whiskers and bushy eyebrows handled the reins, driving the wagon down to a riverfront warehouse. In the spring of '61, the downtown area would have been crowded with cabs, buggies, carriages and wagons, most with slaves managing the reins. Now slaves were digging ores in the mines, fixing railroad rails, sawing and hammering away in the shipyards—or running away to City Point and Hampton Roads.

By the time Bill reached his destination, flurries swirled around him, teased by a blustery wind even though sunbeams peeked through the bleak gray clouds. His scuffed boots proved a poor choice for the icy walkway up to the Goodwin house's stoop. Bill slid on the cobblestones, prompting him to slow his pace. Torn pants at the kneecaps wouldn't impress the ladies.

Upper-crust families like the Goodwins were hanging onto their household slaves. One answered the door when Bill tapped the dog-head knocker. The ladies were sipping tea and eating gingerbread when the darkey peeked his head through the French doors and announced, "Ya've a guest...Captain Bill Stamford."

Bill sidled past the butler. "Excuse me, ladies. I've a wife I need to steal."

Hands pressed against her ears as if she couldn't believe what she'd heard, Franny leaped to her feet, nearly tipping her chair. "Oh my Lord! Darling! You weren't supposed to return until later this week."

With a flip of his hand, Bill motioned for her to join him. "Get your coat. I'm in the mood for a walk."

A widow clad in an old-fashioned mourning dress spoke up, "How did the peace talks go, Captain?"

Scowling, Bill shook his head. "The war continues, ma'am. Too big a gulf between Lincoln and our peace commissioners. I wish it was otherwise."

Fighting back tears, the woman buried her face in her hands. "A husband and two sons dead. Please, Lord, don't take my last one." Shifting her face away from her hands, she glowered at Bill. "George's down at Petersburg. Just seventeen."

A thirtyish woman in a flowery dress rushed to the weeping woman's aid. "Oh, Edith, General Lee won't fail us. He'll pull off another miracle and send the Yanks scurrying to Washington City."

Sobbing, the older woman rasped, "I hope so."

Avis squirmed on a settee cushion. "Where's Charlie? I expected him to be with you, Bill. Is he okay?"

"He went to your parents' house. I imagine he'll be here shortly."

"That was what I was hoping." The relief in Avis's voice was palpable.

Franny patted Avis's knee. "I told you not to worry. Charlie and Bill got to hobnob with Abe Lincoln."

Bill grimaced as the memory of Lincoln's halo flashed through his mind. "Well, not hobnob but we did get to see him aboard his ship, the *River Queen*. He's tall, a giant with the tophat on his noggin. We ate dinner with the Grants. Don't look skeptical, ladies. We ate a turkey dinner with the general and his wife Julia. Avis, please act surprised when Charlie tells you about it."

Franny joined Bill at the doorway. "A walk, eh? It's a bit cold outside, but I do want to hear all about Grant, Lincoln and the peace talks. I'll be thoroughly disappointed if I have to read about it in the newspapers."

With the butler in the lead, they stopped at the coat room where Bill helped Franny into her paletot and her scallop-top boots. At the front door, the butler nervously surveyed the hall. "How much longer ya think the war's goin' to last, Captain?"

"Not beyond the spring." Bill lowered his voice. "Be careful what you ask. These are dangerous times, worse than the Nat Turner days. You don't want to end up hung from an old apple tree."

The darkey nodded. "I knows."

Once beyond the door, Bill and Franny made their way across the porch and down the stoop to the brick footpath. The flurries still tumbled, swirling around them. "I hate snow, even flurries," Franny griped.

"Let's take a walk to the Capitol Square." Bill tucked an arm around Franny's waist. "I predict the flurries will soon disappear."

"A splendid idea, sweetheart. But you're wrong about the flurries." She laughed lightly. Her breath melted snowflakes near her face.

Holding hands, they meandered to the square, kissing at every opportunity. Few people shared the boardwalk with them. Two buggies and a wagon wheeled by during the fifteen-minute walk. He thought Franny would quiz him on the failed peace negotiations. Perhaps the flurries soured her mood. Instead, she chatted about mundane things she'd been doing.

In the square, they sat on a bench overlooking Main Street. Near them, a smattering of folks eyed storefront displays for toys and clothes no one could afford. *Life goes on*, Bill thought, even as Grant and Meade planned their spring campaign.

Her cold-buffed face turning serious, Franny stopped her natter. "What went wrong, Bill? Seddon thought the talks would last for several days."

"Stephens, Campbell and Hunter demanded independence as a starting point. They left Lincoln no wiggle room. The talks ended in just four hours."

"Four hours? Damn!" She smiled grimly. "Ladies shouldn't swear. Damn."

Bill snugged against his wife. "Campbell said Stephens even suggested a joint military mission to Mexico to send Maximilian scampering back to France. Lincoln vetoed that idea."

"Our peace delegates seem to have one foot in the real world and one in a fairytale. How can they still think independence is viable? Our armies are used up." Franny leaned her head against Bill's shoulder.

He kissed her brow. "Our politicians know the Confederacy's petered out. Davis won't face reality. Maybe he doesn't believe Lincoln? Maybe he has nightmares of prison and his execution? Davis can't see Lincoln presented him with an honest framework for coming back into the Union. I think it's the best we can hope for with Grant ready to destroy what remains of our armies. Lincoln favors providing four hundred million dollars to slave owners as compensation. He calls it a fair indemnity." Bill laughed. "Seddon says Seward had an apoplexy attack when he heard Lincoln's offer. I imagine Davis will have one too when he hears the commissioners' report."

"To be brutally honest, my love, Lincoln's plans never stood a chance. The Republican radicals would have wrecked any peace pact." Franny patted Bill's knee then stood. "My belly just growled. We should get home and heat up the stove." Her hand on Bill's chin, she tilted his head upward and kissed him. "Afterwards, I plan to properly welcome you home—in our bed."

Forty-three

The Beginning of the End

Even though Bill knew the meal would taste bland, he dipped his spoon into the pork, beans and boiled corn and took a bite. It tasted lackluster, like every time it was served, which meant most evenings since he returned from the *River Queen* peace conference. A month and counting. Butternut and Union troops still hunkered behind their elaborate entrenchments, waiting for Grant's big artillery guns to open fire, signaling the beginning of the end of Southern dreams. Soon his orders would come, and Yankees thick as flies around a carcass would charge the thinned Confederate lines. Warm spring weather would follow, bringing flowers and death.

As he dipped his spoon into the bowl for another mouthful, Bill knew he needed to chitchat as long as possible with Franny, not reveal what would make her furious. Her penchant for talking proved helpful at times like this.

"Avis is having second thoughts about a wedding at this time." Franny blew on her spoon of steaming stew. "Her gut tells her the war will soon come to Richmond. Everyone else...they have eternal faith in General Lee. They can't believe he'll let the city fall. I see it when I walk to the Capitol Square. No one's packing; no one's dreading the day Grant attacks."

Franny had dragged the conversation in the direction Bill feared, but he had to answer her. "Their wedding's all Charlie talks about since the peace meeting. He wants to put a wedding ring on Avis's finger." Bill absentmindedly stirred the stew in his bowl. "I really don't know this version of Charlie—the lovesick puppy. He's not out visiting brothels sniffing for a tart. The fellow's learned virtue."

Intermingling her fingers, Franny propped her elbows on the kitchen table. "Avis says Charlie wants to get married later this month. She's dubious. I understand her reasoning. Who wants to get married when cannon fire drowns out the vows? Sweetheart, what do you think? Will Grant let Avis and Charlie tie the knot?"

"In a week or two, eh?" Bill lifted his mug to his mouth and drank the water-and-molasses mixture—sweet but warm. "Charlie's been quiet about it, probably waiting to get Avis's consent. He knows if he waits until April, Grant and the Army of the Potomac will likely spoil their wedding plans." He grimaced, knowing he could no longer put off the inevitable. Still, Bill dreaded his new few sentences. "Franny, I received orders today to join the Twenty-Sixth North Carolina at Petersburg. One of their captains took ill and died. Grant could attack at any time, and Lee and his commanders are trying to beef up our lines."

"Damn it, no!" Her face reddening, Franny flicked her spoon, and stew flew across the table and smacked Bill on the forehead and cheek. "At Chancellorsville, you gave your pound of flesh. I won't let you give an arm or a leg or even your life to the Confederacy. It's a walking corpse. Davis won't admit it...it's finished!"

"Orders, Franny." Putting down his mug, Bill dabbed his face with a napkin. "I won't disobey them."

"Here's your orders from me. Make sure I stay safe!" Standing, she took the napkin from him and cleaned the stew from his face, finishing what he'd started. "Yanks will soon march through our neighborhood. Some will pillage and do that other thing. You're my husband. I say it again! Keep me safe!"

Bill fisted his hands and pressed them against his chest. "I'll put you on a Richmond and Danville train this week and send you to my momma."

"I want you with me!"

"I will see this thing through to the bitter end."

Franny gave him the silent treatment for rest of the evening and night. She said nothing as she washed the dishes. When Bill tried to pick up a dishtowel, she pushed him away using three brutal words: "Leave me alone."

Later, when he slipped between the sheets, he expected a cold bed—and it was with Franny sleeping as far away from him as possible. He whispered, "I love you, Franny."

She answered with more silence.

"Please don't torture me, Franny."

Again, silence.

He lay on his back as moonbeams streamed through the window glass and illuminated her naked back. Bill wanted to scoot closer and wrap his arm around Franny's hip, caress her belly and stroke the tuft of pubic hair below her navel.

Without a word, she rolled on top of him, bit his lower lip and dug her fingernails into his back, drawing blood. They made frenzied love—a violent coupling—and at its exhausting, sweaty ending she murmured, "Davis should surrender. It's over. No more deaths!"

~ * ~

"What's wrong with your lip?" Elbows splayed on his desk, an amused Charlie inspected the bruise on Bill's lower lip.

Earlier that morning, Bill had quietly slipped out of bed, not wanting to disturb Franny's sleep. Once dressed in his uniform, he'd eaten a breakfast of cornbread and ersatz coffee then undertook his usual walk to the War Department. Once in his office, he'd been greeted by Charlie, who sported his well-known devilish grin.

Bill tapped the lip's sore spot. "Tessir nipped me during his morning playtime."

"Really? Looks like a lover's bite to me." Charlie handed a fresh mug of steaming counterfeit coffee to Bill. "By the way, Secretary Seddon wants a word with you."

"Good. I want to talk to him as well." Bill sipped the concoction. "Lordly, I'm starting to like this stuff."

A peek out the room's lone window brightened Bill's outlook. The sun ruled an azure sky, except for some dawdling clouds refusing to depart. Folks—too many women in black dresses, soldiers without an arm, youngsters up to no good—were strolling the square without coats. *Grant must be biting at the bit to order the last great campaign.*

"At least we'll get real coffee when the Union's restored." Charlie lowered his voice lest someone in the hallway hear.

Bill turned away from the window. "Franny says Avis's having second thoughts."

Charlie topped off the coffee in his mug. "I'm startin' to agree with Avis. With Grant about to capture Richmond and Petersburg, now ain't the time for a hurried weddin'. I just want her to make up her mind." Charlie winked. "Truth be told she's leavin' me in a dither. She won't tip the velvet until I slip the wedding ring onto her finger." He gestured to his groin. "This fella's gettin' frustrated waitin' to see her naked on our weddin' bed."

"Such frustration! No wonder you're keen to get married. You're desperate to dab it up with your soon-to-be bride, possum."

"Darn tootin'!" Charlie chuckled.

"I'm sending Franny to Kenansville. I think Avis should go with her. Maybe even her parents. Next to Charlestown, Richmond's the most hated city in the South. It won't be a pleasant place when the blue-bellies capture it."

"Her parents won't go. They don't think General Lee will let the city fall. Her ma tells Avis not to worry...there'll be a last-minute miracle."

Irked, Bill shook his head. "No miracles this time, chuckaboo. Make sure Avis takes the train with Franny. You two can get married in Kenansville in April or May. Keep her safe, Charlie."

"I promise I will." Reaching across his desk, Charlie snatched Bill's mug. "No more coffee until after you've seen Secretary Seddon. Now skedaddle!" Charlie pointed to the open doorway and the hallway beyond.

Following Charlie's advice, Bill made the short hike to Seddon's office. Captain Beardsley rose from his chair and turned to knock on Seddon's door. The secretary already stood in the middle entryway. "I've some news I want to share with you." Seddon waved Bill into the inner sanctum.

"Good news I hope." Bill sat in one of the chairs arrayed before the secretary's desk.

"News. Good or bad I'll leave up to you, Bill. I met with President Davis and General Lee yesterday at the executive mansion. Based on what I've learned, I'm countermanding my earlier order."

"I don't understand, sir. I'm not getting that command?" Franny would be relieved. Bill kept his mien pokerfaced.

"I'm going to keep you here to help us maintain order. We're going to have to burn all the government papers and destroy everything in the warehouses. We'll leave nothing for Lincoln to gloat over."

"Gloat over, sir? Lee's going to abandon the city?"

"Soon, Bill. General Lee says he's too thin to hold the line when Grant attacks. So he's going to make the first move. Race to Amelia Courthouse where he'll obtain food and supplies sent by rail from Richmond. Then march south and link up with Joe Johnston's Army of the Tennessee. The two will strike Grant and defeat him before Sherman can march to his rescue."

"Grant isn't Meade. He could strike first." A tumult of thoughts warred in Bill's head. Foremost: get Franny and Avis to a safe place, preferably Kenansville. He spoke the thought aloud, "I need to put Franny and Charlie's Avis on a train to Weldon. Send them down to Wilmington. Lordy, I hope there's enough time."

Seddon stood, signaling the end of their confab. "I don't know, Bill. With Lee marching south, you might be sending them into a battle. Then again, the train might get down to Wilmington before all hell breaks out. It's a gamble, one that President Davis is intent on making. He's put his family on a train, making preparations as we speak."

Bill sneaked a glance through Seddon's office window at strollers down on the square, oblivious to what would soon transpire. "No easy answers, eh?"

"No. But whatever you do, make it quick."

~ * ~

Meowing, demanding attention, Tessir Cat jumped up on Bill's lap. *Lordy, I got to figure out what to do with the cat. Can't abandon him. Franny wouldn't let me.*

Bill had been home and ensconced on the settee for just a few seconds when Tessir decided to pester him. Normally, the cat would have settled on Franny's lap, but she hadn't returned from volunteer work at Chimborazo. Tessir wouldn't be content for long, bedeviling Bill until he cooked up a feline treat. Months ago Bill would have told Franny, "The cat can fend for itself." Not anymore. In good conscience, he couldn't abandon Tessir when it became time to evacuate the city. The cat had adopted them, sharing the bed except when they tipped the velvet.

With Franny at the hospital, Bill couldn't tell her he'd not be joining the Twenty-Sixth North Carolina. Or that he still wanted her and Avis to ride the rails to Warsaw—and take Tessir with them.

The front door always squeaked when someone opened it. The noise alerted Tessir that he had a visitor. If someone he didn't know, he'd dart for the bedroom and his safe spot beneath the bedsprings. This time he turned twitchy on Bill's lap and his whiskered face veered toward the squeaking door as it opened. Perhaps picking up Franny's perfume, Tessir leaped from Bill's lap and shot straight for the door. "Hey, Tessir Boy, Bill forget to give you a treat?" Franny edged beyond the door.

Rising from the settee, Bill strode to the doorway to give Franny a hug and kiss. With one hand nestled around her waist, the other sought and found the doorknob. The door closed as Bill pressed his lips against hers and took delight in their sensual touch. As he released her and stepped back, he wondered if he should tell her then about General Lee's plans and not wait until after supper and subsequent cuddling on the couch.

Eating and cuddling fell by the wayside with her first words to him. "So did you tell Secretary Seddon how I feel?" She knelt and scratched Tessir's head. "Well, Bill?"

"Didn't need to."

"What? I don't understand." Franny quivered and her hand accidentally smacked Tessir on the noggin. Growling, the cat retreated to a perceived safe spot between an end table and the settee.

"The secretary changed his mind. General Lee says he's too weak to hold Richmond and Petersburg. Says the army doesn't stand a chance if the men stay behind their breastworks." Noticing dust clumps congregating along the top of the parlor window, Bill retrieved the duster from its holder and did some fast cleaning.

"Doesn't surprise me in the least. The only ones who will be shocked are the true believers who think the general walks on water."

Bill opened the window and shook the duster, sprinkling dust motes on the yard and boardwalk. The setting sun hung just above the horizon, its diluted light smothering distant buildings in soothing orange. With nightfall minutes away, steeples and towers cast long shadows that shrouded cabs, buggies and freight wagons plying the potholed streets between the brownstone and the James. A sliver moon hung in the darkening sky, presaging little light once the sun disappeared.

Sudden movement caught Bill's eye. A block away, three boys bolted from an alley and accosted two women making their way along the boardwalk. In mere seconds the thugs scurried away with the women's handbags. The scene reinforced Bill's resolve to put Franny on a train bound for North Carolina as soon as possible. Franny's voice interrupted his thoughts.

"Come here, buddy boy. I'm sorry." Down on her knees, Franny snapped her fingers at Tessir. Approaching warily, Tessir sniffed her fingers. He meowed and bumped against Franny's belly, not once but four times. She rose, cradling Tessir as he purred in her arms, then joined Bill at the window.

"I just saw a couple of half-rats blag the handbags of two ladies." Bill nodded toward the scene on the other side of the glass. "It's going to get darn-right nasty when General Lee abandons the city. It's even more imperative that you—and Avis—take the train down to Warsaw. Momma can pick you up and drive you to Kenansville. It has to be done quickly – before the fighting begins. You need to leave tomorrow."

Franny settled softly on the settee's cushion. In turn, Tessir nestled in Franny's lap and purred even louder. "I'm not going!"

Shaking his head, Bill sat beside his wife and petted the cat under his ears and chin. "That's off-your-rocker thinking, Franny. I've got to help oversee the burning of warehouse supplies and government records. I can't be worrying about you." He kissed Tessir's head. "Cat, tell your momma she needs to pack up and get on the train to Weldon. And remind her she needs to find a large birdcage for you. I want you to go with her to Kenansville."

"I've made up my mind, Bill. You know me by now...you can't change it. I'm going to stay and make sure you don't do anything foolish that could get you hurt or dead."

Snaking her arm around Tessir, Franny stroked Bill's thigh. "We'll get away from the city even if we have to commandeer a buggy. Charlie and Avis too."

"Lordy, you're an obstinate woman!" Bill grinned like a circus clown. "That would be quite a sight to behold—the four of us and Tessir crammed into a buggy."

Franny smirked. "Once we get to Kenansville, how do you think Tessir and Indy will get along? You know...two boys."

Bill rolled his eyes. "We'll have our own place."

"Not right away."

Bill tried one more time to get Franny to see it his way. "People'll be in a panic. I don't want you mixed in with a mob."

Franny dismissed his argument with a flick of her fingers. "I'll be with you, so I'll be safe."

Fisting his right hand, Bill smacked it against the open palm of his left hand. "I can't guarantee your safety. I don't want anything to happen to you."

"Remember our first time together? Back at the Yerby Plantation? The boys we nursed? We were a superb team. On that night I knew I had to make you mine." With Tessir protesting her scooting shift, Franny leaned against Bill and nibbled his earlobe. "Just like at Yerby, I'm going to be at your side, Bill, not on a train to North Carolina. We're a team. I'm not afraid of a little danger."

"You'll be the death of me yet, woman!" Reluctance shaded Bill's voice. "Okay, you can stay. But I'm still worried about Tessir."

"We'll figure out something."

Forty-four

Lee Abandons Richmond

The Reverend Peterkin preached a fire-and-brimstone sermon at St. John's Episcopal's April 2 service. As Bill listened to Peterkin pray for God to smite the North's armies, he jerked his head around at the creaky sound of the vestibule doors opening. The preacher stopped in mid-sentence as a soldier tramped down the sanctuary aisle to the pew where Jefferson Davis and his wife Varina sat. The young lieutenant slipped a message into Davis's hand. The president grimaced, and his wife daubed her moist eyes with an embroidered handkerchief.

Bill leaned his shoulder against Franny. "This is it. Richmond's going to fall."

Rising to their feet, Davis and his wife headed for the vestibule's doors. Department heads, senators and representatives followed, scurrying like rats on a fast-sinking ship.

Franny's eyes fluttered, turmoil reflected in them. "It's happening. Look! They know something's up."

Confusion scrawled across their faces, the congregation eyed Peterkin, hoping for guidance. Clearing his throat, the pastor glanced at his notes and continued with his sermon. "The Lord provides miracles for those of strong faith."

Bill tapped Franny's elbow, signaling her to rise. He'd heard enough of the pastor's drivel. No more miracles for the Confederate States of America. He ushered Franny out into the vestibule. Behind him, the murmurs grew in volume. "Please, brothers and sisters, I'm sure it's nothing to worry about. Probably no more than the arrival of General Lee for a meeting."

"Fools!" Franny growled as they pushed open the doors and hurried down the steps. "They still think Lee can walk on water."

Bill caressed his wife's back. "We know far more than them, sweetheart. They don't know the president's fleeing. They won't know it's the end until the church bells toll and factory whistles peal."

They raced for the cabs lined up along the curb, their drivers waiting for the church service to end. Franny's fancy hat flew off her head and tumbled in the breeze. "Oh, no! It's my favorite." She made no move to chase after it. The pins containing her hair loosened and her blonde tresses spilled to her shoulders.

Sunlight poured down on a city awaiting Easter in two weeks, a holiday that would find Yankees patrolling the streets. Songbirds trilling in the trees above Franny and Bill would soon be heard by men from Ohio, New York and Maine. In a matter of days, soiled doves in the brothels would open their legs to soldiers with Midwestern and New England accents.

"Folks need a ride home?" a cabman hollered. "Well, look who it is...two of my favorites."

Bill recognized the fellow atop the one-horse cab. "Howdy, Ernie."

"Ya headin' home, right?"

"Yes, and make it fast as you can." Nodding, Franny saluted Ernie.

As Bill helped his wife up into the passenger compartment, he shuddered as church bells and factory whistles sounded, the long-feared signal that Lee could no longer defend the city. The vestibule doors flew open and jostling men and women surged from the church. A middle-aged woman tripped coming down the steps and nosedived onto the brick walkway. Their eyes awash in fear, men knocked aside the woman's husband as he tried to help her up.

"Please! You're killing them!" the preacher shrieked.

"Get us away from here!" Bill plopped down beside his wife.

Ernie exhorted the horse into a gallop, and the cab wheeled away from the church.

"That poor woman." Franny squeezed Bill's arm so tight he winced.

"It's going to get far worse."

"So Lee has begun his race to link up with Johnston?" Franny shouted over the clang the wheels made as they bounced along the roadway bricks.

"No, not enough time for Lee to prepare for the breakaway. I think Grant has attacked. Our lines have been breached." Bill curled his fingers around Franny's gloved hand.

Richmond's streets teemed with cabs, wagons, coaches and buggies, their drivers racing through intersections with no regard for safety. At one intersection, a two-horse coach T-boned a cab, spilling drivers and passengers. Some lay sprawled on the street, limbs quivering. Ernie guided his cab around the injured and continued wheeling his cab toward their neighborhood.

The cab rumbled to a stop in front of the brownstone. The trapdoor opened. "Don't worry about the fare," Ernie said as steam whistles continued to sound. "That's not worth worryin' about. Anyway, I'm takin' the cab and skedaddlin'."

Standing together on the boardwalk fronting the brownstone's stoop, Bill and Franny cringed as Ernie's cab raced down the street and whirled around the corner on one wheel. He tucked his arm around Franny's waist. "Time to pack. I've got to get down to the War Department. You be ready to leave for the depot when I come for you."

Face grim, Franny nodded.

Even inside their apartment, Bill still heard the screech of the steam whistles. Walls, windows, even the flutter of the breeze couldn't hold back the sounds. They announced: Yankee conquerors are marching into Richmond.

At Bill's feet, Tessir meowed for a treat. Bill glanced into the kitchen, eyeing the bowl on the floor—empty. The cat had eaten the oatmeal remnants Bill and Franny had left him. "You've become a way-too-plump kitty, Tessir." Bill knelt to pet the boy. "Franny, have that birdcage ready when I get back."

"Tessir's going to hate us when we put him in it." Franny glanced past the kitchen to their bedroom. "Time to get into my getup and comb my hair. Go get Charlie, if he isn't already out looking for Avis."

The volume of the steam whistles shot up when Bill opened the apartment door. Tessir darted for the tight space beneath the settee, apparently hoping his new location would provide relief for his ears. Closing the door behind him, Bill proceeded to Charlie's apartment. He knocked incessantly, but Charlie didn't answer. His chuckaboo wasn't a deep sleeper, so Bill figured Charlie must be out lassoing Avis. Hopefully, her family would let her leave with him. A diehard Southern patriot, her father might think she'd be safer with them in their mansion than out with Charlie among the panicky crowds.

The steam whistles and church bells ceased their nerve-wracking blare as Bill made his way back to his own apartment. When he opened the door, he half-expected Tessir to make a break for the hallway and the stairs to the lobby. Instead, Tessir remained huddled under the settee. Maybe the cat sensed the streets wouldn't be a safe place.

Franny paraded into the parlor wearing the daftest outfit Bill had seen since running into Becky in London months before. She wore a man's red pantaloons fastened below her calves to reveal ankle-length black boots. Over the pantaloons a dark blue skirt fell to her knees, scandalous at any other time except when Yanks were only a few hours from entering Richmond. A man's single-breasted tan vest covered a work shirt. A slouch hat sat atop her pinned-back hair.

"Lordy, Franny, you're quite the sight!" Bill showily bowed to her.

"I'm going to help you out doing whatever Secretary Seddon needs done." She fixed her hat's haphazard fit atop her head. "I figure lots of paper needs burning. I know how President Davis thinks. He doesn't want to leave anything useful for Lincoln. The war would have ended in early February if he had any commonsense. Let's head down to the Capitol Square."

"No. I'm taking you to the depot. For once, you will listen to me. These are orders, Franny!"

"Orders? Balderdash! I'm staying with you. When I get on a train, you're to be on it with me."

"You're so obstinate! If I have to, I'll throw you over my shoulder and carry you to the depot."

"You never listen to me!" Franny punched him in the shoulder— hard. He staggered back, shocked. "I'm staying at your side, Bill. You just as well accept it. I won't compromise."

Massaging his shoulder, he laughed. "I surrender. You came all the way from Tennessee to express your love to me. I'm listening, Franny! You can stay with me—for now."

Kneeling, Franny snapped her fingers at Tessir, coaxing him out from under the settee. "Make yourself comfy on the sofa, darling boy. We'll be back for you."

Bill gave the birdcage a once-over before leaving the apartment. They'd have a devil of time getting Tessir into it when they returned. He feared his hands would bear claw and bite marks.

On the boardwalk, they sidestepped women of all ages hurrying helter-skelter, acting like chickens with their heads cut off. With their long-held belief in General Lee's invincibility shattered, the women sought an escape from Yankee marauders only hours away. Some carried carpetbags in one hand and a baby in the other, with toddlers struggling to keep up. Others tugged handcarts filled with children and luggage toward the rail depots crammed full of fearful citizens. Those in buggies and wagons chose a westward journey on plank and dirt roads, hoping to escape the Yankee noose tightening around Richmond.

At Ninth and Franklin streets, hundreds of clerks streamed into the War Department building like worker ants entering an anthill. Bill and Franny joined them. Civilians—old and middle-aged shopkeepers and women of all ages—watched the bureaucrats and soldiers burn piles of documents. There were catcalls: "Liars! Cowards!"

"This is insane! We're turning on each other." Franny kicked at a jagged piece of brick, sending it flying into a budding Moss rosebush.

"And you expected anything less? That's why I wanted to take you to the depot."

Like earlier in the morning, the sun shone in a near-cloudless sky, except for columns of smoke rising from burning documents. The heat coming down from the sky and rising from the fires combined to produce sweat droplets that trickled down Bill's forehead and back.

Bill and Franny found the heads of the War Department congregated in front of Secretary Seddon's office. John Campbell, one of the Confederacy's peace commissioners and supervisor of its conscription program, seized Bill's upper arms. "Sheridan's troops overran our defenses at Five Forks. General Lee's abandoning the Petersburg defenses. Richmond's lost." Releasing Bill's arms, Campbell noticed Franny. "Where did you find this clerk, Captain? Morning, Miss Franny. Terrible day for pleasantries, isn't it?"

"Not for the Yankees, Assistant Secretary. I'm ready to go to work. No hoops for this gal, not today. I'm ready to see what it's like to be an arsonist."

"So General Pickett couldn't hold at Five Forks?" Scowling, Bill clenched his fists.

"No. His lines were just too thin." Campbell sighed. "You served with A.P. Hill, right, Stamford?"

"Yessir. Good general, but too quarrelsome. Always waging a feud."

"He's dead. Shot as he tried to stem the rout." Campbell grimaced.

"Too many good men have died in this damned war." Franny did her own grimacing.

Campbell glanced down the hallway at the stairs. "Stamford, Seddon wants you to take command of the top floor and get the men organized into a fire brigade. Your wife's under your command—if that's possible." Campbell managed a half-formed smile.

Disorder reigned on the stairs. Clerks brought crates of records and files down the steps as others tried to make their way up them. Flustered workers squawked profanities at slowpokes blocking them. A clerk growled at Franny, "Get your butt out of my way before I break your teeth."

"Is that how your mom taught you to speak to a lady?" Clearly, the clerk had mistaken Franny for a man.

The man's eyes widened in embarrassment. "Good Lord! I'm so sorry, ma'am. Captain Stamford, your wife?"

"Yes, Dan. Don't worry. We're all frustrated."

"Your apology accepted, Dan." Franny sidled out of the way, allowing the clerk and his load of documents to pass.

Inch by tight inch, Bill and Franny jostled their way to the fourth floor. Finding a free cabinet, Franny prepared to empty its drawers. Bill climbed atop a desk and shouted, "We're going to bring order to this mess." He pointed to two clerks standing at nearby cabinets. "You two start a line...a fireman's water brigade. It'll run down the stairs and out into the street. Two clerks at each cabinet. One empties the cabinet and hands off the papers to his chuckaboo who fills a crate. Once full, the crate gets handed off to the first man in line."

"Or woman," Franny shouted. The room erupted into laughter.

"Or woman." Bill grinned. "And down the line the crates go until they're out the door and burning on one of the piles."

Franny and another woman—a redhead in a hoopless day dress—squeezed closer to Bill. The redhead pretended to ogle him. "You made a good choice," the young woman remarked to Franny.

"I did, didn't I? And he's quite rambunctious in bed."

The woman's hand flew to her mouth. "Franny, you're terrible!"

As the fourth floor fire brigade began to look proficient, Bill went to the third floor to bring order there. The floor looked even more muddled as he again climbed atop a desk. Only a few clerks toted loaded crates to the stairwell. Too many stood around jabbering.

"Don't embarrass me, men," Bill hollered, gaining their attention. "Schoolchildren could do better than this. You know how a fire brigade works. Form one and let's get all the paperwork down to the bonfires."

By the time Bill reached the first floor, his voice was hoarse. He'd done his job, though. The crates were flowing to the bonfires. Beyond the open front entrance, a hubbub drew Bill outside for a looksee.

Halfway down the walkway to Franklin Street, Secretary Seddon limped toward a rowdy traffic jam where the owners of two buggies and a carriage threatened to break noses. Forced down to one lane due to the Capitol Square bonfires, the drivers found themselves in a bottleneck, unable to advance. Trying to unsnarl it, Charlie with Avis at his side trod toward the arguing drivers and passengers. Seddon, a frail, middle-aged man, could do little to aid Charlie. No one cared an iota about Seddon's prestigious title. Bill, a robust twenty and veteran of the battles of Fredericksburg and Chancellorsville, looked far more menacing. At least that's what Bill hoped.

Charlie poked his finger into the chest of an older man attired in a rich man's suit, a fancy straw hat atop his neatly cropped hair. The well-heeled fellow had been badgering his carriage's darkey driver to push through the blockage, even raised a whip to strike the slave.

Charlie seized the haughty fellow's scrawny arm, preventing him from flinging the whip. "A floggin' won't unjam this mess. Have him turn around. You can't go this direction."

"Mr. Greenstreet, you should be ashamed of yourself," Avis spoke up, distaste in her voice. "I've known you since I was knee high to a grasshopper. You're acting like you've contracted foot-and-mouth disease."

Greenstreet arched an eyebrow. "And you should be home with your parents, Avis Thompson, not here with this mob of commoners." He glared at Charlie, at his stump, but said nothing further.

A buggy passenger, a young man in workman's clothes with a war wound that left his face mangled, leaped down to the brick pavement and snarled at Greenstreet, "If you don't get your carriage turned around, I'm going to bust you up good."

Producing a concealed pistol, Greenstreet aimed the weapon at the disfigured veteran. "Come near me, cur, and I'll have your brains all over the street."

Avis gasped. "Mr. Greenstreet, please don't—"

"Shut up, girl!" Greenstreet eyed his accoster. "You damned soldiers gave up. You're surrendering us to Lincoln."

Seeing madness in Greenstreet's eyes, the ex-soldier backed up against his buggy. Behind him in the buggy...his wife and a child.

Hurrying by Seddon, Bill reached Charlie's side. "Let's be reasonable. We're diverting traffic westward. You can't go east. The only people you'll see are Yanks marching into the city." Suddenly, Bill understood. The upper-class businessman intended to go east to negotiate better treatment for him and his family.

Greenstreet swung his pistol from the buggy passenger to Bill who heard the hammer cock.

Dread widened Avis's eyes.

Bill's revolver remained holstered, a mistake he hoped to remedy if given a chance. "Put that gun away," he said, feigning sternness.

The wealthy man looked edgy enough to shoot. Bill delayed drawing his gun, fearing the businessman would fire before the weapon left the holster.

Belatedly, Seddon reached the snarled-up buggies and carriage. "Mr. Greenstreet, I've always known you as a generous man." Seddon wobbled on his feet. "I don't want to have you jailed, but I will if I must."

"Jailed?" A puff of smoked belched from the barrel. A bullet whizzed by Bill's ear. His whole body rigid, Bill curled his hand around the handle of his revolver. He had no choice... Greenstreet might shoot again.

Another shot rang out before Bill could draw his weapon. Beside him, black smoke corkscrewed away from Charlie's pistol. Greenstreet grabbed his chest as blood gushed through his fingers. The patrician toppled and lay sprawled on the bricks. Avis ran to his side as Greenstreet's wife and teenage daughter wailed. Kneeling, she held his hand. The rise and fall of Greenstreet's chest gradually lessened and he took his last breath.

"I'm so sorry, Bertha," Avis told Greenstreet's wife.

"He was going to shoot my chuckaboo." Charlie sheathed his weapon.

The scarred veteran went to the buggy and looked up at Bertha. "My condolences, ma'am. Your husband didn't lower the gun, didn't put it away."

"I know, young man." Sniffling, Bertha wiped her eyes with her hanky. "I didn't approve of what he intended to do tonight—go to the Yankees. He died a coward and a traitor."

The veteran and the darkey scooped up Greenstreet's body and put it in the buggy.

"I trust you'll get this traffic bottleneck unsnarled, Captain." Seddon turned his gaze to the War Department building. "I need to get back to the bonfires. A curse on my legs and back. I'm too old for this."

As if on a beach, Bill waded into the traffic mess and began issuing orders. His first went to Greenstreet's driver. "Traffic's backing up. Turn the carriage around. Get it out of here. Don't want a floating ember to set your roof on fire." He continued to give directions to the drivers, getting them to maneuver until all the conveyances were wheeling westward.

Bill felt a hand on his shoulder. He turned and discovered Seddon hadn't left—and one more surprise...Franny stood beside him, her face pale as a lily crowned with a moonbeam. "Bill, I told you to take care of yourself. I don't want to wear black."

She jumped into his arms and hugged him so tight he felt like a mouse in the coil of a snake. "Shot wasn't close," he reassured her.

She touched his ear. "Not close? You're bleeding."

He probed his earlobe and knew he'd have to wear his hair long for the rest of his life to hide a tattered ear. "I look a heck of a lot better than the man who shot at me. He's dead, shot by Charlie."

Seddon broke up the lovebirds. "Got another order for you, Captain. I need you down on the waterfront. We're breaking kegs and liquor bottles. Except things aren't going according to plan."

Forty-five

Liquor in the Gutters

Mayhem! The word ricocheted inside Bill's mind as he, Charlie and their women approached the tavern-and-brothel district along the James. Trudging across the chaotic Capitol Square toward Main Street and the waterfront, the four coughed, gagged and rubbed their smoke-irritated eyes. All around them, billowing smoke rose from bonfires of burning ledgers and other Confederate records, darkening the wispy, blue sky. Frazzled men, women and children aboard every conceivable mode of transport careened down Main Street toward the Tredegar Bridge. On the water, canal barges, skiffs and rowboats plied people and their belongings to the far bank and supposed safety. The mass exodus didn't surprise Bill. The unnerved civilians were fleeing as if a fire-breathing dragon pursued them. So many saw the Yankees as demon-possessed and ready to rape women and drown children in the James.

A stench nearly ripped Bill's nose from his face—long before he discovered the reason for the noxious smell. He'd sniffed it before—inside tumbledown taverns and saloons where spilled and vomited beer, wine and whiskey blended together into a concoction not fit for a dog to lap up. Seddon had warned Bill what to expect. The bureaucrats knew what would happen when blue-bellies discovered the whisky, so they'd ordered all the liquor destroyed. Knowing they faced a daunting task and little time to get it done, the Confederate boys smashed bottles and poured kegs into the gutters and street drains outside the saloons and warehouses. "The stench has attracted crowds," Seddon had warned. "We've a mess on our hands. Fix it for me, Captain Stamford."

Bill, Charlie, Franny and Avis turned a corner and found themselves blocked by an overturned wagon, its furniture contents smashed all over Pearl Street. Just beyond, drunken men and women dropped to their knees in front of Pfaff's Saloon and gulped beer and whiskey from the curbstones. Some tottering fellows scooped up the booze in their hats and boots and guzzled before stooping for more.

"Hell no!" Charlie hissed. "A doomed city full of sozzled souls."

Bill sniggered. "The Yanks will march into Richmond and find hundreds of its finest citizens passed out in the gutters."

Like many in the War Department, Bill heard the sordid tales of Columbia, South Carolina. When the Palmetto State's capital city fell to Sherman in mid-February, Union troops swigged stores of whiskey that hadn't been destroyed by retreating Confederates. Whiskey and soldiers are never a fit mix.

Bill must have carelessly spoken his thoughts. Franny muttered, "Neither are whiskey, waterfront thugs and painted ladies."

Bill pressed his hand against his wife's back. "Let's not dilly-dally. Don't want anyone causing us trouble."

Half a block away, two Confederate officers brawled in the gutter, cheered on by soused whores and rowdies. Bill cried out to a sergeant hauling a keg out the saloon doors of Steinmetz Tavern. "Sergeant, assist me!" He turned to Charlie. "Keep the women away. This is bad." Fisting his hands, Bill trod toward the scuffling officers.

Bill dragged the flailing captain one direction while the sergeant jammed his knee against the throat of the curse-spewing lieutenant.

"Now we're fighting each other!" Bill's roar sounded loud enough to burst the captain's eardrum.

The brawlers staggered to their feet, and teetering, collapsed onto their bellies. Grunting, Bill wrangled his arms around the battered captain and heaved skyward until the man stood erect. The sergeant grabbed the lieutenant by his collar and hauled him upright. Both scrappers wobbled yet managed to stay on their feet. Panting, they exhaled rancid breaths that nearly knocked Bill flat. For all their flailing, the two ended up with only bruises, cut lips and broken noses.

"Let 'em fight," a redheaded prostitute goaded.

Liquor and vomit dribbled down the soiled dove's low-cut décollage, sullying her blue blouse. The lower portion of her gray-and-pink skirt looked wet, likely caused when she knelt in the gutter to scoop whisky into her hands.

"Screw you, Tilly!" a greasy blonde growled. "Ya're uglier than pus on a pimple."

If possible, the blonde's dress exposed more flesh than the redheaded dollymop's rig. Bill thought a strong wind might displace her plunging neckline and reveal Cupid's kettle drums. She'd also been on her knees lapping up liquor flowing down the gutter, as evidenced by her dress's dampness.

"Whore!" the ginger-haired woman snarled. "Ya need yur nose broke again!"

"So ya want to fight, Ruby?" Tilly raised her arms in front of her body and flexed her fingers. "I'll yank yur head bald, bitch!"

The doxies flew at each other, exchanged slaps and tugged at each other's hair. Soon they were rolling in the liquor-drenched gutter, scratching eyes, biting noses, ripping off buttons and cheap jewelry, screaming like banshees.

"Lordy, women brawling!" Avis exclaimed, appalled by the scene.

"Not all that unusual." Franny winked at Bill.

He winked back, understanding her meaning. She'd had two tussles with other women—a girlfriend at boarding school and Becky after the Duplin County girl played flirtation games that nearly got Bill killed.

Bill ignored the female scrappers. Instead, he glared at the captain and the lieutenant. The captain still wobbled. Not the lieutenant, though. He stood resolutely, his spine straight, no faltering in his legs. "The war's ending, but I can ensure that everyone in your hometowns will know how badly you behaved as soldiers."

"I'm not drunk and I didn't start the fight," the lieutenant protested. "Captain Mason lost reason. I pleaded with him not to pour the liquor and beer into the gutters until we could post guards to keep the rowdies away. He threatened to arrest me." The lieutenant jabbed a pointing finger at the captain. "Smell him! Drunk as a skunk. I told him I was assuming command. He punched me."

"You're not innocent, Lieutenant," Bill shot back. "I smell liquor on you."

The lieutenant scowled, his frustration growing. "That's from the fighting, sir. We were rolling in the gutter, just like the two dovetails. I've no liquor on my breath."

The whores still fought, albeit in slow motion, their panting louder than their shrieks. Their blouses ripped open exposing bubbies, the women lay on their sides, hands entangled in the other's tresses. Suddenly, Mason spewed his breakfast and toppled against Bill as the women rolled into the vomit. Bill seized the captain by the shoulders, keeping him from falling face first.

"Take command, Lieutenant," Bill growled, shoving the captain toward the fighting women. Mason crumbled atop the females, bringing the fight to an ignoble end. "I'm Captain Stamford and I'm speaking for Secretary Seddon. Post guards. If any drunkards try to force their way past the guards, shoot them."

The lieutenant gave Bill a snappy salute. "Yessir!"

Bill pivoted his gaze to the sergeant who'd helped break up the fight as well as corporals and privates who gawked from the boardwalk. He couldn't let the situation worsen. "I'm putting our captain in your control, boys. Make sure he doesn't interfere. Sit on him if he tries."

A corporal chortled. "Sit on him? Yessir."

The corporal and two privates dragged the captain and the two exhausted doxies up onto the boardwalk where they lay, barely moving. Leaving them behind, Bill stepped toward Franny, Charlie and Avis, now some way in the distance, just as two drunks confronted them. Grimacing, Bill regretted his decision to bring Franny. But what else could he have done? Leave her in the apartment? Not with drunken deserters and hooligan boys prowling the streets and drawn to apartment buildings and valuables inside each flat. No, Franny needed to stay at his side. No doubt Charlie felt the same way about Avis. A coarse voice wrenched Bill from his thoughts.

"Hey, sweet jam, yur bubbies look sweet enough to kiss." The hooligan leered at Avis who turned claret-red and choked out a scream.

"Now look what ya've up and done, Big Joe." The second ruffian slurred his words. Smiling crookedly, he fixed his gaze on Franny. "Those daft clothes ya're wearin', dearie, let's see what's 'neath 'em."

Glowering, Franny produced a stiletto from a vest pocket. "I'll use it. I'm not bluffing."

"Oh, I'm sure ya're not pretendin', sweetie," the thug sneered. "What ya think don't matter, though. I'm goin' to take that tiny knife from ya and cut away those pantaloons."

"No, you're not!" Charlie brandished his revolver.

"Ya lose yur arm in the war, Cripple Boy?" Franny's accoster trod menacingly toward Charlie. "Does it make ya half a man?"

"Yep, Gettysburg. I can tell…you've been a fart-catcher all your life. Even with one arm, I'm more man than you. It's not polite to threaten my possum's wife. On a sad day like this, that's a death sentence." Charlie fired. A hole appeared in the fellow's forehead followed by a streamlet of blood. The goon's eyes turned glassy and rolled up in his sockets. He collapsed and lay motionless.

"Gawd! You kilt him!" A look of astonishment spread across the other lout's face.

Charlie aimed the revolver at the drunkard. "And if you don't run, you'll be next."

Big Joe whirled and took off running, his legs moving like locomotive pistons at full speed.

Reaching Charlie and the two women, Bill tapped his chuckaboo's wrist just inches from the revolver. "Thank you. They meant to rape Franny and Avis."

"You were charging fast, Billy Boy." Charlie made no move to return the revolver to its holster. "You'd have killed both."

"Folks have gone crazy." Franny shifted her stiletto toward its sheath, but stopped in mid-motion. "I may need this again."

"You likely will," Charlie said tersely. "Those were bad fellows. My guess? Even before today they were waylayin' shopkeepers in alleyways. They decided to try their luck at rape."

"I'm not leaving your side, Bill." Franny shivered, like a leaf in a breeze. "I would've stabbed him. But who knows? Maybe he would've wrested the stiletto from me. Thank God for Charlie."

"Yes, Thank God for Charlie," Avis echoed, strength in her voice. "I love you, Charlie. No more waiting. I'm marrying you as soon as we find a willing preacher."

Charlie flashed a wicked grin. "I picked me a good one, didn't I, Billy Boy?"

"Indeed, Possum." Bill playfully smacked his friend's cheek. "The lieutenant back there...he'll run things smoothly from here on in. Well, smoothly as possible considering the riffraff are drunk and looking for trouble. I need to get back to Seddon and tell him how bad it's gotten. When the liquor runs dry, they'll show up at the warehouses looking for food and supplies."

Franny snagged Bill's arm. "Well, let's go." She turned her head for a final look back at Pfaff's Saloon. "The Lord above! The dollymops are scraping again."

Bill swung his head around just in time to see the redhead plunge a dagger toward the blonde and stab her in a breast. The blonde bawled like an infant. "Let's get away from this madness!" *If there's anywhere free from it.*

Forty-six

A Day and Night of Fires and Explosions

Bill felt like he'd just walked through the gates of Hell. Embers drifted down from smoke clouds and burned through his hat and uniform jacket. He ripped the hat from his head and combed through his hair, probing for the sparks singeing his scalp. Successful in his search, Bill jiggled his hat, flinging away more embers, then returned the headwear to his noggin. Grimacing as he eyed the billowing smoke over the warehouse district, he pushed on toward the James, the others in his wake.

Beyond Main Street shops and offices, flames capered skyward, casting the riverfront in dusk colors—hours before sundown. Soldiers had burned the warehouses filled with everything from tobacco to coffee. In turn, vandals armed with improvised torches set fires to riverside mercantile buildings and factories. The late afternoon wind tumbled embers, some that found the faces of Bill and Charlie and their sweethearts. A stone's throw from the two couples a Main Street dress shop caught fire, the newly born flames eating the wood.

"God help us!" Franny glowered as the dress shop's flames spread to a neighboring building, Ephraim's Emporium. "We're going to lose the whole of the downtown. The fools!"

The sounds of shells exploding echoed along the town's brick streets and alleys. Her eyes widening, Avis leaned against Charlie. "The Yanks are shelling us. Our Father which art in Heaven hallowed be thy—"

"No, sweetie." Charlie kissed Avis's forehead. "The Tredegar Iron Works are on fire. The loaded shells there are explodin'."

"We've more dangerous matters closer at hand," Bill told Charlie's fiancé. "They're looting, stealing all they can before the fires burn up everything." He clenched his revolver's grip, but didn't draw the weapon. A moment later, he doubled over and gagged, the smoke overwhelming him.

Near the downtown blaze, men, women and even children dug up bricks and flung them at storefronts. Liquored-up dregs of Richmond citizenry clambered through broken windows and looted merchandise from shelves, barrels and crates. In front of Barnes Jewelers, two boys no older than thirteen and a bear-sized man standing on a peg leg shouted slurred rebel yells. A hoary man with a gray beard down to his belly button limped out of a men's clothing store, shirts and pants draped across his arms. A mad grin twisting his mouth, he bellowed, "Death to Jeff Davis, the lyin' bastard!"

Backlit by the fires, a gramps, granny, their daughter and two grandkids carried looted goods to a wagon hitched to a fidgety horse. The pigtailed girl, likely no more than five, clutched a crate filled with a coffee grinder, dried beans, cigars and tobacco. Tripping on a broken brick, the girl nearly nosedived into the street, but her older brother reached out an arm and steadied her. Miraculously, the boy didn't spill what he carried—toiletries, bolts of cloth and lady undergarments. Draped in mourning clothes, the granny and the younger woman hauled out silverware, plates, mugs and a tea set from a silversmith's shop. At the wagon, gramps dumped board games, dolls and pull toys into the wagon's bed alongside a parlor settee and a mahogany sofa. His thievery finished, the codger straightened his leather apron.

Convalescent soldiers under General Richard Ewell's command stood by and did nothing to stop them or any of the other looters. A corporal with his arm in a sling tipped his hat to the mother of the boy and girl while three grinning privates ogled soused women dancing in the streets, stolen trousers hanging from their shoulders.

Her hair hidden by a somber bonnet, the young mother helped her daughter up onto the wagon seat. "Hello, soldier," the youngster greeted Charlie. "My papa's a soldier too, but momma says he won't be coming home. Jesus needs him. Did Jesus cut off your arm?"

"A doctor did after a mean Yank shot me." Charlie's eyes wrinkled as he grinned.

Bill swung his eyes from the girl to the stolen goods in the back of the wagon. Her eyes shards of ice, the girl's mother took two steps toward him. "Wipe that self-righteous look off your face, Captain. I ain't doin' nuttin' wrong. My husband dies—and then we find out they've been hoardin'. Bastards!"

The old man motioned for the young woman to climb into the back of the wagon alongside her son, then regarded Bill. "Rachael's right. We sacrificed for them. They betrayed us."

"You've been at the warehouses?" Bill turned toward the distant riverside fires. "What happened, Gramps?"

"We watched them open the commissaries." His eyes welled with tears. "God strike dead the corrupt politicians and speculators. Evil men! Those damned warehouses were filled to the gills with smoked meats, sugar and coffee. The speculators won't make a tidy sum now. Their ill gains went up in smoke, but not before we stole us some."

Bill knew the old man considered the stolen goods a dismal trade for his loved one's life. "I can't rebuke you, sir. At the end of his life, Jesus said, 'It's finished.' It's now finished for the Confederacy. We're out of miracles. The CSA's down to hours."

The grandfather nodded. "I pray Lincoln shows us mercy."

"I was at the recent peace negotiations. Lincoln's not a monster." Words of praise for Lincoln came easily to Bill. "I don't think he's looking to punish us into the next century. He knows the war has left the South destitute. I'm hopeful he'll set up conditions that will allow the reunited North and South to prosper in the years ahead." A passing buggy driven by a darkey raced past the rioters. "Without slavery, but with fair restitution for slaveholders."

The old man wiped fire-engendered sweat from his forehead. "I hope you're right."

Bill gestured toward the James. "You need to get your family across the river and out into the countryside. The fires are getting bad, and the Yanks will soon be here."

"That's my plan, Captain. You're a good man. Don't get yourself killed with just hours left in this war." The codger pulled himself up onto the seat he shared with his grandson and the boy's granny.

The kids' mother offered a reluctant apology. "I was wrong about you, soldier."

Taking the reins in his hands, the codger spurred the two horses into a trot. Bill hoped the war would spare them further hurt.

Harried by the downtown fires, the two couples raced beyond the looters, then looped toward the burning warehouses. The springtime sky rained embers as thick as hail in a rainstorm. Even more smoke clouds mottled the firmament, turning late afternoon into night. The fires along the waterfront crackled, the sizzling so loud Bill heard it blocks away. At an open spot with a riverside view, he spotted silhouetted men and women scurrying like wild animals fleeing a forest fire.

"I think I'm seeing a scene from *Dante's Inferno*." Franny clutched Bill's arm tightly, then released it to brush ash from her shirt and his coat. "I'm starting to think we're on a fool's errand."

"We should be running away from this, not charging into the madness." In spite of her words, Avis pressed on alongside Charlie, Bill and Franny.

"Billy Boy's a stickler for orders, ladies." Charlie wiped cinders from his uniform with his hat. "He may think the Confederacy's a lost cause and slavery's an abomination, but he's goin' to do his duty to the bitter end."

"They're your sentiments as well, Charlie, and you're marching lockstep with me." About to make a further observation, Bill noticed Seddon and Campbell painfully making their way toward the two couples. Not just them, but a flood of people escaping the out-of-control warehouse fires. Sadly, they were scampering toward the downtown fire.

Campbell gripped Seddon's waist, helping the lame man walk as they lurched the last few feet to Bill, Charlie and their women.

"You brought Franny and Avis?" Campbell exclaimed, his face scored with shock. "Are you blind, Captain Stamford and Lieutenant Kurtz? Don't you see the bedlam? Your duty must be to them, not us, not the Confederacy. It's over. Union troops will be here in a matter of hours."

"We felt they'd be safer with us, sir," Bill responded, his mouth grim.

Seddon pushed Campbell's hands aside and stood on his own. "Don't come this way! General Ewell stationed fire pumpers at the warehouses to control the fires. They failed." Seddon licked two fingers of his right hand and held them aloft. An ember landed on one finger, but the spit extinguished it. Nonetheless, the War Department Secretary's clothes looked like a pincushion. "The wind's picking up. We're going to have an inferno."

Ewell, once one of Lee's corps commanders, oversaw Richmond's forces mostly made up of convalescent soldiers. He'd lost a leg during General Jackson's Valley Campaign of 1862. His generalship had been questioned at Gettysburg, the Wilderness and Spotsylvania Courthouse. His sentence? An exile to Richmond to oversee its inadequate defenses.

Bill flicked an ember from his uniform collar. "Should we go back to where they're looting? Give me some staff officers, and Charlie and I will see what can be done."

Seddon and Campbell shook their heads vigorously. "Too late. Nothing can be done." Sadness tinged Seddon's hoarse voice.

"Tredegar's flames have jumped to the downtown. They'll soon consume the Capitol Square. There's little you or I can—"

Earth-shaking booms rocked the street. Bill cringed. Storefront windows on either side of the brick pavement shattered, flinging glass shards toward everyone. One stabbed Franny in the chin. Bill quavered as he watched Avis pluck glass from Franny's face. Steely eyed, Franny waited stoically while Avis did her bloody work. Tucking his fingers inside a shirtsleeve, Charlie tore a strip for a bandage to stem the bleeding.

"Don't bother," Franny snapped. "It'll stop bleeding in a moment. What blew up?"

Seddon responded, "Admiral Semmes set his ironclads on fire. I expect we just heard their magazines explode."

"This is an order," Campbell said stonily. "Get to the Richmond and Danville depot. Catch the last train out. Get the women aboard and you with them. Now!"

"What about you, sir, and Secretary Seddon?" Bill pivoted his gaze from the two men to the fierce fires consuming the commissary warehouses, Tredegar armories and the ironclads. "You need to leave with us."

"We're staying." Campbell reached out and steadied Seddon when the war secretary's leg wobbled. "We'll be here when Grant and Lincoln come. I know Lincoln and am hopeful we can get him to show the South leniency. Lincoln's a kind man."

Campbell's words took Bill back to Lincoln's ship and the halo that appeared around the U.S. president. He wondered if an assassin would kill Lincoln as the tall man with his stovepipe hat took a victory tour of Richmond. For an insane moment Bill thought about trying to stop Lincoln's coming death, but realized it could happen anywhere—Washington, D.C., the man's home state of Illinois or Lexington, his wife's Kentucky hometown.

Franny wiped her sleeve across her chin, soaking up trickling blood. "We owe nothing more to the Confederacy. We'll leave Richmond to the greedy speculators and their burned-up tea, coffee, tobacco and clothing. Let's go to Kenansville." She grinned. "But first we need to get Tessir."

Pursued by the proliferating flames, the couples dashed through the downtown. Sots were still looting. Some used torches to set more fires.

In the Capitol Square, Franny spoke up after long minutes of silence. "Bill, your hat's on fire again."

He'd tasted a smoldering smell in the air for at least a block, but hadn't suspected his hat. The waterfront, the downtown, the Capitol Square, flames were consuming everything. Growling under his breath, Bill slapped his hat against his thigh, putting out the sparks.

"They're gone, Billy Boy," Charlie muttered between huffs.

Close to home, they ran at a frantic pace. At clogged intersections, they scampered past tangles of wagons and carts stuffed with the possessions of folks desperate to escape the doomed city. Bill ignored the profanities screeched by the drivers as he led Charlie and their women to the familiar brownstone, The Willows, his and Franny's home since the autumn of 1863. Beyond the last intersection, his head snapped upward at the creaky sound of a sash being lifted. On the third floor of a nondescript apartment building, a thirty-something woman garbed in a patched dress leaned out a window, her gaze fixed on the chaotic scene below her—baby-faced toughs pinching carpetbags from the beds of wagons and skedaddling down an alleyway. She'd chosen to stay behind in her apartment and take her chances with the blue-bellies and possibly those toughs. Bill whispered a prayer for her safety.

Soon The Willows came into view. Settling his hand on the front steps' railing, Bill regarded Charlie. "Possum, you and Avis head to the depot. It doesn't take four people to get Tessir." He turned to his wife. "Franny should go with you."

"No! I won't leave your side—ever."

Charlie rolled his eyes at Bill. "Seems Franny disagrees, possum. Me and Avis will see you and Franny at the depot."

"Looks like you gained an ally, Franny." Bill shrugged, acknowledging his wife would remain with him. "Charlie knows no one can change your mind once it's made up."

Franny nodded. "Charlie's a smart man."

"We need to pick up some things at Father's house before we go to the depot." Sniffling, Avis wiped her sleeve across her runny nose. "Poor Richmond!"

"Your parents took an earlier train, right?" Franny couldn't keep worry out of her voice.

"Charlie finally talked some sense into them. Father agreed to take the train. They should have left earlier."

His hand cupping Avis's elbow, Charlie steered her away from the apartment building.

"Both of you stay safe." Bill nestled his arm around Franny's waist. They took double steps up the stairs and hastened to the apartment. Bill fumbled for his key, and once in his hand had the door unlocked. He could hear Tessir meowing, but couldn't see him even after lighting up a table lamp by the settee.

"Come out, sweetie," Franny coaxed, down on her knees looking under the settee.

An eardrum-jarring explosion juddered the apartment, pitching the room into near-darkness. Pictures on the walls tumbled to the floor. The settee, chairs and end tables wobbled, toppling table lamps including the lit one. Window-glass splinters cascaded throughout the parlor. Slivers buried themselves in Bill's cheeks. Grimacing, he stamped out nascent flames nibbling one corner of the rug, then gently probed his face as he adjusted to the fainter dusk-time light coming through the broken window.

Down on her knees, Franny had escaped the worse of the falling glass. "You okay, darling?" Her voice rose an octave as she said *darling*.

"Some glass shards. Nothing to fret about."

She put off coaxing Tessir out from beneath the settee to help Bill extract slivers from his face. He groaned as she used tweezers to remove the first one. "Oh come on, sweetheart. Don't be a baby. This can't hurt as much as the shell fragment in your back."

"Baby? You're pinching my skin."

"Okay, they're all out." Franny set the slivers on the windowsill. "The bleeding has nearly stopped. Now we'll both have tiny sliver scars."

"Tiny scars? Someone's trying to be funny."

Tessir yowled and then yowled again, reminding Bill the cat still needed to be sweet-talked out from beneath the settee.

"Our boy's spooked." Franny righted the end table and returned the broken lamp to the tabletop. What remained of the glass lampshade lay in fragments on the scorched rug. "It's going to be even harder to get him to come out. Come see Mommy, Tessir boy." She dropped to her knees and scooted closer to the settee. Leaning on her elbows, she peeked between the floor and the settee's underside. "There you are, sonny boy. We're going to take you to a beautiful home where you won't hear explosions ever again. You'll get plenty to eat and kids to play with. You'll have a buddy; his name's Indy." She snapped her fingers. "Tessir, your mommy wants to snuggle with you."

Meows replaced the cat's frenzied yowls. Slowly, Tessir approached Franny's jiggling and rubbed his face against them, familiarizing himself with her scent. Purring loudly, Tessir emerged from under the settee. In the dim light, Franny picked up the cat and crooned baby talk to him.

"Get that birdcage from the bedroom closet, Bill. Lucky for us he's a skinny guy."

Tessir hardly protested when Franny shoved him into the birdcage. One howl and a scratch across the top of her hand.

'Now that was remarkably easy." Bill tapped the top of the birdcage.

"For you." Franny licked the blood trickling from the scratch.

Bill sidled to the shattered window and gazed toward the James River. The twilight sky glowed orange, painting the underbellies of clouds. Explosions continued to rock Tredegar and the ironclads. A miasma of burn smells forced him to step back and turn away from the scene.

"We need to go." Franny struggled to speak above Tessir's whines. "If the fires reach here..." She left her thoughts unsaid.

As shots rang out somewhere nearby, Bill and Franny tore down the stairs into the lobby. The front door rested half on rose bushes and half on the boardwalk. Across the street, an old man lay partway in a flower bed, his feet askew. Charlie and Avis knelt beside him as blood dribbled from a bullet hole in his throat down into the soil, nurturing a rosebush. His money purse and sundry items—but no money—had been left near his ear. He looked asleep, which made the killing more obscene.

"He's dead, died as I held his hand." A frazzled look smudged Avis's face.

"Seen who did it?" Bill drew Franny closer to him. Had he made a mistake? Should he have ignored her protestations and taken her immediately to the depot, kissed her goodbye and then gone to the War Department to do his duty?

Charlie shook his head. "Heard the shots. When we got to him, whoever did this had absconded."

Again, Bill eyed the oldster then pursed his lips. Dangers wouldn't have vanished inside the depot. Franny could have gotten trampled by panicky men and women rushing to departing trains. Or dragged into a broom closet and raped. Inhaling a deep breath, he slowly released the air. He wouldn't doubt himself now. He'd made the right decision. She belonged at his side.

"You two still going to Avis's house?" Bill swung his gaze to the downtown fires.

Charlie laughed sourly. "My woman's insistent. There's a suitcase waitin' to be filled. See you at the depot." The fires painted Charlie's face orange and red.

"Be vigilant, possum." Bill returned his friend's grin.

Bill grabbed Franny's hand, and the two of them sprinted along the boardwalk, their destination the Richmond and Danville depot. Swiveling his head, he sneaked a peek at Charlie and Avis. They were running too—toward the hoity-toity neighborhoods. Behind them, arching flames and dense columns of black smoke hovered above the downtown, the warehouse-and-factory district, and the James River.

Bill toted a carpetbag while Franny carried the birdcage by its leather handle. The more blocks they covered, the louder Tessir's howls became. Buggies, carriages, cabs and wagons headed away from Richmond's snarled the streets. Drivers' cussing voices pierced the night air. On the boardwalk, a throng of people all headed in the same direction—away from the fires. Like Bill and Franny, some lugged suitcases and carpetbags. Others pulled carts filled with steamer trunks. All hoped to board a passenger train.

At one intersection, an elderly couple's cart overturned, entangling buggies and carriages. Most of the walkers hurried around the old pair, ignoring the woman's pleas for aid.

"We've got to help them, Bill." Franny made sure her voice could be heard above the tumult of angry drivers, passengers and pedestrians. One young man who'd likely discarded his uniform for civilian garb knocked the woman down and rushed on without offering her a hand up.

Bill drew her to her feet. "No one has manners anymore."

"No, they don't," she panted. "I hate war. God's punishing us. Well, not you, kind sir." She kissed him on the cheek.

"Two men are always better than one when it comes to righting a cart." Bill wiggled into position beside the elderly husband.

"Yes, two's the better number when it comes to hard work. Thank you, Captain. My name's Maxim."

With the two working in tandem, the pushcart soon stood on its wheels with the couple's suitcases and meager possessions back in it. Bill pushed the cart no more than a few feet when an irate buggy driver upset with the delay shrieked, "Move faster or I'll run you down!"

Besides the driver, the buggy held a woman and a young girl. In less frenzied times, Bill would have never drawn his revolver, but he was at his wit's end. "Wait ten more seconds and we'll have the cart on the boardwalk. Know this! I've no problem shooting you dead." The driver shut his mouth and simmered.

Once back on the boardwalk, Maxim looked curiously at Bill. "You weren't really going to shoot him, were you?"

Franny spoke up, "No. He was bluffing. At least I hope so."

Bill shrugged. "I'd have put a bullet in his shoulder."

"My dear Winnie's right. You're a good man." Maxim shook Bill's hand.

Once Bill and Franny reached the depot, they found the interior standing room only. Bill feared there might be problems boarding the train since he lacked tickets, but everyone apparently lacked them. He cajoled his way up to one of the ticket windows. "My watch for two tickets?"

"No cost tonight, Captain. Compliments of the Confederacy." The ticket agent laughed bitterly. "It's the last train south. I'm going to be on it. There's more people than seats on the *Jamestown*, so you may have to sit in one of the boxcars we're coupling to the train."

"No problem. I've been standing since noontime. What's a few more hours?" Bill could hear the locomotive idling, its release valves discharging steam. Feeling eyes on him, he turned and found his chuckaboo standing beside him. "Hey, Charlie, feels like the inmates have escaped the insane asylum, doesn't it?"

"Saw two men shoot each other on the way here." Charlie gritted his teeth. "Poor Avis! I don't know how much more of this she can take. We talked to one of Avis's friends when we first arrived. They're not issuin' tickets, eh?"

"Normal times have disappeared, and train tickets belong during normal times. Looks like we'll have to fight our way aboard a passenger carriage and sleep on the floor—if we're lucky. We may end up in a boxcar."

"Better than staying here and waitin' for the blue-bellies to march in." Charlie nodded toward Avis and Franny, who were sitting on folding chairs and chitchatting like schoolgirls.

One of the ticket agents appeared amid the throng packed inside the depot, a speaking trumpet raised to his lips. "All aboard the *Jamestown*. Families with children first. Please be orderly and polite. We'll make sure everyone gets aboard."

Bill scanned the cavernous room crowded with people desperate to flee Richmond, mothers in black dresses holding squealing infants against their bosoms, old men and women clinging to each other, politicians too cowardly to stay and face Yankee justice. All stamped out onto the loading platform and pressed up against conductors trying to maintain control at the passenger carriages. Bill decided the depot master should have set up a system for boarding. Maybe write down names and assign them by carriage-car. Instead, chaos reigned.

Bill and Charlie were jostled as they pushed through the crowd to reach their women, and then were jostled some more as they led Franny and Avis out onto the loading platform. The elbowing and bumping occurring all over the platform led to the inevitable. Two middle-aged men swung their canes at each other, landing hits to their torsos. The crowd around them stumbled backward to escape the wild swings. A child fell and cried out for her momma. A conductor reached the girl's side and lifted her into his arms. "Are there any Southern gentlemen left in this God-forsaken town?"

Some of Ewell's soldiers should have been keeping order, but none were present. Fed up, Bill drew his revolver and fired into the air. The cane fight sputtered to a stop. The platform grew quiet. All eyes fixed on Bill, who held his weapon aloft. Beside Bill, Charlie drew his weapon.

"I suggest we all board the train in an orderly manner." Bill's voice remained rock steady amid the bedlam. "Listen to the conductors. Do what they say."

"Thank you, Captain." The conductor who'd scooped up the fallen child returned the girl to her momma. "Now let's board the train like civilized men and women. Don't worry. We'll get you all on board. We've coupled two boxcars. We've extra carriages as well. I promise...no one will be left behind."

The conductor's words turned out prophetic. Everyone boarded without problems except for two young brothers who tussled over a seat. Spankings solved that hitch. Two businessmen gave up their seats so Franny and Avis wouldn't have to hunker down in the aisle. Confined in the birdcage perched on Franny's lap, Tessir yowled incessantly. He'd been abnormally quiet in the depot, cowed by the explosions, the boisterous squabbling, the gunshots close to his ears. "The hard part's over, Tessir boy," Franny sweet-talked as the locomotive chugged away from the depot, its initial stop Petersburg. "Now all we face is a long train ride."

Bill sat in the aisle next to Franny's seat. A convalescent corporal missing a leg handed him a canteen and tin cup. "The cat has probably had nothing to eat or drink for hours." The soldier eyeballed the birdcage.

"Not since this morning," Bill admitted. "I'll say thank you for Tessir. I know he's grateful."

"I also have a stick of beef jerky. I'll cut it up and we'll see what he thinks of it."

Franny poured canteen water into the tin cup and slipped it into the birdcage before Tessir could escape. The cat purred as he lapped it up. The jerky morsels disappeared into Tessir's stomach as soon as Bill tossed them into the cage.

"I'd say the cat has a high opinion of beef jerky, Corporal." A grin flashed across Bill's mouth.

Ensconced in the aisle behind Bill, Charlie puffed a long sigh. "I can't wait until I'm back in the Tar Heel State. I've had enough of battles and drafty winter huts. I've a simple prayer—that the Lord let me live long enough to marry Avis Thompkins and the two of us spend our wedding night in my Kenansville bed."

The corporal reached down and patted Charlie's boot. "Not to burst your bubble, but we could soon be greeted by Yankee soldiers if they've cut the rail line."

"Off with this man's tongue!" Charlie joked. "God couldn't be so cruel...I hope."

Forty-seven

Homeward Bound

Entrenched in the aisle, Bill craned his neck for a view of Richmond as the *Jamestown* chugged away from the gloomy city. Passengers lucky enough to get seats including Franny and Avis blocked his view, but he still managed to get a peek at the scene outside a window.

None of the buildings were aflame. The fires raged miles behind the slowly moving train. In the upper-right portion of the window, scarlet smeared the bottoms of clouds made visible by the conflagration. On Richmond's outskirts, not one candle- or gas lamp illuminated a window in any of the houses. Even when beyond the city limits, the farmhouses were dark, just shadows beneath the sky. Bill checked his watch. Squinting, he made out the hands that read 11:52 p.m., almost midnight. Graveyard stillness ruled the dark land. The only sounds came from snores, the clickety-clack of the train rolling along the tracks and the chug-chug-chug of the locomotive's engine.

Bill swung his gaze from the window to Franny and Avis, both snoozing. Even Tessir slept in the birdcage on Franny's lap. Soon the cat would need to urinate and defecate. If Tessir did his business in the passenger carriage, Bill feared he'd have a riot on his hands. He thought about it through half-closed eyes until a stratagem suggested itself. He'd take Tessir to the train's outhouse-style toilet. If Bill could get the cat to relieve himself, he'd pick up the feces with a tissue and drop the poop down the toilet where it would plunge to the tracks. He'd wipe up any urine and let the tissue find its way to the railbed.

Hoping not to wake any of the sleepers, Bill plucked the birdcage from Franny's lap. Stirring groggily, Franny groaned but didn't wake. Still half-asleep, Tessir loosed a low meow. Cage pressed against his chest, Bill stepped carefully between men sprawled on the floor, his destination the latrine compartment.

Charlie tugged on Bill's pants leg. "Going to the vestibule to toss the thing overboard?"

"That would mark the end of my marriage." Bill reached through the cage and patted Tessir's head. "I'm taking the boy to the latrine. Hopefully, he'll do his business. Go back to sleep, Charlie."

"Can't. I'm wide awake, thanks to you and the cat. If you won't, I'll toss him from the train. He'll land on his feet, and a farm girl will talk her momma into adopting him."

"Wait until Avis wants a dog or cat, chuckaboo."

"I'm expectin' it, but when it happens we won't be travelin' on a rickety train tryin' to escape blue-bellies." Charlie shook his head, as if pondering a future household filled with dogs and cats. "You two lovebirds are madcap crazy to love that animal the way you do."

"Shut up!" an anonymous voice griped. "Little ones are asleep."

Once inside, Tessir did his business as if he understood the reason for the trip to the latrine. Getting him back into the cage proved daunting. Someone desperate to use the latrine knocked while Bill pressed against the cat's rear end, trying to shove him inside the cage. Tessir dug his claws into the floor and refused to budge. On the other side of the door, a male voice yelped, "Let me in! Hurry! I'm about to pee my pants."

Not wanting the individual to have an accident, Bill jostled the protesting cat into the cage, shut the door, and headed back to his perch on the bumpy floor. "Sorry, fella," he whispered to the cat. "I know freedom's precious."

Bill stepped on way too many feet and legs, eliciting tongue lashings. Each time he apologized profusely. In the near-darkness, he saw mostly shadows and heard snoring and whispers.

Finally back to his makeshift aisle bed beside Franny, Bill returned Tessir to his wife's lap and settled on the floor, sitting with his legs crossed. Franny snored softly and never sensed the cage or heard Tessir's meows. Soon the cat snored as well. Tired himself, Bill tried to stretch out the best he could.

"Ready to keep me warm, possum?" Charlie scooted closer to Bill. "Just like our tentin' days, eh?"

"I'd much rather be warming Franny." Bill groaned melodramatically.

"And me warmin' Avis, but we're stuck with each other."

Near them, someone whispered harshly, "Keep quiet! Sleep's hard to get."

Charlie lowered his voice, "I'm scared, Billy Boy."

"Scared?"

"With the war set to end, it's time to do what I promised when I first joined up. Take off my uniform and put on a politician's fancy suit."

Bill choked off a laugh. "That's what you said back in '62. Second thoughts, eh?"

"I'm just a blowhard from tiny Kenansville. Who'd vote for me?"

"Those were good dreams you had back then, Charlie. The Confederacy's dying. Slavery's dying. The South's going to need men like you to help bind our wounds. I expect we'll see some Southerners refusing to lay down arms. You belong in Washington City showing the Stars and Stripes can be our flag again."

"Sounds like I'll get at least one vote." Charlie patted his stump. "I wonder...has there ever been a one-armed U.S. representative?"

"I don't know, Charlie. What I do know is that the Capitol Building in Washington City will soon be filled with veterans missing arms and legs."

"I'm glad we talked, Bill. I'm not goin' to get faint of heart now. Goin' to run for office."

"If the Yanks give you back your citizenship," a voice emerged out of the darkness.

"Hush!" another voice snapped.

"He's right," Charlie whispered. "We need to try to sleep."

Bill couldn't sleep even with his uniform coat puffed into a pillow. While he and Charlie chattered, Bill had hardly noticed the carriage-car's wobbling, but as soon as he drifted into unconsciousness, he was jolted awake. He doubted he got fifteen minutes of sleep over the next several hours.

Sunrise light seeping into the carriage-car proved otherwise. Maybe an hour of sleep, Bill thought. As he rearranged his improvised pillow to provide more cushion for his head, he heard Franny's drowsy voice. "Bill, you awake?"

"Somewhat."

"Your bones must ache something terrible. I've a solution. We'll share my seat. Avis and Charlie can do the same. Wake up Charlie if he's asleep."

Bill elbowed his chuckaboo. "Charlie?"

"You want a shiner? Leave me alone."

"Shut up!" In the dim morning light, Bill could see the voice belonged to a middle-aged man in a crumpled suit.

"Lower your voice," Bill told Charlie, "before the fella gives you a shiner. Anyway, I don't think you're going to get any more sleep—not the way this railcar tosses and turns like a sailing ship."

"I can sleep most anywhere, Billy Boy."

Leaning on the aisle-seat armrest, Franny eyed Charlie. "Don't you want Avis on your lap?"

"What are you talkin' about?" Charlie yawned.

Franny leaned against Avis. "Tell your fiancé our plans."

"You and I are going to share this seat." Avis motioned for Charlie to stand up. "I'm going to make myself comfortable on your lap."

Charlie jumped to his feet, kicking Bill in the butt in the process. "Now that's a most desirable reason to wake up."

While others groaned, their attempts at sleep interrupted, Franny and Avis sidled into the aisle to allow Bill and Charlie to take their seats. Soon, the women were perched on their men's laps. Disturbed by the commotion, Tessir meowed for a spell before settling down.

Franny burrowed against Bill's chest. Her hair, peeking out from beneath her headwear, tickled his cheek. "Awful day and night." He let his words caress her ear. "I apologize for putting you and Avis in danger. So many people turned ugly. I should have put you on the train hours earlier."

"I'm glad you didn't—even with all the scary fires and poor Charlie having to shoot those men." She sighed. "I belong with you—even in times of danger."

"Charlie's always there at the right time to keep me—and now you and Avis—safe." Even with the burning-wood smell in her clothes and hair, Franny smelled wonderful. Bill kissed her neck. "First, God took General Jackson and now the Confederacy. I hope no more need die to atone for slavery." Bill kept his voice at a bare whisper so no one but Franny would hear.

Tessir meowed. Franny slipped her hand into the cage and made kissing sounds as the cat rubbed against her fingertips. "The boy's exhausted. I can't believe he hasn't done his business."

"Oh, but he did. When you were sleeping. I took him to the latrine." Bill chuckled. "Tessir was so grateful."

"It's been a rough trip for the little fella, but better than abandoning him in that hellhole of a city." Franny withdrew her hand from the cage and scratched her neck.

Unable to resist Tessir's forlorn look, Bill stuck his fingers through the cage's bars and scratched the cat's chin. "When the train stops in Danville for refueling, I'll get him some scraps from a restaurant."

Franny patted Bill's thigh. "A few more hours of train travel—well, probably some long, long hours—and we'll be at your mother's. I wish I could take a nap, wake up and find myself in Kenansville with your momma, Laura and Mark on the porch greeting us."

"It's going to take longer than you think, sweetheart. The war's been hell on railroads. The train will get us down to Greensboro and that's it. There's still another hundred and eighty some miles after that until we'll see momma's house."

"A long horse-and-carriage ride then?"

"A Piedmont Railroad growler cab will get us to Raleigh." Doubt crept into Bill's voice. Who knew what the roads would be like with the Confederate government collapsing? "We'll hire our own rig and make our way to Kenansville."

"I'm just happy to be away from Richmond. I don't think I'll ever get the fire stink off my skin and out of my hair."

"You smell like a fireplace at Christmas with stockings hung from the mantle." Bill gently kissed Franny and then exhibited the most scandalous behavior. He slipped his hand past Tessir's cage and caressed a breast through her clothing.

She didn't rebuke his conduct, but pressed her right palm against the back of Bill's neck and forced his mouth against her lips. When sated, she released him and turned away so she could speak. "I like sitting on your lap."

"I like having you on my lap. Lots of folks will be getting off in Danville. We'll be able to have our own seats."

Her fingernails stroking Charlie's lips, Avis said lazily, "Sharing secrets with your sweetheart, Franny? You two are like two schoolgirls whispering about a boy."

"Telling my man I can't wait until I can don a leather apron and help his momma publish her *Gazette*. I've been sweet talking him to convince her to let me do some writing."

"That won't take much convincing," Bill said, joining the girls' conversation. "Momma will be glad to turn over most of the writing and reporting duties to you and me. It'll be a marvelous way to put the war behind us."

Unthinkingly, Franny reached out to stroke Bill's mangled ear, but instead playfully wiggled his nose. "General Lee may have a different idea. He's not surrendered yet."

"Lee's soldiers aren't any different from us, Franny." In turn, Bill wiggled her nose. "They want to go home, so I figure the army's melting away. I do have one fear, but it isn't much of a fear. The last I heard Sherman's army is somewhere around Goldsboro, about thirty miles from Kenansville. I'd sure hate to run into those soldiers, but it's more likely Sherman's marching northward to join up with Grant. That's another reason Lee will never unite with Johnston's army. Grant and Sherman will stop him."

Franny traced a finger along Bill's eyebrows. "So the day of Jubilee will soon be coming to the North." She chose silence for a few seconds, allowing Bill to hear whisperings coming from other passengers. "And much weeping for the South."

"And the North as well." Bill pressed his mouth against Franny's ear so no one but she would hear his next words. "Lincoln's halo... pretty damn ominous. Would a Southerner be so stupid as to murder him?"

Franny turned her mouth against Bill's good ear. "Of course. We've plenty of fanatics who'd love to see him dead. Thank God most of us will be glad for peace and a chance to rebuild our lives. But always that chair at the dinner table will be empty and flowers will decorate the grave of the soldier who once sat in it." She drew her mouth away from his ear. "Enough about your gift. I know one cat who will be glad to reach his new home in Kenansville."

"I'm sure momma's cat Indy will be glad to have a playmate." Bill rolled his eyes at the thought of two tomcats co-existing in the same household. "Tomcats get along about as well as Jeff Davis and his vice president, Alexander Stephens."

"I'll take a couple of hissing cats any day over what we left behind in Richmond." Franny finger-walked from Bill's chin down to where some chest hairs peeked through his uniform shirt. "I'm up to the challenge of getting those two boys to be chuckaboos." She unbuttoned Bill's vest and two shirt buttons and kissed pale flesh.

"And I'm up for another challenge as well—helping Avis and Charlie plan their wedding."

"A wedding?" Charlie piped up. "Just think...it'll be the first one in Kenansville in the era of peace. We'll have it in the Grove Presbyterian Church. Or maybe outside under the red maple. Later we can have a picnic and a square dance."

"That sounds heavenly, Charlie." Avis stroked Charlie's chin.

Franny raised her voice, unconcerned that people might be sleeping around her. "I've a secret I want to share. I'm expecting, Bill. You know...in the family way."

Bill gulped, hardly able to believe Franny's words. "We're going to have a baby?"

"That's what she said, Billy Boy. Congratulations, chuckaboo."

Avis counted on her fingers. "You could have a New Year's baby."

Bill pressed his hand against Franny's belly, prompting a giggle from his wife. "You're not going to feel anything yet."

Glee filling him from the top of his head to his toes, Bill shouted out, "Everyone—we're going to have a baby!"

Someone in the back of the passenger carriage yelped a rebel yell. Mingled male and female voices rang out, "Congratulations. Hip-hip-hooray!"

Now that's the way a war should end, Bill thought to himself. Already, the journey to Kenansville seemingly was going faster.

Meet Michael Staton

Retired after working as a journalist and a technical writer, Michael spends his days researching and writing historical fiction novels. When he's not honing his writing craft, he bowls three times a week and enjoys trying out new restaurants on Friday nights. After living for four years in hectic Las Vegas, Michael has returned to the small Ohio town where he graduated many years ago.

Other Works From The Pen Of Michael Staton

The Emperor's Mistress - Teenaged Stealth is an artful thief with an attitude. Hired to burgle an exiled mage's villa, she tangles with Derrius, an apprentice mage of revoltingly noble birth. Trapped by political upheaval and their own antipathy, Stealth and Derrius undertake a mission to avert civil war.

Thief's Coin - In the river town of Opal, as the traveling players in Balthasar's Dream Palace perform, sorceress Illisandra Zayla's spymaster Jarn Sork captures Prince Derrius Hextor and imprisons him in a tower in the middle of the River Dolor. The prince's lover, the thief Stealth, must employ her cunning to outfox Sork and rescue Derrius, even though she knows her effort might result in his death.

Assassins' Lair - An amnesic girl wandering the streets of a border city holds the key that will decide the fate of the Setor Empire. Plagued with dreams about a queen who commands magic, the girl will soon learn that her body has become the vessel of a tormented soul.

Blessed Shadows Dark and Deep - When the death-predicting halo around Confederate soldier Bill Stamford's buddy, Daniel, turns out to be true, the private turns to a nurse for aid. The nurse, Franny Neale, seeks companionship in Bill's arms. He knows some life-changing decisions lie ahead. As he marches to a place called Chancellorsville, a halo appears around another friend, Charlie from home. Bill has to choose—let the halo win or try to outwit it.

Letter to Our Readers

Enjoy this book?

You can make a difference

As an independent publisher, Wings ePress, Inc. does not have the financial clout of the large New York Publishers. We can't afford large magazine spreads or subway posters to tell people about our quality books.

But, we do have something much more effective and powerful than ads. We have a large base of loyal readers.

Honest Reviews help bring the attention of new readers to our books.

If you enjoyed this book, we would appreciate it if you would spend a few minutes posting a review on the site where you purchased this book or on the Wings ePress, Inc. webpages at: https://wingsepress. com/

Visit Our Website

For The Full Inventory
Of Quality Books:

Wings ePress.Inc
https://wingsepress.com/

Quality trade paperbacks and downloads
in multiple formats,
in genres ranging from light romantic comedy
to general fiction and horror.
Wings has something for every reader's taste.
Visit the website, then bookmark it.
We add new titles each month!

Wings ePress Inc.
3000 N. Rock Road
Newton, KS 67114

www.ingramcontent.com/pod-product-compliance
Lightning Source LLC
Chambersburg PA
CBHW060614100726
47907CB00006B/1611